WARLORDS
RISING

BOOK 1 of WARLORDS
AN ADVENT MAGE NOVEL

HONOR RACONTEUR

 RACONTEUR HOUSE

Published by Raconteur House
Murfreesboro, TN

WARLORDS RISING
Book One of Warlords
An Advent Mage Novel

A Raconteur House book/ published by arrangement with the author

PRINTING HISTORY
Raconteur House mass-market edition/June 2016, June 2018

www.raconteurhouse.com

ACKNOWLEDGMENTS

To all the fans that have been begging for Trev'nor and Nolan's story: Your pleas have been answered! (Don't ask me how Becca snuck in, though, I have no idea.)

To Rosie and Bryce, my Advent Experts, who reminded me of things I had forgotten and double checked my facts. I'd look like an idiot without you.

A very special thank you to Carlos d'Empaire who served as my strategy consultant for this book. I was seriously stuck until we had our Facebook chat session. Thank you!

It goes without saying that I wouldn't survive without my editor, Katie, who puts up with me while I try to figure out book plots. A tip of the hat to her young cousins: Alyssa, Kaleb, and Josh that served as our models for this book. All of you are awesome. I won't ask myself what I'd do without you. The answer is terrifying.

Other books by Honor Raconteur
Published by Raconteur House

THE ADVENT MAGE CYCLE

Book One: Jaunten
Book Two: Magus
Book Three: Advent
Book Four: Balancer

ADVENT MAGE NOVELS
Advent Mage Compendium
The Dragon's Mage
The Lost Mage

Warlords Rising
Warlords Ascending
Warlords Reigning

THE ARTIFACTOR SERIES

The Child Prince
The Dreamer's Curse
The Scofflaw Magician
The Canard Case

DEEPWOODS SAGA

Deepwoods
Blackstone
Fallen Ward

Origins

TASLIM
WATCHTOWER

DUNIXAN

KHOBUNTER

KOLD

MALAK

CARANO

VON

BELEG

BRECON
WATCHTOWER

DILMUN

SAIRA
CHANNEL

RIYU

JASHNI

SHA
WATCHTOWER

RUINS OF
RHEBEN

SAGAR

ALRED
WATCHTOWER

THAIS

TREXLER

ROWE

TIERGAN

RURICK

OLSCHAN

Q'ATAL

"Argue for your limitations, and sure enough they're yours."

\- Richard Bach

WHAT YOU NEED TO KNOW ABOUT ADVENT IF YOU'RE NEW

Welcome to the world of The Advent Mage Cycle. There are four original books, two spinoffs, and now this book. While reading the original six first would fill in a lot of backstory, it's not required for you to be able to understand and enjoy Warlords Rising.

The first four books tell the story of the Advent Mage, Rhebengarthen—Garth. He becomes the dean to a magical academy by the end of the series. Becca, Trev'nor, and Nolan are his students, which is why you'll see them refer to him often.

Garth's story incorporated several other characters, which you'll also see mentioned often. He had a full team of people that helped him rescue magicians through most of the four books. There is Chatta, Xiaolang, Shad, Aletha, Eagle, Shield, Hazard. Only some of them are mentioned or make an appearance in this book. Riicshaden (Shad) is an incredible soldier that Garth rescues from being frozen inside of a crystal in book 2, Magus. Shad stays with him the rest of the series and even has his own book, Lost Mage.

Shad was the one in charge of going into southern Chahir (where all of the mages are from) and rescuing a young Becca, 8 years old, before she could be killed. He takes on the role of Guardian for her, but he's also her parent/older brother that raises her. Or I should say, he and Aletha raise her. They both hold the position of Weapons Professor at Strae Academy, working alongside Garth.

Throughout all of the books there is a magical race called

the Gardeners who keep making appearances. They are the caretakers of the world and their main job is to keep the earth balanced. The whole world to them is a garden that needs tending, and they do what they can to make sure it stays lush and green. They are sometimes thwarted in this, and when that happens, they awaken abilities in specific people to help aid them. These people are often called Balancers. Garth was one, but his job ended at the fourth book. Becca is a new Balancer because of her ability as a Weather Mage. She has spoken to a Gardener personally and was entrusted with straightening out the world's crazy weather patterns. Her task will last her lifetime.

Also important for you to note is that throughout all six books it is understood that Trev'nor and Nolan were special from the very beginning. They are prodigies, with their mage powers awake at five years old, and this is unheard of. Most mages awaken around 15. It was also implicated in the series that there was a very important reason why both boys were awake at such an early age and why they had to meet and become friends. I never gave an answer as to why. Warlords Rising and its sequel is the answer.

Trev'nor was originally found and raised by a nomadic people known as the Tonkowacon in Hain. He is Chahiran by birth, however, and Garth's many times removed cousin. I refer to this every so often. Nolan is Vonnolanen, only prince and Heir to the Chahiran throne. He was supposed to stay at the academy only until he was seventeen and then resume his royal duties at home. So you could say that Warlords is his last adventure.

Weather Mage Riicbeccaan had a plan.

As plans went, Becca thought it a pretty good one. The only potential for things to go wrong lay in that she had yet to convince two particular people to join in. She rather needed both of them for things to work smoothly. That said, knowing them as she did, it was unlikely in the extreme that she would get a 'no.' In fact, she rather doubted that she'd be able to get the full plan out before getting an exuberant 'yes!'

The trick of it was timing. She had to catch these two alone, especially away from any well-meaning adults, or the whole plan would go belly-up like a beached fish. She'd tried three times already today and had been foiled every time.

So when the perfect opportunity landed in her lap, she couldn't be blamed for hesitating a long second and peering in all directions suspiciously. Really, how often were Trev'nor and Nolan alone, in the side garden, quietly reading? If she didn't know better, she would think it was going to storm soon, what with that odd behavior. Well, no, to be fair Nolan liked to read. He was the more studious of the two. It was Trev'nor that couldn't seem to sit still for more than ten minutes before breaking out in fidgets.

She approached cautiously, still keeping a weather eye

out for adults. Trev'nor was flat on his back, book held up above his head with both hands, blond braid dangling over the edge of the bench and in Priya's hands. The little meuritta was having a field day braiding it in that intricately complex manner the Tonkowacon preferred. He was not in his brown mage robes, so she assumed he hadn't been on any sort of job today, although why he was reading so seriously was beyond her.

Nolan was on the ground, back propped up against the bench, his meuritta curled up and in his lap dozing. He sported a small braid on one side, proof that his meuritta had been braiding his hair as well. But the poor soul didn't have much to work with. Contrary to 'mage style' as people termed it, Nolan hadn't let his hair grow out long. In fact, it barely reached his collarbones. He claimed hair that long was sweltering and he was willing to sacrifice a little control if it meant not having to fight through waist-length hair every morning. Becca privately agreed with him. Both had hair that tended to curl, his more than hers, and she had a fight untangling hers every morning. Enough to think about shaving her head bald.

She was a few feet away when Nolan's head came up, eyes blinking as he focused. "Hi, Becca."

"Hi, Nolan." She sank down onto her haunches next to him and peered sideways. "What are you two so engrossed in?"

"Dragons," Trev'nor answered, eyes not wavering from his book.

Oh? Perfect. She clamped down on an evil cackle. "Really. Funny, that's what I was coming to talk to you about."

Nolan peered at her intently. "You're wearing that smile again. The one that says you have a plan and we're going to get in trouble."

Oh boy were they ever. "I have an idea, and if it works out right, we all three get dragons of our own."

Trev'nor snapped upright so quickly she swore she heard vertebrae crack. "And?" he prompted impatiently.

"Let me start at the beginning. I need to go into the Khobunter-Libendorf area. There's something very strange going on up there weather-wise, and I can't tell from here what's going on. Given the political conditions of both countries, Shad is dead set against me going."

Nolan, more in tune with politics than either one of them, grimaced. "Can't say that I blame him. Libendorf is so unorganized it's not even sure what its political stance is from day to day, and Khobunter is worse. There is no cohesive political stance. They're too busy fighting each other to figure it out."

Becca lifted an illustrative finger. "But I need to get up there. I think that the weather might be the reason why the land up that direction is all desert. But if it's not strictly that, I need someone to look at the soil itself and tell me if it's a contributing factor."

Trev'nor pointed a finger at himself. "That's where I come in?"

"Exactly. I think three fully trained mages can waltz through there and come out just fine, don't you? Especially considering the training that Shad put us through." Her adoptive brother had made absolutely certain that magic or no magic, all of his students could fight even the toughest opponent. "And while we're in that area, well, why not go talk to the dragons?"

"It's a sound idea and all," Nolan agreed, scratching at the chin with an idle finger. "But how do I fit in?"

"You're our dragon magnet," she responded promptly.

Trev'nor started laughing. "He's perfect for that!"

Shrugging, Nolan didn't disagree, and in fact smiled slightly. "I suppose I'm also there to talk to them for all three of us, negotiate our way into having dragon partners?"

"You do catch on quick."

The Prince of Chahir took a full three seconds to think about it before asking, "So. When do we leave and how do we get up there?"

"I can't believe you left them a note," Trev'nor complained for what had to be the third time in as many minutes.

Nolan turned around so that he was walking backwards. "We had to tell them something. Otherwise they'd assume the worst and run off in a tearing panic. Who knows what would have happened? And we can't call them via mirror broach—that will let them track our location."

Trev'nor grumbled about it not being a proper adventure when a note was left behind, but Becca agreed with Nolan. It was why she had helped him write the note. It had been rather cryptic, unfortunately—just that the three of them felt that there was a very important thing to do, they were leaving to take care of it, and would be back when things were done. She had been about to add something like 'don't worry' but it would have been a complete waste of ink.

They had wisely left the note on Chatta's desk, as it had a better chance of being found there. Not too soon, of course, just somewhere within a day. Chatta was more organized than any other professor in the school but she could not be deemed tidy.

Not having any other choice in the matter, Trev'nor had used his magic to get them off the island, and at that point they'd taken the first boat that would smuggle them to

Q'atal. Of course they couldn't cut straight through Q'atal, not with the barrier up. Only Trev'nor was able to walk through it freely as neither Nolan nor Becca had been this far north before. So instead they went around, which added a good two days to the trip. From there, they'd continued walking, and after four arduous days of no magic and lots of camping out in the open, they had finally exchanged forest and grassland for the edges of desert.

This far out, they might be able to use Trev'nor's Earth Path again without being detected, but then it would defeat half the purpose of them being out here. Becca had to see the sky in order to know what was going on, which really only left them one choice: walking. So walk they did even as the spring day became progressively warmer. In fact, it really felt like summer out here, not April.

Becca had never seen desert before, not true desert at least. It was very austere and monotone in reds and browns and creamy whites all offset by a stunningly clear blue sky. In its own way, it was rather pretty. Without a lot of trees in the way, they had a clear view of the stars every night, and it had been a breathtaking display of the constellations. Desert life was rather growing on her. The only thing she disliked about it so far was the constant sunburn. Fortunately, with Nolan around, it never lasted more than a few hours as he was able to heal it every night. Still, she'd rather not have it altogether.

Turning to Trev'nor she asked, "Where are we now?"

"Warwick," he answered without a second of thought. "Far western edge, and I think we're only a few hours walk from entering Khobunter."

It never ceased to amaze Becca how Trev'nor did it, but he always knew exactly where they were and very rarely did he ever need a map. He said it was a combination of growing up with the Tonkowacon and his Earth magic, but the last part she doubted. Garth had a terrible sense of direction after all. His only saving grace was his Jaunten blood. No, it must be a talent that Trev'nor just possessed. Either way, she was grateful for it.

Trev'nor gave her a curious look. "What exactly are you looking for?"

Trying not to laugh, she asked, "Did you really follow me all the way out here without knowing that? Just because I said you'd get a dragon out of it?"

Putting on a pompous air, nose lifted in a haughty tilt, he responded snottily, "I cannot imagine letting a delicate female travel alone in such dangerous climes."

Becca lost it and started giggling at his poor impersonation of a courtier. Nolan chuckled as well but wasn't as distracted by this play. "Seriously, Becca, you said that you were looking for something. That something was strange up here. But we've been so busy getting here that we never got a proper explanation. What is it up here that's bothering you?"

She had grown up with these two for nearly nine years now, studying right alongside them, but even then she wasn't sure if she could explain this so they would understand it. Their magic worked very differently from each other after all. "I could go into technical details, but the breakdown of it is this: there's something wonky going on up here. I can't see everything from Strae, of course, but I can tell more or less what is going on in the other countries because of what weather currents come our direction. Air flows like water in many ways. You follow?"

The boys gingerly nodded, so she continued, "Well, Khobunter doesn't flow. It's like I have a steady stream of water that's going along, everything's smooth and in control, and then something happens in Khobunter that tosses a rock into my stream. It throws everything off and I have to constantly rework my currents so the weather is going along as it should."

Nolan pondered on this for a moment before stating, "And from Strae, you can't see what's causing it at all."

She shook her head, mouth tightening in frustration. "Not one bit."

"How long has this been going on?" Trev'nor asked.

"Remember that year when Kaya and her brood first came to visit? The one where we had the epic pillow launch." She wasn't surprised when she got instant nods. That had be one of their more memorable winter holidays. "Ellis was wanting snow so bad that year and I was trying to get it to come to Strae, but something in Khobunter kept messing with my efforts. It took two days longer than it should have. That's the first time I noticed it."

"I think I see." Trev'nor rubbed his hands together in anticipation, a light in his eyes that spoke of pure excitement. "Going off into a dangerous land to find the unknown. Sounds like a proper quest to me."

"Really?" Nolan drawled. "Then why does it feel like a homework assignment or a class project to me?"

Becca slapped a hand against her leg, chortling. "You know, it does! It's just like something that Garth would come up with. 'There's a problem over here. Using whatever resources you have at hand, find the root cause and then give me a solution.'"

Trev'nor pouted at them—a full blown pout. "The two of you are not getting into the spirit of things at all. What kind of homework assignment leads you to a dragon?"

"Well, that is a point," she admitted. "But Trev, I never knew you wanted to go on a grand quest so much." At seventeen, she had assumed that he had more or less outgrown that childhood fantasy.

A very adult expression came over his face for a moment. "Naw, it's not that really. The real work is going to start soon. It's going to get hard, and exhausting, and we're not always going to be sure of the right thing to do. But in this moment, there's nothing like that. So, for as long as I can, I want to pretend we're just on some grand adventure, where nothing can really go wrong."

In that moment she felt her lack of experience keenly. Of the three of them, she was the one that was the most sheltered, at least when it came to actually using her magic in the real world. Strange, considering that Nolan was a crown prince, but nevertheless true. At five, these two had used their magic to alter the course of Hain itself by fixing it so that Queen Chaelane could get pregnant. At seven, they had gone into Mellor and helped stop an ancient plowing system from destroying a whole city. They hadn't even been fully trained.

Because of how potentially destructive weather magic was, no one had let her do anything until she had very precise control; it had been two years of studying and very small projects before Becca had really unleashed her full magical potential. And even then, they had kept her either in Strae or in the safer parts of Chahir most of her life because of who she was. Because there weren't any other like her. She was the last of her line, and if she died without having children, there wouldn't be another Weather Mage ever again.

It was a heavy responsibility and while she understood the reason for being so fiercely safeguarded, it still grated, not being able to go out as the boys had done. That was why, in part, she had snuck out here on her own.

Besides, it couldn't possibly be as dangerous as the adults feared. They were three fully trained mages. A small army wouldn't stand much of a chance against them. How bad could this possibly be?

Day five they finally hit the Great Northern Highway. It shot all the way from the very tip of Khobunter through to Hain, and reaching it meant that they were assured better traveling conditions from here on out. For one, it would mean the ability to stop for food, inns with comfy beds to stay in, and possibly being able to get some information if they played their cards right.

Becca squinted, peering ahead as she walked. The air shimmered, almost a wave, as the suns beat down on the hard-packed earth. The soil here was more crags and rocks than anything, and the air so hot it was a little difficult to breathe. It was impossible to look straight ahead, any higher than the ground as well, because the suns were blindingly bright. "Trev. Is that a town up ahead?"

"Should be Rurick," he agreed, rubbing at his throat. "Which is good. We're out of water and we're going to need a lot if we keep going like this. Maybe we should buy horses?"

Becca thought they should. Or dragoos. Dragoos would probably fare better in this arid heat. "If that's Rurick, then it means we're properly in Khobunter now, right?"

"Right." It took a second for him to catch onto her meaning. "Ah, want me to look at the soil now?"

"Please."

Trev eased his pack to the ground and squatted on his haunches. To the outsider, it looked like he was idly poking at the ground with a finger, but she could see the magic swirling around him and the intense concentration on his face. When he sat back, he peered up at the two of them.

"Part of it at least is the soil's condition. There's absolutely no soil moisture in here."

Despite growing up with these two, there were times they said something that went completely over her head. Like now. "How is that important?"

"Um. Hm. How to explain..." he trailed off, staring blankly at the ground. "Healthy soil, what we call rich ground, isn't just minerals. It's a mix of things, water and earth and compost all mixed in. So if there's nothing but minerals in the ground and loose particles of sand, then it hardens like cement."

"So even if Becca called down rain right here and now," Nolan ventured, "then it wouldn't be able to penetrate the ground? It would just stand there?"

"You got it. It's like this whole place is a giant fountain. The ground is that tough and impenetrable to water."

Becca turned in a slow circle, staring hard at her surroundings. The area was relatively flat, no standings of sand or much in the way of hills, and there was sparse vegetation indeed. "I could flood this place if I bring in too much water at once."

"Easily," Trev'nor confirmed. "I'd have to change the composition of the soil first, and I'd need water to do that with. We'd have to work together to pull it off. If you really want to change this desert, Bec, it's not going to be an easy stop and go project. You're talking months, here. Maybe a full year in one place."

A year. In each part of this country? She could only manage about twenty square miles at a time. It would take a lifetime to do all of Khobunter. And what about Libendorf? It was just as bad. Possibly worse, judging from Krys's descriptions of it.

"You might be jumping to things too quickly," Nolan

advised. "For one, you don't even have permission from any of the warlords here to tamper with their territory."

Becca felt like slapping herself. Yes, of course, what was she thinking? This place wasn't her responsibility. Why she had thought for even a moment that it was baffled her. Actually, why had she felt that way?

Trev'nor gave a loud groan. "Oh man, I'm glad it's not our job. Can you imagine? Having to go to every warlord and getting permission to work in his territory? There's what, eight of them?"

"Five," Nolan corrected. "Five that govern specific sections. There's no unifying government or leader, though, like there is in Empire of Sol. It's just those five contending with each other."

"Five is not much better. Just getting permission from one person is usually a fight as they have this garbled understanding of what magic can do. And for some reason they always have this idea in mind of what you need to do." Standing, he put his pack back on, adjusting the straps. "Never mind how feasible that is. Sorry, Bec, but this class project I'll pass on."

She snorted. "Don't blame you. Well, we didn't really come up here to fix the desert anyway. We came to find who's been tampering with my weather patterns."

"Yes, we did," Nolan agreed, relieved. "So? You detect anything yet?"

"He or she is quiet at the moment. I don't have anything to go off of specifically. But I think they're further north than here." Past experiences said so, at least. "For now, let's walk."

"Just curious," Nolan had a funny expression on as he asked, as if he were ready to start laughing, "but so far you haven't mentioned a thing about Tail. I mean, we left our meurittas behind on purpose because we didn't know how they'd fare on this trip. But what about Tail?"

The question was perfectly reasonable as her Jaunten cat/familiar was intelligent enough to get out of the way when he needed to. He was as smart as any person, in some ways smarter. "He's at an age where it takes constant pain reducing potions to keep him moving," Becca responded, all logic. "And he gets tired quickly."

"Uh-huh." Trev'nor didn't buy this. "You know that he would have argued with you about coming, don't you."

Becca grimaced. "You two are so lucky with your familiars, you have no idea. A Jaunten familiar knows when you're doing things without permission. They're the worst tattle-tales on the planet."

Trev'nor laughed. "I bet. So do you have a plan on how to soothe his ruffled fur when we get back home?"

"No, I do not," Becca retorted primly. "But I'm open to suggestions."

They walked. And walked. Distance was very hard to judge in the desert. Things that looked close were actually quite far. The only person not fooled by this optical illusion was Trev'nor, of course, who could feel quite well the distance in the ground.

Rurick was not quite what Trev'nor expected. No one really chose to travel into Khobunter by choice, as it was well known to be chaotic even in the best of times, so he had never heard a first person description of the place. They just had maps and rumors to go off of. Still, for a militaristic country he would have expected stouter walls, more fortifications, something more fort-like. The walls were stout enough, but not very high, and there was a light guard on the main gate they walked through. It was also very strange being here as they were obviously the only foreigners passing through. Most of the people here were dark skinned, black hair, black eyes. The three teens stood out like sore thumbs.

Trev'nor looked at the other two and asked, "Divide and conquer? Someone go after dragoos, someone go after food, someone else get water?"

Nolan was tilting his head this way and that, almost as if he were slowly shaking it. "Something's very wrong in this place. The vibe I feel is not a good one."

When a Life Mage said something like that, a wise person paid attention. Trev'nor looked around, paying better attention to the people, and he had to admit that he didn't like the attention they were getting. He saw quite a few passerby stop and stare suspiciously before continuing on. These people were not used to travelers, which was strange, as they were very near the border. Still, they were fully trained mages, what could possibly pose a danger to them here?

Becca rubbed her arms in an uneasy motion, her eyes darting around. "I don't like this place. Something stinks, I just can't put my finger on what."

"In that case, let's really divide and conquer," Trev'nor suggested. "Let's get what we need and move on quickly."

Nolan was slow to approve this plan. "Keep your weapons in hand and stay alert. I'll get the dragoos. Becca, water. Trev, food. But nothing like cheese, it'll spoil fast here."

"Right." Trev'nor used his nose to figure out where the local market street was and went that direction. He kept the hat on his head held low, trying to disguise his hair a little, and put his braid down the back of his shirt, but it didn't help that much. He was more tanned than the other two, spending more of his time out of doors, but he still wasn't anywhere near the skin tone of the Khobuntian people.

Roughly two blocks down, he found the heart of the market. He started with the first stall, taking a look at what they offered. Most of it was fresh, which didn't do him much good, as he needed travel food. Shaking his head, he went to the next stall, then the next. He tried to keep an eye around him at all times, but it was hard to do with this many people in such a narrow space. Eventually he gave up on that idea and just kept a close eye on his purse and made sure his pack was in front of him all of the time. A pickpocket wouldn't find him an easy mark.

Hmm. This stall sold dried fruit of different sorts. Now, that would make a good traveling food and it would give them a welcome break from jerky and bread.

He paused long enough to dig his purse out of his pack. When he couldn't immediately lay hands on it, he became worried and twisted it about to get a hand more firmly inside. Nope, still no purse. Frowning, he quirked a mental finger at the ground and created a mini-pedestal to set the bag on so he could search it easier. It took some rummaging, but he found it at the bottom of the bag and hauled it out with a victorious "Ha!" With money in hand (hopefully they accepted foreign currency), he turned back to the stall, letting the dirt settle back down into the road as he moved. Most Khobuntians spoke Solian—it was an almost universal trade language north of Hain—so he cleared his throat and tried that. "What types of fruits are these? How much for a bag of each?"

He never got an answer. In the next second someone grabbed him roughly by the shoulder and spun him around. Trev'nor didn't fight it, instead flowing with it, and hit the person grabbing him with as much force as he possibly could. His attacker folded over the fist in his gut and went down. But it wasn't just one man attacking—it was about six and they were all strong fighters. Trev'nor dropped his pack, freeing up his arms, and lashed out in every direction, trying to find himself some breathing room. He couldn't put up a wall in this location, too many people crowded around him, he'd hurt someone by accident if he tried. He twisted about, trying to get a visual so he could sink his attackers into the stone under their feet.

Something heavy dropped around his neck, and before he could figure out what, something else hit him hard in the back of the head. A sharp, lancing pain went through the back of his skull.

The world went black.

He woke up slowly, head throbbing, a terrible stench in his nose. Groaning, he put a hand to his head. "What hit me?"

"A slaver, likely," Becca responded quietly. "How are you feeling, Trev?"

"Like a hammer was taken to my skull. Nol, could you—" he broke off as he finally got his eyes open and the first sight of where he was penetrated. All around him was grey. Or maybe it just looked like that in the dim torchlight. He was in a cave-looking place of some sort, iron cages lined up in tidy rows, with a good hundred people all crammed into them. Alarm shot up his spine as he realized he was one of the people in those cages. "Becca. Where are we?" the question came out more than a little panicked.

It was Nolan that answered. "In the slave pens of Rurick."

Trev'nor had to turn his head slowly to keep it from screaming at him, but he still shifted so that he was no longer leaning against Becca's lap and could face both of them. "We're where?!" his voice rose uncontrollably.

Someone else in the pen prodded him in the side with a foot and hissed something in a language he couldn't understand. Tone was enough for Trev'nor to understand that it was a command to keep it down before he called the attention of the guards.

Trev'nor studied the man with hysteria climbing in his throat. He looked old, but that could have been because of the grime clinging to his skin, deepening the wrinkles in his face and hands. His hair was kept back in a messy knot at the back of his head, clothes obviously the wrong size and not laundered anywhere in the past year. He was quite obviously a slave, and a poorly kept one, at that.

Nolan reached out, gripping him by the arm, and grounded Trev'nor a little. "Trev. Breathe."

"I'm breathing. I'm just also hoping I'm dreaming."

"Me too," Becca sighed. "Really, how did this happen? We knew the place had a bad vibe to it, but we were all on the lookout for trouble, and they still got the drop on us."

Nolan shook his head. "These men were professionals. And they wouldn't take chances with three mages. We're too powerful for them to face. They had to ambush us or risk losing us entirely."

Tre'vnor started paying better attention and really looked at the man. "He's a wizard."

The man had a bitter look to his face as he looked away, not interested in their conversation.

"Untrained," Nolan added on quietly. "I can see the raw power in him, but at a guess I'd say he'd never had any sort of training. I wonder if he speaks proper Khobuntish?"

"Do you?" Becca asked.

"Some. Let me try." Nolan cleared his throat and carefully spoke a question. The language had a certain rise and fall cadence to it that was very alien to Trev'nor's ear.

The man didn't respond.

Nolan shrugged. "Either he didn't understand me or he doesn't want to talk."

Becca put on her most charming smile and scooted over closer, ducking her head to catch the man's eyes and drawing him back up again. In Solish she said, "Sir? My name is Riicbeccaan. What's yours?"

He eyed her dourly but finally pried open his mouth and

spoke in halting Solish, "Riicbeccaan. I thought you were Chahiran." He cleared his throat, a wet, hacking sound that spoke of an infection in his lungs. "I'm Orba. I'd give up hope of getting free of this place, young Mages. I've been here since birth. There won't be a rescue."

Trev'nor highly doubted that. It might take a few weeks for people to figure out where they were, but there certainly would be a rescue, and it might level the city. His family and mentors were not known for their tolerance about this sort of thing.

Nolan gave him a smile as well. "Call me Nolan. This is Trev'nor."

Orba looked confused for a split second. "You're not Chahiran?"

"We are," Trev'nor clarified. "I was just found by the Tonkowacon as a baby and raised by them. So I carry their name. If you want my Chahiran name, it's Rhebentrev'noren."

For a split second, Orba almost smiled. "Mouthful, that one."

"You think that's bad? You should try my cousin's wife's name. She's Hainish so when she got married to Garth, her name became Rhebenl-chattamoinitaan."

Orba did smile at that one, although it was faint. "Sounds like a disease."

"Doesn't it?" Trev'nor agreed. Wait, how had they ended up talking about this, anyway? That wasn't even what he needed to know. Granted, it had seemed to draw the man briefly out of his shell. "Orba, what do you mean by you've been here your entire life? And why were we taken?"

"Khobunter doesn't recognize anyone with magic as citizens. We're slaves. Property. We fight for them, build for them, create for them. The older slaves teach you a skill, whatever it is your magic is suited for, and that's what you do for the rest of your lives."

Trev'nor darted a look at Nolan but the crown prince of Chahir looked just as surprised by this as he was. So, this wasn't an official policy that Khobunter discussed with the other countries. It was a dirty little secret that no one outside of the country knew. Well, actually, that made sense. The Trasdee Evondit Orra would never have tolerated having magicians kept as slaves. If they'd known about it, they would have marched on Khobunter in force and taken the place by storm.

"But even travelers?" Nolan objected. "I can see why they think they can get by with it if a person is born in Khobunter, but travelers too?"

"Not many choose to travel here," Orba responded, tired. "Those that do are traders desperate to make a coin. And you three are too rich of a prize for them to pass up, I guess. Resign yourselves. You won't be going back home." He rolled over, leaning up against the bars and looking listlessly out, signaling he was done talking.

Trev'nor looked at the other two with a growing sense of frustration. "What do we do?"

Nolan pointed at the amulets hanging around his neck. "I recognize these. They last twenty-four hours, sealing all magic, although they're made for wizards and witches."

"Which is why they undoubtedly put five of them on us." Becca tried poking at one and got zapped for her efforts. She yanked her hand back with a wince. "I can't feel my magic core at all. You?"

Trev'nor shook his head, throat tight. Nolan did the same.

"I knew that they had slavery in Khobunter," Nolan whispered, voice barely audible. "But I had no idea some of them were magicians. As far as I know, only Chahir and

Hain really produce magicians. Where did the bloodlines for this even come from?"

A good question that no one had an answer to.

Becca shook her head. "That we can figure out later. What we need to ask is how do we get out of here? I'm not sitting still for the rest of my life."

"We have no access to magic or weapons," Nolan responded bleakly. "That's going to make this harder."

Harder, yes, but not impossible. Shad and Aletha both had taught them how to escape just in case they were in a situation like this one. Not that anyone had ever thought they would be. This was not at all the grand adventure that he'd signed up for. He was wishing, too, that the note Becca had left behind actually did give people a hint of where they had gone. They might need the rescue.

Becca eyed the bars, mouth twisted up and to the side as she thought hard. They were sturdy, those bars. With her magic, she could force her way out as easily as snapping twigs. But without it, she couldn't do a thing about them. Not barehanded, anyway. The question was, how to get past the bars?

Strategy was admittedly not her strongest talent. She was decent at it, but most of the time her battle strategy came down to: Charge! Only sometimes was she able to look at a situation and see what Shad or Aletha had taught her, and able to use actual tactics. They had certainly trained her on how to break free if captured, but right now, she wasn't seeing any sort of escape routes. Even if she saw one right this minute, she wasn't sure if it was the best idea to move. They didn't know the routines of their guards at all. The first day they'd been here, they were out cold for most of it.

Today was their first full day in the slave pens and she planned to use it for observation. It was doubtful that the routine from day to day would change much.

After they had a better idea of what they had walked into, then she would figure out how to get past those bars. Maybe Trev'nor had an idea. He had learned quite a bit of blacksmithing from Krys and Garth over the years; surely all of that experience and knowledge would pay off. Now would be a good moment for it.

The doors clanged open and an official looking man with a beer belly and rich silk robes strode through. He wasn't dressed like anyone else Becca had seen in this country but the way his nose was lifted in the air, an orange peel pressed against it, told her that he was pompous. And a slimeball. If he didn't like how it smelled in here (she personally didn't blame him for that part, she didn't either) then why not put some water and soap in here? Heavens, the whole crowd in here could use the wash.

He stopped in front of their cage and pointed at them. "What are you?"

Not who? Where are you from? Becca slowly stood. At least he spoke in perfect Solish so she could understand him. "My name is—"

The guard at his side moved like a viper, almost a blur of motion, and struck her in the mouth. Or tried. She dodged and it was more like a graze, but it still smarted and left a trickle of blood inside her lip.

"What are you," the official repeated, bored, as if this reprimand for not answering his question was only to be expected.

"Weather Mage," Nolan answered carefully, coming to stand just in front of her, subtly pushing her out of range of the guard's reach. "I'm a Life Mage. He's an Earth Mage."

"Weather?" he repeated with the first flicker of curiosity. "Life? There are no types of magic like that."

So he was an idiot on top of it all. Becca gingerly dabbed at her lip with the cuff of her sleeve and glared at him. She didn't feel like straightening him out.

The guard lifted a triangle that all of them recognized, holding it up so the official could see for himself. Of course, for each person, it glowed a different color. The men looked at the triangle for a long moment, not commenting.

Finally the official let out a growl of half-frustration, half-resignation. "We will have to ask the warlord what to do with you two. For now, you, Earth Mage. You will help rebuild the walls. Come out."

Trev'nor did not look at all happy to be separated from them. The idea frankly terrified Becca. But he didn't have much of a choice and he stepped out gingerly. This wasn't fast enough for the guard and he yanked him completely free of the cage door before slamming and locking it shut again.

Becca went forward, a protest half-formed on her lips, but Trev'nor shot her a look that made her freeze in her tracks.

No one was waiting to see how she would react. They trooped back out, taking several other slaves with them, and left with a very loud clang of the door.

Shifting, Nolan put an arm around her shoulder and hugged her against him. "This might be good, Bec. In order to do any magic, they'll have to take at least one amulet off of him. He'll also have a chance to really study the outside. If we know how many soldiers there are, and where everything is, we'll know how to break free of this place while minimizing the danger."

All of that sounded good, but it still felt very wrong to send Trev'nor out there alone. "How could they recognize what an Earth Mage is but not our types? I mean, it makes sense with me, but not with you."

"It's a very interesting question. I'm puzzled myself. I think we can assume that they've seen Earth Mages before. Which means there is a Rheben line in this insane country somewhere."

"But not a Von line."

"Right." Nolan took a good look all around them, regarding the slaves as they huddled together or slept. "Wait, I'm not sure we can assume that. There is a city up here called Von after all. Maybe they just haven't seen one down here? Argh, I don't know. I have this feeling that later, after we've gotten more information, that this will make perfect sense."

She really hoped that he was right. Right now, Becca was desperately short on answers and she didn't appreciate that feeling at all.

Hours crept by, slower than a slug moving uphill in a snowstorm. Without windows, it was hard to have any sense of time, and it bothered her. A lot. Becca's habit was to check the skies every morning and evening, making sure that the weather was moving like she wanted it to. Not being able to do that was like an itch that she couldn't scratch.

If she didn't get to see the sky soon, she might go stark raving mad.

Nolan spent his time popping his knuckles, then his neck, and finally his toes. After he went through all of his joints three times, Becca finally rounded on him. "Will you stop that? My joints are aching in sympathy just listening."

"You try shapeshifting on a regular basis and see what happens to your body," he returned easily, not at all bothered by her attitude. "My joints are a little confused sometimes on where they're supposed to be."

Becca nearly snapped that he was the all-powerful Life Mage, he could fix that problem himself, then realized that with those amulets on, he couldn't. Feeling contrite, she asked in a gentler voice, "Do they hurt?"

"It's more annoying than anything. There's no pain involved, it's just discomfiting." Nolan shrugged as if it was no big deal.

She had a feeling there was a little lie mixed in with truth but let it lay.

The door clanged open and the slaves taken earlier trudged back in. Becca shot to her feet and huddled near the doors. Nolan just as quickly stood, but grabbed her by the shoulders and hauled her back. She resisted automatically against the restraint until she realized that the guards were ready to smack her again for being too close to the doors.

Trev'nor looked as if he had been in the suns all morning, cheeks sunburned, dusty, and had only four amulets on instead of five.

Becca noticed this with interest, as four amulets meant that he could indeed work some magic. Before she could blink, the guard whirled Trev'nor around forcibly and a slave magician—slightly better dressed than the others—dropped an amulet around his neck. Then he yanked off the other four and replaced them.

Shrieking hinges, so they realized that with mages the amulets wouldn't last as long? Frustrated, she obeyed the beckoning motion and allowed the amulets to be replaced. She expected the guards to leave at that point but the guard pointed a finger at her and Nolan and asked in a thick, accented Solish, "What can a Life Mage do?"

Nolan seemed to expect this question as he had a ready answer. "Heal. Anything living, I can heal."

The guard seemed interested in this. "Heal what?"

"Anything."

"Anything, anything?"

"Anything living. I cannot do anything with the dead."

Wise man for saying that. Becca had a feeling that they would try to get Nolan to raise dead soldiers if he hadn't clarified. But she also found his answer interesting. Healing was certainly within a Life Mage's abilities, but it was considered to be one of the lesser talents. They could do a great deal more than just heal. What game was he playing?

Satisfied with the answer, the guard stabbed a finger at her. "You?"

In a split second, she decided that Nolan's answer was a safe one and it would behoove her to answer likewise. "I can make it rain. Or sunny."

He went alert at her words for some reason. "Big storms?"

"No," she denied, which was certainly the truth if they expected her to work with four amulets on. "Soft rains. Planting rains."

Not being able to call on storms to use as a weapon was a disappointment, but in this desert climate, any rain was very welcome and he still seemed quite excited about her answer. "You both work tomorrow. Bring in rains and you will heal our soldiers." With that order issued, he did an about-face and left.

As soon as the door shut, Becca caught Trev'nor's arm and asked urgently, "What was it like outside?"

"Not good." Trev'nor dropped wearily to the ground, arms dangling over his knees. "They seriously work you hard out there. I wanted to tell them that if they would just take off another amulet or two, I could do the work they were wanting a lot faster, but the slaves working with me advised against talking much at all. You talk when you have something important to say and that's it."

"Guards?" Nolan pressed.

"I couldn't get a good headcount, sorry. I tried. But they had me outside the city and the guards with us were basically breathing down our necks. They were nervous about escape attempts, I guess, but where can you possibly go?" Trev'nor shook his head. "Me, I could make it fine, after the amulets fell off. But anyone else in here would struggle to survive. It's literally sand and rocks for miles and miles. I can't see even a small pond in any direction."

Literally suicide to escape the city without their magic. "Easy to run down escapees, I would imagine."

"Sure. There's no place to hide." Trev'nor rolled his head around on his shoulders. "Busted buckets, I'm tired."

"What did they have you doing, exactly?" Nolan asked him, sinking down to sit nearby. "Building a wall, they said."

"Apparently they were attacked by a neighboring city or warlord or something about three months ago. There's holes in the walls, although not many. They were very impressed that I was able to repair them so easily." Grumbling, Trev'nor added sourly, "Although if I'd had my full magic, I would be done already. At this rate, it'll take another three days."

"I doubt they're going to release your magic just to get the job done faster," Becca informed him dryly.

"Pity, but true," Trev'nor agreed. "They asked me some questions about you two, and I basically told them what you just did, so I'm glad you gave the same answers. It didn't occur to me that they would double check what I said."

"It's rule number five," Nolan said with a cheeky grin. Seeing that expression seemed so out of place in this dismal environment that it was more comical than it should have been. "Never let your enemy see your full potential."

Oh, was that his game? "You do realize that Shad's rules are totally whimsical and the numbers change depending on the color of the sky and whether he's had coffee that morning, don't you?"

"No, the first five stay pretty consistent with us," Trev'nor disagreed. "The top two especially."

"What, 'I always win' and rule two being 'You always lose?'" Becca snorted. "I don't think those rules help us much at all in here."

Nolan shook his head, disagreeing. "Don't assume anything just yet. Rule five came in pretty handy just now. Shad's got more experience in situations like this than all three of us combined. I think we need to judge every situation by what Shad would do and try our best to emulate him."

"Our chances of surviving are better that way," Trev'nor agreed quietly.

The words struck like a physical blow and it wiped out any sign of mirth. Becca had to blink hard, several times, as the conversation made her desperately wish Shad was with them now. If anyone could get them out of this mess, it would be him.

Trev'nor snuggled into her shoulder, using her as a pillow. "I'm bagged out. Wake me when dinner gets here."

Under normal circumstances, Becca would have pushed him off for treating her like furniture and pinched him to boot. But her heart wasn't in it and she let him stay where he was. In truth, she needed the contact after worrying about his safety most of the day.

They absolutely had to find a way out of here. Soon.

They went to work the next morning.

The guards barely gave them time to eat before hauling them out and into the city. Becca had hopes that she could work in the general area of the boys but the hope quickly died when Trev'nor was again towed outside of the city to work on the walls, Nolan was taken to some area of the city to heal people, and she was taken to the highest point of Rurick—the government building.

It was clear what the building was because of the huge banners hanging on the walls and the people bustling in and out, all on business. They had 'government officials' written all over them. The two guards with her gave her no chance to slow down or ask any questions, just took her up an outside staircase made of stone and directly to the roof.

Someone had assumed that in order to perform weather magic, she must be at a high point, near the sky. This was far from true but she wasn't about to correct them. After two days of living in a hole, she was so happy to see that blue expanse that she nearly cried. The slave magician in charge of amulets had already taken off one of hers, giving her the freedom to work her magic, and she was quite happy to do so. Becca's routine of magic working was a daily thing, sometimes three or four times a day. Not being able to feel her own magic core had felt beyond strange.

The guards were literally within arm's reach of her, not varying their positions, and while having someone breathe on her while working was hardly pleasant, Becca knew better than to protest. It would have only earned her a cuff to the head.

One of them poked her hard in the back. "Work magic."

She gave him a look that most girls aimed at slimy frogs. "Be more specific. Rain? Do you want rain?"

The official from the first day sauntered up the staircase, sounding off like a fog horn as he did so, "You said you could make it rain. Why are you asking questions?"

Because she didn't want to cause trouble and get hit for not giving them what they wanted. If she could avoid injury, Becca was going to. "How long do you want it to rain? I need more information before I can do anything."

He came within two feet of her and stared with a molten look in his eyes, anger and disgust brewing on his face. "You do not ask questions. You obey."

Oh for the love of…was he a complete idiot? Becca had suspected he was a half-wit, but this was more than she'd anticipated. Giving up, she turned her attention the sky. If all they wanted was rain, without caring when it came or how long it stayed, then rain she would give them until they got sick of it and told her to make it stop.

It took a few minutes to find the right wind current, and hook some moisture into the clouds, but she got a rainstorm formed and heading for them.

The official stabbed a finger in her direction, nearly vibrating with impatience. "You said you could make it rain!"

"The storm is coming," she answered as neutrally as she could. "I can't make instant rain clouds in a moment's notice." Not with four amulets on her, at least. "I have to find a weather current, tweak it so clouds can form, then guide it here. That's going to take time."

He blinked and stared at her as if she had just spouted some complex mathematic formula. Perhaps, for him, she had. Most people didn't have a good sense of how weather worked after all. After processing this for a long moment, he settled on the one part he could understand. "How much time?"

Probably an hour. "Three hours to get it here and make sure it doesn't break up before it can arrive. If you want it to stay the whole day?" He gave her a belligerent 'of course I do' look, so she continued, "Then I need to stay up here a good portion of the day and divert any other wind streams from taking off with it." Not necessarily true, but the less time she spent in the slave pens, the better.

"Then stay up here all day."

With his orders given, she expected the official to leave, but instead he eyed her up and down like a man would a prize mare. "I have never heard of a Weather Mage before you."

How to answer this? Becca didn't think she should say anything at all and stayed quiet.

"How many are in your family?" he demanded.

If he thought he could track down her family, he was sorely mistaken. "I'm the only magician in my family. I was adopted." Both true, if very misleading.

This didn't deter him like she thought it would. Instead he gave a leer. "Then we need to make sure it doesn't stay this way."

What was he suggesting? Her head canted as she stared at him, perplexed at his meaning.

"The Life Mage or Earth Mage, either will do. Get pregnant by one of them." The official turned to go, then paused to add, "Anyone will do, if you don't prefer them, but I want a child out of you by the end of the year."

Becca's jaw dropped. What did he just say?!

As if he hadn't just said anything spectacular, he returned the way he had come, retreating back down the staircase. She watched him go, certain that her ears had betrayed her. Either that or this was a nightmare. A nightmare of nightmares.

"Work," the guard to her right commanded brusquely.

Becca trained her eyes on the sky as if focusing, but in truth, her mind whirled like a twister. Were slaves nothing better than dogs to that man? Did he think he could just order them to breed when he wanted to?! She tried to imagine having a child by either Trev'nor or Nolan and gagged. They were brothers to her, not lovers. And she certainly couldn't imagine doing it with anyone else in the slave pens. Khobunter was an absolutely revolting country.

It was so revolting that she nearly let her storm system escape and had to track it down and pull it back into the right direction.

Rain. She would think about rain today. Rain and nothing else.

Four days into staying in the slave pens, and they had the routine down. A chamber pot was shoved into a corner of their cells every morning and taken away again at night. They all did their best to give each other what privacy they could, turning their backs so no one saw something, but there wasn't much dignity in such situations. Their meals were shoved in on metal plates twice a day, usually something hard and of poor quality, and they had to stand at the back of the cages when someone came to deliver the food and take the plates away again.

Once a day were they told to come to the front of the cage, and that was right before breakfast was served. Only then was a wizard of some sort there to renew their amulets. He always put the same five types of amulets on them, one on everyone else, and it was a quick on-and-off thing. He had this down to a science after doing it so many years. Becca found being anywhere near the man to be revolting but the one time that she had flinched from him, he'd slapped her hard across the face, so she hadn't dared to do anything again.

Orba was quick to grab them, yanking them this way and that, for fear of them doing something that would get them all in trouble. He would shush them if they tried to talk when the guards were in the pens with them. Even if the guards were out of the pens, in the guardroom, he would only let them talk in whispers.

Everyone grew tired after working full days in the hot desert suns. The only relief came after Becca brought in the rains, but those were sporadic, as they discovered it wasn't a good idea to let it rain all of the time after that first day. From then on, she was brought out in the mornings to let it rain for a few hours, and then shoved back into the pens. It was blissful outside, terrible inside, and she fell to talking to the people around her to distract herself.

She had discovered a man in the adjacent cage more talkative than the rest. Roskin was his name. He had only a bare grasp of Solish, but he was willing to teach them Khobuntish, and between his lessons and Nolan's, she started to pick up the basics. It was similar enough to Solish that it didn't give her too much trouble. Well, the sentence structure and the basic syntax at least.

Most of the slaves here had been slaves their entire lives. Few had been captured and even the ones that were captured had been slaves for years. They didn't really talk to each other. There was little to talk about. They slept, or stared listlessly toward the ground, or sometimes taught magical techniques to each other. Becca listened in on these conversations and winced. Even with her understanding only one word in five, it was obvious that they had no concept of magical theory at all. It was just: do this, you get this result, do this, and this will work. How had they not destroyed something or burned out their magical cores already, that was her question.

Dinner arrived, and Becca was hungry enough to eat, even though the food was just as unappetizing as usual. She ate every crumb then put the plate back toward the front of the cage and retreated to her usual spot in the back corner. It was nice here, as Nolan normally slept next to her, keeping her warm, and Roskin sometimes talked to her. He was one of the few that still had a sense of humor to him.

Roskin came back to his corner, sitting down facing her, legs crossed comfortably. His hair stuck up in every direction after sleeping on it but he didn't have a mirror to tell him that and appearances didn't matter at all in the slave pens, so she didn't point it out. "Hey, Becca. I was wondering. Why does your friend keep his hair so long?"

"Trev?" At his nod, she struggled to phrase the answer. "Mages' power in body. All body. Hair too. So more power if hair long."

"But Nolan keeps his shorter."

"I can't stand long hair," Nolan answered, eyes still closed as he leaned against Becca's side. "That's why."

"That explains it."

Seeing that Roskin was in a talkative mood, she tried to get a few answers to some questions. "Just wizards and witches here? No mages?"

"No, there's mages too," Roskin assured her.

Nolan didn't sit up, but she felt him tense against her shoulder, so he was obviously paying attention now. Trev'nor, too, had stopped slouching and was looking at Roskin with keen interest.

"Really." They'd suspected as much as the slimy official had none of some types. Becca leaned forward, hands wrapping around the bars. "What kinds?"

For her sake, Roskin spoke slow and pronounced clearly so she could follow but even then she lost words here and there. "Hmm, we don't really know the types. Just heard that there was some. Before I was throbough here, I heard of a mage ani north that was being used diesorl. Rumor said that the warlord des him because he kept any attacks from ginhap." Roskin shrugged, silently stating that was all he knew.

Frustrated, she glanced at Nolan. "He was being used as what?"

"A soldier by a warlord," Nolan filled in, frowning.

Was that what they were going to do with them, too? But if they wanted them to fight, they'd have to take off a few amulets at least first. Wouldn't that give them the chance to escape? Or…no, they'd do something to them first to make sure they wouldn't fight back. Like the Star Order would have done.

Becca sat back and leaned into Nolan. These people were as evil as the Star Order ever was. Her doubts about being rescued from here grew. Trev'nor still believed they would be rescued, but this world was huge, their magic was sealed off and undetectable, and their families had no idea where they had gone. It would take a miracle to find them.

Nolan wrapped an arm around her shoulders and leaned

against her ear to whisper fiercely, "Don't you dare give up. We will get out of here. My word as a Von on that."

She managed a wan smile and nodded as if she believed him. Becca fervently wanted to but she had been in this situation before, or something very like it. She knew better than the other two what ruthless men would do. No, if they were going to leave this place, it would be under their own power. Not someone else's.

Trev'nor carried on the conversation as if she hadn't fallen into abrupt silence. "Orba says they make magicians work, most don't, just..." he paused, visibly searching for the word. "Nolan, how do you say 'sitting around all day.'"

"Jothanen da sou," Nolan supplied.

Rosking nodded understanding before explaining, "This is a holding ground. We're here giwai until a slave caravan comes and buys us. We're only giwai here another few days before ubury comes for us. I'd be pahi of here and get some sun."

"Huh, is that so."

Move? They were going to be moved? Becca's heart sank at the thought. If they were moved from place to place, that would mean possibly splitting up the three of them. Standing alone against a whole country was not a thought she liked. At all. No, she'd better go back to her first idea and get free of here fast. Although she still had no idea how to get past the bars. Waiting for the moment when they were taken out, with one amulet taken off, was not a good idea. After two days of being outside, she realized that the place was crawling with guards. She did not want to tackle them without Nolan and Trev'nor at her back. Not on minimal magic power at least. Splitting up in this place was a terrible idea and broke at least three of Shad's rules.

Nolan leaned in again, whispering into her temple,

"Remember, Shad, Aletha, Garth, and Chatta are experts at finding hiding magicians. They did it for nearly two years. Also, if nothing else, the Gardeners cannot afford to lose you. They'll go and tell someone where you are if we can't be found. As long as one of us is found, they can find all three of us."

It made sense, what he was saying. But still, if they wanted to get out of here, she had the feeling they'd be better off doing it on their own.

Not for the first time, Trev'nor blessed that he was an Earth Mage.

It didn't seem to matter where he went, people always needed something fixed. Walls, buildings, wells, streets, there was always something majorly broken in a city. Even a town as small as this was no exception. Garth once told him that being an Earth Mage often opened windows where there were no doors. He hadn't really understood that until Rurick.

The guards treated every magician as if they were some sort of subclass human, little better than an animal. The citizens of Rurick weren't much better. They certainly weren't going to talk to Trev'nor, no matter how charming he might be. Aletha had taught him that there was more than one way to connect with people, and he used every trick she had taught him.

The first two days in Rurick, he was outside of the city and repairing the wall. But eventually he had to move inside to work on the interior of the wall. He couldn't do it all at once. (Which wouldn't have been the case if he had his full power handy, but the guards weren't about to believe him on that.) That was when he was finally presented a window.

As Trev'nor walked through the streets, fixing the wall,

he would catch other things that were damaged. He would automatically stop to fix those too. At first the guards poked him hard in the back, not understanding what he was doing. When they did that, he would turn to them with a look of absolute confusion plastered on his face and say, "But you want me to fix this too, right?"

Having a slave that looked for work to do was inconceivable to them. They really didn't know how to react. But it was true that other things aside from the wall needed fixing, and he was faster than conventional methods, so they let him do so.

That was their mistake.

The people of Rurick got used to seeing him. He was radically different in appearance from them—it sure wasn't hard to find him in a crowd—and the braver ones came to tentatively request his help. It had happened twice yesterday. Trev'nor would bet his eye teeth that he would be swamped by requests today, and the guards would likely let him, as the first section of wall was mostly fixed now.

A woman that everyone called the Rikkana came with a young man in tow. Trev'nor had met her twice before, as no one would approach him without her at their side. She always spoke to the guards first, as protocol likely demanded.

"The grill pits are splintering," she informed them. "We need this mage."

Guard A (as Trev'nor thought of them) jerked his chin at the young man standing behind her. "Noogre can't fix them?"

"Beyond repair," Noogre replied with a helpless spread of the hands. "I'd have to rip them out entirely and fix them, and that would take a solid week. At least. We don't have enough food laid in for me to do that."

Food was very dear to men that worked all day in

the suns. The guards immediately saw his point and gave Trev'nor a grunt that meant, Let's go.

Trev'nor of course started walking, but he greeted them both politely. "Rikkana, Master Noogre, glad you came to see me."

Noogre blinked at him as if a dog had just started talking. Only the Rikkana, an aged woman with silver hair and years of experience etched into her face, wasn't startled. Then again, he'd spoken to her twice yesterday so of course it wouldn't surprise her. "Why are you glad?"

"Because I like to eat." He grinned at her, a boyishly charming grin. "I'm still growing, y'know."

If he had tried to speak to anyone else, it likely wouldn't have worked, as the guards would have shut him down. But this woman was highly ranked in this society (somehow, he was still figuring out how) and if she thought it was appropriate to talk to a slave, no one was going to argue with her about it. "You do not mind the extra work?"

"I like to work. I was raised to work. If it's work that puts food in my belly, I'm all for it."

This answer threw everyone listening. They didn't know what to make of it. Trev'nor wanted to shake them until they gained some sense. Of course the magicians did exactly what they were told and nothing more. They had been trained from birth to obey orders and nothing more. No one learned initiative that way. They certainly didn't gain a work ethic.

Was this whole country full of idiots? Corrupt idiots?

It took fifteen minutes to walk to where the firepits were. Trev'nor counted every guard, noting their positions, as he moved. It had slowly dawned on him that the guards had their own sections of the city they were in charge of and they didn't really communicate with each other until the end of the day. Why they were organized so, he didn't know, but he had a feeling that they could really take advantage of this.

The pits were worse than he had imagined. They were nothing elaborate—brick structures as long as two troughs with metal grills or spits hanging over them. They were meant to roast a huge amount of meat at a time, and from what Trev'nor had seen, it was likely these pits that provided meat for both slaves and soldiers alike. The amount of meat that could be cooked at once seemed about right, at least.

Trev'nor knelt down and examined it, looking at every angle, and really spending more time on it than he needed to. This was a beautiful opportunity to talk and get more information. "How often do you use these?"

The Rikkana, as usual, answered, "Twice a day."

"Ah, makes sense." Trev'nor leaned his head over to investigate the interior of the open brick enclosure. "Some of these bricks are cracked clean through. Let me fix those first, then I'll worry about the thing as a whole."

Noogre stood nearby wringing his hands. "But you can fix it? Soon?"

"Sure, sure." Trev'nor sat back on his heels and blinked up at him, shielding his eyes from the suns with a hand. "You need this soon?"

"I have to start the meat cooking in two hours."

"Oh, I'll be done by then," Trev'nor assured him. No way was he drawing out this show that long. "Go ahead and start prepping the meat."

Relieved, Noogre bobbed his head and took off for the nearest building, which Trev'nor assumed was the kitchen. It smelled like it, anyway, as there was a pungent mix of spices wafting from that general direction.

"I'm surprised this hasn't already been fixed. It's been past the point of needing repair for a while now to get this bad."

Guard B snorted. "Trexler doesn't spend money on things like this."

Trev'nor found that reaction highly interesting. The man sounded bitter about it.

"No, he'd rather nidh another campaign," Guard A agreed, sounding just as bitter but also resigned. "Why he keeps trying to win against Riyu is pare me."

"We should be more focused defending against the east instead of the north," Guard A agreed. "They attack us more often."

As if spurred by this thought, Guard B prodded Trev'nor with a flat palm—gently, for once, "Hey. You can improve the walls, can't you? Make them more abhe."

It didn't take a genius to know that last word was probably something like 'impenetrable.' "Sure I can," Trev'nor agreed amiably.

"That's a great idea," Guard A agreed, noticeably perking up. "But you think it will kam if we suggest it?"

"No way, we're just gaard. Rikkana," his tone became very respectful, "would you put in the suggestion for us?"

Was it Trev'nor's imagination or did she glance his way first? "I can. Perhaps we should ask how long this will take?"

"Depends on what you want me to do," Trev'nor responded. There, bricks were fixed. Now it was time to deal with the structure as a whole, make it a little more fireproof. "I've seen one section of the wall for myself. Is the whole wall built like that?"

"It is," Guard A answered, seeming to forget temporarily just who he was talking to, although he still spoke in the ruder, more casual form of the language.

"How do you want me to improve on it?" Trev'nor asked. "Thicker walls? I can draw up bedrock from the ground, reinforce them with stronger stone." He had to default to

Solish to explain all of that, but no one seemed to mind. They were instead excited about this new possibility as their walls was made of the same material that their houses were. Trev'nor thought of it as hardened sand dunes.

They drew him almost naturally into the conversation as they discussed the best way to improve the walls. Trev'nor learned more about their defenses in an hour's conversation than he had in three days of observation. Aletha was right: when in doubt, keep them talking.

He finished up with the fire pit, much to Noogre's excitement, then Trev'nor dutifully followed them through the town and to the headquarters for Rurick. As a slave, he was not allowed to step inside and speak to the commander, but he didn't need to. Knowing the building's location was enough. The Rikkana went in with one of the guards to put in the request. They were in and out in five minutes, which was probably all it had taken to explain the idea and get a hearty approval.

Stepping back out, the Rikkana informed the waiting men, "It has been approved. You start immediately."

Guard B actually smiled, and before that moment, Trev'nor hadn't thought that possible.

A relaxed smile on his face, Trev'nor said, "Alright then. Let's go get bedrock. Where should I start?"

"Let's do east section first," Guard A suggested. "Thank you, Rikkana."

She inclined her head to them, the three men bowed back—Trev'nor had quickly learned to treat the woman with full deference and decorum—and then she left as quietly as she had come. Her work was done, after all; she didn't have to troop after them for the rest of the afternoon.

It took some skill and substitution, but Trev'nor kept his guards talking as they exited the city and he farmed up some bedrock, and they were happy to suggest improvements to him as he worked. They were also just as happy to complain about their warlord. The more Trev'nor heard about him, the more he realized that Rurick wasn't an exception when it came to corruption and callous treatment of human life. The whole province was this way.

And that thought made him boiling mad.

He didn't let his anger show, but instead looked sympathetic and lent a willing ear as they moaned and bickered about which place was the worst one to serve in. He learned a great deal that afternoon and had every intention of carrying every single word back to Nolan and Becca.

He stopped working when the light failed and they dragged him back to his cell. After being in the suns a full day with little to drink or eat, he was exhausted, and his plan to talk to his friends failed. After eating dinner he fell fast asleep next to Nolan.

Ah well, morning would be soon enough.

By the tenth day, they stopped talking to each other except to pass along information they had learned. Roskin would draw one of them out, sometimes, having them tell stories about what life outside of Khobunter was like. But in their own group, they didn't say anything to each other. Everything that could be said had been in the first three days. They silently moved to accommodate each other, curling in close for warmth and comfort, but they had become as silent and withdrawn as Orba. It was exhaustion that made them act so, or so Trev'nor believed. After working a full day under the blistering suns, he felt drained in more ways than one, and usually fell asleep as soon as he had eaten.

Becca started having terrible dreams, memories of those days when she had been only eight years old and abandoned by her parents to face the Star Order Priests on her own. The cave she had found as shelter reminded her of this place the pens were in. She woke up many a time with a silent scream in her throat. Nolan or Trev'nor would grab her, hold on to her, until the dream had left and the shaking had passed. Sometimes Nolan would even purr, like a mother cat easing a baby kitten. But sleeping became an uncomfortable thing for her and she avoided it as much as she could, just drowsing while sitting up, avoiding true sleep altogether.

Trev'nor became very, very worried about her. Becca was taking this harder than either he or Nolan. Being detached from the sky for most of the day was highly uncomfortable for her. It was as bad as Nolan being cut off from most of his magic. Between being cut off from the weather and having severe sleep deprivation, she wasn't holding up well at all. She was becoming more fragile with every passing day, although her spirit and determination to win free of the cages hadn't changed. Trev'nor just wasn't sure if her strength would hold out much longer at this rate.

Guard A came to stand in front of their cage and he had a highly unhappy turn to his mouth. "We just received word. You'll be taken to Trexler the day after tomorrow. So whatever projects you started need to be finished tomorrow. We won't let you eat or rest until they're done."

With that said, he turned on a heel and left as abruptly as he'd come in.

Trev'nor watched him go, an uncomfortable tightness in his chest. Moving to Trexler would not be good.

Nolan moved, jarring Becca out of her comfortable spot, and stood. It was the first time in days he had fully stood up instead of just crab-walking to one side or another of the pen. It drew Trev'nor's attention completely and he stared up at him in surprise.

Nolan lifted his chin, projecting an aura of confidence that no one in these abysmal pits had. In spite of the dirty clothes, the grime on his skin, the oily hair hanging around his face, he looked like the prince he was. "It's time."

Trev'nor and Becca both looked at him blankly, not understanding at all what he meant by that statement.

"It's time to go, don't you think?" the Prince of Chahir clarified.

Becca frowned up at him, words coming out uncertainly. "We don't have an accurate count of the guards right now. I thought we needed to do that before we moved."

"I'd normally agree and wait a little longer but if we don't move now—"

"—we get separated," she finished, chewing on her bottom lip. "We'll have to do this by the seat of our pants if we go now, but you're right, that's better than possibly being separated tomorrow."

"I agree, but we have a slight problem, remember?" Trev'nor objected. He pointed to the five amulets still hanging about his chest. "What about these?"

Nolan smirked. On his grit-streaked face, the expression was more macabre than he probably intended. "We are students of Riicshaden, the best soldier Chahir has ever seen. We can't use our magic. So what. I look around me and you know what I see?" He splayed his hands to gesture in every direction. "Weapons for the taking."

Trev'nor looked around as well but didn't see what his friend meant. At first. Then the lessons that Shad had taught him, the methods of fighting that didn't have anything to do with a proper staff or sword in hand, but in using everything in their environment to fight came to mind. They came slowly, through a fog of half-remembrance, but they came. The second time he looked around him he saw slave chains hanging on hooks, iron food trays, stakes for nailing the chains to the floor, and oil lamps that were already on fire. He saw weapons.

"I can tell from your face," Nolan said softly, triumphantly. "Now you see it too."

Well, if he was serious, and Trev'nor was inclined to agree they needed to go now…. Shrugging, he deftly pulled out two slender picks made from granite and pulled them free from his braid. Reaching around, he put them both into the lock and wiggled them a little, springing the lock free.

"Now when did you get those?" Becca demanded.

"I made them a few days ago," he answered absently, his mind debating on what would make the better weapon. "While I was working on the wall, I slipped a little granite away and crafted them before they put the fifth amulet on."

"If you had those, then why haven't you used them earlier? Or mentioned them? I've been racking my brains for days trying to figure out how to get out of this thrice-cursed cage!" Becca's voice rose uncontrollably at the end.

"I was waiting for the right timing," he defended himself.

"We will have a long talk about your sad communication skills later, don't think we won't," she muttered, aggravated. Becca cracked her knuckles against each hand, then her neck to either side. "I call chains."

"That's the spirit."

Nolan went for the nearest stack of stakes on the ground, arming himself the way he would have two daggers.

Orba grabbed him by the arm, dragging him to a halt. "Don't," he pleaded. "You'll be killed. We'll be killed."

Nolan looked down at him with one of the saddest, gentlest smiles Trev'nor had ever seen. "You live worse than an animal would, Orba," he said quietly. "If you're willing to keep living like this, it means that means you're already dead. Your body just hasn't stopped moving yet."

Trev'nor met Becca's eyes for a moment, feeling a shiver go up his spine as he realized that Nolan might be more right than not. Fighting, no matter the outcome, was better than just sitting here.

For the first time in ten days, Trev'nor walked out of the cell like a free man. It was a liberating feeling. Becca eyed the door with mixed emotions, trepidation and eagerness at war on her face. "How do we do this? It's, what, a few hours after dinner now?"

"We don't know how many are in the guardroom," Trev'nor started.

"Four," Nolan instantly replied. At their looks of surprise, he grinned. "My magic is shut off, not dead. From here, I can tell at least that much."

"Four in the immediate vicinity." Trev'nor wished he had more information about the guards' schedules, but all he knew was what he could see, and they always locked them away in this room after dinner. The little he did know was what they did in the daylight hours. "We know what the guardroom looks like. Should we fight as far as there and then decide?"

"If we can fight and escape the city completely, I vote we do so," Nolan confirmed, stretching his arms high over his head. Even from here, Trev'nor could hear his joints pop. "Ow. Hunching over like that is not good for the back."

"Tell me about it," Becca grumbled, also stretching, although she focused on her waist. "If we can't escape the city completely, what then? Find a defensible position and hold until the amulets drop off?"

"Sounds like a plan to me." Trev'nor grabbed iron bars so

that he had one for each hand. Tearing off his vest, he ripped it in half, then tied off cloth on both ends before grabbing a lantern and soaking it with oil and igniting them.

"Nice," Becca approved, holding chains in both hands. "We ready?"

"I am," Nolan replied, stepping to join their sides. "Are we taking prisoners?"

Trev'nor snarled the word, "No."

"Good." Nolan strode forward, stakes in hands, then paused. "Come to think of it, Becca, you're going to have the most reach with those chains. You'd better go first."

"Gladly." She didn't have an ounce of hesitation in her as she entered the short tunnel.

"—hearing some strange noises," one of the guards ahead was saying.

"They're in cages or weighted down with amulets, you kabat, what do you think they can do?"

"Quite a bit," Trev'nor responded conversationally.

Becca breached the door like a whirlwind, spinning on her toes in a never-ending pirouette that sent cast iron slicing through the air and connecting to anything and everything around her. One cuff on the edge of the chain found the jaw of a guard as he jumped to his feet in alarm. The other solidly hit someone else in the head with a meaty thunk, sending him instantly to the ground.

She didn't stop until she ran out of room, almost at the wall, and then she put her back to it, changing her grip on the chains so that she could whirl them vertically instead of horizontally.

Her pause gave Trev'nor and Nolan the time they needed to come inside. The guardroom wasn't much—a single square with four men on duty—and slaves had never revolted, so they were ill-prepared to face three armed and very upset teenagers. Trev'nor tackled one guard with his flaming bars, Nolan the other with his stakes, and the guardroom went completely still within minutes.

Nolan put his stakes down and looted a sword from one guard. He eyed it critically and made a face. "Not the best quality or condition. But better than what I had, I suppose."

Trev'nor made the same evaluation and declared, "I think I like my bars better."

"I would. If there had been more than two of them, I'd have grabbed those instead." Nolan inclined his head toward the doorway. "What's our plan for out there? Becca, want to go first again?"

"I can? But it won't be as much of an advantage as it's all open air outside. I can only give you enough clearance to get out the door without a fight."

"That's enough," Nolan assured her.

Trev'nor propped up his bars against the table, making sure they weren't going to accidentally set something on fire, then found cuffs for the guards. He didn't check if they were alive or dead. He didn't want to know that yet. Shad, Chatta, Aletha, and Garth had all taken lives in the line of duty. He knew that. They'd been very frank about how rattling and awful it felt afterwards. Right now, they couldn't afford to be sick or have any hesitation. So he just made sure they couldn't cause trouble if they woke up again, and stood. To Becca, he said, "We've got your back, go."

She didn't so much open the door as kick it aside and stride through. Trev'nor and Nolan were at her heels. In the few seconds it took to clear the doorway, Trev'nor kept his bars held high in a guard position. But it turned out that everyone outside was so stunned to see three slaves come out that no one knew quite how to react.

Becca took advantage of their hesitation. She rushed

toward the nearest group of slavers and attacked with such savagery that one would think she was a starving wolf.

Trev'nor swore aloud and raced to her, spinning and putting his back to hers, making sure that nothing could attack her from behind. He did leave enough distance between them that she didn't accidentally brain him, though. Just in case. Nolan moved with him, positioning himself on her other side, forming a triangle.

"Move as a unit!" Trev'nor yelled to them over the clangs and shouted orders of panicking slavers. If they tried to go their own directions, they'd be cut down in short order.

Trev'nor had never gotten a good headcount, but he knew that the ratio of slaver to slave was very unequal. He saw just how disproportionate it was when slavers and guards started pouring out into this narrow courtyard they were in. There were far more slaves than guards. It made sense, after he took a second to think about it. Even slavers had to sleep and the Night Watch would have fewer guards. People rushed him from all sides, and he had to focus to guard his right even as he attacked with his left, but he still got a rough idea of what they were up against. If there were more than twenty men in there with them, he'd eat his boots.

Shad had stacked the three of them up against worse odds than this during their training. Was this really all that had been holding him back in there? Twenty men that weren't particularly well trained in combat, and having their magic sealed off? Granted, they'd had little information about what they were up against the first few days. But still, they could have moved sooner than this. They should have. He let out a bloodcurdling war cry and watched them flinch back.

He couldn't watch his friends, couldn't turn to check on them, but he kept his ears open, and Becca's chains never faltered. They constantly whirled through the air or hit something with a hard cracking sound. Nolan's breathing was a little ragged, but steady, his borrowed sword clanging against others'. Those sounds let him know that they were alright and it gave him the strength to fight that much harder.

An arrow of magic and fire whizzed past his nose, barely an inch away, and Trev'nor flinched and rolled in sheer instinct. He came up ready to roll again, head snapping from one direction to the next as he tried to spot his attacker. There, in between the guards. Trev'nor wasn't sure in this dim lighting, but the man looked familiar, one of the magicians the guards trusted to keep the rest of the slaves in line.

Staying low, he put on a burst of speed and went directly for the man, which scared both the magician and the two guards next to him. They stood their ground well enough, but he could clearly see the whites of their eyes. Trev'nor was ruthless and quick, utilizing every skill Shad and Aletha had taught him on how to combat another magician. One of the guards fell to Nolan's sword, the other to Trev'nor's staves, and then the magician tried to turn and flee.

Ha, wasn't very confident with his magic, was he?

Trev'nor tried to dredge up some pity from somewhere. It seemed he was temporarily out. He'd have to gather some up later. The man was more or less out of reach at this point so he used a little magic to scoop up a handful of street and chuck it at the man's head. The magician went down without a whimper of sound.

Turning, he reclaimed his spot next to his friends. It became a blur of faces, and hands with swords, and bodies falling one after another. The pounding tempo of his heartbeat in his ears almost drowned out everything else, and the sweat pouring off his temples threatened to fall into his eyes. Trev'nor blinked furiously and kept moving even when he couldn't see clearly. His bars swept one side, then another, and didn't encounter any resistance. He stopped, breathing hard, and swiped quickly with a sleeve to clear out the sweat enough to see.

No guard was left standing.

He stared incredulously at the litter of bodies on the ground. "Did we…win? That couldn't have been all of them."

"Everyone in this city we have to fight…" Becca trailed off uncertainly. "Or at least, everyone in this section of the city that got word we broke out. Most people have already reported in for the night and gone to bed, I don't think word is going to spread very fast. Trev, go build us a nice wall to block the entrances until we can get these amulets off."

"I can't," he reminded her sardonically, "until the amulets are off."

Becca closed her eyes, aggravated. "Right. Sorry."

Nolan stared down at the ground, sometimes using a boot to flip a body over. "Do you remember who it was that always put the amulets on us?"

"The snarky guy with the fat nose," Trev'nor responded promptly. "Why?"

"Well, I don't know much about the amulets, but it seemed to me that he never used magic to take off the old amulets and apply the new ones. He just lifted them off. Could he have constructed them to recognize his magic and respond without him having to invoke a spell for each one?"

From what Trev'nor understood of magical theory, that was entirely possible. From what he knew of slavers, it was highly likely. Now that he understood what Nolan was thinking, he started searching faces as well. Becca maneuvered to a spot where she could see out both archways, keeping a lookout while they were preoccupied.

"Found him!" Trev'nor crowed, hauling the man fully over onto his back. From the limp way that he moved, he was either very, very unconscious or dead. At the moment, the young Earth Mage wasn't entirely sure which he preferred. "Now what? Put my amulet in his hand and see if it falls off?"

"Sure?" Nolan stared at the array of amulets around his neck with worry.

Trev'nor went down on one knee and picked up the slaver's hand the way he would have a dirty dishrag. Gingerly, he put the grubby hand near the amulets. Two promptly fell off but the other three stayed stubbornly on. Sighing, he leaned back. "But why won't all of them come off?"

"Maybe they're on a timer?" Becca offered. "Not all of the amulets can work the same, not when they're harnessing someone with our power."

That did make an aggravating amount of sense. Curse it. Or as Garth liked to say, shrieking hinges.

Nolan knelt down and tried and the same two amulets fell off with the other three remaining stubbornly on. He sighed as he sank back on his haunches, partially in relief, mostly in regret. "Ah, that does feel better. I won't be able to transform, but should be able to heal and talk to animals. Trev?"

"Can fight and mold stone some, but nothing earth-shattering." He grinned, a little giddy at their success so far. "Pun intended."

"Yes, yes, ha ha ha, you're so funny. Come guard the entrances and let me get some off," Becca commanded.

Trev'nor willingly switched places because truth told, he wanted Becca's magic active as much as possible. She was a scary fighter with her magic in full swing. "Let's see," he said, keeping an eagle eye out for anyone coming down the street, "they put amulets on right after breakfast, which was…when?"

"I lost track of time in that place," Nolan admitted. "Fourteen, fifteen hours ago?"

Becca lifted her head to the sky. "It's nearly midnight now. These things last a full twenty-four hours. So we have to hold out for another seven, eight hours?"

Trev'nor's impromptu staves had long since gone out and he looked around for something to relight them even as he gave them a twirl. "I think we can do it. Especially if we just take down anyone that tries to stop us. Last time, we were ambushed, and that was how they caught us."

"No problem." Becca's lips curled back in something that might be called a smile. "I don't have any mercy left in me after what they did. So, what do we do? Free people first or last? I vote last."

"Last," Trev'nor concurred. "They'd be too easily taken and used as hostages."

"Agreed," Nolan said slowly, eyeing the door to the slave pens. "Although…do you think if we combined our magic, we could erect a ward on that door to prevent anyone from going in there?"

"I don't see why not." Trev'nor eyed the door in question. It was the only one leading to the pens and it would keep everyone safely out of the way until this was done. "Let's do that. Afterwards, then what? Wait until our magic is fully released before continuing?"

Nolan eyed the sky. "While I'm not really in the mood to wait…"

"It's safer not to go on like this," Becca finished wryly. "Yes, I feel the same way. Until someone comes after us here, I vote we don't move on. We've got water, food, and a defensible location. Why waste it?"

It was a good argument and Trev'nor didn't have any objections to doing things that way. Well, not if he were listening to his head. His heart wanted to just charge ahead and slay any enemy within range, but he knew better than to do something that foolish. "Then let's get the ward up in case we do have to leave here. And I could certainly use something to drink."

In order to build the wards, of course, they had to be inside of them so that the ward would recognize them as friendly. Once inside, they realized that actually the most defensible area was inside the guardroom itself. They stayed in there, out of sight, and waited as the suns climbed.

The guards had infinitely better food than what the slaves did, so they had a very nice meal while they waited. Then they divided up the remaining hours into a watch and took turns napping. People who had nothing to do with the slave trade had no reason to be on this side of the town after all. It gave them peace and quiet for several hours.

Eventually their luck ran out, and two hours before breakfast several guards came over to see where everybody was. When they found a magical ward on the guardroom door that barred their entrance, and multiple bodies on the ground, they leapt to the right conclusion and ran for help.

Becca watched this play out just inside of the doorway, smirking. "What are the odds that they have a magician that can get through the ward?"

"Low," Nolan said. "They don't have any formal training, just hand-me-down tricks passed from one generation to another, and I don't think any of them know the first thing about wards."

"Besides, we're the ones that put it up." Trev'nor leaned around the doorjamb to see for himself what the situation was like. "Even with limited power, we're still more powerful than a wizard would be. They'd need a full circle to get through this ward. And they don't know what a circle even is, much less how to form one."

"So we just have to sit tight for another two hours until these amulets fall off." Becca glared at the offending objects as she spoke, mouth in a flat line of distaste. "My question is, how did all of these magicians get up here? I mean, we were always told that Chahir and Hain produced the magicians, not anyone else."

"It's a question we need to investigate," Nolan stated, finally getting up to get his own look of the situation. "Sadly, none of the slaves are likely to know. They don't talk about things like origins or where they came from. It'll take digging on our part to get an answer."

Becca had a feeling it was an important answer that they needed to find.

More men poured into the street and some of them went to the ones that were down. Becca had seen some of the men they had defeated twitch or move slightly, but not many. An uncomfortable pit yawned open in her stomach. "How many men did we kill?"

Trev'nor clamped a hand down on her shoulder, the grip almost bruising. "Don't ask yourself that question. Not yet. We're not able to face that yet."

He'd apparently already thought of this. He was right, though, she couldn't afford to think about it. It was hard to redirect her mind, to not focus on the dead, but fortunately the men that were coming toward the guardhouse created a good distraction.

She didn't recognize the face, but a man that had red

stripes on his shoulders marched forward brusquely. The stripes, she had come to understand, denoted rank. She didn't know what red meant, though. He demanded of them in broken Chahirese, "You. Out now."

Nolan stepped forward and said in fluent Solish, "No. We will not leave here until we are ready to do so. Evacuate this city. Get all of the innocents out. When we leave, we will level this place and anyone left here will be deemed a combatant and treated accordingly."

Becca grinned at him. That sounded like a marvelous plan. She was in the mood to channel Garth and destroy a few buildings.

The slaver curled a lip at them but responded in Solish, which was a language he obviously knew. "You were easily captured. We've seen you work for days. We don't buy your bluff."

"You got the drop on us. You have no idea what our fighting power is really like." Nolan shook his head, dismissive. "I won't argue about this with you. Believe me or not, that is your choice."

Stepping back, the slaver gave a brusque command she didn't understand a word of. His slang was so thick it could be cut and served on bread. It became obvious soon enough when four men took axes and tried to hammer at the wall. They were instantly blown back, knocked out cold from the impact.

Becca couldn't help it—she laughed. "What, did they think we only put a ward up on the doorway? They really don't know how wards work, do they?"

"We're safe as houses in here," Trev'nor remarked, lounging back in his chair. "Seriously. The past four days of gathering intel seems like a complete waste of time right now."

Nolan looked pensive for a moment. "But it might have been better in the long run that we stayed. We learned their culture. We learned a great deal about the people living here. We know the layout of this city. Strategically speaking, maybe we didn't learn much more, but I learned a great deal about what's wrong in this country. It's good that we stayed put as long as we did."

There was that. Although Becca was of the opinion that they could have cut it short to just two days and not done this extended stay. If she had known how to get past those bars, she would have moved sooner than this. Well, it was water under the bridge now; it was time for her to think about what to do next. "So after we level this place, then what?"

"We fortify this city first and then move on." Trev'nor looked at both of them. "I've got it half-done anyway, I might as well finish the job.

"The people here are kind, even if they are extremely prejudiced against magicians." Nolan had a hard look in his eyes. "They treated me decently, even when they didn't know how to respond to me. It's the government at fault here, not the citizens."

Becca studied him from the corner of her eye. Sometimes, not often, Nolan went into what she had dubbed Prince Mode. Now was such an occasion. He had a different perspective on this situation than they did, where he analyzed the underlying problem, and who was at fault for it. "The government officials here think of magicians the way a man would cattle. To breed and use and nothing more. I didn't get to interact with the people like you two did. They didn't have that opinion?"

"Not at all," Trev'nor denied vehemently. "They were a little lost at first on how to react to me, sure, but they weren't callous like the guards were. I got them to actually talk with me a few times and they weren't keen on who was in power. I'm with you on this, Nol. I'm not going to just ignore what they're doing here. I vote we go to each city and free all of the slaves. Who knows? We'll probably run into Becca's weather-tamperer while we're at it."

"Sounds like a plan to me." She let an unholy smile cross her face as she said this. She was really, truly, looking forward to pounding all of the slavers into dust. If the boys were right about the citizens, she'd help them. If not, she'd focus on freeing the slaves and let her friends do as they wished.

The men outside became more frantic to get inside. They picked up shovels and tried to dig under the wall, only to be blown back again. Becca laughed, a little hysterically, and enjoyed the show. "They really have no idea how wards work. Idiots. Of course the ward wraps all the way around the building. How else do you prevent an Earth Mage from popping up underneath?"

"Not to mention it's stronger if it's a full ball shape or full square," Nolan observed. "Becca, you can see the sky better; what time is it?"

"About time, I would think." The sky was streaked with golds and pinks and hints of grey-blue.

They waited some more, enjoying seeing their former slavers panic. They no doubt knew that as soon as those amulets fell off, they were going to have a real fight on their hands. Becca's lips curled back into a snarl. They didn't know the half of it.

Without warning, an amulet fell off her neck with a clink as it hit the floor. She clapped her hands together, doing a celebratory bounce. "One's off!" The words were barely out of her mouth when the other two fell in quick succession.

Her magic flared up like a bonfire in a windstorm. She felt more alive than she had in ten days. Turning, she checked on Trev'nor and Nolan and found their amulets were off as well and they had set aside their impromptu weapons. To her magical eyes, their magic was building up, coming off of them in visible waves. They were more than ready to fight. "Do we have a plan?"

"I'm going dragon," Nolan informed them, as calmly as if he was announcing that he wanted a cup of tea. "I'll level anything and everyone. What about you two?"

"I want to take out the governor's residence," Becca stated frankly. "Trev?"

"That sounds like a good target to me. I'll go with you. And the guards' barracks, if they have any."

"Targets acquired." Nolan circled a finger in the air and pointed forward, which was totally a Xiaolang mannerism. "Move out."

They passed through the ward easily. Becca, knowing that when Nolan went dragon he became the size of a building, quickly moved out of the immediate area. Trev'nor was hot on her heels. Slavers tried to swarm them, of course, but Trev'nor was quick to react this time and the earth opened up underneath them, burying them up to their necks.

A bellowing roar rang behind them, loud and sharp enough to hurt her ears. Becca put her hands over them, trying to avoid a burst eardrum, and turned around to look. Nolan was in full dragon-mode, glimmering gold in the dawning light. He spread his wings, head lifted toward the sky, and gave another earth-shattering roar. Then his tail swept out, leveling the guardroom they had spent the past few hours in, rock and debris flying everywhere.

The few people still standing frantically ran for their lives, taking any escape route that they saw. Becca gave a casual salute to her friend and went back to her mission. Nolan would be fine. Nothing could harm him in dragon mode.

She went three streets over before she stopped dead. "Trev?"

"Sure." He knew what she was asking without her spelling it out. Grabbing her by the waist, he held her against him as a support as he lifted the ground under their feet and rose twenty feet into the air. It gave her a bird's eye view of the city and, for the first time, she saw Rurick as a whole.

As cities went, it wasn't impressive. Strae Academy was only a little smaller than this place. It had thick stucco walls, rounded from either design or wind wearing at it over the years. It was almost all the same color, a tannish cream, with only a few buildings looking different. In the very heart of it, to her right, there were three buildings made of stone and mortar, banners flowing from the roof toward the ground in a language she couldn't read. Pointing, she said, "Government buildings. Should that be our only target?"

"We'd best stick to them, otherwise we risk injuring people," Trev'nor agreed, squinting against the light. "Nolan can get the barracks. There's three for us, so…I'll take the big one?"

"I'll hit the smaller ones. Leave me up here, it's a good perch." Becca did her best fighting from a distance, when she could see all of her targets.

"I'll widen it for you." Trev'nor never admitted as much but he had a slight fear of falling. Not enough to prevent him from getting up on high buildings or creating towers for himself, like now, but he always took the precaution of either having lots of room or being strapped in somehow. He widened the platform so that it had a flat mushroom top, giving her enough room to lay down if she so desired. Then he splintered off a small section of it and used it to go back toward the ground.

Becca rolled her sleeves back, hands reaching toward the sky, and called forth a mother storm like these people had never seen before. Dark clouds formed overhead, winds picked up, and the air became heavy with a feeling of rain. Satisfied she had the conditions right, she pointed a finger at one of the smaller office buildings and directed a lightning bolt to hit it squarely in the middle. Lightning arced and crackled, setting fire to the building. From this distance, she could see people frantically bail out of windows and doors. Not many, though, as most were still coming in to work.

Cackling, she called forth more lightning. This was fun! No wonder Garth levelled buildings when he got mad. It was wonderful for relieving stress. Two targets were simply not going to satisfy her need for destruction. If Trev'nor didn't hurry, she was going to fry his building too.

Trev'nor saw the second building get struck by lightning and grinned even as he ran. Becca was in full form. She could hit the head of a pin with lightning if she were of the mind to, which today, she apparently was. The whole city could hear Nolan screeching and buildings being stomped flat, so they were gathering up children and whatever belongings could fit in their arms before racing out of the city. Trev'nor had ended up on the rooftops because of that, as it was the only clear space to maneuver without fear of being trampled. It delayed him and he hit the government square just as Becca lost all patience and aimed not one, but two lightning bolts right at his target.

Miffed, he turned and shook a fist at her. "THAT'S

SELFISH, BECCA!"

She couldn't hear him, but she could see him, and she waved cheerfully. Not apologetic, eh? That figured. Her lightning strikes had set the buildings ablaze so he focused on them. He should probably stop the fire from spreading. None of them really wanted to level this whole city—after all that would impact innocent people—they just wanted the government to be taken down. He focused on the building nearest to him, taking out its foundation, watching it sink into the ground a foot at a time. Magic still working on that one, he flung out his right hand and hit the other building with a magical burst, doing the same to it.

It took them ten minutes to destroy the governmental center of Rurick. Trev'nor didn't find that his anger had really dissipated yet, but he didn't feel like he was on a homicidal rage anymore either.

He found a higher point, another roof ledge behind him, and climbed up in order to get a broader view of the city. From what he could tell, there wasn't anyone left inside the walls. No one living, anyway.

Nolan swept up into the sky, angling around and gliding past low enough to catch Becca in his talons. Then he flew directly to Trev'nor and carefully dropped Becca to the rooftop before flying up and around in a tight arc, easing back into his human shape as he landed.

"Feel better?" Trev'nor asked the pair of them although he didn't need to—the flushed exhilaration was bright on their faces.

"Much." Nolan stretched his arms out high above his head. "Feels good to have the kinks out. Now what do we do next? Let everyone out of the slave pens?"

"I can do that," Trev'nor offered. "But what do we do then? I mean, the citizens here are used to thinking that magicians are slaves. We can't just turn them loose and leave, not without knowing how they'll be treated later."

"I think we scared everyone off, though." Becca frowned and peered toward the south, where most people had fled. "Should we wait for them to come back and try to talk to them?"

"Or we go out to meet them halfway and try to talk." Nolan didn't sound sold on this possibility. "I'm not sure if they'd let us come anywhere close, though. Not after seeing all of this."

"Better to deal with the slave pens and wait," Trev'nor agreed. "Bec, Nol, you deal with the people. Once they're all out, I'm going to bury the place."

The aftermath of the battle was not a pretty one.

Becca let the former slaves out of their pens but most refused to move, not believing that they could after a lifetime of being kept in chains. She didn't argue with them, figuring that hunger would drive them out eventually. Nolan went in and healed those that needed it, speaking to the whole group as he worked, explaining who they were and what had happened.

Because Trev'nor couldn't really help with that, building detail fell to him. In Nolan's rage, he had smashed quite a few buildings that they actually needed. Trev'nor wandered up one street and down the next, repairing buildings. While doing that, he came across multiple bodies that obviously didn't have a breath of life left in them. Shad had said once that no one could mistake a dead body. Trev'nor now understood exactly what he'd meant. It wasn't just the stillness, it was the lack of all animation in them, the absence of a soul itself. They were like macabre wooden puppets, badly damaged and strewn about by a giant's hand. Or, in this case, a dragon's claws.

Ignoring it only lasted about two streets before he fetched up hard against the side of a building, dry heaves wracking his stomach. Trev'nor put his head against the cool, pitted surface and breathed deeply. He could not imagine a feeling more terrible than this—to walk through a battlefield and know that it was partially his hand that had robbed these men of their lives. It tore at his own soul and robbed him of breath.

Trev'nor spent a small eternity hunched over, shaking and sick. Eventually he forced himself upright, using the back of his hand to swipe at wet cheeks. If he was like this now, then odds were it was going to hit the other two soon. It would be worse for them. Nolan's magic and gentle nature would tear at him for this. Becca had lived through a situation similar enough that it would shake her up again, dark memories bombarding her as much as the reality. He couldn't let either one of them be alone until they got a handle on this.

He went to Nolan first, as he knew where the young prince was, and Becca was currently on a rooftop somewhere keeping an eye on the city as a whole. The slave pens were empty save about two dozen people who stubbornly refused to leave. Most of the slaves milled about the city, pointing things out to each other and exclaiming over the damage done, but there was no fair head of hair to be spotted. Eventually Trev'nor had to use his magical sense to help find him.

In a very narrow alleyway, Nolan was hunched over in a dark corner, retching. Trev'nor winced even as he lengthened his stride, heading for him. He hadn't made it in time. "Nolan."

Nolan staggered back a few steps, wiping at his mouth with a dirty shirt sleeve, eyes a little wild. His magic arced around him in short bursts, his control finicky. Trev'nor grabbed him up in a strong hug and just held on.

His friend gasped and shuddered, clawing at Trev'nor's back with a weak grip. There might have been more than a few tears soaking into his shoulder, too. Trev'nor didn't think him any the weaker for it. To Nolan, it wasn't just a dead body. It was the very absence of life where there should be an abundance. It would be completely repulsive to his magical sense.

It took close to an hour before his breathing changed, becoming less ragged and more even. Nolan gently pushed back, regaining his center, and looked at Trev'nor with red-rimmed eyes. "Becca?"

"I'm worried about her too," Trev'nor admitted. "Are you alright?"

"No." Nolan tried for a crooked smile and failed. "But I will be. Just...give me some more time to come to grips with this."

"I can bury the bodies real quick if you need me to?" Trev'nor mentally kicked himself for not thinking of that earlier.

"I think that will help, yes, but go find Becca first. Of the two of us, you're handling this better."

It took strength for Nolan to admit that, and Trev'nor gave his friend a supportive nod. "You're doing fine. Your magic must be going ballistic about this."

"It's certainly not helping."

Nolan really did look as if he were pulling himself back together. Trev'nor trusted that he would be fine, at least for a little while, and took himself out of the alley. Well now. Where would Becca be?

It took him more than a few minutes to find her. Becca had always had this knack for hiding in the most obscure places. She'd always won in 'hide and seek' as a child because of that. Trev'nor now realized that it was likely a carryover from when she had been hunted by the Star Order Priests. Her mind subconsciously found the best places to go just in case she needed to hide.

She was tucked up against the side of a chimney, facing the setting suns against the far horizon, her knees up against her chest. From the back, he was terribly afraid she was crying. Slowly, he came in from an angle, not wanting to startle her (bad things normally followed that), and trying to get her attention without being pushy about it. But when he came around far enough to see her face, he found that she was completely dry-eyed. Her expression wasn't just blank, it was actively not-there in a way that suggested she was trying to escape from reality as much as possible. At least for a few minutes.

Should he leave her be, come back later? Or sit down next to her? Trev'nor couldn't read people like Nolan could, so he wasn't sure which was the best way to go.

"Trev." It was barely audible although distinctly said.

That sounded like an invitation to him. He came around to sit at her side, close but not touching, and pointed his face toward the sunset. "Hey. Next time, try to hide somewhere that an emotionally upset woman would hide? It was really hard to find you."

Not so much as a twitch. Busted buckets. Had it all finally caught up to her?

"Trev," she repeated, tone hollow. "We killed people today, didn't we."

That was clearly not a question. He puffed out his cheeks and blew out a breath before admitting, "We did."

"Aletha was right. It's a really terrible feeling. It feels like someone has a stranglehold on my gut but I can't seem to throw up."

Nolan had, earlier. Trev'nor almost had. He was surprised Becca hadn't, but then she had always been more world-tough in some ways than they were. Trev'nor tried to find some words of comfort but what came out instead was, "Do you regret it?"

Finally, she looked at him, still with those hollow eyes, as if he were speaking in words she couldn't understand. "Regret it? I do. But I don't."

As contradictory as that sounded, Trev'nor understood exactly what she meant. "Garth talked to me about this once. I didn't understand what he meant then but I do now. He said that before you go into a fight, you have all of these reasons—some of them important, some of them not. You go in thinking about your country, and justice, and all sorts of justification for fighting. But while you're fighting, you realize that none of that really matters. What's most important is keeping yourself alive, and the people that are important to you, and that's it."

"Keeping myself alive," she whispered and finally some animation returned to her face. "If we hadn't killed them, they would have killed us."

"To them, we were loose cannons," Trev'nor confirmed bleakly. "They wouldn't put up with anything else other than complete obedience. And we wouldn't have been able to keep our heads down like that forever—eventually we'd snap and do something that would get us killed. We had to fight today, Becca. We had to wipe them out of existence. Remember, though, they were the ones that brought the fight to us. We didn't ask for it."

Her mouth curved up in a wan smile, a barely-there expression. "I know. I wish Shad had talked to me more about this. He never really did. I think he always believed that I wouldn't have to fight because Chahir had finally found peace within itself."

While that was true, it didn't sound like Shad to believe in peace so strongly that he wouldn't arm his foster sister just in case that peace ever broke. "He really never said anything?"

"He told me war stories from time to time. I learned something from them. But really, the only advice I got from him was about three years ago. I asked him if he believed in killing or if was just something he had to do as a soldier."

Now that was an interesting question. Trev'nor scooted around a little so he could face her easier. "What did he say?"

"He said he did believe that sometimes it was just necessary. It wasn't like some people should never have been born, or they didn't have the right to live, it was just that because of what they had done they lost the privilege of continuing to live." Her rigid posture relaxed and she leaned her chin against her knees, still staring out at the sunset. "Because of what they had done, they lost the right to live on this world anymore. He said the problem comes when it takes someone with power to make that judgment call and it takes someone else to give them that power. I guess, what I'm really struggling with here, is whether I have the right to take on that power."

They rather had played judge, jury, and executioner in this city without a second thought. "They were trying to enslave us. I think that gives us more of a right than anyone else, don't you?"

"Really, I can't argue." Becca tilted sideways so that she fetched up against him, head on his shoulder. "And it fits Xiaolang's definition of evil to a tee: the purposeful destruction of innocence."

"I don't think we were wrong, Bec. I think it's just hard. This whole situation is just hard. We're going to lose sleep over it, we're going to have nightmares about it, and we're always going to wonder if there wasn't a better way to deal with it. But we were fighting for our very freedom and survival. I don't think anyone will judge us harshly for what we did here."

"What we did here, no. But Trev, even Nolan said we can't let this slavery continue. Even he said we should continue going on through Khobunter and end this situation. Do we have the right to do that?"

"Look at this way. If we had gone into some other city instead of Rurick, do you think the slavers there would do anything differently?"

Her mouth opened, paused, then closed. "No."

"There's your answer. There's nothing to like about fighting. It's just necessary sometimes because the only thing an evil man responds to is brute force." Right now, facing this situation again felt repugnant in the extreme but he couldn't deny the dire need for it. Maybe, a week or two from now, he would be able to face the future more head on. Tonight, though, he didn't think it was something that any of them needed to focus on. "Come on, come down. This hit Nolan hard and I think he'd feel better seeing you."

She leaned into him a second more before pushing her way up to her feet. "What about you?"

"I have bodies to bury."

It took nearly three days for the inhabitants of Rurick to return.

At first it was the young men, the bolder ones that dared to risk an enemy occupied city. But when they were met with tentative hellos and welcomes, they went back and reported that it was safe, and more poured in after them.

Becca didn't quite know what to do with them at first. Her grasp on the language was shaky at best and they sometimes used slang on words that didn't make any sense to her. They didn't know how to respond to her either. Or to Nolan and Trev'nor. Magicians were slaves. That was the tradition they had been raised with and they had never questioned it until their city was torn apart. They oscillated between thinking along traditional lines and being overly cautious of the three powerful mages walking around in their midst.

Two days after the populace had returned, they finally sat down and spoke with someone who was the de facto leader of Rurick. Rikkana Sumi was her name, an older woman that looked to be a grandmother. She came to them as they struggled to teach some of the magicians the basics of magic and tapped her cane on the ground once, as if calling for their attention. "I want to speak with you."

Becca frowned in concentration, trying to understand

her. Sumi's Solish had a very thick accent. "Rikkana Sumi, we can speak," she carefully replied. "Now?"

The Rikkana found a bench in the shade and plopped down on it, her black robes flaring out, expression impassive.

Now, apparently. Trev'nor and Nolan picked up on this as well and found seats that faced the old woman. Becca shifted as well, although she was content to let the boys do most of the talking.

"What is your goal here?" the Rikkana asked the three of them.

It was Trev'nor that responded, "Our goal is to right the order of things in Khobunter. You have been taught that any magician should be enslaved. This is not right. Every other country honors their magicians. They respect them. They are not slaves."

Whatever the Rikkana had expected, this was not it. Her dark eyes narrowed in suspicion. "You conquered this city. It is now yours."

Trev'nor shook his head. "We did not fight to claim this place. We fought to free ourselves. This city is yours as it has always been."

"You freed your kind." The Rikkana inclined her head to indicate the magicians avidly listening in this conversation. "You will take them with you?"

"They can go wherever they want," Nolan corrected. "They are free. We will contact home and inform them there are magicians here who need training. Where they go is up to them."

Becca wasn't sure about leaving the magicians here. She had seen for herself how long it had taken Chahir to accept magic once again. The tradition in Khobunter seemed just as engrained. The fact that they were sitting here and having this conversation was proof enough that hearts and minds did not change overnight.

Frustrated, the Rikkana pointed a finger at Nolan. "You want something."

"I do," Nolan agreed with a brilliant smile. "I want magicians to be free in Khobunter. I want slavery to end."

He might as well have announced that he wanted the suns to be green and the sky to be pink. The Rikkana did not understand this wish at all.

Trev'nor cleared his throat and offered, "Rikkana Sumi, as magicians we make...ah, how to explain this? We make oaths to protect people. To prevent wrongs." Trev'nor jerked a thumb over his shoulder to indicate the silent onlookers. "Our oath is to protect them."

This, at least, rang a bell with the old woman. She nodded somberly. "To honor an oath is a good thing. In Chahir, all magicians honor this oath?"

"All of them," Nolan confirmed.

"I see." The Rikkana sat back and considered things for a moment, her eyes blankly focused on the dirt under their feet. "Our governor here was bad. Rotten. We are glad for what you did."

Becca had heard enough grumblings from the citizens about the government to believe her. "Then we did you a favor?"

"You did," the Rikkana agreed with a bleak smile. "Even though you fought to honor your oath, you did not harm the people and only struck at the government. We are thankful."

So the Rikkana wasn't upset by what they had done, most of the city wasn't either, they just weren't sure what the new conquerors wanted? Becca could work with that. "Rikkana Sumi, we will not stay. You can do what you want."

"Right," Nolan backed her up with a nod of agreement. "Do what you want. Right now, we intend to move on, get some answers, then call home and tell them about the magicians here. Can I ask some questions?"

The old woman seemed relieved that all they wanted was some answers and waved her hand, gesturing for Nolan to ask.

"Magicians come from…" Nolan stopped, frowned, and rephrased. "Magic comes from families. From our records, no one in Khobunter should have magic. We would like to know where they came from."

"They have been here since living memory," the Rikkana answered, spreading her hands slightly in a shrug. "We cannot tell you."

Since living memory? Was that was she said? Becca rubbed at her chin. "Do you know of any old documents, or records, that might tell us?"

The Rikkana just shrugged, indicating she had no idea. "Old stories do not mention magic."

"Oh."

From behind, Roskin came around and gave a formal bow to the Rikkana, recognizing her, before he said to Trev'nor, "I heard you say your Chahirese name. What was it?"

"Rhebentrev'noren," Trev'nor responded. "Why?"

"Chahirese names, they have upana first?"

"Upana first," Nolan affirmed. "In this case, Rheben is the upana."

"There is a place north of here." Roskin turned and pointed in the right general direction. "Khandahr of Rheben."

"Khandahr?" Trev'nor repeated in confusion.

Nolan shook his head, not getting the word either. "City?"

"Old city," Roskin explained patiently. "No one lives there. Half-destroyed."

"Ruins," Becca breathed. "Khandahr probably means ruins. Ruins of Rheben."

"Something like it," Nolan agreed, visibly perking up. "Now why would a city in Khobunter be named with a Chahirese name like that?"

"My family name, no less." Trev'nor stared north and the way his eyes looked, it suggested he was looking far ahead with his magical sense more than his physical sight. "Now that does bear investigation. That place might have answers."

"I'm certainly inclined to go look." Nolan flashed Roskin a smile. "That was helpful. Thanks."

Roskin beamed back. "Glad to help."

"Is it straight north from here?" Nolan asked.

"Adhirk." Tone said 'mostly.' Roskin cocked his head and offered doubtfully, "Four days?"

Four days to get there by horseback? Or dragoo.

Trev'nor waved this away. "I can get there fast. Roskin, we want to go up and look at this place."

"Investigate," Nolan tacked on. "Chhaan."

"Right. Get some answers. Then call home. Tell them about all of you."

"That's fine," Roskin assured him. "We will practice what you taught."

Becca didn't see how the delay would hurt. They'd only need a week or two of poking around in the ruins to see if there was anything to discover. That way, when they did call home, they'd have a great more information to report instead of half-baked theories and conjecture. Half-baked theories would not get them out of the hot water they were already in. Solid information would ease them out of the tight spot and into a more secure location.

"Then we will leave in a few days for a look." Trev'nor looked to the two of them to see if this was alright as he spoke. "We want to spend some time here fixing everything we broke before leaving. After we go to the ruins, we'll come back in a week or two. Good?"

"Fine by me," Nolan acquiesced.

Becca lifted her shoulders slightly. "And me."

Khobunter apparently had very strict laws about female-male conduct. Becca didn't pick up on it at first, as slaves didn't abide by any kind of rules aside from the ones the guards set, so it took a day of being free in Rurick to catch on that most of the citizens here found her relationship with Trev'nor and Nolan strange. Bizarre, even. Family would interact the way they did, or spouses, but nothing short of that. The women did not speak with a man one-on-one unless another woman was with her. Becca freely went wherever she was of a mind to and spoke to whomever she pleased and the women did not agree with this behavior at all.

At first she assumed that Rikkana Sumi followed them about because of what they were doing. Nolan went off to heal anyone that was injured while she and Trev'nor surveyed the damage and discussed what needed to happen. Then Trev'nor went off to start on the government buildings and she split the other direction with a totally different project in mind, and Rikkana Sumi immediately followed her.

Becca stopped dead in her tracks and turned to the woman. "Is there a problem, Rikkana Sumi?"

"You cannot be alone while walking," she responded with that overly patient tone reserved for a person that asks stupid questions.

She blinked. Then blinked again as the full import of that sentence registered. "You mean a woman does not walk alone? At all?"

"Covana women can," she explained.

Covana meaning, what? Becca had an inkling but tried the Solian word to clarify. "Married?"

The Rikkana nodded. "Married women."

So, in other words, because she wasn't married she shouldn't be walking around alone. "My countrywomen are free to do what they want."

The Rikkana didn't like this response at all. She frowned at her, a very maternal look on her face. "Not safe."

"Rikkana, I can fight off any man. Trust me." Rather, Becca had the opposite problem of boys being afraid to approach her. Having the Super Soldier as a brother-parent might have something to do with that. Well, that and her habit of chucking lightning at anything that bothered her. Deciding that a change of subject was in order, she asked, "We did lots of damage. Food stores fine?"

The Rikkana really, really wanted to pursue the topic but food was very important in a desert land like this one. A mulish expression on her face, she nevertheless responded, "Need to check."

"Then let's check."

Seeing that Becca was willing to follow her, and she wouldn't have to worry short-term about her being inappropriate, the Rikkana relaxed a tad and led off. Becca relaxed as well and schemed. She'd get Nolan over here later and have him explain Chahiran culture. No way was she living under these kinds of restrictions; they were patently ridiculous. Women normally moved in groups because they were social and it was more fun that way, but being forced to? Just to step outside the house? No thanks.

They stopped at a building that was thicker than most, the walls nearly wide enough that she couldn't put her hands

on either side. When she stepped inside, Becca felt that the
air was much cooler, with only two lamps inside providing
light. Two other women were already there, both near
her age, their hair tied back in kerchiefs. They greeted the
Rikkana with high-pitched excitement, which Becca took as
a good sign.

As the Rikkana spoke with them, she looked the building
over in general. It was quite the warehouse, really, with
enough food in here to feed the town for at least two or three
days. Bins were lined in rows, different types of vegetables
poking out of them. Becca went and investigated as they
rarely got anything more than flat bread and meat in the
slave pens.

There was wheat, watermelon, corn, some root vegetables
like tarot and carrots, but there wasn't much in the way of
variety. Perhaps the rest were stored elsewhere? Come to
think of it, there were practically no fruits here either. At
least, none that she recognized.

The Rikkana came back to her and introduced, "Raya
Becca, this is Chanda and Bala."

Becca gave the Rikkana a weary look. She had protested
this, several times, but the Rikkana insisted that raya was the
proper way to address her. Nolan had translated the title as
meaning 'lady,' roughly. No matter how many times Becca
denied this, and that just Becca was fine, the Rikkana would
not yield.

She gave up on the point for the time being and focused
on the two girls. They had to be sisters. They had the same
heart-shaped faces, wavy dark hair, and slightly prominent
nose bridge. Their smiles were identical too, sweet but shy,
and a little nervous. Considering Becca had leveled a good
section of the city three days ago, she couldn't blame them
for being nervous. Trying to show good intentions, she

smiled and gave them a quick bow. "I'm Becca. Hello."

Melting under her smile, they bobbed their heads to return the greeting.

"Food stores safe?" she asked them. The building didn't look impacted from here, but she could only easily see about half of the area from here.

"Perfectly," Chanda assured her.

That was reassuring. "All of it?"

They looked puzzled, although why, Becca couldn't fathom. She thought it a rather straightforward question.

The Rikkana stepped in to clarify. "This is all."

"Just this building?" Becca spluttered. They hadn't passed many farms coming in, granted, but surely this building wasn't meant to feed the whole town! Belatedly she realized that she had spoken in Chahirese and tried to rephrase in her limited vocabulary. "Just here? No more?"

"No more," the Rikkana verified carefully. "This is plenty."

Becca shook her head firmly. "No." Making a snap decision, she turned to the three as a whole and demanded, "Show me water. Well for town."

Bala caught on first what she wanted to see and gestured for her to follow. Becca went right on her heels as they left the building and headed for the outer wall. They passed Nolan as they walked, who was kneeling next to an injured dragoo with a pitiful expression on its face. Becca called to him as she passed, "Meet me at the well over here when you're done."

Nolan sank back onto his haunches to respond, "Is there a problem?"

"I think so. But finish there, then I'll explain."

He waved a hand in acknowledgement and bent back to the dragoo.

Fortunately the well was right around the next corner, so

Nolan wouldn't get too lost trying to find them. Becca bent down to give it a thorough examination.

With no Weather Mage other than herself in existence, there wasn't a ready teacher for her. Garth had instead cobbled together a curriculum of history books and two professors from Coven Ordan to give her some idea of what she could do. She had been taught by both an Air Mage and a Water Mage, and so had the basic teachings of both. She used that knowledge now to trace the water source as far as she could feel, but eventually she lost track of it. What she could feel did not seem adequate to really supply a town of this size with enough water.

Frowning, she stood up again and found Nolan right behind her. "Problem?" he prompted.

"Nol, I'm not liking what I see," she stated, gesturing to the well. "This is the main water source for the town, but I wouldn't think it could support more than half of this population comfortably."

Nolan leaned so that he could peer down the well. "My water sense isn't nearly as strong as yours, but it doesn't seem that deep."

"It's not. Also, I checked their food storage, and what they call 'food storage' for a town is ridiculous. They have about ten varieties of vegetables. That's it."

His eyebrows shot up. "You're kidding."

"I wish I was. We want to do something to make up for the damage we did here, right? Then I think we should create an aqueduct system, a water reservoir, and create a garden with more variety of fruits and vegetables. To them, it will seem like a luxury."

Nolan flipped a hand up. "It should be easy enough to do if the three of us put our heads and magic together. Want me to call Trev'nor?"

"Yes. I refuse to leave for the ruins until this is done."

She had no argument from him. To the three waiting women, he explained what they intended to do. It was funny to watch their reactions because even though he spoke in their native tongue it was clear they had no idea what he was describing. But then, how could they, when they had never seen the like before?

Nolan gave up and said to her, "I'll get Trev. We'll have to just show them; they don't even really know what the words mean."

"I caught that. Go, go. I'll start studying the layout while you fetch him. We have our work cut out for us here."

"It will take more than a day," Nolan agreed. Then grinned.

She knew that look. "You're looking forward to playing, aren't you?"

"What's the fun of being a mage if you can't be creative?"

Creative? With plants? Oh dear.

Trev'nor greeted her idea with an enthusiastic, "Great idea! It's perfect for what they need here."

"In other words," Becca drawled, struggling not to laugh at his enthusiasm, "any excuse to play in the dirt will do."

"Yes?" he responded as if this were perfectly obvious.

Boys. Give them a dirt pile and they were happy. "I've studied the area a little and I think I have an idea of how to work an aqueduct in here."

"Hey now, I'm the builder in the group," Trev'nor objected.

She pointed toward her own nose, "And I'm the one that understands best how water flows."

He had his mouth open for a retort only to think better of it. "I see your point. Together?"

"Probably for the best. Since you're building the things. Nolan, do you have an idea of what we can plant out here?"

"More or less but some of it depends on how much you're going to build and where. Some plants require a lot of space to grow in, others can't survive in full sunlight, so I'll need at least partial shade for them."

All valid points. "Follow along, then, and let's figure out how to do this."

The Rikkana more or less came along for the ride as the three mages went throughout the town and talked to anyone willing to stop and speak for a minute. They asked many questions, sometimes struggling to get their points across, as they tried to understand just what the needs were for the town and where they could build without it interfering in people's businesses. Becca's vocabulary grew by leaps and bounds during this process as she picked up words here and there.

Chanda and Bala turned out to be in charge of food storage for the town. Nolan pulled them aside and asked many, many questions about their storage abilities. The girls seemed a little enthralled with his politeness and looks as they would sometimes clutch each other and giggle.

It did not go unnoticed that Nolan seemed to appreciate the attention.

Half the day was spent talking to the citizens and planning what could go where. Trev'nor wasn't even able to break ground until late that afternoon but of course an Earth Mage didn't need the same amount of time as a regular construction crew to do the job. He had the water reservoir built and three aqueduct lines in place before the light failed him.

Nolan got sucked back into healing ailments but came back to the outer wall of the city and gave the area a long look. "Trev," Nolan intoned with an unhappy look narrowing his eyes, "you didn't change the soil for me."

"Ah, oops? Wait, was I supposed to do that first?"

"Yes," Becca inserted with a roll of her eyes. "It's more time efficient that way, remember? That way Nolan can be planting things while you build."

"Ah. Double oops?"

Double oops, he said. The man needed a keeper some days. "Too late now. I guess do it first thing in the morning."

"Sure," Trev'nor agreed easily. "I'm almost done, Bec, I

think we can finish everything up tomorrow. You want to call in a storm tonight and fill up the reservoir?"

"Not a bad thought. I'll do that." Almost belatedly she realized that Sumi and another woman that she didn't know where standing nearby, clearly waiting to catch her attention. Waving the boys on, she went over to the women. "Hello."

"Raya Becca, this is Asha," the Rikkana introduced.

Asha looked like she was a well-established matron that likely had at least five kids. She wasn't particularly portly but her face had a roundness to it that gave her a certain charm. With a bow, she greeted, "Raya Becca. You will stay with my family."

Oh?

Seeing her confusion, the Rikkana explained, "It was her house that you stayed in the past three days."

Ahhh. They had chosen a house at random to sleep in. So Becca's room was in Asha's? "And the boys?"

"They have been moved to stay next door."

In other words, it was Not Appropriate for them to sleep under the same roof as she did. Becca decided not to bring up that she had camped out with them for nearly two weeks before coming here. It was best to not trip into that dangerous ground. "I will be glad to stay with you, Mistress Asha."

They both looked relieved at this response. "You are done for the day?" the Rikkana pressed.

"I am not," she denied, trying not to show any amusement at her impatience. "I have a storm to call. But after that, I can go back."

Asha and the Rikkana exchanged looks and it was clear they were working out who would stay with her. Becca didn't even try to argue that she was fine by herself. Those words would fall on deaf ears. "Ten, fifteen minutes. Tops."

Since it was a short time, they were more amiable, and

the Rikkana indicated Asha could go back first. Then she planted herself and made it absolutely clear that she was not leaving Becca's side.

That was fine as Becca wasn't sure she could find the house again in the dark anyway. To the boys, she said, "They've apparently moved you two into the house next to the one we were in."

They weren't surprised by this change—after all, they had just crashed it someone's house; with the owners back, of course they would have to move—and Trev'nor gave a flick of the hand in acknowledgement before finishing up what he was doing.

Nolan and Trev'nor left, likely to find dinner and bed, leaving Becca to work. She focused on the sky and patiently called in the right wind currents, the right moisture, all culminating in a storm that would give them steady rainfall through most of the night. She wanted that reservoir as full as she could get it before leaving. Having moisture on the ground for Trev'nor to work with in the morning wouldn't hurt either.

With her work done, she finally consented to go to bed, which relieved the Rikkana. The woman must be dead tired running all over the city all day. They barely got within sight of the door when Asha latched onto her upper arm and pulled her inside. "Raya Becca, it is late," she said in reproving tones.

Becca bit back a sigh, or a groan, and went along. That was another rule: a woman should not be out after sunset. "Asha, this place has too many rules."

"Good rules," the older woman told her, still with that frown on her face. "Protect you."

"From what, exactly? You do remember that I can level this city if I want to?"

"Protect your heart."

And what in the world did that mean? Becca had no chance to follow it up with another question as she was dragged into the house and bombarded from both sides. "Whoa! Chanda, Bala, what?"

Both girls had visible hearts in their eyes as they looked at her. The words nearly tripped out of Chanda's mouth, she spoke so quickly. "We heard. Raja Nolan is prince?"

"Trev'nor called him so," Bala added, nearly vibrating in place.

"Ah, yes. Nolan is Prince of Chahir."

The girls let out high pitched squeals and bounced in a tight circle, gripping each other's hands and talking so quickly that Becca barely caught one word in five.

Asha's eyes were crossed. "Truly? A prince?"

"Only prince of Chahir," Becca confirmed. Well, technically his father was too. It was too much trouble to explain that and she let it go with a shrug.

"Does not act like prince..." Asha trailed off uncertainly.

"No, he's nice. Not arrogant." Becca had to wonder what their impression of princes were but if the government and warlord here had been any indication, then they were not nice men. Certainly not the type to go around healing people and talking with them. Seeing that Asha was worried about this, she ducked her head enough to give the matron a smile. "Nolan came as Life Mage. Not as prince. Treat him as mage. Yes?"

"But is a prince," Asha responded, her sense of propriety flaring to life.

Oh dear. Maybe Becca shouldn't have said anything. "Is also mage. He came to work as mage. Respect that."

Asha visibly struggled but finally nodded reluctantly.

Seeing that she had a chance to break for freedom, Becca

took it and headed for the kitchen, finding that a plate had been made up for her. After not eating most of the day, she was starving and ate it quickly up. She had every intention of washing up afterwards until Asha elbowed her aside and shooed her up the stairs. This was likely another etiquette thing but Becca was too tired to ask and figure it out. Instead, she went up the stairs to her second story bedroom.

The room was as she had left it. It barely had space for a single bed, washstand, and a chest to put clothes into. She closed the door behind her with a nudge of the hip before stripping down, then washing with the tepid water from the washstand. Running around in a desert didn't make a person sweat, not really, but it did leave traces of sand on the skin that was uncomfortable to sleep in.

Pulling on a loose slip, she crawled into bed, leaving the covers pooled around her waist. The desert had extremes of hots and colds. It was scorching hot during the day, very cold at night, but after sunset like this was a middle ground to where it still retained some heat. She'd need the covers later but not right at this moment.

Laying back, she pillowed her arms under her head and stared sightlessly at the ceiling. Absolutely nothing about this trip had gone to plan. First capture, then fighting to get free, and now having to convince people that she hadn't come in to conquer their city. Well, no, Sumi more or less believed them. Really, if she had to pick an argument to win, it wasn't that one. Trying to convince them that magician didn't automatically mean 'slave' had been a more than uphill battle. The people here seemed to think that the three Chahirans were an exception to the rule because they were a different type of magician. Mages weren't slaves. Witches and wizards were.

It was like trying to argue that magic wasn't evil in

Chahir all over again, it was so engrained in Khobunter's culture. Becca felt like screaming.

The only saving grace was that the people of Rurick did understand this: they were not to try to enslave the magicians again. They would have three very upset mages if they did and they wanted to avoid that at all costs. Becca could live with that, for now. It did beg the question, though, of what to do later? Obviously they couldn't just charge into a city and release the slaves and then go on their merry way expecting all to be fine.

Agitated, she flopped over to lie on her side, staring at the wall instead. This might be a moot point, at least in the near future. Trying to set up several magical academies here in Khobunter would be near impossible. The Trasdee Evondit Orra would likely want to just relocate all of the magicians from here and train them in Hain, or in Chahir, which would be the more sensible approach. She envisioned Garth's reaction when he had several thousand students come into Strae and snorted laughter. Oh dear. He'd be torn between elation and panic.

Honestly, none of these were really her problems to fix. What she should do was go investigate the ruins, get answers, then report home on what they had found here. After that, she would go back to searching for her weather-tampering magician and free any slaves that crossed her path in the process. That was her task.

Putting aside the questions she couldn't solve, she closed her eyes in a determined way. She had to get up early tomorrow to travel to the ruins and it would be best to get a full night's sleep. Trev'nor was a notorious early bird.

As she slipped into sleep, one more errant thought floated through her mind. She hoped, wistfully, that she would be able to meet up again with everyone at the Academy after she returned home. She'd made friends with them, these past two weeks. It would be fun to show them what being a respected magician was like out in the rest of the world.

The next morning they were out again, finishing up the job they had started. Becca's storm had done its job and filled the reservoir half-full and given the ground a good soaking. Well, as much as this soil could handle, at least.

Trev'nor surveyed the results inside their walled-in garden space with a satisfied expression. "Perfect. I needed moisture to really get the soil to optimum conditions."

Watching an Earth Mage work was nothing like watching a Life Mage, or an Air Mage, or any other type. They didn't have to concentrate in quite the same way. Trev'nor's eyes seemed to go blind to his immediate surroundings as he saw something below the level of the ground that the rest of them could not detect.

But even she could see the results. A great deal of powdery substance and hard pebbles were shifted to the side in a rubbish pile. The earth around them became dark and rich, perfect for planting. She glanced at Nolan and found him rubbing his hands, eager to get started. "Perfect?"

"Perfect," he agreed.

Trev'nor stepped back and gave Nolan a grand flourish and bow. "My apologies for the delay, My Lord Magus. Do proceed."

Nolan punched him in the arm, playfully, and stepped past him with a grin on his face.

"Did you see that?" Trev'nor mock-complained to her. "I do the man favors and get abused for it."

"You poor baby," she cooed. "Should I kiss it and make

it better?"

"Ew. Becca, seriously, ew."

Snickering, she turned to find that Bala was in her shadow. Of course she was, someone had to be. She looked between the two of them with a blush on her cheeks and Becca could just see the girl jumping to the wrong conclusions. "Bala. Quit that. I was teasing him, that's why he's grossed out right now."

She looked confused for a split second. Then she lit right back up. "Ah, then it's Raja Nolan that you favor?"

Becca buried her head in both hands and groaned, loud and long. "No. No, I do not. Trev, stop laughing and help me out here."

"I've been trying for three days now to convince people that I'm not interested in dating you." Trev'nor sounded quite cheerful about the whole thing. "They refuse to be convinced. I'm alright with them misunderstanding you and Nolan, that's much funnier."

For that, Becca slugged him in the arm.

Bala gasped. Something about her horrified, befuddled confusion got Becca's undivided attention.

"What?" Becca demanded of her.

"Raya Becca, you mustn't touch a man casually if you are not attached to him," Bala scolded in a shocked whisper, as if afraid one of the elders would overhear. Although who was a good question—they were the only ones in this section of town at the moment.

It was close, but Becca didn't start screaming in frustration.

"Breathe, Bec," Trev'nor advised, amused and sympathetic all at once. "Breathe. Miss Bala, our culture is radically different than yours, you probably won't get it if I explain. So do us a favor. Treat us like siblings."

The girl blinked at him as if she had never heard the word. "Siblings?"

"Right. Like brother and sister. Because that's basically what we are, siblings. We grew up together like them."

She did not seem able to wrap her mind around this idea either but seemed more game to try. "I see. I will try."

"Good, good." To Becca, Trev'nor said, "While he's playing, let's go eat something. I think we skipped breakfast."

"It's too early for lunch," she pointed out.

"Then we'll go for luncfest."

"Trev. There has to be a better way to combine those words."

He gave her a sweet smile. "We can debate the matter over food."

Becca gave up. "Fine. Food."

Nolan joined them an hour later looking more than a little dirty but with satisfaction all over his face. He dropped into the chair next to them, eyeing the remains of the dishes on their table the way a stray dog would leftovers. "You left some for me?"

"We did, but shouldn't you clean up first?" Becca eyed him from head to toe, wondering aloud, "How did you even get this dirty?"

"I had to form a few plants by hand and then bury them more firmly into the soil," he explained. "Trev, hit me."

Trev'nor waved a hand expansively in his direction, like a stage magician would. "Dirt, I banish thee."

The dirt leapt to obey and fell off Nolan in one fell swoop. It left the Life Mage looking clean but not exactly pristine.

Nolan grabbed a clean plate from the middle of the table and started filling his plate. "So I planted seven different fruit trees, more vegetables, a few grape vines, and the like. I tweaked them a little so they're hardier and they'll produce longer. They'll also go dormant on their own without needing much care, but we need to run the proper way to take care of the garden by a few people. We don't want them killing things by accident."

Becca wholeheartedly agreed with that. "We also need

to teach them what to do with all of these plants. They won't know how to eat them, or cook them, or store them, or anything."

Nolan nodded with his mouth full.

"How fast are these plants of yours growing?" Trev'nor asked with a slight frown. "Will we be able to show them all of this today?"

Nolan shook his head and reached for his cup, chugging it down. Once his mouth was clear, he said, "No, the plants will reach full maturation tonight. We'll need to stay one more day."

This surprised Becca. "Even the fruit trees?"

"They won't be very big, but they'll produce at least some fruit by morning. It'll take years for them to reach full maturation."

Well, that was a surprise. Becca had no experience with young fruit trees so she hadn't realized even the small ones could bear something. "I'm guessing you used a lot of magic putting the garden in, that's why you're starving?"

"In a nutshell," Nolan verified before pointing at a dish near her elbow. "That looks spicy."

Nolan couldn't handle any level of spice at all. He had no tolerance for it. Becca felt a spark of mischievousness take hold.

"It is—" Trev'nor started, only to clam up when she kicked him in the shin under the table.

"—n't," she completed smoothly. "It just looks that way because of some spice they used. But it's safe for your tongue."

Not suspecting a thing, Nolan popped a bite into his mouth. He probably intended to say something, but his reaction to the hot dish was almost immediate. His eyes bugged out of his head, his face flushed, sweat started dewing on his temples. Choking, spluttering, he downed another glass of water but of course that didn't help much. Swearing unintelligibly around the mouthful he couldn't (politely) spit out, he lunged to his feet.

Becca instinctively jumped up to follow him, which attracted the attention of everyone else on the street. They slowed as they watched their foreign mages react in a crazy fashion. Nolan stripped off his jacket, kicked off shoes one foot at a time, and headed for the nearest open aqueduct. Without a word to anyone, he climbed up, turning into a seal as he did so. Flopping inside, he ducked under the water and stayed there for a solid minute.

Of course Trev'nor had followed along, and seeing what his friend did, doubled over in laughter. "Bec, you're mean!" he gasped out.

"You say that, but you're laughing," she responded, chuckling herself. "Why is he so bad at spice?"

"I have no idea. My question is, why does he constantly believe you when you tell him something isn't spicy? This is like the hundredth time he's fallen for it."

Yes, it was close to that. Becca enjoyed pranking every time too.

Nolan finally surfaced. Bracing his front fins on the side of the aqueduct he leveled a seally glare at her and squawked indignantly, making honking noises.

"I'm sorry, I don't speak seal," Becca responded with false contriteness.

The townspeople around them gathered in closer, awed and a little amused at this scene. Rikkana Sumi approached and studied Nolan with something akin to trepidation. "This is…?"

"Nolan," Becca answered forthrightly. "Life Mages can assume the form of any animal they wish to."

The Rikkana regarded the transformed teenager for

another long moment. "Why...?"

"He ate something spicy," Becca explained, still acting innocent. "He's very bad at spice."

Nolan gave another indignant protest that no one could understand.

"By that, she means she tricked him into eating something spicy," Trev'nor explained, still chuckling and wiping a tear from the corner of his eye. "Ah, this never gets old. He goes into a different animal form every time."

Yes, he did. That's why she did it. Adopting a business-like expression, she snapped her fingers at him. "Alright, enough, climb out now and put your clothes back on. We need to finish eating lunch and return to work."

Nolan gave her another glare, and a huff, and dove back into the water.

"I don't think he trusts you anymore," Trev'nor drawled.

Wise man. There was still another dish on that table she'd planned on making him eat. Well, another time would do. Feeling happy and light for the first time in many days, she skipped back to her lunch. Maybe Nolan wouldn't come out of the water anytime soon, but she still planned on teaching the people in this city some of the joys of life before leaving. Fruits were high on that list.

Nolan stifled a yawn behind one hand. "Trev. Why are we up before birds are even awake?"

"Half-asleep people aren't as prone to panicking," Trev'nor explained cheerfully as he took them down into the earth. His magic wrapped around them in muted tones of green and brown.

They had spent two days longer in Rurick than anyone

had planned, mostly because it had taken that long to teach people how to tend the garden and what to do with the food it yielded. She did not regret the extra time because it let her learn more about them. Becca liked to think she had formed friendships among the people and not just the magicians that she had shared such a horrific experience with.

Because of that, it was only this morning that they were finally leaving. Becca had extremely limited experience when it came to using the Earth Path. In fact, she had only been on it perhaps thrice before in her life. She wouldn't begin to say that she was an expert, but to her Trev'nor's path felt a little different than Garth's. How, she couldn't say, as it wasn't something that she could put a finger on. It just did. Although, being down here did bring up a thought she hadn't considered before. "Trev. How do you navigate down here?"

"Same way Garth does. By the feel of the land. I know by the map where cities are, and I can feel things like mountains and lakes and such. I use them as landmarks and navigate." Pausing, he thought for a moment more before offering, "Also, the buildings that we're going to are really old, right? I doubt anything else standing has quite the same feel to them so I'm searching for something that feels ancient."

That made a great deal of sense. Most of magic was common sense application, really, although an outsider didn't always see it that way. "You can tell how old a building is?"

"The age of it is very obvious," Trev'nor admitted absently, focusing.

Nolan sidled up to her and whispered, "Try not to distract him. It's hard for him to navigate in a place he doesn't know and I'd rather he not trip over a ley line."

Oops. Becca clamped her mouth shut and didn't dare to

utter another peep for the rest of the trip.

She had no way of sensing time, but it seemed like not even an hour had passed before they rose to the surface, the ground melting away from them like reverse quicksand. The morning sunlight was just turning to true day, still in that hazy wash of sepia tones and cool blue. Laid out before them was a small ridge of hills, like a miniature mountain range, and nestled into the basin sat a spread of what must have once been a magnificent city. The buildings sat half-destroyed, there were no roofs to be found, but the pillars of carved stone still stood straight and tall, forming archways and partial walls. Some of the buildings stood several stories, others were so demolished that barely anything of the original structure stood, just one brick on top of another. Even in its ruined state, it looked breathtaking.

Becca's voice came out hushed as she asked, "How old is it?"

"At a guess? About thirty or so years after the Magic War ended." Trev'nor pointed to the far right. "This part is newer by about a decade. The central part here is the oldest."

Nolan tilted sideways to look around Becca, eyes fastened on Trev'nor. "What? You have the strangest look on your face."

"Two things," Trev'nor said hoarsely unable to look away from the ruins. "One, most of what we're seeing was fashioned by magic."

Her breath caught in her throat as Becca took in his meaning. This was a magically constructed city?! Was it something like the ancient form of Coven Ordan?

Oblivious to their reaction, Trev'nor continued, "Two, there's a memory stone here."

She had to catch her jaw and slot it back into place to demand, "Memory stone? Are you sure?"

"Positive. It's calling out to me very strongly." Trev'nor started forward as if sleepwalking, moving as quickly as he could without taking any more than the basic necessary precautions.

Becca and Nolan had to scramble to keep up with him, he moved that fast. Becca caught flashes here and there as Trev'nor used magic subconsciously to speed him past any obstacles that would take more than two seconds to get through. She had no time to examine any part of the city, as he moved too fast for her to have that luxury. Instead she focused on keeping up with him, and it wasn't until they were near the middle of the ruins—at least it felt like they were— that Trev'nor abruptly stopped, pivoted on his heel, and went directly to the right. He reached out with both hands, touching something just out of her sight, and immediately froze with a look of wonder on his face.

Stepping around, she got a look over his shoulder and found the strangest looking stone in front of him. It was huge, large enough to put an ancient tree to shame, and it had lines of magic flickering over it in an abstract pattern that made no sense to her. The way it writhed and shifted colors, it looked alive. "That's a memory stone?"

Nolan nodded, cheeks flushed from the exertion of keeping up. "Did you ever see the one in Coven Ordan? Or the one we have on Strae?"

"I always meant to, but didn't. Garth said that it's almost alive but…" she trailed off, still studying it. "Is it?"

"Not in the sense you mean," Nolan disagreed. "It's alive with memory, with history, with the recordings of the magician who last touched it. But it doesn't have any will of its own. Memory stones are by nature crafted largely by Earth Mages and then used by everyone else. I think that's partially why they call so strongly to any Earth Mage nearby."

That did make sense. She tilted her torso and looked up at Trev'nor. He stared straight ahead, expression changing from one second to the next as he responded to something that she couldn't hear or see. Waving a hand in front of his face, he didn't blink, nor seemed to realize she was nearby at all. "Is he in a trance?"

"Of sorts," Nolan confirmed. He came around to study Trev'nor's face as well. "Last time this happened, he was more or less held prisoner by the stone until it had told him everything. I think it's going to happen again this time so we might as well be patient and wait him out."

Becca didn't like the sound of that. "But what if something dangerous happens?"

"We can yank him away by force if we need to," Nolan assured her. "It's just not advisable unless it's a true emergency. It's very jarring to be taken out forcefully and it gives the body and mind an unwelcome shock. I'd rather we didn't try it unless we absolutely have to."

Not being a Life Mage, or having anything more than basic training in medicine, she couldn't begin to evaluate if Trev'nor was in danger or not. She'd have to trust Nolan's judgement on this. So she nodded and turned, looking about her. "Then, why don't we put a ward up around him, just in case, and go exploring?"

"We might as well." Nolan turned and looked as well. "I think this is going to take a while, so why don't we find a fresh source of water, if we can, and some place nearby so we can sleep."

It was the sensible thing to do, so she agreed. "Any idea of how to find water out here?"

"Not a one," Nolan admitted cheerfully, already bring his magic to the front, preparing to create a ward. "But we'll figure it out."

It took minutes to set up the ward and then they set out, slowly exploring the ruins. The outer walls had come down in multiple places, baring the interior, which gave her an interesting view. All of the doorways were arched—not round per se, but with a definite diamond tip to the top. Other places looked strongly Chahiran, with the traditional architecture that she was used to.

Nolan held out a hand as they went down a crumbling staircase. "Watch your step."

She took the offered hand and was more than grateful for the courtesy as the stone shifted a little under her weight. "This place grows more bizarre as I look at it. Parts of it match up with Chahir so well and other parts, like the doorways, look very in tune with what we've seen in Rurick."

"It's growing increasingly obvious to me that the original builders to this place must have been Chahiran magicians." Nolan looked around. "That shimmering over there, does that look like water to you?"

"Possibly?" It glinted in the light like water would. If nothing else, she wanted to see what it was. "Let's see."

Nolan led the way, making sure to keep his pace so that she could easily keep up, and continued where he had left off. "The memory stone alone says that an Earth Mage was up here at some point. I think this is conclusive evidence. But none of the records show that we had a large number of Chahiran magicians come and settle into Khobunter."

He said this so confidently. "How do you know?"

"When Garth and Xiaolang were first given the task of finding the magicians out of Chahir, they spent their off time studying the indexes and matching them up with whatever records they could find," Nolan explained. "And when they found that huge stash of records at a pool in Chahir, it was all carted back to the Sojavel Ra Institute and studied even more there. Believe me, if there had been a record of a group traveling up into Khobunter, they would know about it."

Becca pondered on that for a while, trying to match it up with what she had been taught in school. "But wasn't the situation right at the end of the Magic War a complete mess? I mean, they lost track completely of the only family of Weather Mages in the confusion of evacuation. No one even knew about Coven Ordan until they decided to come over and say hi."

"That…" Nolan gave her a sharp look. "That is a good point. What are you saying? That it's possible the builders of this city were evacuees from Chahir at the end of the Magic War?"

"It's possible, isn't it? And it fits the timeline too well to be a coincidence. Trev'nor said this place had been built a few decades after the war. Even with magic, wouldn't it take a long time to build this city?"

"Several decades, I would think." Nolan's steps slowed as he took another, more contemplative look around. "But Becca, if that's the case, then the magicians here in Khobunter are likely the descendants of this ruined city. That means that the magicians here are Chahiran."

"Several generations removed." The idea didn't sit well with her. She hadn't thought of the magicians in Rurick as Chahiran because they hadn't looked the part. There hadn't been a hint of blond hair or fair skin to be found anywhere on them. But the magic that sang through their veins was proof enough. "I don't like this. We don't have the evidence to prove it, I know, but if we're right?"

"I think we are," Nolan said grimly. He had to duck and slip sideways to get past a fallen pillar that was leaning at an angle and resting in between two buildings. "It makes too much sense and fits in too neatly with what we know.

If we're right, it means that a whole generation of Chahiran magicians tried to take refuge in Khobunter and rebuild their lives. Only it didn't last. They were taken and turned into slaves."

The thought made her blood boil. Bad enough that magicians were treated like animals to begin with, but if they were originally Chahiran, her own countrymen, it was a different matter altogether.

"Don't get angry just yet," Nolan counseled, although from the sparks arcing off of his bare skin, it was clear that he was not following his own advice. "We don't have proof. And that memory stone likely holds most of the answers that we need. We wait for Trev'nor to get done and then tell us what we need to know."

"You're assuming it holds all the answers."

"It doesn't need to. It just needs to answer two: Were the builders of this place Chahiran? Were they taken captive by the people of Khobunter? That's all we need to know."

The building right behind the memory stone was largely intact, with the second floor still standing and acting like a roof for them. They chose it to stay in that night, sweeping the floor clear of sand and pebbles to make a smoother bed, with a small fire going for warmth. Their dinner was a cold one, made of the food they'd packed for the trip, and Nolan was the one that coaxed Trev'nor to eat. Feeding someone while still in a trance was interesting. At least, Becca found it entertaining. It took Nolan nearly an hour to feed Trev'nor a full meal, one small bite at a time.

If Trev'nor had been with them that night, instead of glued to the stone, he would have made the ground softer so that they weren't literally sleeping on a slab of rock. Becca, not used to such a hard bed, tossed and turned, only falling asleep in the wee hours of the morning. When she awoke, she felt fuzzy headed and her back half-numb. Some strange music thrummed near her ear, too. It sounded somewhat like birdsong, but not quite, with a strum of a vibrating string mixed in. What in the wide green world…?

"Becca. Don't move."

She blinked open both eyes and lifted her head enough to see. Nolan was sitting comfortably on his bedroll, legs crossed, with the strangest looking creatures covering him from the shoulders down. They were small, about the size of a man's closed fist, completely covered in fur with a long tail that trailed out and big, liquid eyes. They seemed to come in every possible hue of color from the brightest of blues to muted tans.

"Ah...."

"No idea what these are," Nolan answered, as if she had asked the question aloud. He was petting two of them with careful fingers, a grin on his face. "But they're very affectionate. And soft. I woke up this morning completely buried in them."

Seeing that she too was buried in them from the waist down, Becca eased up onto her elbows and got a better look at them. They were all more or less the same size, and seemed to have legs under all of that fur, but really they looked like furry eggs. Large furry eggs. "How are they making that sound?"

"Their tails are vibrating at high speeds. It's rather like a cat's purr, I think. It's a sign of happiness." Nolan slid one finger under and scratched at the belly of a yellow one and the tail went so fast that it made a blur of sound. "Haha, they're ticklish!"

Becca tentatively reached out as well—just because they liked Nolan didn't mean they'd like her, he was the Life Mage after all—and stroked the head of one near her hand. It blinked at her and then crawled into her hand, tail vibrating in a faster movement. "They are soft. Where did they come from? We didn't see a hint of them yesterday."

"I felt them yesterday," Nolan disagreed, "but I didn't know what they were. I just thought it was rats or something as they were small and fast. I couldn't get a clear sense of them. I guess they got used to us being here during the course of the night and couldn't resist coming in closer."

Nolan's magic had that effect on animals. "They can't be native to Khobunter, though, can they? I mean, Rurick didn't have them."

His eyes on the animals in his hands, Nolan said quietly, "They're Life Mage constructions."

Becca's breath caught in her throat. "You can tell?"

"The magic isn't strong in them anymore, it's been multiple generations since the first one was created, but it's like looking at a meuritta versus looking at a normal cat. To me, it's obvious that one was created and the other is natural. These are created."

So a Life Mage had obviously been up here too. "Nolan, this is looking pretty conclusive to me."

His mouth went into a flat line. "I'm convinced. But I want to hear what Trev'nor has learned from the stone."

"Me too." Becca gave her situation another study. "Say, Nolan?"

"What is it?"

"How do I convince them that I need to move?"

"That is a very good question. If I knew the answer, I would have done it myself."

"But you can communicate with them, right?"

"Sure, but…how do I say this? I can talk to them but they don't quite get it. I ask them to move, and they gladly do, but it's like three inches. Max. I can't get them to leave either one of us alone."

"Slowly roll to our feet and give them time to move? I can't think of a better plan."

Nolan shrugged and rolled up to his knees, fuzzy creatures bouncing off in all directions. Even though they didn't land on their feet, they didn't seem hurt by the movements and were upright again in moments, tails still making those musical sounds.

Seeing how resilient they were, Becca wasn't as cautious in getting out of bed and gaining her feet. It helped that she wasn't as popular as Nolan, so she had fewer of the creatures to watch out for as she moved.

They spent the rest of the day exploring and dodging their new fuzzy friends. They went back at noon for lunch, feeding Trev'nor as well, and making sure he was hydrated under the hot desert suns. Then they continued their foray, exploring a different section of the city. Aside from what they had already discovered, nothing else leapt out at them. Becca and Nolan didn't really know how to analyze what they were seeing, but at the very least when they were home again they could dump their memories into a crystal and show it to other people.

When they came back that evening, Becca tried making something over their small campfire, as she was tired of bread and jerky and sliced fruit. The fuzzies had led her to a clear underground well, giving she had fresh water and some vegetables, so she stewed them together and hoped for the best.

Nolan sat and helped her, peeling a potato, when his head abruptly snapped up. "Trev'nor's out of the trance."

"Finally!" Dropping everything in her hands, she raced around the wall and directly to Trev'nor's side. "Trev."

He was sprawled out on the ground, breathing hard, a grimace on his face. "How long have I been standing? My legs are cramping something awful."

"Two days." Nolan knelt at his feet, hands reaching out for Trev'nor calves. He glowed a muted red as he magically eased the cramps. "You need to drink."

"I need more than just to drink." Looking a little embarrassed, he eased back up to his feet. "Where's, ah…?"

Nolan pointed him out of the building. "Go down, first

doorway on the right."

"Thanks, back in a bit."

It took Becca a second to get it. Oh, right, of course. They'd been pouring water down him for two days but because of the trance he couldn't go to the bathroom. His bladder was probably screaming. A little amused, she went back to making dinner, cutting up the rest of the vegetables and throwing them into the cookpot.

Trev'nor came to them looking tired but relieved and plopped down next to the fire. "My brain is wrung out. Shouldn't there have been a safety spell in place on that thing? It's not supposed to hold you captive like that for more than a few hours."

"I have a feeling that spell failed over the years," Becca offered, brushing the last of the water from her hands. "It's several centuries old, after all. But tell us what it was showing you."

"Sure thing, but…" Trev'nor pointed down at the creature that was happily leaning up against his crossed ankles. "What's that?"

"A fuzzy," Becca replied promptly.

"Becca!" Nolan protested. "We have to give them a better name than that!"

"They're little, walking fuzzballs, what else are you going to name them?"

The Prince of Chahir spluttered incoherently.

"They're very sweet," Becca assured Trev'nor, who was now poking at the fuzzy with the tip of his finger, making the creature vibrate with musical pleasure. "Not very bright, but sweet. The noise its tail is making is like a cat purring."

"And they like humans, I take it?"

"You'll probably wake up completely buried in them," Nolan warned cheerfully. "We were. These are Life Mage constructions, by the way."

"Not surprised." Trev'nor blew out a breath, expression troubled. "I'm not sure how much the two of you have figured out in the past two days, so I'll just start from the beginning. Some of the families that evacuated from Chahir during the Magic War came here. It was a slow journey—some of them actually took two years to get here, as they tried living other places first—but they gradually all came here. My many times great uncle, a Rhebenhughen, was the one that created the stone and set up the core of the city. Other magicians gravitated here when they found out about the place and it eventually grew to," Trev'nor gave an expansive sweep of the arm, "this. It was a trade hub, and because of the magic of its citizens, it was like a garden. A paradise in the middle of the desert. They had no trouble setting up trade with the neighboring cities and it flourished very quickly. Eventually, other people started marrying in, and they started to look Khobuntian, even though they retained their magical heritage."

Hence why the slaves didn't look Chahiran anymore.

"And then about a hundred years ago, give or take, their neighbors started to get greedy. They didn't want to abide by the terms of the trade agreements anymore. They didn't want to live in their desert cities. They wanted this place, Rheben." Trev'nor rubbed at his temples with both hands. "Keep in mind, I'm condensing this a lot for you. There's too much to recount if I don't."

"We figured as much considering the stone kept you for two days," Nolan assured him. "We'll put it all into a memory crystal later, record it for history. But keep going."

"There were a lot of recordings of different skirmishes and battles that they had with their neighbors. It eventually came down to a battle of attrition and then a massive betrayal at the end. Rheben was conquered in force." Trev'nor's eyes grew sad. "The person that last recorded, Linsallahan, was actually killed while trying to record. So I don't know what happened after that. I think anyone that fought back was killed, anyone that they could capture was sold into slavery, and the place was looted."

"Odds are they weren't able to stay in here for long." Nolan looked grieved by this account. "I mean, most of what we've seen took magic to operate. Even the irrigation canals required someone with magic to keep the water flowing. They might have had a few months to enjoy their new city before it started falling apart on them."

"So senseless." Becca stared at the city, now shrouded by nightfall, with sad eyes. "They destroyed the very thing they were trying to have. I wonder why the original group chose this place. Why here? Why not somewhere in a country more peaceful?"

"They tried other peaceful places first, but magicians were in such high demand they couldn't stay there for long without being fought over. They chose this spot because nothing was here. It wasn't desirable to anyone. Even the underground lake here that fed the canals wasn't here to begin with. A Water Mage and Earth Mage together crafted it." Trev'nor pointed toward the stewpot. "Is that done yet?"

"Give it a little more time," Becca cautioned. Reminded, she leaned over and gave it a good stir. "So we know the answers to our questions. The current day slave in Khobunter is originally from Chahir."

"And they were enslaved at first because of jealousy and now out of...what? Engrained habit? Ease of living? Profit?" Nolan shook his head in violent denial. "Poor excuses, all of them."

"I now feel a little better about what we did in Rurick."

Trev'nor had a ghastly expression on his face, lips stretched into a feral baring of teeth. "So. We have answers. Now what?"

"Now we go back to Rurick," Becca opined. "I think we should be there when we call home so that if they ask us questions we don't have an answer to, we can ask someone there."

Trev'nor lifted a shoulder in a tired shrug. "Agreed. I think we need another day to think about this anyway before we call home. Besides, when we do call, they're going to immediately demand we go back. But Becca, we haven't found your answer yet."

"And we don't have our dragons yet," Nolan reminded him. "I think we should call home, make arrangements, and then quickly get out of Rurick before they catch us. We still have things to do up here."

Becca agreed. She wasn't done up here yet and wasn't about to go home. Yes, Khobunter was dangerous, but they now knew exactly how dangerous. A slaver wouldn't get the chance to catch them again. Forewarned was forearmed. "Then let's eat, sleep, and figure out what to say to everyone back home."

"I'm sleeping in late tomorrow," Trev'nor told them firmly. "And getting a good look at the place before we go back to Rurick. You two got to explore this place but I didn't. I want to see it all before we go back."

"Fine," Becca acquiesced. It wasn't like they had a firm deadline after all. Besides, she wanted to play with the fuzzies a little longer. She's grown strangely attached to the little things. Really, she was of half a mind to take one home with her, although it might be a little dangerous to do so.

How to convince Tail that the fuzzies were not toys? That was the question.

Trev'nor's 'take a day to explore' turned into three days. He hadn't intended to take that long, but it was a large place, and he found himself stopping in certain parts of the ruins and telling the other two the full story to the place. The stone had recordings of every major building and he recounted them as they walked about. They had an energetic audience, as the fuzzies followed them around, actively looking for scratches and pets. Nolan could barely shift two feet in any direction without bumping into a dozen of them. Trev'nor was used to his friend being an animal magnet and didn't find it strange. He still found it funny, though, even after so many years.

They were all a little reluctant to leave, but they'd promised to be back in a week or so, and they'd already spent more time in Rheben than they'd really needed to. So the morning of the following day, they packed up and headed back to Rurick.

Since he'd already come this direction once, Trev'nor more or less knew where to go, or thought he did. When he came close to the right area, he slowed abruptly, senses straining. "Wait."

Nolan and Becca looked at him strangely.

"Something's not right." Trev'nor felt like they were a few

marks north of the city and rose abruptly to the surface.

"What's not right—?" Nolan turned to face the city as he asked and the sentence died unspoken.

Before they had left, Trev'nor had made sure to put all of the buildings to rights as much as possible and to repair the wall around the place to give them more security, until the city could form up a new guard to protect it. The wall was now in shambles, crumbling in various places and there were clear signs of a battle being carried out.

"They're gone," Nolan breathed, voice shaking. "The whole town is gone."

"WHAT?!" Becca demanded incredulously. "But I'm seeing movement! Surely someone's in there."

"Not our people," Nolan denied instantly, eyes still glued to the town. "Different people."

Trev'nor felt like someone had reached into his chest and tugged his heart out of place, hollow and cold, breathless with denial. "They can't just be gone."

A slightly hysterical note rang in Becca's voice. "Where are they? It's a whole town; where could they disappear to in six days?!"

Nolan grabbed her by the arm, his grip tight and reassuring. "Steady. Steady. We'll find them. First question really is, what happened? And who are these soldiers that we're seeing in the town?"

Eyes narrowed against the brightness of the suns, Trev'nor peered intently ahead. "Nol, didn't you say before that the warlords in Khobunter are in constant conflict with each other? Always fighting over land or water rights, is what you said."

Head flopping back, Nolan groaned in realization. "It's the neighboring warlord's men. He took advantage of the confusion and lack of soldiers and conquered this place, didn't he?"

It wasn't really a question but Trev'nor answered it anyway, "That would be my bet. It'd be the perfect opportunity to strike. I mean, that's Strategy 101."

Becca looked at the town she thought she'd saved with hollow eyes. "We set them up for this."

"Yes." There were unshed tears in Trev'nor's eyes. "Yes, we did. Some heroes we are. Why did I think just building a bigger, stronger wall around the town would be enough to keep them safe?"

Shaking his head, Nolan said softly, "None of us thought this through well. We were too impulsive. Too mad to think straight. But we have to think now. We have to. Our mistakes already cost lives. We can't afford to make another one like this." Grabbing them by the arms, he towed them back the direction they'd come. "We need to find a safe place to make camp. We have to talk this through and decide what to do."

Trev'nor stumbled along behind him, not thinking of anything at all. Or at least, trying very hard not to think of anything. He didn't want to imagine what must have happened after they left.

Nolan jostled him. "Trev, focus. We need a safe place to stop. Somewhere shady, somewhere with water if that's possible."

Rarely had Trev'nor had to use the training that Shad put him through. He used it now to force himself to be rational, to function, even as his heart screamed. He took in a deep breath, let it out in a steady stream, then took in another, bearing his mind and magic on the problem at hand. "No water within fifteen miles that I can feel. Ahead and a little to the left there's a craggy sort of ravine with a lot of overhangs. Lots of shade."

"That'll do. Guide us."

Putting one foot in front of the other, Trev'nor took his friends to a place of relative safety. The overhangs weren't large, barely enough for three people to lie down underneath, but it would suffice for a camp. Not trusting anything, he put a ward up immediately so that he could at least breathe without worrying someone would ambush them from behind.

Becca dropped like a marionette with its strings cut. Tears streamed down her face, mixing in with the fine dust on her skin, so that it looked like dirty trails on her cheeks. Nolan went to her and gave her a hard hug, and Trev'nor saw for the first time that tears were in his eyes too. Every one of them had grown attached to the people in that town. They were friends. After what they'd been through together, that was understandable. And now those friends were missing, possibly hurt or dead, and Trev'nor had no idea where they had gone.

He felt like killing something.

"Our mistake was thinking that we really are heroes." Nolan's voice sounded jarringly loud in the silence. "Our mistake was thinking this really was a grand quest where we could swoop in, save the day, and leave with the sunset. But this country has never been peaceful. There are not any centralized laws here, no one to make sure that things are just and right. Might of arms is what rules Khobunter."

Trev'nor felt Nolan's words like barbs aimed at his heart. He gasped from the pain of it. "Nolan, we can't just leave. We can't ignore it because things went wrong!"

Nolan turned his head and looked at him. In that moment, Trev'nor knew he was not looking at his childhood friend. He was looking at the Prince of Chahir. Those clear blue eyes nailed him in place, seeing right through the very heart of him.

"You have one of two options. We either stop right where we are and call home, call for the reinforcements we should have called for when we realized that we were in over our heads, and let an army do the job. We go home."

Becca shook her head, still unable to speak a word past her tears, but adamant in her refusal.

Glancing down at her, Nolan continued, "Or, you two realize that you're in this for the long haul. I can't stay in Khobunter forever, I have my own country to rule. So it would have to be you, the two of you, who do this. You take this country on as your own. You conquer it, you rule it, and you stay here for the rest of your lives. Nothing short of that dedication will safeguard it as you wish."

Stay here...forever? Could he even do that?

"It has to be one or the other," Nolan said adamantly. "There is no middle ground on this, no compromise. Trev, you said on the way up here that things would likely get to the point where it would be beyond hard and we won't know what to do. Well, guess what, we've landed. We're now at that point. You and Becca have to decide just how important it is to you that you rescue all the magicians in this country yourselves."

"I..." he started, only to falter.

"Don't you dare answer right now." Nolan jabbed a finger at him. "I won't take any answer you give me. It'll be from impulse. You sleep on it, Becca you too, and then give me an answer in the morning."

Trev'nor was actually grateful for the reprieve because his mind and heart were in such a muddle that he wasn't sure what he wanted to do. His heart said one thing, his mind another, and they weren't agreeing on much of anything. So he gave a ginger nod, arranged his pack, and laid down with his head pillowed on top of it. It was still plenty light out, it wasn't like he was that tired either, but the gravity of the decision weighed on him. He needed to lie down and just ponder it for a while.

Shad's training had finally fully kicked in. His mind whirled with questions, most without immediate answers. Say he did stay and called this place home. How did he defend each city from being re-conquered? How could he manage that when he had no resources of his own? Did he have to stay long enough to train the magicians of that town how to fight before he could move on to the next place? In that case, conquering Khobunter could well take a decade. It took at least two years to train a magician up to a good fighting level. And he had no resources to train them with. Cripes, that was another problem. He didn't have the faintest idea on how to train a witch or wizard to begin with.

But did he really have to leave each city to fend for itself while he moved on to the next? That seemed like a poor strategic choice. They could put up wards, certainly, but that was a restrictive way to go about it. It was half-prison to the inhabitants, as they wouldn't be able to do any trading or true communication with the outside world. That was a temporary fix, nothing more. They needed a real solution.

Trev'nor, being initially raised Tonkowacon, was not one to be really attached to places. He'd been constantly on the move since he was two. The only place he'd really stayed for any length of time was Strae Academy. Was his attachment to these people really so strong that he could consider this place home for the rest of his life? In this moment, it felt like it, but would that feeling fade?

The questions whirled around in his mind even as night fell, becoming snarled and then untangling themselves again as he boiled it down to the more essential questions. Could he just go home and ignore the people here? No. Could he call for reinforcements, hand this problem over to someone else, and hope they did a better job than he did? No. Could he live with the fact that he had seen and experienced incredible evil firsthand and didn't try to stop it? Absolutely not.

Somewhere in the predawn, he realized that while he had been arguing with himself, his subconscious had already reached a decision. He was staying. He was going to fight this whole country until he was finally able to rescue every last magician imprisoned here.

Trev'nor had always been aware that a Gardener had spoken to Garth about him and Nolan. It had been no secret. The adults had talked about it openly for years in front of him. Why had it been so important for the two of them to meet and become friends? Twelve years later, Trev'nor still had no idea. But he hoped that if this problem wasn't the one that the Gardeners wanted him to fix, that it was somewhere in this country. Because no matter what came, he would not leave Khobunter.

Dawn teased the horizon, washing the desert in tones of cool blues and whites. Trev'nor hadn't slept a wink. He rolled over to find Becca wide awake as well, curled up and looking at the rising suns with one of the calmest expressions he'd ever seen from her. He knew by looking at her that she had reached a decision too. Nolan was the only one that had tried to sleep, but he kept tossing and turning fitfully.

"Nolan." Trev'nor waited until Nolan rolled to a sitting position and was looking at him. As Trev'nor said the words, the weight of the responsibility he was taking on settled over him like a heavy mantle. "I'm staying."

Nolan searched his eyes, looking for resolve, and found it. His smile came slowly over his face, speaking of pride. "I thought you would. Becca?"

"You can't pry me out of this country," she responded without turning her head. "I'm staying. I will not let this nightmare continue."

Trev'nor understood her sentiments perfectly but he still had to wonder, "Will they let you stay? Considering who you are?"

Now she looked at him, eyes fierce. "I will fry anyone that tries to stop me."

He had seen her chuck lightning bolts at things. She was scarily accurate. He wouldn't cross her. So he made a peaceful motion with his hands. "Noted. Alright, Nolan, you have our answer. Now what?"

"Now we go back, study the situation, and come up with a strategy of how we're going to do this."

Becca's forehead crinkled into a frown. "What about the townspeople?"

"I was thinking about that last night. Odds are they're sold as slaves and carted off to the next warlord. Which one is a bit of a question—there's three within distance of Rurick. I think that if we systematically go from one place to another, we'll run into them."

Trev'nor couldn't fault the logic. A warlord in Khobunter was not one to waste resources or the chance to make money, and selling that many slaves would make him a lot of money. Odds were good that he hadn't gone in and massacred the whole town. The thought eased his mind and he could breathe a little easier. "Right. Breakfast first, and then let's go figure out how to conquer Khobunter."

Becca gave him a flat look. "Really. Breakfast first?"

"I can't think on an empty stomach," Trev'nor protested. "I don't know about girls, but men sure can't."

Nolan coughed, the sound suspiciously close to a laugh. "We need to keep up our strength, Becca."

She threw up her hands into the air. "Oh, fine. Breakfast first. Who's cooking?"

The benefit of having to re-conquer a city was that one knew the layout extremely well. Becca knew exactly where to strike, how much power it required, and which weak points to exploit first.

The garrison of soldiers, dressed in cream white uniforms that she didn't recognize, didn't stand a chance. They received no warning that they would be fighting three very enraged mages. Trev'nor took down his wall, what was left of it, which threw them into a tizzy. Then Nolan went dragon again and took out the original wall and garrison, further disrupting their chain of command. Becca was perched up high—thanks to Trev'nor—and watched it play out as she struck her own targets with bolts of lightning.

Rurick fell within an hour.

Anyone left standing immediately retreated, running from the city like their lives depended on it. (Which they did.) Becca noted the direction they ran to, due east, with interest. So, they were from a city over in that direction? That narrowed the field of likely suspects quite nicely. Maybe they could recover their friends sooner rather than later.

She was just about to call for Trev'nor to get her down from her earthen pedestal when something caught her attention. From the corner of her eye, there had been specks that had blocked out part of the suns for a moment. Hmm? What could possibly do that, when there wasn't a cloud in the sky?

Turning, she looked harder, lifting a hand to shield her eyes. Three distinct shadows were in the sky and coming in closer. Becca did not mistake them for a bird as nothing in the world had a wingspan like that except one species: dragons.

Becca's mouth went dry as she stared up at them. Dragons. Three wild dragons. What in the wide green world were they doing all the way down here? This was not anywhere close to their nesting or hunting grounds! Dragons didn't normally attack humans, granted, but they didn't normally venture this far from home either. Their behavior was completely unpredictable at the moment and Becca had no desire to figure out if they were in the mood to snack on humans or not.

Frantic, she spun this way and that until she spotted Trev'nor on the ground two streets over. Drawing air into her lungs, she shouted as loudly as she could, "TREV!"

His head snapped around and he yelled something back, so faint at this distance she could barely hear it.

She energetically pointed toward the sky with both fingers.

Turning, he looked up in that direction and even from here she could see him stagger a step backward as he realized what was coming their direction. Fighting a few squadrons of soldiers? It would be tough, but doable. Fighting three dragons? No way. Becca wasn't sure they'd come out with their skins intact.

They didn't have long before the dragons came over their heads. Becca's primary fear was for Nolan, still in dragon form. They would probably make a beeline straight for him and she wasn't sure if that was a good thing or not. They would either view him as an interloper on their territory and get huffy about it, or they'd be welcoming. It was a coin toss on which reaction it would be.

Nolan either noticed them or sensed them because he climbed half-up onto a building, letting his front legs balance there, and stretched his neck toward the sky. A long, almost haunting sound came from his throat as he called out to them.

He was the Life Mage, not her, so she had to believe that he knew what he was doing, but...wouldn't it have been better to go un-dragon and see if they would just pass by?

All three dragons dropped sharply toward the ground. They came in close enough for her to get a good look at them. Two of them were small, dainty like Kaya was, one a deep sapphire blue and the other a muted cream. The third was huge in comparison, an earthen green, and looked much older.

It was the oldest dragon that responded, voice low and rumbling. If an earthquake could be given a voice, it would have sounded like that.

Trev'nor abruptly popped up next to her, snagged Becca around the waist, and took them quickly back down to solid earth. "We do not want to be up high when they come in for a landing," he said as much to himself as to her. "The backdraft will likely knock us down."

Oh, true, it would. Becca paid little attention to where Trev'nor put her, as her eyes were glued to the dragons. The daintier ones settled along the rooftops near Nolan, but the largest one circled around until he could settle in a clear spot. Afraid that the buildings wouldn't hold up to this weight? Becca certainly would be, if she was that size.

Even with them on the ground, with buildings in between

them, the backdraft was enough to send her skirt and hair flying. She felt buffeted by them, although not enough to upset her balance. Thank heavens Trev'nor had thought of it, though, as she would have fallen off her perch if he hadn't reacted so quickly.

Nolan didn't seem the least bit afraid of them, turning his head to greet each one in turn, body relaxed. He didn't look like he was expecting a fight.

Trev'nor was tense against her side, also staring hard in their direction. "I vote we stay right here until Nolan says otherwise."

"Why?" She managed around a tight throat. "Because humans are crunchy?"

"And we taste good with barbecue sauce, yup, that sums it up." He managed a brief, fleeting smile.

They waited edgily as Nolan spoke, which seemed to involve a lot of nose touching, as he was constantly craning his neck this way or that to bump noses. The tip of his tail twitched sometimes too in what Becca recognized as a pleased manner. Kaya did that same thing when she was happy about something.

Minutes dragged, and the day warmed up enough that sweat started pouring in a thin line down her spine. Becca began to think that they would be safer sidling into a building and waiting this out when Nolan looked at them and gave a beckoning wave of his hand. Claws. Whatever.

"If he says its fine, then…" Trev'nor took in a breath and strode confidently that direction.

Becca prayed that Nolan knew what he was doing and followed suit.

As they walked, they lost sight of Nolan briefly, and when they rounded the corner and came into the marketplace courtyard, they found that he had shifted back to human form. The dragons didn't seem upset about this change or surprised, so they must have realized at some point that he was not a dragon like they were.

"Hey." Nolan greeted them with a boyish smile. "So, you're not going to believe this, but they're from a far northern clan of dragons. They said they heard me down here going into battle mode when we escaped, and they were worried, so three of them were dispatched to see what was going on."

"They heard you?" Trev'nor demanded incredulously. "Nolan, do you realize how much distance is between here and the northern dragon lands?!"

"A lot," Nolan answered, tone awed. "But it apparently doesn't matter to dragons. They can communicate with each other no matter the distance."

"You don't say," Becca breathed, regarding the pretty blue dragon near her with open wonder. "I wonder how?"

"It's not something they question, as the ability is innate, so I'll have to study to figure it out." Nolan's tone said plainly that he would figure it out. "Anyway. They heard 'young male dragon in trouble' and came over as quickly as they could, but when they got here, I was of course no longer in dragon mode, so they couldn't find me. They've been circling this general area for the past few days, not knowing what to do, until they heard me again just now."

Hence why they'd come in at such blazing speed. "And now what?"

"Hold on, you came in mid-conversation." Nolan turned back to them, neck stretched, mimicking their movements as closely as human anatomy would let him.

Becca watched and found that she couldn't follow what they were saying at all, and yet she could, somehow. They seemed to speak in some combination of body language, and sounds, and something else that she was missing. Telepathy? Although it wasn't the type that a human could pick up on, not like a nreesce's. The sounds were growls, or snorts, or soft wuffs of air, like and unlike nonverbal communication that a human might employ.

They at first seemed to be listening to Nolan more than anything, only occasionally making some sound that might have been a question or statement. Then all three flared up, wings snapping out, ridges on their necks going into sharp spikes, and steam coming out of their mouths. Becca flinched back in alarm, as she had never seen an angry dragon before. The sight of them would have given a guilty man heart failure.

Whatever Nolan said next, it made them even more angry, as the large green dragon let out a roar of sound that was nigh deafening and a short burst of flame.

Trev'nor put an arm around her waist, leaning in to murmur, "I'll drop us onto the Earth Path if they start torching the city."

Becca had intended to catch a strong gust of wind and ride it a short distance to the outside of the city. She'd learned the trick from one of her professors. But it would be vastly safer underground with Trev'nor, so she nodded adamant approval of this plan.

Their fears proved groundless as Nolan continued talking. The dragons simmered down into a cold anger, their wings came in to be half-furled, but the alarming steam disappeared.

Nolan stepped back and turned to them with an update. "Well, I explained to them the situation and what's been happening to us. They're very, very upset about it all. In their living memory, the magicians have always been their friends. Not all of them are willing to be paired up with magicians, of course, but they still like us fine. So to hear that this whole country is enslaving magicians has them..." Nolan paused here. "This doesn't translate to human speech very well. They had a particular phrase for it. 'Head in an egg' I think is the best way to translate it."

"Extremely frustrated?" Trev'nor offered.

"And angry, too, yeah that's the kind of feeling. Anyway." Nolan gestured very politely to the oldest dragon, using not an arm, but his whole torso to lean toward that direction. "He is an elder in the dragons, very old and respected, and is in charge of younglings like these two. It's part of the reason why he came, because I'm also a youngling, so I fall under his responsibilities. He said that he thinks the clan will be willing to help us."

Becca felt the world tilt on her. She either hadn't heard him right or she wasn't understanding what Nolan said. "Help us. How?"

"Fight, protect, guard the magicians." Nolan was bouncing on his toes in excitement. "Isn't it great? We were wondering what to do, since we didn't have an army, but if we ask it right then the dragons might be our army."

"Because they'd be protecting magicians?" Trev'nor's head was half-shaking, half-jerking back as if he couldn't quite process this. "Nolan, how'd you convince them of that?"

"Well, I haven't really, we need to go to their clan head directly to talk about this. But we're invited to go now and speak to them." Nolan blinked ingenious eyes at them, all innocence. "Want to go with me?"

Trev'nor response was immediate. "You bet your life I do."

"You are so not leaving me behind," Becca replied fervently.

"Then load up," Nolan offered, hand outstretched. The Life Mage almost glowed in anticipation. "I'll bring you with me."

The green dragon lowered his head to where it was more eye level with them and gently bumped his nose against Nolan's side. He blew out a long stream of warm air from his nostrils, eyes dipping and flaring open, revealing eyes of pure gold.

"Oh, really?" Nolan cocked his head and translated for them, "He says it's better if we each ride a different dragon. It's not that we're heavy or anything, but they're afraid that their hands will cramp up after a certain point if one of them tries to hold onto all three of us."

That made sense. Becca knew, from Krys, that it was not feasible to ride a dragon's back without a saddle first. Riding along in their claws was the only option. "I'm game?"

"Me too."

The elder dragon blew out another stream of air, head inching in closer.

Nolan responded in kind, eyes flaring and narrowing, blowing out a breath, tilting his head. What it all meant was a mystery to Becca. "What's he asking?"

"He wanted to know what kind of mages you two are. He also said it might be best if I ride in with him; that way he can set me down straight in front of the clan head." Nolan rubbed at the back of his head before offering, "Sounds like there's some sort of hierarchy in place and the two younger dragons can't directly go to the clan head's side without permission."

"You're the one that needs to talk to the head, not us." Trev'nor waved him on. "Go for it."

"Right. First, though, let's eat lunch and drink lots of water. The dragons are hungry and thirsty too; it would be best to do all of that before we leave here."

"I think we need to do more than that," Trev'nor disagreed. "Let's take care of the worst of the damage, erect a ward around the town to protect it from scavengers and anyone else that gets the notion to conquer the place. Then we can go."

"I agree completely. Trev, if you'll start repairing buildings? There's large watering troughs over there," Becca suggested, pointing in the right direction. "I saw them while I was up high. I can lead them that direction if you can find them something to eat?"

"They'll do their own hunting, but the water is a good idea. I'll find us humans something to eat instead. Maybe pack a few things for us too considering there probably won't be much available in their home grounds."

Erk. That wasn't a comforting thought. "Trev'nor?"

Trev'nor looked discomfited by this idea too. "Krys never did tell us details like that, when he went back with Kaya. I think Nolan's right, let's prepare for the worst. Nol, you go for the market. I'll start repairing some buildings."

They split up easily, each going their own way. Becca was slightly in awe that she had three overgrown dragons following her like obedient dogs toward the troughs. They were meant for large herds of cattle and dragoos, so they were long and deep, serviceable enough for the dragons to use. She used their aqueducts to refresh the water and offer something that was cooler and hadn't been sitting in the hot suns all morning.

The dragons drank deeply and all of them gently touched noses to her side in thanks. Not sure if it was appropriate, but not able to resist the urge, she patted them in between their nostrils and smiled up at them. Were all dragons like this? They were as kind and gentle as Kaya was.

Perhaps they were as intelligent as Kaya too? Willing to test the theory, she pointed toward herself and said, "Becca."

The elder dragon's eyes narrowed and zeroed in on her.

"Becca," she repeated again, enunciating clearly.

"Be-ca?" he repeated, tone rumbling.

"Right. Becca." Oh good, they were just as intelligent.

The two younger ones crowded in, heads jostling against each other. For their sake, she repeated her name, and was delighted when they both picked up on it quickly.

It was a rare chance, so she dipped her hand into one of the troughs and said clearly, "Water."

"Wa..." the elder dragon's head cocked. She had the distinct impression that was a way of frowning and asking for a repeat.

"Water."

"Wa-ta."

"Water."

"Water." He blew out a breath and flipped his tail, happy that he got it right.

"Right, water."

"Water," the blue dragon repeated, interest rising. She clawed at the ground and cocked her head.

Now asking for words? "Ground."

"Groud."

Oh, right, dragons struggled with 'n' sounds. "Ground."

"Grouund."

Close enough. "You're all very smart. I wonder if I can learn to speak your language too, or if it's something that a human body can't really duplicate?"

"It's not something you can duplicate," Nolan said, coming around the three dragons to stand at her side. "I have to cheat and use magic in order to get my full point across. But that said, you can say a few words and phrases to them. They'd be delighted if you did. Dragons like to learn things. They hoard knowledge as much as they hoard gold."

"Really?" Trev'nor joined them with two huge sacks in his hands. "I thought it was just Kaya that was like that."

"Oh no. Her brood is just as insatiably curious." Nolan jerked a thumb at the bags. "We have enough food to last us about four days. I think that's enough. Are we good to go here?"

"I don't know." Becca lifted both shoulders in a shrug. "They only drank water here."

Nolan tilted his face up and switched to dragon-speak. He got a response that made him blink. "They said there's not enough game here but not to worry about it as they had a large feast last night. They stumbled into a flock of nekons, it sounds like."

Becca knew that was the favored food of dragoos, but dragons too? "Oh. Then they're not really hungry?"

"Sounds like it. Alright, well, in that case let's sit down and eat a quick lunch and go. I found the fixings for flatbread and cheese. We have some vegetables and fruits that were ripe enough to pick, too, but not much. Whoever came in here cleaned the place of anything good." Nolan led the way to a shaded table off on the side as he spoke.

She had eaten far too much flat bread since entering this country but it was true they wouldn't have a lot of ready-made options in this twice-conquered city. Resigned, she followed Nolan to the table and prepared a quick lunch, consuming it while guzzling water. It was easy to dehydrate in this desert land.

Nolan spoke to the dragons as he ate, sometimes smiling, sometimes teaching them words. They lapped up the attention, enjoying the learning process.

Trev'nor wrapped up the rest of the food, tying it securely

in large squares of cloth. "Nolan, did you ask them how long of a flight this is going to be?"

"They said almost two days, and we'll probably arrive in the wee hours of the morning."

"Is it safe to fly at night?" Becca couldn't help but wonder.

"Sure. They have eyes like a cat's. Krys avoids doing it just because he can't navigate in the dark. However, we will stop at some point for a rest." Nolan turned back to the dragons, speaking to them, then instructed, "Trev, go with the white dragon, Becca go with the blue one. Don't worry about hanging onto them, they know how to grip you without hurting. Just try to be still as much as possible to make it easier on them."

Becca said a prayer that this would go smoothly as she climbed into the proffered claw, one of the sacks of food in her lap. As she settled, she caught a glimpse of Trev'nor's face. His eyes were scrunched tight and he had the bag in an iron clutch like it was a lifeline. "Trev?"

Without opening his eyes, he responded, "I'll be fine. I just won't look down."

Said the boy who wanted a dragon.

They really had to do something about his nervousness when it came to heights.

Trev'nor had been fine with heights up until he was nearly thirteen. He'd been on a scaffold, five stories up, helping to fix a particularly tricky part of Strae Academy, when the scaffold was jarred and it lurched sideways. It knocked him off his feet, although thanks to Garth's quick reflexes, not off the scaffold entirely. Still, he'd come this close to taking a head dive toward the ground, and the incident had somewhat scarred him.

If he were on a wide platform, or in a place where he knew he absolutely couldn't fall off, then he was able to tolerate it just fine. A dragon's claws weren't quite the stability he needed, and it took steady breathing and whole-hearted concentration on his part to make sure he didn't lose the contents of his stomach.

Most of the flight was sensations for him more than visual as he refused to look down, just up. The air whipped around his face, often pulling strands out of his braid so that hair got into eyes and mouth. He now understood why Krys kept his hair short. It felt good up here, though, exhilarating in a stomach-dropping sort of way. He was torn between wanting his feet on the ground and staying up here for a little longer.

The dragon that carried him often tilted her head so that

she could peek down, checking on him. It relieved him to know that she was keeping a careful eye on his wellbeing. In the long history of the world, the dragons had always been good friends to the magicians of every type and in every age. Their loss had been keenly felt when they migrated to the far north, out of the range of human civilizations. That was why Kaya had been such a joy to all of them when she adopted Krys.

They went through a cycle of hot air, cool, hot, and cool again as they went from day to night and back to day, continuing to fly steadily for their destination. Downright cold, actually. Part of that was the season, part of it was being this far off the ground, but another factor was that they were much further north now than they had been. Trev'nor couldn't see much as it was pitch black and the thin crescent moon wasn't able to illuminate much. There were mountains. He gathered that much. Maybe big trees too.

His dragon carrier banked a hard right, descending rapidly enough to make his cheeks flap out. He felt like holding on for dear life, only there was nothing really to hold onto. His dragon's claws were like an iron cage around him—he definitely wasn't going anywhere—although he slid backward into her grip from the force of the descent.

Trev'nor's head snapped back as she abruptly back-flapped, braking hard in midair before touching down with only one front paw and two back feet. Trev'nor opened his eyes and found that she had turned her head around to peer at him intently.

"I—" He cleared his throat and tried again, the words coming out husky. "I'm good. Thanks. Nice flight?"

She didn't know any of those words, but she understood something from his tone as she bobbed her head in a pleased fashion and let him all the way to the ground. Trev'nor was heartily glad to have both boots on rock after being in the air most of the day. Looking around, he spied Becca and hailed her softly.

Neither of them could see much in this place. Trev'nor felt rock under him, but also a massive amount of trees—come to think of it, the trees were unusually large. They made the ones around Q'atal look a little on the small side, and he'd seen people carve houses out of those trees. But it was only his earth sense that gave him any sense of navigation. Becca was clearly uncertain about trying to move far as she had no light to see by.

He went to her, offering a hand to steady her. "How are your legs?"

"A little shaky," she admitted cheerfully. "But that was a fun ride. How are you?"

"A little nauseous," he responded, swallowing hard. "I'm just glad it didn't last any longer than it did. I wouldn't suggest moving any further than this without me guiding you. We're on a rocky ledge with massive trees all around us."

"I can kind of see that," she allowed, peering hard in all direction. "My eyes adjusted enough to see silhouettes, at least. Nolan is way above us, isn't he?"

"On an entirely different ledge," Trev'nor confirmed, craning his neck to look up, although that was a futile gesture. He couldn't see a thing, not with his usual eyes. Magical sense just let him see Nolan standing like a bright spot directly above him, and lots of rock and vegetation. "I assume he's talking to the dragon king. Do dragons have kings?"

"You're asking me?"

Right, their animal expert was not with them. "Well, what do you want to do?"

"Lead me to a place where I can take care of some private

business and then I guess we find somewhere to settle in while we wait for Nolan. I am rather hungry, though, are you?"

"Not right this minute, but give my stomach a little time to settle, and I will be." Part of being a growing teenager was a perpetually growling stomach.

Trev'nor played guide for Becca to make sure she maneuvered around without falling off the ledge. They shifted around the dragons as they moved, who seemed to be growing in number every time Trev'nor turned around. Word must be spreading among the...herd?...of dragons that there were visitors and they all wanted to come and take a look for themselves. The bolder ones stretched out their noses to get a long sniff, and Trev'nor carefully did what Nolan had instructed and laid out a flat palm so that they could do so.

The blue dragon, which had carried Becca, didn't venture far from their sides and seemed intent on being next to them at all times. After Becca had eaten, the little dragon nudged the pair of them closer to her with a tail and encouraged them to settle in against her side. Trev'nor was extremely grateful for the offer as he hadn't a clue where to lie down without encroaching on someone else's nest, and he didn't want to offend his hosts. He really, really didn't want to do that.

"Oh, she's warm," Becca sighed in delight, curling in next to that smooth hide. "I'm glad she's snuggly like this. It's rather cold out here."

"I thought dragons don't like cold, like dragoos don't." Trev'nor was rather sure of that, actually.

"They might be forced to deal with it in order to have a source of food." Becca sounded uncertain. "I think a lot of them are snuggling up with each other to share warmth."

"You can see that?"

"More like I can hear it. It's the same sound as when Kaya's brood snuggled in with her."

Ah, now that she said it, it was a sound he recognized.

Becca stroked a hand along the hide and leaned in. "You're a nice dragon. Thank you."

He recognized that tone in her voice. "Are you seriously going to sleep without waiting on Nolan?"

"He'll wake us up when it's time. And I'm tired. I didn't sleep last night."

Trev'nor hadn't either and he was absolutely exhausted, but he found himself too on edge to think about sleeping. Becca had always been the sort that could turn her mind off when she wanted to rest but he had never been able to develop that talent. So he sat with his shoulder touching hers, soaking in the warmth along his back, and waited with as much patience as he could muster for Nolan to come down.

At some point, who knows when, he fell asleep. And dreamed. They weren't good dreams. In fact they were confusing and scary, dreams where he was being chased and cornered, forced to turn and fight. It was like a mashup of the last two battles he had been in, only he wasn't against normal soldiers this time, but some sort of demonic version of them. He fought and screamed and tried to find Becca and Nolan in the madness, but no matter where he turned, it all looked the same to him.

Something hard and warm settled on his lap, the weight of it knocking the breath out of him just enough that he flailed awake in sheer panic. He found himself staring at the elder green dragon dead in the eye, clear golden that had warmth and sympathy for him.

Knowing he wouldn't understand the words, but hoping he'd understand the tone, Trev'nor breathed, "Thank you."

"It looked like a bad dream," Nolan said quietly, coming around to stand at both their sides.

The green dragon had not budged, so Trev'nor was not able to sit up like he wanted to. "It was a mix between memory and nightmare."

That golden eye rolled toward Nolan, and he obviously said something, as Nolan picked up the roll of translator. "'You are afraid of fighting?' he asked."

"No," Trev'nor responded honestly, "but the weight of the lives I took is heavy. And I'm scared of losing people dear to me in battle."

Nolan dutifully translated, listened, and repeated, "You did not choose to fight. You chose to survive. Anyone that enters a battle chooses life and death. Their souls are not yours to carry."

For days now, they had assuaged themselves by saying they hadn't had a choice—and they really hadn't. They'd had to fight. They had to survive. They'd had to rescue themselves. But this reasoning hadn't helped Trev'nor accept what had happened and he wasn't sure why. Was it because they honestly hadn't been prepared for an all-out battle like that one and they kept feeling that with their magic, they should have been able to win the conflict with less bloodshed? Or some other reason entirely?

These words, given to him by someone from a different species, who was who-knows-how-old, struck a chord in him when nothing else had had any impact. "I'm not responsible for their lives."

"You are not," Nolan translated. "Only family and leaders are responsible for the lives of others. You are not either."

Trev'nor reached out and found the exact spot on the nose bridge where Kaya always enjoyed being scratched. "You are wise. Thank you."

The dragon's eyes fell to half-mast in a sign of pleasure and he heaved out a warm sigh, which felt very welcome in the cool morning air.

"He said you have wonderful hands and you can keep that up until your arm falls off," Nolan informed Trev'nor dryly.

"Kaya tells me the same thing." Trev'nor found it relaxing, soothing, to have such peaceful contact with another living being after that nightmare. So he kept it up for longer than he normally would have. "What did the dragon leader say?"

"Wait, let me get Becca up first so I don't have to repeat this." Nolan bent down and nudged her in the side. "Bec. Wake up."

Becca's eyes sprang open, not unusually, as she wasn't a deep sleeper in unfamiliar places. Especially in a place like this, she would be sleeping very lightly. She sat up and stretched her arms above her head, taking in Trev'nor's guest with a startled laugh. "Making friends, Trev?"

"This must be a universal spot for dragons."

"Must be." Turning to Nolan, she cocked her head. "What did the dragon chief say?"

Nolan plopped down to the ground, crossing his feet, looking beyond tired. Then again, he was the one that had stayed up all night. "First off, he's really mad. Like, steaming mad. I literally saw steam coming out. According to dragon memory, the magicians have always been friends and allies, and that's proven true even in this generation after Krys visited with Kaya. So the idea that we've become slaves? He's ready to go tear the country apart right now."

Trev'nor felt a flash of panic. "You did explain to him

there are innocent people over there too? Not just bad guys?"

"He realized on his own, and he's not going to, but he's eager to help us. He said, 'Bad men must go squish.' I'm not paraphrasing when I say that, those were his exact words. We talked a good portion of last night on how he can help us. First off, he wants to let each of us partner with a dragon."

Becca let out an unintended squeal, which got the attention of every dragon around her. Trev'nor had to settle for a pump-fist of victory, as his lap and other hand were still occupied.

Nolan grinned at them in perfect understanding. "I know, right? At least something about this trip is going according to plan."

"Do we know who wants to partner with us?" Becca asked.

Shaking his head, Nolan explained, "Too early to tell. He wants to talk to everyone first, but he said he'll try to stay out of it leave it up to us and his own dragonlings to decide. Next, he's saying that he'll make dragon…um…" Nolan paused and frowned. "Not sure how to translate this. Covens? Clans? Wards? Groups of dragons that live together in designated areas."

"Let's go with clans," Becca suggested. "Dragon clans in Khobunter?"

"Right. This area is nice enough but they've grown too large to comfortably support it, and if they keep hunting in this area, all of the game will be gone in a few years. He wants to divide dragons up and send them to different areas, make mini-clans, so that they can live safely but have enough to eat. Trev," Nolan had a distinct twinkle in his eyes, "you said before that we couldn't conquer Khobunter because we didn't have an army or a way of safeguarding the cities after we conquered them."

"I think a clan of dragons will manage that just fine," Trev'nor managed hoarsely. The mental picture in his mind was throwing him for a loop. Dragons as guardians? Dragons as comrades in arms? Was the world supposed to work this way? "To clarify, they'll fight alongside us?"

"They will, but their main task is to protect the areas we assign them to. He doesn't want them to be always in battle, just for as long as we need them to be, as otherwise they'll be sucked into being battle mounts."

"That's actually wise," Becca allowed. "He's right, putting dragons into warfare will just make the carnage more intense. And it'll make people want to hunt and enslave dragons. It's better not to open that door."

"I agree." Nolan blew out a breath, tired but victorious. "So. Did I do alright in my first international negotiations?"

"We couldn't have asked for a better ambassador."

"Relieved to hear it." Nolan rubbed at his eyes, fatigue in every line of his body. "I was seriously flying by the seat of my pants all night. I realized five minutes in that Krys didn't tell us the half of his trip to dragon territory."

"You're telling me." Trev'nor looked around, or tried to, but he still had a dragon partially in his lap. "I'm not even sure if we're allowed to explore this area freely."

"The dragon chief assured me that we had free rein to the area, although he asked that we stay out of the nesting grounds. You can't mistake the place for anything else, there's remains of shells littering the area."

"Duly noted," Becca responded. "I take it that he wants us to stay several days?"

"He does. To get acquainted with everyone but also so that I can help them. Some of the dragons have a few ailments or birth defects that he wants me to address."

That made sense to Trev'nor. If they were allies, then of

course they would trade favors like this. "We should tell him too that I'll help as I can. If he needs the landscape changed at all, I'm ready to work."

"I'll pass that along," Nolan promised, fighting back a yawn.

Gently pushing a giant head out of his lap, Trev'nor sought to stand. "Well, first things first."

"Breakfast?" Becca drawled.

"It's like you read minds."

"The day you stop thinking with your stomach first, Trev, is the day that I know you're dying." Becca levered herself up to her feet. "Breakfast first, and then I think we should explore and introduce ourselves to the dragons."

"Great plan," Trev'nor enthused. "Sorry, Nolan, you'll have to nap later."

"Much later," Nolan responded with a look over his shoulder. "You can't see it from your angle but we literally have a line of dragons wanting to meet us. Funny, I don't remember Krys mentioning that mages are popular with dragons."

"I have a feeling that Kaya had something to do with that." Becca dug through her pack, laying out food as she did so. "Remember how possessive she was, especially in the beginning?"

Trev'nor tilted his torso, trying in vain to see around two dragons blocking his view, and caught no more than glimpses of a multitude of different colored hides. "What are the odds that our new dragon partners are going to be the same way?"

Around a mouthful of jerky, Nolan informed him, "Really, really good."

"I had a feeling you'd say that."

Becca stepped out to the ledge of what she had assumed to be a cave, only to find it was nothing of the sort. The dragons here apparently did use caves—she saw some tails sticking out of the mountainside, as well as a few noses—but the majority of them lived in trees. The trees here were massive, large enough to hold full sized cabins, and could take a dragon or two with ease. The ledge she stood on was actually inside the trunk of a tree, hollowed out so that there was room to stretch out in. Some of the tree openings looked too uniform to be natural, but others were obviously natural growths.

Slowly, she did a full turn, looking around her. Three massive waterfalls shimmered in the morning light, making a soft roar of never-ending sound. The scents of greenery, of running water, of rock baking under the suns, permeated the air. Mixed in with all of this lush scenery was the multitude of dragons. From the purest of whites to the darkest of blacks, and every color in between, they were everywhere. A dragon lover would have keeled over on the spot in sheer happiness at such a sight.

Nolan shifted to dragon form—which garnered a roar of delight and approval from the watching dragons—long enough to get Trev'nor and Becca to a plateau further down.

This turned out to be a wise decision as the waiting multitude wanted to touch noses to them. She could just picture having all of those dragons trying to squeeze into the hollow of a tree. They would have been squished like a grape.

Surrounded by dragons on all sides had to be one of the most unique experiences in the world. Becca turned, hands outstretched, touching noses and looking into their eyes. The suns were warming up, reflecting dully off their hides, and making the musky smell of their scales a little stronger. It was not an unpleasant experience but definitely overwhelming.

Becca and Trev'nor, not knowing how to communicate, let themselves be bombarded with noses and the dragon equivalent of nuzzling. The tamed version, fortunately, as their usual approach could throw human beings a good fifty feet. Nolan was the one that was actually talking to them and being constructive.

He waved them closer, then pointed at the dragons hovering nearby. "I'm doing a very rough translation of their names, alright? This is Wind Soars High and his mate, Blue Sky Before Storm. They said that they would like to have Rurick as their territory."

That cemented Becca's attention. "They do understand that no one's there right now and that they'll probably have to fight often to keep it? At least until we have the surrounding cities conquered?"

"They do. In fact, the elder dragon that came to get us first? He suggested that what we actually do is bring all of the mated pairs that want to go with us and then they can sort out themselves who gets what territories. They will just branch out to the next conquered city when it's time to do so; that way there's always a large group ready to fight until we have all of Khobunter under control."

Becca gave an approving hum. "That's smart. He's right, that's the best way to do it." Turning to the mated pair, she said, "We would love for you to guard the place. It is an important city to us."

Nolan dutifully translated both ways. "They said they understand this and will keep it from being conquered again."

"Glad to hear it." Trev'nor looked around him slowly. "Ah, Nol? Are you saying that every dragon that's around us wants to go?"

"Of course," Nolan said slowly, puzzled. "I thought you understood that."

Becca's jaw dropped. "What? Seriously?!" There had to be a good hundred dragons crowding around them!

"These are our volunteers," Nolan explained, laughing at their reactions. "Most of them are mated pairs, and they're not interested in pairing up with us, so they want territories of their own to guard. A few of them are hopefuls wanting to partner with us, if we feel like it would be a good match."

This was far, far more than they had hoped for. To have so many willing to go was nothing short of astounding.

"They're not sure what Khobunter looks like," Nolan continued. "Trev, can you do that thing Garth does? The mini-map?"

"Sure, sure." Trev'nor spread his hands out wide, encouraging dragons to back up. "I mean, it's not going to be completely accurate, as I haven't been there myself, and I'm going off a map mostly. That still work?"

"They just need an idea right now, so they can talk it over and start divvying up territory," Nolan explained. "And make it larger than that, you have a huge crowd here."

In more than one sense of the word. Becca stepped back too, giving Trev'nor space, as he created a topical map of the whole country. The cities and Ruins of Rheben were almost miniatures popping out of the ground, the streams and oasis represented as close to what could be found in nature as possible with only stone to work with. Really, the amount of detail that Trev'nor could pull off was amazing. He might have a finer hand at this than Garth did.

Finished, Trev'nor looked up at Nolan. "That work?"

"Garth would be proud," Nolan assured him with a low whistle of appreciation. Distracted, he twisted to look up at the elder green dragon, the two of them clearly speaking with each other for a moment. "Huh. We've apparently mentioned Garth enough that he's picked up on the name. He wanted to know who it was we're speaking of."

Interesting that he would do that. "That means he's paying very close attention to everything we're saying."

"I've actually been teaching him words," Nolan told her. "He's been one of the more avid students. Anyway, back to this. So, this is Rurick?" Nolan pointed to a city at the bottom of the map.

"Right. And that's the Ruins of Rheben." Trev'nor played tour guide on his map, pointing out cities, pausing to give Nolan time to translate. By the time they were through the map, some of the dragons were trying out the names of the cities, although the pronunciation was usually off.

Becca was relieved they were trying to learn Chahirese, as she couldn't begin to figure out how to communicate with them. Even Nolan had to cheat outrageously with his magic to pull it off.

A sapphire blue dragon came and nudged against her side, blinking pale gold eyes at her. After a startled blink, Becca recognized her as the dragon that had carried her here. "You're coming too?"

Nolan caught this exchange and answered, "She was one

of the first volunteers. She saw for herself firsthand what Khobunter's like, what we had to do to survive, and she's very, very angry about the whole thing."

This touched Becca, to have someone she barely knew be so angry for her sake. Reaching out, she rubbed at the sensitive spot on the blue dragon's nose, which earned a happy rumbling purr. "Thank you." Struck by a thought, she twisted and mouthed to Nolan, 'Mated?'

He shook his head no.

Oh, so this was one of the hopefuls? Becca found the dragon to be stunning in looks and she had a sweet personality. Perhaps this would be a good pairing? Wanting to test the theory out, she requested, "Nol, translate for me? Ask her if she'd take me for a short flight around this area. I want to study the weather patterns up here and it's easier if I can do it up high."

"Sure." Nolan slipped around two dragons to be more in line of sight and asked. "She said she'd love to. She said, as a prearranged signal, double tap her to get her attention and point where you want to go."

Smart of her to think of that now. "I will."

Trev'nor levied himself off his knees, brushing the dirt off as he stood. "Well, I think you're set here, Nol. You can talk to them about all of this. But I don't think we should just stand around here and take what they're offering. Can you ask them if there's anything they need help with?"

Nolan gave him a knowing a look. "Tonkowacon manners kicking in?"

"Can't take without giving back," Trev'nor responded with a shrug.

True, it was bad form to do that, especially with as much help as the dragons were giving them.

"I can ask, sure."

With the boys occupied, she patted the blue dragon to get her attention and then pointed skyward. "Shall we go up?"

The dragons did indeed have things that needed to be done. Trev'nor got quite the "Magus-Do-List" when he offered his services—everything from creating more nesting caves to extending rocky areas near the falls so there was more ledge room. The green elder dragon was the one that took him around, showing him what needed to be done, with Nolan playing translator.

Trev'nor wasn't quite sure why the elder dragon liked to be around them so much. He was clearly done with his initial duty but he stayed nearby anyway. Part of it might be curiosity, as he seemed more determined than most of the dragons to learn how to speak in human languages. He absorbed words so quickly that it almost put Kaya to shame. Part of that, though, might have been that Nolan was the one teaching.

It took him the whole day to get the nesting grounds right. There were mother dragons up here that were specifically charged with watching over the eggs and making sure that all was well. Trev'nor had the equivalent of six mothers-in-law following him around and making sure that he got every detail exactly right. By the end of the day, Nolan looked as harried as Trev'nor felt, and both boys were glad that finally, finally, the nesting grounds met their collective approval.

The dragon chief came down himself to take a look. It had amazed Trev'nor, the size of him, as he didn't think anything living could get that big. How did he even fly, that was Trev'nor's question. He looked the whole area over with a thorough scrutiny before turning and, via Nolan, stated, "You have done well here, Earth Mage. You have our thanks."

With the chief's spoken approval, even the mothers-in-law had to agree, which meant Trev'nor was finally free. He thankfully escaped back to the perch he had slept on the night before and fell immediately to sleep.

Day two in dragon territory wasn't nearly as taxing. All he did was extend ledges and create more tree hollows for nests. The hardest part about this was making sure that the new ledges could hold the weight of several dragons. The green dragon and some of the fledglings happily tested them out for him. The rock didn't even shift under their weight.

Satisfied, he went to the next project.

Nests, as it turned out, were a very personal thing. Trev'nor and Nolan had to speak to each dragon requesting a new nest, asking for their preferences, before he could start on one. It also took their combined powers to grow tree limbs the right direction and then hollow them out without harming the tree in the process. Trev'nor shifted rocks and dirt about to act as an anchor for the trees as Nolan tweaked them to grow just right. It was anything but a simple process.

After doing six nests in a row, he'd had enough, and wanted nothing more than to get off his feet for a while. Taking the canteen from his waist, he guzzled half of it. "Break time."

"I can go with that." Nolan flopped immediately to the ledge, not minding that the waterfall was close enough to mist him with spray.

Trev'nor found the spray refreshing and plopped down right next to his friend. He twisted so that he lay on his back, looking aimlessly toward the sky. Overhead, he saw the sapphire blue dragon and Becca fly past, making a wide circle around the area. "Becca sure is spending quality time up in the air."

"She said there's something wonky about the weather patterns up here," Nolan responded almost absently. "She's almost got it figured out, I think, she's just double checking to make sure she hasn't jumped to conclusions. But have you noticed? It's always that dragon that takes her up."

"I noticed." Trev'nor grinned skyward. "How much you want to bet those two pair up?"

"I don't take sucker bets."

The green dragon laid down next to Trev'nor and put his head squarely on Trev's lap. Only Trev'nor's feet poked out the other side. Used to this, he obligingly scratched, sending the dragon into rumbling purrs.

"Speaking of pairings..." Nolan drawled. "You do realize by now, I hope, that this particular dragon likes you?"

Trev'nor froze, head creaking around to stare at Nolan with wide eyes. "Come again?"

"Our options of pairings are not just the young ones," Nolan chided, eyes laughing. "Is that what you thought? Some of the elder dragons, like this one, don't have mates and so are willing to go into Khobunter."

Actually, no, Trev'nor hadn't realized any of that at all. He could barely tell ages when it came to the dragons. He only knew this one was older because he was bigger than most of the adolescents and Nolan had told him he was an elder. Otherwise there was nothing about his range of motion or actions to indicate his age. But it was true, in the time he'd known the dragon, he'd followed Trev'nor around like an oversized puppy. And he could admit that he'd grown rather attached.

A dark gold eye opened and locked onto Trev'nor's. "Like Trev," he rumbled in a voice deeper than mountains.

Trev'nor had a moment where it was honestly hard to

breathe. There was this sense of hovering on a thin line, as if his future could go either direction. It was a little scary. He felt a surge of anticipation shoot up his spine and he had to wet his lips twice before he could speak. "Do you really? I mean, we've known each other four days. Are you sure?"

"Sure," the dragon answered promptly.

"They don't need to think like we do, Trev," Nolan inserted quietly. "Their instincts are a lot better than ours when it comes to others. Remember, Kaya knew Krys all of five minutes before attaching herself to him."

That was a very valid point. In fact, that threw the situation into an entirely new light, as it had been watching the bond between Kaya and Krys that made Trev'nor want a dragon to begin with. They were such amazing friends, such good partners, that it would make anyone want a dragon.

For the first time, Trev'nor decided to trust in another's instincts more than his own doubts. If this dragon thought they would be a good pairing, then he wanted to believe that, and work to make it true. So he took a deep breath for courage, or maybe just to fight down the butterflies in his stomach. "Then, want to partner up with me?"

That considerable tail flicked back and forth in a happy wag, and he raised his head long enough to give a very human-like nod. "Partner. My partner."

Trev'nor sat up enough to lean against that massive head and breathe deeply. "Good," he whispered against warm skin.

"Your habit of making snap decisions is going to scare ten years off of me," Nolan complained to him.

Not worried, Trev'nor just laughed and sat back. "It was the right snap decision."

"It usually is," Nolan allowed, making a face, "but still. Alright. I guess we need to think of a name for him?" Nolan confessed to the dragon, "I have no idea how to translate your name into Chahirese. It's very long and complicated."

This was the first Trev'nor had heard about him having a name. Well, of course he did, the dragons' had their own sense of naming. "Really? How complicated?"

"Seriously, I have no idea how to even try. It has to deal with a certain feeling of wind and air and sky that only Becca would probably understand."

The dragon's eyes bounced between the two of them, only partially following all of this. There was no way he had the right vocabulary to understand. Trev'nor tried to break it down into simple terms for him. "Can't say your name. Too long. Can I give you one?"

Head canted, his dragon looked at him for a moment before declaring. "Garth."

Trev'nor blinked at him, not following. What did Garth have to do with any of this?

"Name me Garth," the dragon stated, then blew out a breath, satisfied with his own words.

"Ahhh…" Trev'nor looked to Nolan, lost on why his dragon wanted Garth's name.

Nolan looked just as confused, so fell to Dragonese to ask for an explanation. It must have been a good one, as he got that look on his face that said he was going to start laughing any second.

"Nol?" Trev'nor prompted impatiently.

"This is good." Nolan bit his lip but even so a chuckle escaped. "Right, so, we've been mentioning Garth on and off for days, right? Apparently he's figured out that Garth is an older person that is wise, or at least has a lot of authority back home. I explained Garth as a mentor and teacher, but he's taken his understanding past that. So, to him, Garth is a powerful name and one that is suitable for him."

"Garth," the dragon maintained, growing stubborn.

"He won't hear about any other name," Nolan tacked on, finally losing the battle and laughing outright.

"But that's going to get really confusing," Trev'nor complained, although even he saw the humor in it. "I mean, how do we keep the two separate? Magus-Garth, Dragon-Garth? My Garth, the other Garth?"

"I guess so." Nolan shrugged, looking innocent, but he was still laughing on some internal level. It was clear in his expression. "Either way, he's not changing his stance on this. You're stuck with Garth the Dragon."

It looked like he was at that. Well, Garth would likely get a kick out of this later, when they finally did call home. Resigned, more than a little amused, he faced his dragon and said, "Garth it is."

Garth gave a contented purr and settled back down for more scratches.

The man really was a legend in his own time. Even dragons wanted to be named after him. Trev'nor looked forward to the day when he could spring this surprise on his old teacher. "Nol, you are hereby banned from telling Garth this over mirror."

"And miss his reaction? Wouldn't dream of it."

Becca descended from the blue dragon's claws with a small sigh of relief. She truly enjoyed flying, no doubt about that, but her hair kept flying into her face and there was only so much of that a girl could take. She really had to come up with a method of keeping her hair secured that worked more than five minutes. She patted the dragon on the leg as she descended. "Thank you. Good flight."

The dragon purred back at her, bumped her gently with her nose, then took several steps back before taking off again. She was no doubt hungry, after having carted Becca around for a good portion of the day. Becca certainly was, as she'd skipped lunch entirely. They were coming up short on foods to eat, but with a Life Mage in tow, she was certain that it wouldn't be a problem for long. All she had to do was find Nolan.

Due to common sense, she did not cook up in any of the trees. For one thing, she didn't want to set the whole forest on fire. For another, she needed a ready source of water. After asking, the dragons pointed her in the direction of a shallow depression near the water that shielded her cookfire from the wind, while at the same time giving her the space she needed. It wasn't perfect, but no campfire ever was. It worked and that was all she cared about.

Before leaving this morning, she had put several lines into the river in the hopes of catching something. Really, the situation called for a net, but she didn't have one to use. She went there first to check but not only was every line empty, there were a few that looked frayed at the end. She eyed one of them suspiciously. "I think something is amok."

"You would be correct," Nolan answered, coming to squat down next to her. "The fledglings figured it out this morning that fish could be found here. The adults tried, but they're sneaky when it comes to food. By the time they caught them, they already had the fish in their mouths."

She let out an aggravated growl. "Scamps."

"You know, that's exactly what the chief said?" Nolan chuckled and shrugged. "The young don't always do what they're told. It's part of growing up."

"The older ones don't do it either."

"Like us?"

"Like us," she agreed. "Well, Nol, since you're here, catch me some fish."

"That I can do." He turned an intent gaze into the water.

Now that she thought of it... "Does this bother you? Luring in animals to eat them."

"It did once, when I was about six and I figured out where the yummy meat on the table was coming from," he answered almost absently. "But really, to a Life Mage, plants have as much life force as any animal. Eating vegetables and fruits only doesn't make it any better for me. I had to learn to be alright with eating both plants and animals because I couldn't really differentiate between the two. To do otherwise is a path to madness."

"And starvation," she observed practically. "How much of a struggle was it?"

"I couldn't hold anything down for about three days.

But, well, I got over it." He shot her a quick grin. "For a six year old, cookies can be a powerful motivating tool."

That made her laugh. "I think that's true at any age."

"How many fish?"

"With Trev? Better give me six."

"Six it—" Nolan cut himself off and glanced up. "Huh. It looks like you didn't need me after all."

Before she could ask what he meant by that, her blue dragon friend returned, settling gently some feet away from them. In her claw was a fish the size of a man's torso. She hopped forward and gently laid it in front of Becca.

Becca was no fool. She knew good and well what this meant. Still, she had to ask, "Nol, any particular reason why she's feeding me?"

He had an enigmatic smile on his face as he answered, "I think you know the answer to that."

Yes, so she did. She didn't really know what to do with it, though. Swallowing hard, she did not give the verbal thanks that she normally would have given but instead tried to emulate the dragon equivalent, one where she cocked her head and peered upwards with a soft sigh.

This delighted the blue dragon to no end, her tail thumping hard enough to leave cracks in the top of the rock. She stretched forward to nuzzle against the top of Becca's hair before bouncing once and taking off in a flurry of wings.

Becca felt more than a little battered but she stayed her ground, somehow, and regarded the fish with open amazement.

"You can't find a better partner than her," Nolan stated quietly, still resting on his heels. "I asked around, and spoke to her several times, and she's one of the best fighters they have. She's also one of the more intelligent. If you're looking for a partner that can watch your back, Bec, I think you found her."

She'd had a feeling for the past two days about this dragon but still, the idea was a bit much to take in all at once. "I'm cooking dinner and sleeping on this."

"That's fair. I'm glad at least one of you isn't impulsive."

That was an odd statement. She gingerly picked up the fish and took it to the river to clean. "What do you mean?"

"Trev'nor partnered with a dragon about an hour ago."

She nearly dropped the fish in the river. "He did what?!"

Nolan gave an eloquent shrug as if to say he had no part in any of it, he was just the messenger. "I'll let him explain it."

"You talking about me?" Trev'nor sauntered up and viewed the situation. "That is a huge fish. Good, I'm starving."

"Trev, put your stomach aside for a moment and tell me how this happened," Becca demanded. "How did it happen? Your partnering?"

"First, what are we doing with this?"

"Fish stew and jerky. Only way to keep it all from spoiling."

"I'll handle jerky if you handle stew," Trev'nor offered.

"Deal. Now start talking."

"Nolan flat out told me that Garth was hoping to partner with me. And I realized that I had grown to like him over the past few days. Honestly, Bec, we really can't spend weeks and weeks getting to know every dragon before picking one. I mean, human judgment isn't always right in choosing relationships. The dragons are better at it than we are. I chose to trust his instincts."

"You always make these snap decisions," Nolan muttered to the air in general. He took over the cleanup, which was only fair, as they were the ones doing most of the cooking.

With her hands finally free, Becca looked at Trev'nor

squarely.

"You named your dragon Garth?"

"I didn't name him that," Trev'nor corrected her, "he named himself that. We tried to talk him out of it, honest, as it's bound to get confusing. But he's adamant. He likes that name, and it's the only one he'll answer to."

Becca sat back and roared with laughter. "You are not allowed to tell Garth this without me present. The look on his face is going to be priceless."

"I bet it is," Trev'nor agreed, rubbing his hands in anticipation. "I swore Nolan to secrecy until we can see Garth face to face. It's going to be a complete waste to tell him this over mirror."

"Truly." Becca leaned over to stir the soup, but idly, as the fire wasn't hot enough to make the soup instantly burn. Putting the spoon aside, she turned and crossed her legs, getting more comfortable. A thoughtful frown tugged at her forehead. "I do admit, though, you make a valid point. I've been struggling with the question myself because we have so many dragons that want to go. But it's the blue dragon that I'm the most comfortable with."

"It's been obvious to me and Nolan for a day now that you two are a good match," Trev'nor offered. "I don't understand why you're hesitating, to be honest."

"It's more like, I need a little time for the idea to settle before leaping."

Nolan's head came up and he said, "Be back in a few minutes." He promptly got up and left, heading for a cluster of dragons that were staring hard at the Life Mage.

The newly partnered dragon swooped in and landed as delicately as a feather touching to ground, which considering his size, was amazing. He then went directly to Trev'nor and bumped him with his nose, arranging it so that he was curled up with his human ensconced against his side. Trev'nor indulged this selfishness without even a twitch and leaned back against Garth.

"Welcome, Garth," Becca said to him with the appropriate dragon gesture to accompany. Or as close as a human could emulate. "We are glad to have you with us."

He of course didn't know all of the words she said but the sincerity came across just fine. Garth gave a happy snort. "My Trev."

Becca nodded sagely. "Yup, just as bad as Kaya."

Trev'nor rolled his eyes but didn't deny it.

As they waited for dinner to finish cooking, they all watched as Nolan tried and failed to extract himself from the group for the umpteenth time. "You think you have it rough picking a dragon partner? Put yourself in his shoes."

Garth stirred and pointed with his nose dead ahead. "Her."

Becca looked to where he pointed, but there was at least a half dozen dragons that Garth could mean. "Which one? White, black, green?"

"White."

"What about her, Garth?" Trev'nor lifted a hand to shield his eyes from the setting suns.

"Nolan needs her." Garth canted his head, thinking, then rephrased. "She needs Nolan."

Now that was interesting. Garth, of course, had been in charge of the fledglings up until this afternoon, when he partnered with Trev'nor. He would know the younger dragons very well, being one of the guardians that raised them.

"Why?" Trev'nor pressed.

Garth hummed, thinking, probably trying to figure out how to use what words he knew to explain. Finally, he offered, "No words."

"No words?" Becca repeated slowly. "Do you mean she can't speak?"

"Speak?" Garth's tone suggested he had an idea of what this word meant but wanted to be sure.

"Words from me," Trev'nor pointed to his own nose before pointing to Garth, "Words from you. Speak."

Garth's head bobbed up and down a fraction. "No speak."

"A mute dragon. Wait." Becca twisted to get a better look at her. "But I swear I heard her say Nolan's name earlier."

"She has," Trev'nor confirmed, staring hard at the dragon in question. "She hangs around Nolan often. In fact, I think this is the first time I've seen her not at his side. She repeats his name all the time. Garth, what do you mean 'no speak?' We heard her say words."

"No dragon speak," Garth explained patiently.

"Ahhh," Becca breathed, enlightened. "She can't speak the way dragons can speak, so they consider her to be mute. But her vocal chords work fine, obviously, so she can speak with Nolan easily. That's why you think he should pick her? Because she can't talk with them anyway, so living in Chahir will be easier for her."

It made a great deal of sense. The dragons here understood that Nolan would only be in Khobunter temporarily, that he would be spending most of his life in Chahir. It had dismayed quite a few of them, as they realized that they would rarely get to see a member of their own kind if they chose the Life Mage. But with the white dragon, it wouldn't be as much of a struggle for her, as she could communicate better with humans anyway. It would also be a bonus for her because if she did miss flying with other dragons, Nolan would likely just go dragon and play with her. After all, Nolan looked for excuses to go dragon all of the time.

"Likes Nolan," Garth informed them.

"Good to hear." Part of the mystery was solved, but… "What do you mean by Nolan needs her?"

"Strong." Garth opened his mouth, paused, and let out a frustrated huff. Lifting his head, he turned to Nolan and asked a question in Dragonese. "Ah. Strong fighter. Fast."

True, out of all the mages, the Life Mages had the lowest combat skill. That didn't mean Nolan was defenseless, not by any means, but he had to physically fight while the rest of the mages could do ranged fighting. It put him into danger that led to injuries more often than not. To have a dragon fighting at his side that was strong and fast would be a blessing for Nolan. "That's a good argument, Garth. You think Nolan will pick her?"

Garth got this look in his eye that said 'He'd better.'

Right. Becca and Trev'nor exchanged a look and silently agreed right then and there that they were going to stay out of that little discussion. Neither of them wanted to put themselves between a rock and a hard place, no sir.

Nolan finally won free of his adoring crowd and plopped himself down next to Trev'nor. "Becca, tell me dinner's almost done."

"Almost," she agreed. "Meat's not quite there, it needs another few minutes. You starving?"

"Completely." Wiggling about, Nolan looked at Garth from the corner of his eyes. "Why are we talking about a certain dragon, hmmm?"

Trev'nor started to roll up to his knees probably intending to escape, but Garth caught him around the waist and held him fast, tail pinning him down. The dragon's head never turned as he spoke one-on-one with Nolan but the way he reacted made it clear that he had at least one eye on Trev'nor.

Becca had to bite the inside of her lip to keep from

laughing as Trev'nor's expression clearly said, busted buckets.

Nolan got a disturbed frown on his face and turned to look at the white dragon. "She's really that ostracized? I mean, I knew that no one tried to speak to her, but…"

"Can't you fix the problem, whatever it is?" Resigned to being pinned in place, Trev'nor gave his dragon a dirty look.

"To be perfectly honest with you, I have no idea how it works," Nolan confessed, palms spreading outward. "This is one of those 'magic follows intents' moments. Not even the dragons have been able to explain to me how it works. It's almost telepathy, but with body language and certain tones from their vocal chords all blended together. Something in her mind is blocked, I think, so that she can only communicate with body language effectively. Even her vocal chords don't seem to work the same way theirs do."

This confused Trev'nor. "But it works well enough for human speech?"

"Our sounds are short, compact," Nolan explained. "Theirs are long, deep, sustained. She can't do sounds for more than about three seconds before her voice fails her. I took a look at her almost as soon as we arrived, as the dragon chief is worried about her, but I honestly can't point a finger and say 'this is the problem.' I don't understand enough about dragon anatomy to begin with. It will take a lot of time and in-depth study before I can figure out the cause and how to correct it."

"So to the dragons, she's essentially mute."

"Worse," Nolan sighed. "She's basically deaf, too, as she can't hear what they're saying on most levels. They're kind to her, but they don't know how to deal with her."

No wonder she had been glued to Nolan since his arrival, then. It was probably the first time she had been able to speak to someone since her birth. "What is she like, personality wise? I mean from what I saw she seemed nice."

"Absolute sweetheart." Nolan drew a leg up so that he could prop his chin on his knee. "Really, I think she'd be easy to live with. I'm just not sure I should offer a partnership because she needs my help. That seems a little…."

"She needs Nolan," Garth maintained firmly.

Nolan fell to conferring with Garth in Dragonese again, so whatever they spoke of went over both Becca's and Trev'nor's head. After several minutes, Nolan looked away, toward the ground.

"What did he say?" Becca prompted, voice quiet.

"That she won't ask." Nolan looked sightlessly forward, not meeting any of their eyes. "She thinks that she's abnormal, strange, and so doesn't deserve to be my partner."

Ouch. Well, the low self-esteem made sense, really. Becca felt even more sorry for her now.

"Do you remember?" Nolan asked, voice so small that it could barely be heard. "When we were told that we were mages, and that we could no longer live with our families, that we had to go somewhere else. Do you remember what you thought?"

Becca did. Vividly. Even being eight years old hadn't dimmed that memory. "That I was strange, and that's why they didn't want me anymore. It took a long time before I understood why they had made the choice to send me off on my own."

"It took me years to dispel that idea," Nolan admitted sadly. "I felt wholly abandoned, no matter what anyone said to me, as I only understood that it was my magic that made me unwanted. I was always so glad when I could play with you," he glanced up at Trev'nor with a small smile, "because I knew that I wasn't alone. I think our situation might be similar to hers, but it's different too. We eventually were put into a place where magic was normal, where everyone had a type of magic, and we grew up with them. She has no future like that."

"That's just too heartbreaking." Becca got that look on her face, the one that said she was going to get her way and destroy anything that tried to stop her. "Nolan. You talk to her. If she doesn't want to go with you, then I'll take her."

Nolan threw up a hand. "No. You know which dragon should be your partner. It'll break her heart if you choose someone else. In fact," Nolan's tone went dry, "put me out of my misery and go ask her, will you? She's driving me crazy."

"I'd like to, but…" Becca trailed off uncertainly, giving the white dragon a glance.

"I'll speak with her." Nolan pushed up to his feet and walked to the white dragon, determination ringing with every step.

Trev'nor watched him go, chewing on the edge of his thumbnail. "Are we all sure about this?"

"Likes Nolan," Garth assured him confidently.

"And I think Nolan likes her," Becca chimed in, taking the soup pot off the fire and giving it another good stir. "Really, I think the main reason why he's been hesitating to choose a partner is because he knows that the dragon will be like Kaya, cut off from the clan. Even with this dragon, who can barely communicate with everyone, that's going to be hard emotionally."

"Well, sure, but she's partnering with the future King of Chahir. I mean, you know she's going to be spoiled."

"Rotten," Becca agreed cheerfully. "Which is why I think this is a good idea. She'll have a much better future with Nolan, and I honestly think she adores him."

The tableau held its breath as they watched Nolan talk to the other dragon. She had crouched down so that their eyes were more or less on the same level. Becca knew the moment that Nolan had gotten the full question across, as the dragon literally pounced on him. Wings, head, tail, all of it wrapped around the Life Mage in the most all-encompassing embrace the world had ever witnessed. Not a hair of Nolan could be seen.

"I think that's a yes," Becca laughed, her heart warming at the sight.

Trev'nor chuckled. "Look at them. She's practically glowing with happiness." He went taut for a moment. "Ah, Garth? The other dragons won't pick on her because Nolan chose her, right?"

"Pick?" Garth parroted, obviously not understanding.

"Tease?" Becca offered.

"Be mean?" Trev'nor waited for a beat, but when his dragon didn't show any signs of comprehension, he rephrased again, "Not nice?"

Garth shook his head (he was really adopting human mannerisms) in reassurance. "Stay nice."

Oh good. Dragons apparently weren't the type to bully. Relieved, Trev'nor sank back against his dragon chair and watched as Nolan came back to the cookfire, this time with his own dragon in tow. Nolan had a smile bright enough to be a third sun, so happy that he couldn't contain it. "So, as I'm sure you saw, she agreed to be my partner."

"We saw," Becca assured him, giggling. Standing, she made her way to the white dragon and stroked her nose. "Welcome, pretty one. We are glad you are coming with us. Garth says you're strong and fast, which is good. We leave Nolan in your care."

Someone, either Garth or Nolan, was translating Becca's words as their newest addition was able to follow this seamlessly. She pushed into Becca's touch, the tip of her tail thumping in a happy rhythm. "Becca-friend nice."

"Oh? I didn't know you knew my name."

"She made sure she knew before coming over here," Nolan explained.

Becca understood what Nolan had said before, now that she was paying proper attention. Most dragons when they said words had a kind of echo effect to their voice. But not this one. She spoke the way a human would speak.

Trev'nor rose up to greet her as well. "You know my name too?"

"Trev'nor," she responded promptly.

"Wow." He sounded sincerely impressed. "I have yet to meet a dragon that can pronounce the 'n' sound so well. You speak like a human would."

He got hugged for that, a wing and arm gathering him up into her chest. With an oomph, he settled against her, hugging her back. "I take it that made her happy?"

"Like you would not believe," Nolan said, amused.

It was probably rare for her to be praised, after all.

"We haven't settled on a name for her yet. I thought we could throw some out over dinner, see if we can't come up with something she likes." Nolan sounded hopeful about this request. Actually, it was more like a demand. Didn't want to think up all those names himself, eh?

"Sounds fine to me." Becca went back to the soup pot, rustling up the bowls from their bags. "It's all ready. But Nolan, don't you need to report to the chief that you're partnered with her?"

"I will after dinner," Nolan answered, diving for his dinner bowl. "I'm too hungry to wait, for one thing, but he's out hunting right now anyway."

Nolan always seemed to know where all the dragons were at any given time. It probably had something to do with his magical senses. Just like Trev'nor could tell what the geography looked like.

Becca, not being a starving teenage boy, was the first to offer a name before taking a bite. "Chellie?"

The white dragon settled in around Nolan, curling up like a sphinx would, giving her human the perfect 'chair' to lounge against. "No," she said firmly. "N."

"Something with an N in it, eh?" Becca shot Trev'nor an amused glance. Apparently that little praise had gone directly to her head.

From the expression on Trev'nor's face, he couldn't think of a single N name at the moment.

"Thanks, Trev." Nolan rolled his eyes.

"This is not my fault. Besides, I just saved us time, there's only so many names with an N in it anyway."

"I'll remind you that you said that later, when we're stuck and can't think of any other names."

That might happen sooner rather than later. Becca seriously couldn't think of a single name that didn't already belong to a person they knew. One dragon doppelganger was enough. They really didn't need two. Nolan was right, this…might take a while.

They spent a total of five glorious days in dragon territory. Becca turned into a teacher after she got done with her own research. At any given time, she had at least twenty dragons sitting around her, plaguing her for more words. Anticipating where they would go, Becca taught them mostly Solish words and what Khobuntish she knew. Sometimes Nolan stepped in, when she couldn't figure out how to explain a new word, but most of the time it was just her teaching. The dragons, in turn, taught each other so that by the time they left everyone had a basic vocabulary of about three hundred words. And growing.

An interesting part that was finally explained to Becca, now that the dragons had the necessary vocabulary, was that distance didn't matter too much to them when they needed to speak to each other. As they explained it, they could hear each other, just not full speech. Becca still puzzled over full speech. She had an idea that dragon telepathy worked like a mirror broach. They could hear voices, but the tone and body language were lost. Dragons relied on all three to get a full message across. To them, just telepathy was a pale imitation of true communication.

Becca's dragon leaned her head down so that she could sniff as Becca packed everything into her bag. She had to push the massive head away. "Stop that. I can't see what I'm doing."

After a lifetime of traveling, Trev'nor was of course a pro at packing, and he was relaxing against Garth's side as he waited for the other two. "She's a curious one, your dragon."

"Like a cat," Becca responded, exasperated and amused in turns. Ever since she had asked her dragon to partner yesterday, she'd been faithfully followed around and rubbed up against at every opportunity. It was clear to her that the blue dragon was so delighted that she seemed about to burst from happiness. It had not prevented her from being picky about names though. Becca had spent a good majority of yesterday trying to think of a name and failing.

Nolan's dragon nearly knocked Becca flat as she turned her head about, nudging against the saddle strapped to her back. This earned a scolding from Becca's dragon, which had the other cringing back.

Reaching up, Becca caught her own dragon's nose and brought her back down. "Easy, easy, she didn't realize she was that close."

"It's alright, Llona." Nolan stopped packing and rocked up to his feet, reassuring her. "You'll get used to this. Is the saddle too tight?"

Trev'nor, in a flash of creative genius, had used wood and flax fiber to grow their saddles. The bulk of the hardware was all hard wood, seamless in its craftsmanship, with tightly woven fiber in intricate braids making up the rest of the harness. Becca had never seen anything else like it, but Trev'nor said this was similar to how the Tonkowacon saddles were fashioned, just adapted to fit a dragon form. He'd spent the majority of the past two days making them so that they didn't have to be carried in their dragons' claws anymore.

Of course when Nolan asked this, Trev'nor responded first, as he was still making adjustments to make sure everything was perfect. "Is it?"

Nolan touched a bottom ring. "She said this part is starting to chaff."

"That's not good." Trev'nor reacted immediately, going to Llona's side and bringing his magic to bear on the problem. "Tell me when things don't fit right," he told the dragon as he worked. "Alright?"

"Alright," she responded, voice mellow and happy.

Concerned now, Becca looked at her own dragon. "Saddle still fits fine?"

"Sure, sure," the dragon assured her, head bobbing.

That was such a Trev'nor move. Now when had she picked up that?

They'd had no chance to practice flying with their new partners. Trev'nor had finished up Llona's saddle this morning. They were trusting Nolan to give whatever instructions needed to be said, and were going to fly off by the seat of their pants. There was a sense of urgency pressing down on all of them, a feeling that they had perhaps stayed too long as it was, and needed to go. So even though it would be wiser to linger for a day or three, learn how to fly with each other, none of them wished to do so.

This morning, they would leave for Khobunter.

Becca threw her pack on behind the brand new saddle, strapped it in, and then paused and really looked around her. Part of her heart ached at the idea of leaving this idyllic place. It had been so peaceful here, so inviting, that she almost wished she could just stay forever. "We can come back here, right?"

"I think we'll have to," Nolan opined, also strapping his bag into place. "We didn't do near the setup that we need to really carry our plan into the future. This is totally a stop-gap measure."

He did have a point there. "How does it feel, anyway, to have completed your first international talk with dragons?"

"I really, really wanted a guide book. A manual. Something," Nolan informed her fervently.

Laughing, Trev'nor pointed out, "None of those would have helped you. In fact, I don't think a guide book exists."

That was probably true. "In fact, Nolan, you'll probably be the one that has to write it."

"Neither of you are helping," Nolan moaned, which made them laugh again. "Speaking of, I should probably pay my respects to the chief one last time before we go."

"Shouldn't we all go?" Becca asked uncertainly. She hadn't actually spoken to him face to face the entire stay here.

"That...is a good point. Yes, we should all go. Trev, ready?"

"Ready." Trev'nor patted Llona's saddle. "That good? Good. Nothing else chaffing or pinching, right? Glad to hear it. Tell me if that changes." Satisfied Llona was set, Trev'nor carefully climbed onto Garth's back, settling into his saddle with an air of caution.

Becca felt the same way about her new saddle, as she was not convinced she had all of the straps tight enough yet. And she did not want to fall out, thank you very much. The only person that could safely fall would be Nolan, who would likely transform into a dragon or bird or some such thing and just merrily fly with everyone else after that. She double checked everything to make sure that she had a little wiggle room, but not enough to risk slipping out. It should be alright. Maybe.

Their dragons waited until the humans were settled

before taking off and doing a long, lazy turn to the upper ledge where their clan chief liked to lounge. Krys had always claimed that dragons were more cat than anything, and seeing the chief of this entire clan sunbathing made Becca think he was right. Tail often did that exact same thing.

The chief raised his head, making the black scales gleam dully in the sunlight as he spotted their approach. He sat up more properly as they landed, looking far more massive than any other dragon present. Becca hadn't been told his age, but she had to wonder, did dragons just get bigger as the years passed? It seemed to be a common theme. If that was the case, just how big was hers going to get?

Like a parent seeing off a child, the chief leaned in and touched noses with each dragon, lingering there for several moments in a tender gesture of farewell. Then he pulled back and looked each mage squarely in the eye.

"He asks that we take care of his children," Nolan translated quietly. "He knows we're going into danger, that's unavoidable, but try to not enter into a situation where we know the odds are stacked against us. Don't hesitate to ask for more help, either. He doesn't want us to feel that we only have this much help from him and that we're to manage the rest of it on our own."

Truly like a parent. Becca smiled at the realization. "Tell him we will. We don't want anyone hurt."

Nolan lifted his head, expression softening as he conversed with the giant clan chief. "He says, safe flight, and don't try anything reckless. Fly quickly. There's a storm coming."

Becca turned toward the sky, checking with her own magical senses, and frowned when she realized the dragon was right. That storm had moved faster than she'd predicted. She'd spotted it two nights ago but had thought it would hit tonight, not sooner. Now, they would be lucky to get ahead of it. "I'll divert it some."

"We're really glad you're with us for things like this," Trev'nor informed her fervently. "I hate traveling in storms. Well, let's go. Thank him for the help and hospitality, Nol."

"Sure." Nolan said the last farewell and then tapped Llona on the shoulder, signaling it was time to leave.

All of the dragons that had promised to come with them lifted into the air at the same time, making the air swirl in chaotic patterns as wings beat it back and forth. Becca had taken the precaution of tying her hair firmly back in braids, then a bandana on top of it all, and even than a few strands escaped to sneak into her eyes. Clawing them away, she blinked and found that while she had been temporarily blinded, they had already gained altitude and were flying away from dragon territory. Twisting a little, she looked behind her, seeing a hundred dragons flying in her wake like a moving, breathing rainbow. It was a breathtaking display. It was moments like this that made her fervently wish she had some kind of talent in painting, as this would be a scene well worth capturing on canvas.

Well, maybe she could put it into a crystal and commission it done.

The flight back into Khobunter took just as long as the journey out of it had been. Becca had taken the precaution of packing a few snacks in a bag hanging off her front saddle rim, so she didn't starve on the almost two day-long trip. They had stopped for the night, but still, it was late afternoon of the next day by the time that Rurick came into sight, and she was beyond ready for real food at that point. Not to mention getting off her dragon. The flight had been smooth, but Becca wasn't used to riding anything at all. She basically hadn't really been on a horse since Shad had taken her to

Strae. Her inner thighs were killing her, the cramps were so
bad. Massaging them while sitting only helped a little. The
minute she was off, she was pestering Nolan for help.

The ward glimmered slightly in the afternoon suns. No
one camped near it, which rather surprised Becca. Surely
they'd noticed by now the city was claimed by magic? Or
had they tried to get in, failed, and retreated for the time
being until they could figure out how to break through? The
last was a more real possibility.

Wards were strange things. Being developed by humans,
with human magic, they were easy to set and take down but
they had odd limitations. Most of the time, wards could only
be made to keep out one of three things: people, power, and
everything. Becca understood this in theory, but watching
the dragons easily pass through the wards and settle in
and around the city walls felt a little nerve-wracking. She
had to remind herself, several times, that dragons were not
humans. Human beings would not be able to go through the
ward like they had.

Their dragons settled near each other, in one of the
open marketplace courtyards. Trev'nor looked around as he
hopped off, sliding out of the saddle and easily to the ground.
"Looks like they didn't figure out how to get through the
ward while we were gone."

"Odds are they didn't even recognize what they were,"
Nolan observed, also sliding neatly out of the saddle. "Or,
if they did, had no idea what to do about it. Wards are
somewhat complicated to build, magically speaking. It's not
something intuitively obvious."

Becca only half followed this as she struggled to get out
of her saddle. Undoing the straps was easy enough but her
cramping legs wouldn't let her maneuver free. She hissed
in a pained breath and stopped in an undignified position,

one leg over her dragon's neck, the other dangling free and throbbing.

Of course Trev'nor noticed and pointed it out to Nolan. "I think she's having trouble. What's the matter, Bec?"

"I'm not used to riding," she retorted acerbically. "I don't normally leave Strae, remember? And how can you just walk around like you didn't spent two days in the saddle?"

"Because I'm used to riding?" Trev'nor offered artlessly, coming toward her with arms outstretched. "Uh-oh, I know that look. You hate me right now, don't you?"

"SO, so much," she gritted out between clenched teeth. "Riding a dragon and riding a horse are different."

"Very different," he soothed, motioning for Nolan to go ahead of him. "Can you help with the cramps?"

"Sure, hang on." Nolan reached up and grabbed a handle on the saddle to pull himself even closer. Leaning into the dragon's side, he put both hands flat against her thighs and let out a thread of healing magic. "Becca, getting mad at Trev'nor solves nothing."

"Ridiculous. It makes me feel better."

Trev'nor grinned widely. "Is that why you hit me all the time?"

"No, I hit you because you ask for it."

Nolan paused and gave her a strange look. "You don't hit me."

"You don't ask for it." What was that? Was that a pout on his face? "Nolan, are you seriously pouting because I don't hit you?"

He ducked his head to focus more on her legs. "I'm not pouting."

It sure looked that way from here. What, did he feel like her hitting Trev was a sign of closeness or something? That he was being left out because she didn't punch him occasionally? Boys were strange creatures sometimes.

Her muscles stopped cramping under Nolan's treatment and with Trev'nor's help, she slid her way to the ground. Never had the feeling of dirt under her feet felt so good. "Thank you, gentlemen. Now, we've arrived. What shall we do first?"

"Dinner?" Trev'nor responded, looking at both of them to gauge their reactions. "Then I think we need to sit down and have a proper strategy session. We can't just bank on having a hundred dragons and forging ahead."

"I agree." Nolan looked around them, eyes going semi-blind as he saw further than their immediate surroundings. "I think I can scrounge up ingredients for dinner easily enough. Becca, get a fire going? And make sure the dragons are settled. I'll be back shortly."

His was the hardest task, in her opinion. Where was he going to find food still viable after nearly ten days in a hot desert? But if he thought he could do it, Becca wasn't about to stop him.

She looked about her and decided that the first order of business was unsaddling her own dragon, as the boys had theirs. Then she'd build a fire and talk with everyone so they knew where to get water. "Everyone, you're free to hunt!"

Dragons touched noses, extended their heads to greet her, sometimes nudge her, then took off in different directions. Becca hoped they had enough resources on hand to feed a hundred dragons.

When Nolan said he could find food, he wasn't exaggerating. Trev'nor was actually impressed with how much he found. Perhaps it was his Life Mage sense that made him so good at it, but the prince came back with several jars of pickled meat, fruit, and enough ingredients to make flat bread. Even a few pans.

Becca had chosen a house that had a large veranda and courtyard so that their dragon companions could stick their noses inside with the people if they wanted to. The three borrowed the kitchen and cooked companionably together, each taking the dish they were most comfortable making, then sitting down for a late supper. Trev'nor was very glad for solid food to be in his stomach, as snacking had not really done the trick.

They put off doing dishes, sticking them in the sink to soak before returning to the table. Trev'nor had found a map of Khobunter in the house's study, which he laid out flat so they had something to reference. "Alright, I now declare this strategy session in order. We have a hundred dragons at our beck and call, minus the four that will stay here and guard Rurick. What shall we do first?"

"Rurick is part of the Trexler Warlord's territory, right?" Becca nibbled on the edge of a thumb as she studied the map. "He can't be much of a warlord if another came in and carted away the whole population."

"Warlord territories fluctuate," Nolan stated, frowning. "Even if this map is, what, two or three years old? It could be inaccurate. Rurick is between Rowe and Trexler, it gets re-conquered by warlords all of the time."

"So it could belong to Rowe." Trev'nor scratched at the back of his head. "Well, that's not confusing. So do you know anything about the warlords here?"

"Not really, no. I do know that every warlord basically has a non-aggression treaty in place with its neighboring country. Rowe has one with Sol, Riyu and Von have one with Libendorf. They mostly suffer from internal conflict."

"What you're saying is, we don't actually know which warlord's city we conquered, and it doesn't matter to either Sol or Libendorf that we did so, as long as we don't take the war to them?" Becca blew out a long stream of air. "That's good and bad news."

"At least we don't have to worry about one of those countries sending aid," Trev'nor observed. "Although I think we should be careful moving forward so that they don't get nervous and think we're going to conquer them next."

"That is a very good thought," Nolan seconded firmly. "Please, please let's not do that. For one thing, I don't want to explain it to either Da or Granda. Or the Trasdee Evondit Orra, come to think of it."

"Or Guin," Trev'nor grimaced. "Or Shad. Or Garth. Especially not Chatta or Xiaolang."

"There's a whole list of people we don't want to explain that to, so I agree, let's make sure we don't land in that pitfall." Becca tapped Rurick's symbol on the map. "We took this place by surprise, so we won easily. But I think we should practice fighting with the dragons, get used to coming at a city directly. I think we should start off by taking another, smaller city first."

She did have a point. Trev'nor admitted to himself that the way they'd taken Rurick was more than haphazard, and it likely wouldn't work to just charge blindly in on the next city. They'd probably have the element of surprise on their side for the next city but not after that. So if they were going to practice fighting together, a smaller city would be a good way to do it. "In that case, Tiergan."

Both of them looked at the map, seeing the city he named, and went 'Ahhh' in immediate understanding. Trev'nor hadn't expected any other reaction. A student of Shad's would instantly see the logic behind his choice. Tiergan was in a unique strategic position. It was next to Q'atal, nearly on the coast of Saira Channel, and so was protected on two sides from attack. It was also located near Rurick, almost dead west of it. If their plans went seriously wrong, then they had two places to retreat to, both of them with protective wards up: Q'atal and Rurick. It was the perfect choice for testing their mettle. "No objections?"

"None," Nolan agreed. "Although it does beg the question of what to hit after. Sagar? Trexler?"

"Sagar would be nice simply because it's smaller and doesn't have the defenses of Trexler." Becca circled an idle finger around both cities as she spoke. "But I'm not sure if it's viable. I mean, we have to go around Trexler to get to Sagar."

"Surely the Trexler Warlord will retaliate after we take Tiergan?" Nolan followed up his own question by shaking his head. "I don't think we have enough information to make a decision on this right now. We don't know the strengths or the personalities of the warlords involved. Let's take Tiergan first. If we succeed, then we get more information and only after that point do we sit down and figure out what to tackle next."

That sounded reasonable to Trev'nor, and frankly, he was ready to be horizontal for a while. "Let's wash up dishes and go to bed. We can't continue this discussion any further without the dragons being involved, and they're still hunting, I think."

Nolan's eyes went blind as he checked. "About half of them are, I think."

"So let's continue this in the morning," Trev'nor concluded.

"Sounds good to me." Becca stretched her arms above her head and even from across the table, Trev'nor could hear vertebra pop. "I'm bagged out. I chose the first bedroom in the hallway, so choose somewhere else to sleep."

Trev'nor couldn't see how assigned bedrooms would matter, considering they'd be here at most two days, but girls were fussy about things like that. "Alright. Good night."

For whatever reason, Nolan was always the first to rise. It might have been sheer habit by now, as the royal family had to get up early in order to see to all of their duties. The only times that Trev'nor had seen his friend sleep in was if he had either been up all night or was dog sick. This morning was no exception to the rule, as Trev'nor found his friend sitting at the table, a cup of something hot and steaming sitting at his elbow, a studious expression on his face as he stared at the map.

"Morning," he offered as he came in.

"Morning," Nolan returned, glancing up. "There's hot porridge and tea on the stove."

He knew he was friends with Nol for a reason. Happy to

have breakfast already cooked, he dished out a large bowl, filled up a mug, and joined the other at the table.

"Becca still sleeping?" Nolan asked, sitting back a little to take a leisurely sip at his mug.

"She is, and no, I will not wake her up. I'm pretty sure that the only thing that can safely wake up Becca is a dragon."

Nolan snickered. "Why, because they're fire-proof?"

"Exactly. Well, Tail manages it somehow, but I'm pretty sure he's lost a few lives in the process. Despite cat reflexes."

"It's funny, she doesn't exactly sleep late, it's just she's really stubborn if some outside influence tries to wake her up. Except for when she barely sleeps at all." Nolan pondered this for a brief second before shrugging and dismissing it. "Changing topics, I'm not sure what to think of that city named Von."

Trev'nor paused, spoon hovering in the air, to gauge his friend's reaction. "You realize that if there's a place called 'Rheben' and it was built by an Earth Mage, then…."

"Von would mean that someone from my family built that city, yes. That's highly probable. For that matter, I find Sha to be very suspicious as well. That's a family name for a magical line too. How much of Khobunter was built by Chahiran magicians?"

"Apparently at least some of it. How that history was so easily lost, that's the next question. Have they deliberately altered the history books?"

"They must have." Nolan shook his head sadly. "Abuse of power always brings such sorrow."

Unfortunately true. And to think, all of it started because the magical council in Chahir had gotten it in their heads to limit the power of a mage. If they hadn't been afraid of their own mages, the world wouldn't have turned upside down and taken so many lives in the process.

"Well, I've slept on it. I still feel like Tiergan is our best bet. You?"

"I haven't changed my mind. I spoke briefly to our dragons this morning and they assured me that the four who are going to stay here in Rurick have already been decided."

Trev'nor did appreciate how the dragons were divvying themselves up without making their human mages decide. It made his life much easier.

Becca wandered out of her room, a hand up to cover a yawn, bed hair going in every direction. "Do I smell breakfast?"

"On the stove," Nolan answered.

"Bless you." She shuffled that direction, humming soundlessly in a happy note. Apparently she was glad not to need to cook breakfast either.

Trev'nor turned sideways in his chair and gave her a quick study. "You're oddly tired this morning."

"It's the fatigue of traveling, I think," she answered as she ladled porridge into a bowl. "I'm not used to it like you are. Nolan, this smells wonderful. Are those figs?"

"They are. I found them stored in the pantry here."

"Perfect, I was craving fruit." Becca settled at the table with her breakfast, coming a bit more alive with every bite. "So what are we talking about?"

"Battle plans." A sudden thought struck Trev'nor and he slowed down so he could talk. "You know, Becca, I think I've only seen you actually fight with your magic twice."

"Here in Rurick, you mean?"

"Yup, just then. I mean, I saw you practice sometimes, but never actually fight."

Nolan glanced between them. "Come to think of it, Trev and I have fought together multiple times but never once with you. Before we go talk to the dragons we'd better get it straight first on what we can use to fight with that isn't going to clash with someone else's magic."

That was an amazingly good idea and Trev'nor wholeheartedly approved of it. He did not want to be accidentally zapped by lightning.

"I think, for the first several battles at least, that I need to fight in dragon-mode," Nolan stated. "That way it's easier for me to communicate with our dragons and show them where they need to go. Since that's the case, it's really a matter of knowing what you two will plan."

Trev'nor tapped the symbol of Tiergan with a forefinger. "From what I can feel from here, this is basically all flat land, with a few ravines and some sloping toward the coastline. Lots of loose ground to work with, I think. I can box people in with quick walls, bury them up to their necks, block off entrances and exits, sink buildings, throw rocks at troops, and of course lob large boulders to destroy buildings. If you want rock armor, I can do it, but that takes more time as it takes control."

Becca took a large swallow of tea before asking, "How many can you bury at a time?"

"Basically what I can see, so about twenty. And before you ask, I can do very large quick walls at a time, but only if I have the vantage to see exactly what I'm doing."

"Which you will on a dragon's back." Nolan quirked a brow. "That isn't all you can do, though."

"For group tactics like this, that's my main strengths. The rest of it comes down to individual fighting."

Nolan's open palm conceded the point. "And you, Becca?"

"You've seen my lightning strikes, right? I can also do mini-tornadoes, although those are more destructive and harder to control, so I'd rather not do it on a populated city.

I can use very strong winds as well, to force people different directions. I can also do misdirection, with blinding rain, or mists, to confuse the enemy with." She popped a bite into her mouth, chewing as she thought. "For group tactics, that's about it. Theoretically, I can also heat the air to the boiling point, but that's hard to keep to a certain location, and I risk hitting allies as well as enemies, so I'd rather not use it. There's a few other things that I can do that can cover whole areas, but I don't see how it would help to fight with, not really."

"What it sounds like to me is that Becca should focus on strategic strikes and pushing soldiers into the same area. Once she's herded them together, then Trev'nor can box them in and keep them from attacking." Nolan stared blindly forward. "The dragons can be used as guards to keep them from trying anything, but also as a scare tactic to keep them from forming up any ranks or utilizing their defenses properly."

"That will be not only the best way to use them, but the safest," Trev'nor agreed. He felt privately relieved about this as they had promised the dragon chief that they wouldn't put his dragons into dangerous situations if they could help it. "Becca, I think this is a pretty good plan. It's rough, so I think we should form up and do a few practice runs at Rurick today until we have a feeling for it."

"Practice runs only work if someone's defending," she pointed out. "Should we take turns being the enemy?"

"Why not? I'll go first if you want me to." Trev'nor wanted to do this for the simple reason that it would give him a chance to really study the city's defenses, which was information he would need to know later to attack them properly. Hopefully Tiergan's defenses were similar. That would be extremely helpful if they were. "Nol, if you want to explain to the dragons?"

"Sure. Meet you outside in an hour."

They spent a full day doing dry runs at Rurick. Becca was fervently grateful for the boys' insight on this, because it was apparent on the first try that the dragons had a limited grasp on what they needed to do. It took three runs before they were all in the right places at the right time, and five before they stopped flying into each other.

Becca also learned, really learned, how Trev'nor and Nolan thought as they battled. She'd fought along with them as sparring partners, so when it came to non-magical fighting, she knew how to predict them. But on an open ground with large group tactics, they didn't necessarily fight the same way, and she'd lost three mock battles in a row before learning that lesson.

Really, they could stand more practice. That day had done them a great deal of good, but no army can form itself up in a day, even when formed at the core with three childhood friends. They just didn't feel like they had time to keep sitting around practicing. It was a miracle that no one had come to bother Rurick again, in Becca's opinion.

They left the next morning on dragon-back, more equipped than when they had started out. The three had gone scavenging for the supplies they needed and now had proper goggles and leather helms to keep hair out of their faces. Becca had thrown out basically every skirt she'd brought with her and now solely wore pants. Wearing a skirt on dragon-back was completely impractical.

In terms of flight time, Tiergan was very close, barely four hours away. They did not issue a warning to the city, or declare anything to them, just flew in fast and hard. Becca called in a storm as she rode, and it hovered over them in a rolling mass of dark clouds. It was surely an odd sight to the inhabitants of the city. They saw storms coming in off the ocean, certainly, but never from the east before.

Nolan and Llona veered sharply left, coming in and around the city. Trev'nor and Garth dropped further toward the ground, probably to give Trev'nor the best vantage possible. Becca's task was to take out the government buildings as quickly as possible, leaving the garrisons up to the boys. Her targets were clearly defined by the large banners hanging off the sides of the buildings. They were the same color and design as the ones in Rurick, so the map that they had been looking at was accurate—Rurick was part of Trexler. Did that mean that with this city, they would halve Trexler's fighting force?

Part of Becca felt that was a little optimistic.

She had to be very, very careful in how she struck. In Rurick, Becca had been mad enough that if a few buildings aside from her target went up in flames, she hadn't cared. But here, they couldn't afford that kind of carelessness. Part of the reason why she had a storm raging above her head, rearing to be released, was to put out the flames after she started them.

From here, she couldn't hear much of anything, but she could see people frantically running around. They were about the size of ants from this distance, but it didn't take seeing their expressions to know they were terrified. This area of the country hadn't seen a dragon in living memory, after all. Even Kaya was likely nothing more than rumor mill to them.

Becca urged her dragon to fly in tight circles so that she could not only strike her key targets, but monitor them afterwards. With a flick of the wrist, she hit three main buildings with lightning and watched with a sort of macabre satisfaction as they sizzled and burst into flame. People launched themselves out of the building left and right, using windows if they couldn't get to a door. Seeing people flee for their lives actually relieved her. It would be fewer bodies to count for her.

Spying two other buildings, she urged her dragon up and around toward them, then struck them with the same precision. They weren't nearly of the same size, so rather than burn, the lightning nearly demolished them in one strike. She was quick to encourage rain in that area, to douse the flames before they could spread to the whole city.

Coming back around, she found that her attention had lingered a little too long on her secondary targets, and the flames had hopped the street onto another building that didn't look like it had anything to do with the government. Oops. Well, Trev'nor would help her fix it later. Becca called on the rain here, too, dousing the fire.

Anywhere else? She couldn't see any more banners, at least. Soaked to the skin, she guided her dragon to fly out of that area of the city and toward where the boys were fighting. Or where they had been fighting, at least. When she went back toward the front gates, she found almost the entirety of Tiergan's guard locked up in an impromptu rock jail made by Trev'nor, with several dragons perched on top of the wall and looking at the guards as if they were contemplating a mid-day meal.

Becca knew very well that dragons did not eat people. Was she going to stop and explain that to any of the guards? Well, perhaps later. Much later.

Without her direction, Becca's dragon back flapped hard and came in to land next to Garth. The elder dragon had draped himself along the wall, next to Trev'nor side, and toyed with the guards by idling poking at them with the tip of his tail. The guards were white and shaking, trying to dodge, but there wasn't enough room for them to maneuver more than two feet in any direction.

"How is it going?" Becca asked Trev'nor.

The Earth Mage looked up with a shrug. "I think we have most of them. How many guardsmen did you see inside the city?"

"They ran to the front defenses pretty quickly. I didn't see anyone lingering."

"Then we basically have only the ones left on the top of the wall." Trev'nor frowned in that direction. "This city looks an awful lot like Rurick, did you notice?"

She had, actually. "The layout's a little different, but the center of the city was almost an exact replica. Are all of the cities like this?"

"Surely not. Maybe it's because they're all of the same warlord's territory?"

That could be it. "Where's Nolan?"

"He went dragon at some point and is flying around to make sure that we got everything. He's communicating with me via Garth."

Flying around as she had been, Becca wouldn't have been able to hear much of anything that her dragon said, so it was probably wise that she had been given a separate task from the boys. Becca surveyed the area again, a frown forming. "This was far easier than Rurick had been."

"It really was," Trev'nor agreed, almost disapprovingly. "I think it's because of where they're located. They're in the far corner, protected on all sides, so I think they don't get attacked more than once a century. The guards were like sloths responding."

That did make sense. And it was part of the reason why they had chosen to strike Tiergan first. "Well, I guess that means we've won?"

"We've won." Trev'nor puffed out a breath. "Now comes the hard part."

This was not a repeat of Rurick in one simple way: none of the citizens had been allowed to flee. With dragons perched on top of the walls in every direction, no one had dared to get close to the gates, and so instead huddled in the middle of the city like confused sheep. This made the mages' job easier as they didn't have to wait for people to get brave enough to return to their homes.

Becca went with Trev'nor and Nolan to the center of the group, noting that some people were hiding in their houses, or any building they felt safe in. Only a few were brave enough to be out in the open still, although they were huddled together under a stone portico to shield them from the eyes of their aviator guards.

Being the best in Khobuntish still, Nolan went a little ahead and gave the group a proper greeting. "I am Vonnolanen, Life Mage of Chahir. I wish to speak with the governor or Rikkana of this city."

There was a moment of taut silence. Everyone stared at Nolan as if he had announced he was a mythical being come to life. Which, maybe, he had. For all that they had witches and wizards here, Becca had yet to see a mage. No one in the crowd moved, or even seemed to breathe, for several long moments until finally one man in front cleared his throat and offered, "Governor's dead."

"I see. And who might you be?"

He didn't shrink at gaining Nolan's undivided attention although he looked as if he dearly wanted to just jump into a hole and pull the ground in over him. "Sosa. I'm Head of Artillery Construction."

Becca leaned closer to Trev'nor. "A civilian doing a military job?" she whispered.

"Maybe," he whispered back. "Or maybe he's part of the guard but only does construction work."

"A pleasure, Master Sosa. I'm sure you're wondering—" everyone within earshot was included in this 'you'— "why we have conquered this city."

"Yes," the man agreed carefully, uncertain how to address someone with magic properly. "Yes, we are."

"In truth, it's because of how you treat your magicians." Nolan's smile hadn't faltered but there was a hard set to the expression that made him a little scary. "Magicians are not slaves. We will not tolerate having them treated as ones."

Sosa glanced at the people around him and there was a low rumble as people muttered to themselves. Becca picked up a random word here and there but mostly she heard confusion.

Nolan launched into an explanation of exactly where the magicians originally came from, what had happened to the three of them when they traveled into Khobunter, and why they were fighting to reclaim Khobunter to right the wrong. He started using words Becca didn't know, and her attention wandered, since she knew more or less what he would say anyway.

No one knew what to make of it. Becca watched their expressions, their body language, and saw that the people here didn't understand his reasoning at all. They understood that they had three fully trained mages that were angry with them and that was all they were truly getting.

"Trev."

Trev'nor turned to her, head cocked, listening.

"This isn't working."

"It's not," he agreed. His own words spurred him forward and he stepped up, clapping Nolan's shoulder, stopping the other mid-sentence. Leaning in, he whispered something, and Nolan nodded slowly in support.

Decided, Trev'nor looked up and gave the audience a smile. "I'm Trev'nor, an Earth Mage of Chahir. One question for all of you: do you like your government here? Do you like your warlord?"

No one dared to speak out.

Trev'nor tried again. "It's alright to answer the question honestly. I'm just curious, as the people of Rurick hated him. I'm not asking if your warlord is a good one or not, just if you like him."

There was some uneasy shifting and glances, but people didn't respond still. No one said any praise, or offered any support to the government and warlord they had. The silence spoke volumes.

"Right, then, we'll simplify this for you. We," Trev'nor pointed between himself and Becca, "are going to conquer Khobunter and replace the government you have. It will be far more fair and tolerant than what you've been living under. The only demand we have, aside from your cooperation, is that you treat the magicians as citizens of Khobunter and not slaves."

They didn't know what to make of that, either. Becca

knew that it wouldn't be a simple matter to change their minds or the traditions that were engrained here. Notifying them first of what their conquerors felt was only an initial step and nothing more.

Nolan heaved out a somewhat resigned breath. "Just… keep that in mind. The dragons are here to make sure this place stays under our control. They will not hurt you." He paused, waiting to see how this was taken, then continued, "Where are your slaves?"

Since Sosa had already spoken up, he was unanimously voted as the spokesman for the city. Very uneasy, he stepped forward and led the way.

As Becca followed him, she truly felt like she was reliving an echo of the past. It felt eerily similar to walking through Rurick's streets. Why were the cities so similar? Even Sol, which had a set pattern for their cities, had more variety than this. Was it a matter of lack of building supplies, perhaps? They had precious little wood to work with in this desert landscape after all. And where was the Rikkana? Were they sheltering her from the evil conquerors? Likely so.

Sosa took them into a building that had the earmarks for a slaver's pen all over it. Becca's skin crawled at the first look of it and the thought of having to walk into that building made her stomach turn over in a hard lurch. Steeling herself, she forced her shoulders back and went in after the men.

For whatever reason, Tiergan didn't have as many slaves. Less need for them, perhaps? Becca scanned, doing a quick headcount, and came up with a little over one hundred slaves. Most of them seemed to be young, few elderly mixed in with them, and quite a number of children. Odd, Rurick had a complete mix of people of all ages. Why was this place different?

"I've got the door," Trev'nor stated simply and turned to

face the doorway, feet planted shoulder length apart. "Master Sosa, you stay with me."

The tension riding in Becca's body eased knowing that he had a watchful eye on their backs. In this warring country, conquering a city did not mean the inhabitants would blindly follow whoever had defeated their government. They were used to war, and used to being fought over. Becca did not think them cowed and she had been afraid that someone would try to pounce from behind and take them unawares.

With her worries set aside, she paid better attention to the people. Not all of them were magicians, but the majority certainly was. She could clearly see their magic underneath the magical amulets subduing them. Actually, the amulets were distorting her vision enough that her eyes nearly missed the obvious entirely.

"Nolan," she breathed, jerking back around, convinced her eyes were playing tricks on her. "Is that...?"

"We have mages," he confirmed, equally hoarse. He took a step forward as if he wanted to make a beeline straight for them, but all of the magicians were standing up now and creeping cautiously closer.

Becca thought this was a different reaction from the usual. Why were they looking so awed, so hopeful? Realization kicked in and she felt like smacking herself. Of course they would react so. Three powerful mages just waltzed in without amulets or guards. Free magicians must be an awe-inspiring sight, like watching unicorns walk past. Clearing her throat, she tried to be as clear and distinct as possible. "My name is Riicbeccaan. I am a Weather Mage from Chahir. With me is Vonnolanen, a Life Mage, and Rhebentrev'noren, an Earth Mage." Using the Chahiran names helped as the surnames of the boys rang a bell with everyone in the room and they looked more interested than before. "We are here to free you." At that point, her limited grasp on the language rather failed and she looked to Nolan to cue him.

Nolan picked up the explanation of why they were there, what they hoped to accomplish, and so forth. As he talked, Becca found the key ring and started with the people nearest to her, unlocking shackles and ripping off amulets before crushing them under her heel. She made it almost halfway around the room before he stopped talking and waited for a reaction.

A young woman with a heart shaped face and pretty dark eyes sitting in front of Becca tentatively reached out to take her arm. "Free?"

"Free," Becca responded firmly. "You can go. Or stay. Will help you train magic." Frustrated by her lack of vocabulary to explain all of this, she turned to Nolan and requested, "Explain to them what their options are."

The woman tugged at her arm. "Will you fight all of Khobunter? Take back all of the slaves?"

Grateful she'd understood those questions, Becca met her eyes and said, "Yes. All of them."

Tears brimmed in her eyes. "My husband, children, you will help me find them?"

Wait, what? "Were they taken?"

"Yes. They were sold four days ago and sent up north." The woman's grip on her became so tight it threatened to leave bruises. "You will go that far?"

She felt Nolan come to stand behind her and she looked up. Nolan's mouth twisted as if he had bitten into something rotten. "Busted buckets, I didn't think of that. Of course they would have no regard for families and would sell people anywhere and everywhere. We're going to have a fun time later, trying to reunite people."

Becca felt her stomach, already upset, twist a little more.

Had they really paid no regard to families whatsoever?

To the woman, Nolan smiled and reassured her gently, "Everyone. We'll free everyone and make sure that families see each other again."

A sob escaped her mouth before she burst into tears. Becca felt like she'd been thrown into the past in that moment, reliving when she had been forced to say goodbye to her family. Even to this day, she had not been able to see them again, as it was still dangerous in southern Chahir. Feeling perfect empathy, she reached out and hugged the woman tight, rocking her slightly as if comforting a child. "We'll find them. My oath as a Riic."

From the other side of the room, a tall man that looked to be in his forties stood and made his way to them. He looked rough, long hair pulled back in a ponytail, beard scraggly and un-kept, skin dark from long exposure to the suns. He caught Becca's undivided attention as this was one of the mages, a Water Mage, by the looks of it. "I am Ehsan. I have questions."

"Ask," Nolan encouraged.

"Only three of you fight?"

"Three of us," Nolan admitted openly, mouth twisting up in amusement, "and about a hundred dragons."

That shocked the room back into stillness.

"Dragons?" Ehsan parroted incredulously.

"The dragons are friends of magicians," Nolan explained simply. "Always. They have agreed to help fight Khobunter and free magicians."

Ehsan searched their expressions, then turned to Sosa. "He speaks truth?"

"He does," Sosa answered although he had a strange expression on his face, as if he had just bitten down the impulse to say something nasty to a former slave for speaking out of turn. Wise man not to do that, as Becca was in such a mood that she would have gladly jumped down his throat for it.

Thinking this over for a long moment, Ehsan finally concluded aloud, "With dragons, you might win. I am tired of being a slave. I will fight with you."

Nolan reached out, taking off the amulets, and crushing them under his boot. "You are a Water Mage, and powerful. We welcome your help."

A fierce light came into the man's dark eyes. "I am powerful? Like you?"

"Like me. Like Becca. You and the Elemental Mage over there." Nolan turned to look at the woman that had still not moved. "What is your name?"

"Azin." The woman slowly rose, revealing her full figure for the first time. She was a slender little thing, small enough to make Becca look large, dark hair in a matted braid over one shoulder, skin paler than most of the people around her. "I am not powerful. I can work with metal, a little."

"And water, and earth, and air, and fire," Nolan corrected, walking to her. "But your best element is metal. Isn't that right?"

Stunned, she nodded dumbly. "You can see that?"

"Part of that was a guess," he denied cheerfully. "But most Elemental Mages are very strong in metal, perhaps one or two other elements, and then can sort of work with the rest. That's normal. Once we get these amulets off of you, and I have time to do some proper training, you're going to be a powerhouse of a fighter." Nolan happily flung off the amulets as he spoke, destroying them with a smirk on his face. "I know that all of you have a lot of questions. But let's get these chains off, and the amulets, and get out of this hole first. Then we can talk."

The slaves didn't know what to do with themselves. Becca realized that before they had even left the building and took charge of them. With Sosa's reluctant help, she found three inns and commandeered them, getting people into bathing chambers and finding clean clothes for them to wear. Once they were properly bathed and fed, then it seemed to sink in that they truly were free.

Some of the braver ones went out in the streets, walking about and testing their new freedom. Of course the dragons noticed them, and a few came down into the streets to talk. Becca caught one exchange in between bustling from inn to the other. The two magicians in the street looked ready to bolt but the dragon was careful in its approach, slow, showing no aggression. Becca thought she recognized the dragon in question, a young male that had been one of her better students, and he tried out his language skills in a low rumbling voice.

Hearing human words out of a dragon's mouth surprised them, but put them at ease, and they cautiously responded. Becca smiled as she watched them grow more comfortable in the exchange. It did not escape her notice, either, that the other inhabitants of Tiergan were also watching and taking special note of this. "That's right," she muttered to them under her breath, "the dragons like your former slaves. Keep that in mind."

Her dragon had been lounging along the roof of the inn but dipped her head down to talk to Becca. "Guards now in hole."

"Hole? Oh, you mean where the slaves were?" Becca had referred to it as a 'hole' several times, that was probably where she'd picked up the term.

"Yes." Her golden eyes flared with a spark of anger. "Bad men?" she asked, tone relaying that she was perfectly amiable to frying them for Becca if needed.

"Don't know," Becca admitted. "Some probably are. Some were probably just defending the city. We'll have to see."

Satisfied, her dragon sat back again, stretching out in her new sunny perch.

"You're seriously like a cat, you know that?" Becca felt, watching her, that she had another feline familiar.

"Cat?" the dragon repeated, interested.

"Right, cat. You sunbathe, you chase things that move, your mannerisms are all like a cat."

With a feline rumble of pleasure, she repeated, "Cat."

Becca's forehead compressed into a quick frown. "Wait, you like that word?"

"Like. Name."

"You want Cat to be your name?" Seriously? Of all the ones for her to choose. Not that it wasn't accurate, but still….

"Name," her dragon stated firmly.

"Well, alright, Cat it is." Watching her dragon's tail twitch happily, she shook her head. Strange, strange creature. "So, Cat, can you see everything up there?"

"Yes. Trev'nor—" her mouth tripped a little over the 'n' sound "—have guards locked up. Nolan talk with people."

"Which people? Magic people?"

"No. City people."

It was very interesting to Becca that the dragons could tell a difference between the two. And it wasn't like they were asking to verify, they just knew in a glance. Were dragons sensitive to magic? There was so little really known about them, yet somehow Becca had no doubt that they could. "Can you hear what he's saying?"

"Yes. People confused. Don't know what want."

Didn't know what Nolan wanted? True, they had rather divided up duties here, with Nolan taking the lead in establishing a temporary government. It worked rather like Chahir's martial law, as that was one they were all familiar with, and knew well enough to implement here. Besides, any government was better than the one here. "Does he need help?"

"Will ask." Cat's head lifted, eyes intent for a long moment. "Says no."

Nolan was more up to the task than she was.

Trev'nor came around the bend, spotted her, and made a beeline directly for her. "Bec. You know what just hit me?"

"What?"

"Our mages have no limiters on their powers."

It took a second to click, but when it did, she groaned. "And they only have a basic grasp of how to use their magic. We're sure to have magical accidents at this rate."

"It's seriously a problem. Not just with them but the witches and wizards. I think we better have some quick lessons on magic."

Becca whole-heartedly agreed. After all, the three trained mages in this city might or might not have the right skills to fix whatever broke. "How much should we teach them?"

"Even the basics will help right now."

Mentally, she held a debate with herself. "Which one takes higher priority, teaching our magicians some basics or making sure this city doesn't revolt on us?"

"Magicians," Trev'nor responded promptly. "Nolan has enlisted the dragons to make sure that people obey the martial laws."

That was not something they had discussed beforehand, but Becca had to admit that was brilliant. Nothing escaped a dragon's hearing, after all, and they might not have all of the vocabulary to understand human speech, but they could certainly communicate to Nolan when people were misbehaving. "The dragons don't have a problem with this?"

"Actually, I think they volunteered. Nolan said their duty was to protect the city, from both inside and outside. It helps us tremendously."

It truly did. Becca had been plagued by nightmares when she thought of trying to move on to the next city without properly governing Tiergan first. "Well, if we're going to do magic lessons, I vote we do it outside of the city."

"Where there's less breakables around?" Trev'nor grinned at her in complete understanding. "Sounds good to me. Garth and I will go out and build some wards, if you want to gather people up and meet me out there?"

"Alright. I'll be out there shortly."

Gathering up the magicians didn't take much time at all, and most were glad for an excuse to be outside of the city for once, so Becca didn't need to do much more than call them. The hard part was explaining the fundamentals of magic. Becca had extensive training as a mage, mostly in weather patterns, but even with all of that knowledge, she didn't know everything. In fact, most of the basics that she was trying to teach were things she had studied as an eight year old. To say that her memory was a little rusty was putting it mildly.

Their saving grace came from Trev'nor's teaching abilities. He didn't try to explain when he could demonstrate, or physically and magically walk a person through step by step. People crowded around him, intently watching his every move as he demonstrated how to properly activate magic, use it, then release it to let it idle again.

Someone had broken into a storage room that contained magical items, and they'd brought them along. Mirror broaches, small scrying bowls, a few triangles, and one bon'a'lon, which took Becca by surprise. Trev'nor used all of them to demonstrate how to properly use magic.

The lesson took three hours. Becca called a halt after that point before people could make any stupid and dangerous mistakes due to fatigue. It was a good breaking point anyway, as everyone understood the basic concepts and were no longer a danger to themselves or the populace in general.

Trev'nor regrouped with her as people trudged the short distance back into the city, talking animatedly amongst themselves. "I think that went well."

"Extremely well. They were like sponges, soaking up everything you had to say. I didn't know you were good at teaching like this."

"Ah, that?" Trev'nor's sight turned inward. "In the early days, before Strae Academy had a full roster of professors, I would often act like a teacher's aide for Night."

Having sat through Night's class on History of Magic, Becca nodded understanding. "I remember liking his class. He's a fun teacher."

"He is. I don't think I ever helped out with your class, though."

"No, you must have had a class at the same time. In fact, I think the only class we ever had together was Weapons."

"Huh." Trev'nor pondered that for a moment. "I think

you're right. Anyway, I basically adopted his teaching methods, and Shad's, as those seem to work the best. I don't think there's much more that I can teach the wizards and witches, not with what I know."

"Even if you knew more, you wouldn't be able to teach them much past this anyway," she observed pragmatically. "You don't have all of the potions and tools you need."

"That's a good point." Trev'nor watched the last of his students enter the city and asked softly, "Is it safe to leave them here?"

"More than safety, I think it's necessary to leave them here."

Garth, trailing along at Trev'nor's other side, gave a deep hum of agreement.

"You see what I mean?" she asked him.

"Do," Garth stated with a slight nod of the head. "Tradition deep. Must change."

Trev'nor cottoned on at that point. "True, the people of Tiergan aren't going to learn to change their minds about magicians if we don't leave magicians here to influence them, but Bec...that's a really rough position to put them in. I mean, our magicians still have a lifetime of habit to overcome. They're going to be deferential automatically."

"Then they, too, need to learn better."

"We help," Garth assured them both. "All young need raising."

Trev'nor tilted is head around to look Garth in the eye, tone suspicious. "Just how young do I look to you, anyway?"

"Baby chick," the dragon rumbled, amusement rumbling in his chest.

Somehow this answer didn't surprise Becca and she giggled. "Compared to him, I think most of the world are baby chicks. But I think we can trust the dragons to herd people in the right direction while we focus on the rest of the country."

"Probably right."

"Besides, Trev, look at this objectively: can we really take half-trained magicians in with us to the next battle?"

He winced. "Nooo, that's a bad idea."

"Right? Especially when they're unarmed. They don't have the tools they need to do magic with. It'll be suicide."

"But that doesn't apply to our two mages," he objected. "In fact, I think we should take them with us. They've got a half-grasp on their magic already. With some more training, some practical experience in doing something outside of their norm, they'll become formidable."

True. Becca did have some doubts about them, but mage powers were more volatile than a witch's or wizard's because they didn't require a focusing tool to release. A few hours of training wouldn't teach them everything they'd need to know. "It would be nice having some additional fighters."

"Wouldn't it?"

"But are you sure we can train them well enough in the next few days that they'll be battle-ready?"

"I actually spoke with them a little earlier. Our Elemental Mage worked directly with the artillery in building and maintaining siege weapons as well as defenses. She's been doing it for nearly four years."

"Then she already has the experience she needs." Becca felt hope rise up. "And the Water Mage?"

"He's been at this for about fifteen years. Mostly they used him to find water in the desert but he said he's fought in a few battles too. On the rare occasion they had a navy come in from the coast, he was the one that fought them off."

That poor navy. When Becca imagined what a Water Mage could do with an entire ocean to work with…normal ships wouldn't stand a chance. "So really, what we're doing is fine tuning their control and teaching them what they're really capable of."

"Yup." Trev'nor could read her reaction well enough to grin. "See? We need to take them with us."

Becca was half-sold on this idea but still had reservations. "Let's put it to the test first, then. I had a thought this morning as we were flying in. You know how we changed part of Rurick's landscape, put in a garden, etc?"

"Yes, what about it?"

"Well, after we conquer everything, I don't think we're going to have a lot of spare time on our hands. Like, ruling a country is going to be really demanding. Do you think we'll be able to roam around the country fixing the landscape later?"

Trev'nor shook his head. "I really doubt that. So what are you suggesting? That we fix the land as we go, take time after we win each city to work on the land?"

"Like we did in Rurick, yes. You have a better solution?" she challenged.

"Naw, not really. In that case, you want to spend a few days working here before we move on, and use our new mages to help do it."

"Two birds, one stone."

"I can't disagree. Alright, let's talk to Nolan. We need his help after all."

It really was going to take all three of them to put Khobunter back to rights. That and about twenty years. Strangely, this thought didn't daunt Becca like it should have.

"One more thing we should do before leaving is get a full list of everyone's names." Trev'nor glanced between both dragons. "Can the two of you help with this? You have such amazing memories, can you remember every person's name?"

"Can," Cat assured him. "Why?"

"To help reunite people later," Trev'nor explained. "Say, we go into the next city, we can recite the names to the slaves there so we know if there're family members. We might not be able to reunite everyone all at once, but if we can start locating them, then I can always transport them real quick to the right place. I don't see why they have to wait for us to win before seeing their families again."

It was such a sweet, sweet, thought. Becca couldn't contain herself. She slung an arm around his shoulders and hugged him to her. "I knew I liked you for a reason."

"My devastating charm and good looks?"

"Nope, that wasn't it."

Trev'nor mock-pouted at her, which set her and both dragons grinning.

"Cat," Becca instructed, "tell Nolan our plans and ask him if he wants to join us out here."

"Cat?" Trev'nor repeated, tone climbing. "You named a dragon Cat?"

"This was not my choice, trust me. She's strange."

"Like Cat," Cat defended, miffed.

"Yes, dearling, I know." Although heaven knew why, Becca was not questioning it. Her brain was completely tired of playing Name That Dragon. If she liked Cat, Cat it would be.

"You want us to fight with you?" Azin repeated incredulously.

Trev'nor had taken the precaution of bring all both mages out of the city before having this discussion. He did not want anyone to overhear them talking. The dragons were taking the time to hunt, although Becca noticed that either Garth, Cat, or Llona would fly lazy circles over their head, taking turns keeping an eye out.

Becca anticipated that today would go more smoothly than yesterday for the simple reason that Ehsan and Azin both spoke some Solish. Ehsan used the occasional Khobuntish word when he couldn't think of or didn't know the Solish one. Azin would stop and re-phrase entirely if she got stuck. But it saved Becca from a headache, trying to explain everything with her limited vocabulary. She'd improved by leaps and bounds over the past few weeks, of course, but she was not conversational in Khobuntish yet.

"We do," Nolan confirmed. He had listened to Becca last night for all of a minute before agreeing that it was a good choice. "There are two reasons for this. One, we would like to have help in the upcoming battles. It's a little rough with just three mages, even with this many dragons. But every time we conquer a city, we lose at least one pair of dragons to guard the city. We need to augment our fighting force or we'll be in trouble later."

"It's a good argument," Ehsan agreed, expression and tone unreadable. He stood with arms crossed over his chest, as if determined not to move until he had the full gist of the situation. "What else? There is something else."

"We can't teach the witches and wizards more than we already have," Becca picked up the explanation smoothly, "because we don't know as much about their magic and we frankly don't have all of the right tools. But we can teach you. It's safer to teach you, actually, than to try to leave you on your own to manage your magic. You're not used to managing it day-to-day as your power was always sealed when not in active use. This is dangerous, for both you and the city as a whole. We'd rather take you along with us so that we can properly train you as we go."

"We'd also be grateful for the help," Trev'nor added. "I'm not sure if you've heard this already, but one of our goals is to change Khobunter back into the fertile land it's supposed to be."

Ehsan and Azin blinked at him as if he had gone mad. "Fertile?" they repeated in stereo, doubt dripping from the word.

Trev'nor gave them a sad smile. "Hard for you to believe it now, I know, as you've been in this desert your whole life. But it was not originally like this. It was the change of weather patterns that slowly made it this way. Its state now is such that it will take the combined powers of an Earth, Life, and Weather Mage to get it back to its former glory."

"And that's rather a tall order, for three people to change a whole country," Becca tacked on. "Two more people will help speed the process along."

Ehsan looked at them long and hard before puffing out

an incredulous breath. "You're serious."

"Dead serious." Nolan grinned at him. "Oh, it'll take a long time. Decades, probably. But wouldn't you rather live in a place that's lush and green with abundant life in it?"

Azin seemed caught up in some internal vision. "I certainly would. You think I can help?"

"You can," Trev'nor assured her promptly. "See, there's too much of a mineral deposit in the soil right now, and not enough moisture and compost. I need help extracting some of the minerals to soften the ground up enough to be able to accept moisture. I figure that we can use what's taken from the ground to build irrigation canals and wells. You have experience building walls, right? This is basically the same thing."

"Our part," Becca informed Ehsan, "is the water. I have rain clouds forming and on their way this very moment," she had in fact started that this morning right after waking up, "but Trev'nor needs water now to moisten the soil. Otherwise when my rain gets here, it won't be able to penetrate."

Ehsan turned his eyes to Nolan. "And you?"

"Plant life. But I can only do my part after the rest of you are done." He paused, thought about that, and re-phrased, "Well, actually I will need to come out here before Becca's rain comes in. A good, soft rain is perfect for watering seeds with."

Did she have a soft rain coming? Becca had been a little foggy this morning; she barely remembered getting a storm started and heading this direction. She'd need to check what type it was.

"You're all crazy," Ehsan informed them. A grin broke out over his face. "I like it."

Azin was smiling too, almost laughing, although the laughter was born more from self-defense, it seemed. She looked more than a little overwhelmed.

"We're not going to just turn you loose," Nolan assured Azin, tone gentle. "Let's go over the basics of power before we start. I know that your education in your ability was basically passed down like an oral tradition more than anything."

Putting a hand to her heart, Azin gathered herself again, nodding. "That would be good."

Trev'nor formed up earthen benches for them to sit on, which everyone promptly used. Becca, already tired of the sunburn she had gotten yesterday, decided she would not repeat her mistakes today. While they talked, she formed a miniature cloud to float over their heads.

Pausing in mid-sentence, Trev'nor glanced up. "I have this feeling that I'm under a dark cloud. Sure enough, I am. Bec?"

"You might not burn," she responded frostily, "but I certainly do. I want shade, thank you very much."

"No argument from me," Nolan said cheerfully. "I'm tired of burning too. Go on, Trev."

Smiling still at the absurdity of it, Trev'nor continued his lesson, asking questions more than anything. Becca listened very intently to the answers, as it was important for her to know as much about their new allies as possible. Basically, it seemed as if they had a foundation of how their magic was released and used. They just had no bearings on how to store it, control it, and limited understanding of how intent could form magic.

They talked for half the morning, making sure the basics were ground into Ehsan's and Azin's heads before daring to get back up again and work.

When they were ready to start, Nolan went back into the city, wanting to check on how things were going. Becca gestured for Ehsan to follow her even as Azin went off some distance with Trev'nor. On the wind, she could hear snatches of their conversation and she frowned. "Azin doesn't know how to draw ore and minerals from the soil?"

"She never had to before," Ehsan explained. "She was always given either raw ore to work with or metal already forged."

That did make sense. "What about you? Have you ever had to hunt for water underground?"

"A few times, in the dry seasons, when they needed new wells." He took the initiative and led her to the far right. "There's underground streams here, and another that joins up over here."

"Is that all in this area?"

"No, there's a few more. Most of them feed into the sea."

That made perfect sense.

Ehsan stopped abruptly, expression warring as emotions clashed. "I don't understand you."

Becca blinked up at him. "Sorry?" Had she been using words he didn't know?

"I don't understand you," he repeated, more forcefully. Rounding on her, he leaned forward, almost looming over her. "You're all powerful mages, fully trained, with connections to prominent people. One of you is an actual prince! Why don't you call for help? Why don't you bring armies into here?"

Oh, that sort of not understanding. This man was a good decade older than she was. He was more mature in many ways, so perhaps to him her decisions made no sense whatsoever. Becca admitted (to herself at least) that her emotions were at the root of what she had decided to do. Logic hadn't played into it much at all. How to explain this all to him? "Did you know that we were captured as slaves too?"

Ehsan stopped dead. "Even you? How?"

"How is that even possible?" Her mouth twisted into a grimace. "We weren't expecting that much trouble. We were overconfident, I guess, and we waltzed into Rurick thinking that we might stumble across a pickpocket or some such, but nothing more serious than that. They caught us unawares, blind-sided us, and we were down before we properly understood what was happening. I lived in a slave pen for ten days, and it was a hellish experience. I fought my way out of there and swore that no one would be forced to live like that, like an animal, not as long as I breathed."

This he seemed to understand. In fact, was it her imagination, or did he appear more relaxed? "But why don't you call for help?"

"I have a very hard time believing that absolutely no one knew that they had magical slaves up here in Khobunter. This has been going on for at least a hundred years— that much we can prove. Khobunter might be somewhat isolated, since it's up here in the far corner of the world, but it's not that isolated. Someone had to have known." Becca privately hoped that neither Vonlorisen nor Guin Braehorn did. If they had, they would have reacted by now. Surely, they would have, given how they had actively been rescuing magicians in Chahir. "So, at least some of the governments in this world are choosing to ignore the problem."

Ehsan's face fell into grim lines. He had no counterargument for her.

"I'm not sure if my own country's leaders are the same, in fact I rather doubt it, but it still falls down to a matter of politics: they would have to arrange non-aggression treaties to bring an army over the Empire of Sol's territory just to get here. And then they would have to fight their way through this country to rescue all of the slaves. After that was done, then they would come down to the argument of what to do next. Treat Khobunter like a conquered nation and rule it? Abandon it now that the slaves were out?" Gentling her tone, she smiled up at him sadly. "Do you see? Most countries can't afford to front a war in a far-distant country to begin with. You add politics into the mix, it becomes impossible to do, no matter how the kings in question might feel about it."

His dark eyes searched her face. "You thought all of that through and still chose to fight? You have no allies up here."

"I make my allies as I go." She grinned, not in the least daunted. "I decided, weeks ago, that I would not leave this country even after the slaves are all freed. Someone has to stay and properly reconstruct this country; otherwise other atrocities are going to be committed up here, and no one will stop them."

"If you've fought two battles and gained a treaty with dragons, I suppose I shouldn't underestimate your determination." Uncertainty and tension had been riding high in his body language, but as Ehsan said these words, it visibly dissipated. "But you really have no intention of returning?"

"No. Nolan can't stay, he has his own country to rule, but Trev'nor and I are staying."

Satisfied with her answers, Ehsan settled into a content expression. "Alright then." He took in a breath before bellowing, "Trev'nor!"

Trev'nor's head snapped around, as that was the first time Ehsan had called any of them by name. Delight exploded across his face even as he called back, "What?"

"How much water you want right now?"

"Soak all the way to the under crust! No more than that!"

Grunting, Ehsan knelt and concentrated. His power, not having any constraints on it, leapt to obey. Swearing, Becca slammed a hand against his back, her own power coming to bear. "Whoa, not that much. Back it down."

Ehsan gasped and shook, breathing all over the place. "Is this what it's like? Is this my full power?"

"Yes, yes, it is, but you don't need that much right now. Let some of it go."

He seemed overwhelmed by his own power, so much so that it took several minutes for him to come to grips with it. Becca patiently waited him out. Rushing matters like this did absolutely no good and often a great deal of harm. One of the truest things she had learned from Garth was the art of patience.

The Water Mage's power seeped down into more normal, working levels and he cautiously went back to work. Becca just as slowly withdrew her hand, although she remained ready to leap back in and help contain his power if need be. It proved unnecessary as he encouraged the underground water to come up and soak into the ground.

As he worked, Trev'nor and Azin made their way closer to him, changing the soil composition as they walked for miles in either direction. Watching Trev'nor in action had always amazed Becca. Her power worked so differently from his, almost ethereal in its formation, if not in its execution. But Trev'nor's magic was very tangible and solid. His seemed the more permanent of the two.

When they hit the patch of ground that was soaked and waiting for them, it turned from a golden sand to a more rich dark brown color. "That looks much better."

"Soil's almost perfect right now," Trev'nor agreed, proud and satisfied. "Having Azin along is speeding up the process a lot."

Azin blushed and stammered and looked anywhere but at their eyes.

Trying to extract the girl from her embarrassment, Becca informed them, "Ehsan says there's two underground rivers right under our feet."

"Oh really?" Trev'nor asked him, "How large?"

"Sizeable, as thick and deep as the city's walls."

"In that case, let's build a canal here and start it toward the city. Azin, draw all of our excess over here and let's put it to work."

Becca stood back and watched as the three fell into a companionable working atmosphere with each other. Her job right now was just to be on hand in case someone's magic went out of control; it wasn't like she could do any good until her storm arrived. Considering how fast they all worked, though, she gave it three days before this entire area became fertile and bursting with new buds.

The thought made her smile.

Becca found Nolan bent over a table with Sosa at his side, and two women that she didn't recognize. He'd sent a message to her via mirror broach that he wanted her and Trev'nor to meet him in the main marketplace, but she hadn't expected there to be a crowd of military men standing around him. As she slid in between people, forcing her way to Nolan's side, she saw signs that this was an information broker's table, as there were charts hanging from several lines and a collection of colorful maps strewn out on top of the table. "Nolan."

The Life Mage glanced up and pointed her into a stool next to him. "Bec, Trev, glad you came so fast. I've found out some very interesting information."

Is that why he was vibrating in his chair? "Like what?"

"Well, you know how we were talking about what to do with Trexler once we captured him?"

"No," she denied pleasantly, "I don't."

"Ahhh…" Nolan trailed off, an almost visible question mark on his face.

"She'd already gone to bed before we started talking about that," Trev'nor reminded him.

"Oh, right. Right. I'd forgotten."

Becca felt mildly irritated at both of them. "Did the two

of you discuss something important and make decisions without me?"

"Bec, I know better than to wake you up," Trev'nor drawled, not in the least worried. "You zap people when peeved. Besides, considering the cultural rules here, I didn't dare."

If he had barged into her room to wake her, the two of them would be considered automatically engaged, so she was rather glad he had stifled the impulse. It also robbed her of an argument, though, so she huffed out a resigned breath.

Nolan leaned in a little and whispered, "You two need to be especially careful. People know that I'm not staying, that you two are, and they're already forming conjectures about when you'll marry."

"Again?!" Trev'nor squawked.

"We already disabused the notion in Rurick. Are we going to have to do it everywhere we go?" Becca groaned.

The two looked at each other in disbelief, then in unison, spat out, "Ewwww."

This made people in the crowd chuckle. Becca flushed and realized that she had automatically been speaking in Solish, as that was the only language she'd been really using these days. Habit was such a wonderful thing. At least some had understood their exchange and were getting a good laugh out of it. Clearing her throat, she tried to regain her dignity. "You were saying about important discussions held in the middle of the night?"

"Ah, right." Nolan sat back and returned to a more normal tone. "We were talking about what to do with Trexler once we had him in hand. It seemed like a bad plan to just execute him and move on. Taking Tiergan has taught me that we have to stop and spend at least some time straightening out governmental affairs, cleaning house, and such before we can move on."

That had become very obvious to Becca as well. Conquering Tiergan had been an eye-opener in several ways. It wasn't like taking Rurick at all in some aspects. "You two thought of a plan?"

"We can't just be young upstarts to these people," Trev'nor explained to her. Well, explained to everyone, as he certainly had everyone's attention. "We don't want to be an outside source pressuring them into something they don't want to do. Instead, we need to make them a part of our revolution."

"So," Nolan picked up the thread smoothly, "we thought to really examine the laws of Khobunter, especially Trexler's brand of laws, and see if the man is guilty of violating his own rules. Then we choose people from Tiergan and the army, and have them sit in judgement over him. That way, we're sharing joint responsibility for what happens."

Once outlined, it became apparent to her that it was a wise way to go. Half the trouble they'd had the first day in Tiergan was because no one had wanted to bow their heads to three teenagers. "You two actually thought of this last night in the wee hours of the morning?"

"From the ethers of desperation comes inspiration," Nolan intoned. "As Garth loves to say. What do you think?"

"I think it's great. It's better he's judged by the people than us doing it. I take it you've been researching that all morning?"

"Not quite me," Nolan denied. "I was planting half the morning. Sosa and…forgive me, have you met anyone else at the table?"

"I have not," Becca denied before standing and giving them both a quick bow. "I am Riicbeccaan."

"This is Yasmina," Nolan introduced the woman to his immediate right, who looked to be in her late sixties, as there was not a strand of black to be found in her silver hair, "who is the equivalent of a city historian, in our terms. Her title here is Rikkshana."

"A pleasure to exchange names," Becca and Trev'nor said, almost together. Yasmina smiled and inclined her head toward them.

"In Rurick, we met their Rikkana, which apparently is a universal position in Khobunter," Nolan started only to stop. "Sosa, can you explain this? I want to make sure I'm not confusing them."

"In this land we have experts on law and tradition," Sosa stated, words carefully expressed and slow. He knew how shaky they were with the language. "The Rikkan and the Rikkana. They are male and female, always, one expert in female laws and the other in male laws. They sit in judgement or offer advice for the city."

"Sorry," Trev'nor held up a hand to stall him, "I'm seeing a similarity in all of these titles. Do they mean something?"

It was Ehsan, standing behind them, that leaned in over their shoulders and broke it down. "Rikk meaning living, sha means history. An and ana are the male and female versions of ann, or law."

So their titles literally meant living history and living law? "Thank you, Ehsan. That makes it easier to remember."

Sosa seemed glad someone else had explained. His Solish wasn't always the best. "Our Rikkan and Rikkana are Shiva and Akbar."

Becca wasn't clear if these two were married or not but they certainly looked like they were. They sat closely enough that their shoulders were overlapping, perfectly at ease with their close contact. They looked of the same age as Yasmina, which made Becca wonder, was advanced age a requirement in this job? Or were you stuck with the position until death after you were hired? The similarity, even in her head, created a sharp pang in her chest when she remembered that they still had no idea where Rikkana Sumi and the rest had been carted off. Becca had to stop and breathe through the pain for a moment before she could manage in a level voice, "A pleasure to exchange names, Rikkan, Rikkana."

They smiled at her greeting but it was Akbar that responded in a creaking voice, "Blessings on you, Raya."

"Also with us are Danyal, Commander of the Tiergan forces," Nolan continued with a gesture toward a very stoic man with closely cropped hair, still in the sand-colored uniform of the military, "and his two captains, Nima and Hadi. When I explained to them what we wanted to do here in Khobunter, they readily swore allegiance to us."

Just like that? Becca was very surprised to hear this, as she had been under the impression that not many leaders in Tiergan were willing to switch sides. "Thank you for the gift of your names."

Danyal gave them a sharp salute. "Raya, Rajas, we have been given an oath by Raja Nolan that you will serve the people. As long as you do so, we will serve you."

In that moment, Becca felt like she was speaking with Xiaolang. Or a more serious, darker version of Shad. She scooted her stool back and snapped into the same military bearing, exchanging the salute. "We will honor them, Commander. My word as a Riic."

Every person at the table appeared surprised except her two childhood friends. The commander and his two captains actually smiled at her as Danyal dropped the salute.

"Where did you learn to do that?" Ehsan wondered aloud.

"I was raised by two soldiers," she drawled, dropping back into her stool. "You pick up things. Alright, Nolan, I think we know everyone at the table. Tell me what you've discovered."

"First off, Trexler has not been a good ruler."

Trev'nor tsked mockingly. "Color me surprised. How many major rules has he broken?"

"At least three that we can prove. I'll let each of our experts explain. Rikkshana Yasmina, if you could start off?"

"Raja Nolan asked me what the first laws of this land were," the woman stated, speaking in careful Solish. Her accent was thick enough to slice and serve on bread, so Becca paid max attention to make sure she understood her. "I would need to lecture him for a week to answer this question completely." She might have winked at Nolan before continuing, "I think perhaps I should answer the question he truly wished to ask. In the beginning, slavery was not allowed at all in Khobunter. All of the warlords agreed on this. When the magicians came in from the south and created Rheben, the laws started changing at that point. When Rheben fell, and the magicians taken, then the laws were altered to allow magical slaves."

Becca seethed in anger. "That was very convenient."

"People in power always change the rules to benefit them," Trev'nor stated, more rhetorically than anything else. "It's how the world spins. Rikkshana, has the law changed at all after that? Is it still only magical slaves allowed?"

She did not answer but turned to the two living law experts. Akbar seemed to study the three before carefully stating, "It has not changed."

Giving a growl of satisfaction, Becca rubbed her hands in evil anticipation. "Then we have him dead to rights there." Glancing up, she realized that only the magicians understood what she meant by that. "You do realize, I hope, that while magic can be inherited, not all of the slaves you have are magicians?"

Becca got a lot of blank stares in response.

"In fact, in this group, you have six that aren't," Trev'nor clarified.

It was Nima, one of the captains, that had to demand, "Are you sure?"

"Very sure," Nolan stated. "We can see magic. It's clear as day to us. Are you seriously telling me that in the past hundred years you've been enslaving magicians, you didn't realize that some of them couldn't do magic?"

"We…thought they had little talent and so couldn't perform magic like the others," Rikkana Shiva offered weakly.

Becca felt like banging her head against the table. Trev'nor actually did, which made a few people jump.

Nolan had more patience than either of them although his frustration bled into his voice. "No, magic can skip a generation like any other talent. It's not guaranteed to have a magician just because both parents are one. I actually hadn't thought of that angle, Becca. We knew we had him on this because he routinely takes any citizens that he conquers and makes them slaves."

"Like what happened in Rurick?"

"Exactly like that. It's apparently a common practice with some of the warlords."

That thought made her anger burn all over again. "So that's a major one. What else?"

Rikkana Shiva seemed glad for a chance to move off this uncomfortable topic. "We have a particular tax here called the War Tax. It's quite high, forty percent of a man's income, and is to be used strictly for war funding."

Nolan winced. "That's very high for a tax. How long have you been paying this?"

"Years, now. The laws stipulate that it is not to be used

for more than a year at a time unless actively in war."

"You weren't actively in war until we showed up," Trev'nor stated more than questioned.

"That is correct, Raja. He has violated the law by leaving it in place so long."

Danyal cleared his throat. "Permission to speak, Raja."

"Please do, Commander."

"I know for a fact that the money from the War Tax has not been given to us here. We've been on short pay as long as I've been stationed here."

Becca let out a low whistle. She knew all about 'short pay' from growing up around soldiers. It was not a good idea to leave soldiers indefinitely on that. They got very cranky very quickly. Badgers with toothaches were known to be more pleasant than soldiers on short pay. "And how long has that been, Commander?"

"Seven years, Raya."

She stood so fast her stool toppled over. "Seven—!" she blurted out, past astonished. "Why haven't your men revolted?!"

The commander gave her a bitter smile. "Nowhere to go, Raya."

That was so wrong on so many levels.

"It gets worse, Bec," Nolan warned her. "Tell her, Commander."

"We can't take leave, Raya."

Becca was absolutely certain that her ears were not working. That was the only explanation for it. He couldn't have possibly said what she thought he'd said. Maybe it was an internal mistranslation on her brain's part. "I'm sorry?"

"He said the men can't take leave," Nolan repeated in Chahirese. "You heard him right."

She stared at him, jaw dangling, simply past words.

"Do you mean to tell me," Trev'nor demanded of the commander in a hoarse voice, "That once you've joined the army, you can't take leave? Ever?"

"You may return home when discharged," Captain Hadi answered succinctly.

"No," Becca blurted out. "No, no, no. That, that…I can't think of a curse word strong enough!"

"Scumbag? Prick? Pillock? Ratsbane?" Trev'nor supplied helpfully.

Becca flipped a hand into the air. "All of the above. Trexler has turned his own army into slaves!"

That turned the area around her deadly silent.

Commander Danyal went totally expressionless, as still as a statue. "We are not slaves."

Becca rounded on him, slapping a hand against the table top, sounding it off like a wardrum. "You are conscripted into service without any option of refusing, then are confined to a specific area without the ability to leave. You have no way to see your family or friends when you wish to. You must obey orders otherwise you're jailed or executed. He pays you a pittance which pays for…what? All food, clothing, daily expenses except housing? Yes, I thought so. How is it different?"

Commander Danyal's mouth opened. Closed. Not a word escaped.

"The soldiers of a country should be a leader's pride and joy," she argued. "They are asked to do tough things, to follow orders even if they don't agree, to fight under hard circumstances. In return for that loyalty, you deserve the right to go see your families. To be paid as you were promised. Not be treated like this."

He had no rebuttal for her. Neither did the captains. In fact, they couldn't meet her eyes.

Trev'nor, more practically, asked Nolan, "Can we fix this?"

"Right this minute? No. But I think we can at least give them leave. I have only the most basic grasp of what the economy and finances are like." Was that a trace of a smile on Nolan's face? "I knew you'd be the most passionate about this, Bec, when you found out."

"You try being raised by the Super Soldier and see how you feel about military service," she shot back in Chahirese. "Not to mention Aletha."

"No argument," Nolan responded, hands raised in surrender. "In that case, I'll let you work with the military and figure out who needs to go where. It goes without saying that anyone from Sagar or Trexler cannot be given leave yet?"

"Of course. But we'll do that as soon as we can," she promised, facing the three officers. "How many of your men are from those areas?"

"Roughly half, Raya," Captain Nima answered. "All of them, once they hear your promise, will be willing to swear loyalty to you."

After learning that they had been paid mere pittances and not been given leave for years, Becca was not surprised to hear this. "Let's go talk to them, then. Nolan, is that your full report on things this thickset varlot has done?"

"That we can immediately pin on him, yes. I think that's enough to execute him for, don't you?"

"Just one was bad enough." Trev'nor pushed back from the table and stood. "Becca, I'll help you sort out who needs to go where and transport them myself."

Oh, right, he'd need to for Rurick. The ward was still up after all. "Wait, should we send anyone there now? I mean, no one is there."

"If we don't send anyone, then the city will be in disarray

and the garden we planted will be dead," Nolan pointed out. "We need to send in a work crew, to do everything that we didn't have the time to do, or the city will be in shambles still when we finally do track down the citizens and return them home."

Becca was of the opinion that they still needed the manpower here, but he was right in that the garden needed tending, and the city did need cleanup. "I think we should give them the option of whether they go or not, though. They might choose to stay and fight with us instead."

Commander Danyal had a soft expression on his face. Was that possibly a smile? "I will ask them, Raya."

They likely would be more frank with their commander than they would with her. It was engrained military training to always go where the boss wanted you to. "Please do."

Heaven help the warlord when she got her hands on him. He'd be lucky to live to his day of judgment with the mood she was in.

"Bec," Nolan stalled her. "One more thing. Commander Danyal wishes to form up a militia and work with us."

She stopped mid-stride. "Truly?" She'd assumed they would stay to protect the city, no more.

Danyal met her eyes and Trev'nor's without flinching. "We have seen your fighting abilities. We are not sure how much help we can be to you on a battlefield. But we would like to help where we can."

Trev'nor rubbed at the back of his neck. "Commander, honestly, I'm not sure how much help you can be either. At this point, you're not trained on how to fight with a magician. It's a very different thing than your usual tactics. But off a battlefield, we will need all the help we can get. Especially when we go into Trexler. We welcome your support."

Trev'nor yawned his way down the stairs, navigating toward the main room of the inn through blurred vision as his eyes weren't properly awake yet. He had not had enough sleep the previous night, because as soon as they had finished working outside of the city and returned, they'd been surrounded by dozens of people. It had alarmed Trev'nor to see that many people waiting for them, as it looked like a mob, but it became clear quickly enough that they weren't angry. Flabbergasted, awed, perhaps a little afraid, yes, but not angry.

Apparently, in the long course of remembered history, no one had really invested in Tiergan. Because it lay near the coast, its first goal was to do as much trade as possible and then pass that wealth onto the warlord's city of Trexler. The citizens thought they knew how to handle conquerors. They'd assumed that they knew what Trev'nor, Becca, and Nolan wanted. But the mages had turned those assumptions on its collective head. They hadn't demanded war funds, or tribute, or anything like that. They hadn't turned the people into slaves or demanded soldiers. Aside from locking up the government officials and some of the army officers, they hadn't done much of anything. Trev'nor heard people whispering to each other and knew that they were actually relieved to have different people in charge now. The last regime had not been a good one. Just all of that might have been enough, but seeing five mages work all day to improve the land and make it fertile enough to become an oasis destroyed every preconception Tiergan had left.

Trev'nor half-expected their newly appointed leaders to come and talk to them, but it was other people as well, everyday citizens that wanted to speak one-on-one. Nolan handled this flawlessly, accustomed to hearing people's complaints and addressing them. Trev'nor and Becca both felt more than out of depth and overwhelmed. Still, he struggled to face each person and honestly listen to them. It took time, but they heard every person, and the citizens left satisfied. Mostly, it wasn't anything serious, but questions of what the future would hold or if such-and-such was possible. Trev'nor answered more magical questions than not as he explained the limits and possibilities of his power.

It had taken most of the night to discuss everything with them but Trev'nor didn't regret the lack of sleep. He felt now that they had won a tentative trust with Tiergan. The people of this city didn't really like their warlord, yet they didn't want to readily accept anyone that came along either for fear of the new version being worse. Trev'nor could understand that.

Ehsan met him at the foot of the stairs. "I was about to wake you."

No one woke up someone unless it was important. Trev'nor's brain whirred into a more alert state. "Problem?"

"I don't know." Pointing a finger toward the roof, Ehsan said uncertainly, "Becca has been up there for a half hour looking at the sky."

"Ah, that. Don't worry about that. It's a habit of hers to study the sky first thing after waking. She wants to make sure that none of her weather currents have gone astray while she's sleeping."

That put the man's mind to ease a little. "Also, Nolan is sleeping outside with his dragon."

That didn't surprise Trev'nor either. "Just his dragon? It's not his dragon, other dragons, cats, dogs, and two dozen birds?"

Ehsan gave him an odd look. "You already knew?"

"No, I just know Nolan. As a Life Mage, he attracts creatures to him all of the time. He spends half of his life sitting on the ground so that animals can easily access him. I'm not surprised he's sleeping outside with them." Trev'nor stretched his arms over his head and finally felt like his blood was flowing. Breakfast first, then he would have to sit down with the other two and come up with a battle plan. They'd discussed going after Sagar first, hitting the remaining smaller town before heading for Trexler, and Trev'nor felt that was the best plan. They had two new mages with them, after all; it would be best to take on a smaller target and iron out any kinks.

There were other magicians awake and sitting at the table. Trev'nor found an open chair and joined them. "Dilshad, Fatemah, Hamide, morning."

The three gave him automatic smiles and returned the greeting.

"Raja Trev'nor," Dilshad said in excitement, "the master in the market asked me if I wanted a job."

He absolutely couldn't have heard that right. "A job?" While amazing news, that a citizen of Tiergan would respect a magician enough to employ them, Trev'nor had to wonder, "What kind of job?"

"Sagas."

That word meant nothing to Trev'nor. "A what?"

"A finder," Ehsan clarified, taking the free seat next to him. "Someone who finds lost objects for a fee."

Dilshad apparently knew enough Solish to follow and nodded in agreement. "Yes, that. He saw me use scrying bowl." Uncertain, he asked, "Magicians work like this?"

"Exactly like that," Trev'nor assured the man firmly. It felt a little odd to do so, as the other man was a good decade older, but in terms of magical training and experience Trev'nor was definitely the senior. "That is a job a magician will take."

Relieved, Dilshad grinned at his friends, more than smug.

Granted, it was him more than the others that had grasped scrying and its nuances quickly. But he wasn't the only one that could use the bowl. Trev'nor had to wonder if others would acquire jobs like this, now that they had one person to forge the trail for them. "What kind of things do you search for?"

"Lost or stolen things."

Made sense. "Do you start today?"

"I do." Seeming to realize the time, he quickly finished off his plate, bowed at Trev'nor and then took off for the door.

"He's not the only one hired," Ehsan informed him. "Three others were hired this morning as well by an information broker. They're using the mirrors to communicate across the city about market prices and such."

While very glad for this news, as it meant that the city was starting to accept the magicians as actual citizens, Trev'nor had to wonder at the timing. "Were they influenced to do this after watching us work yesterday?"

"No one says that," Ehsan responded dryly. "But that is my guess."

Whatever worked. Trev'nor was not questioning it.

Danyal slammed into the main room, eyes hard. Trev'nor popped out of his chair automatically because he knew that look all too well. The commander came directly to him, vibrating with urgency. "Raja. You say this city is yours. You say you will protect the people. You mean this?"

Trev'nor tapped Ehsan's shoulder and gave him a meaningful look and jerk of the chin. The other mage understood that signal and quickly got up, heading for the roof to get the other two.

With him dispatched, Trev'nor looked Danyal dead in the eye. "I do. What's happened?"

"We have been mirror signaled. Trexler knows the city has been taken. He is coming."

Silence crashed through the room, so absolute that people stopped dead in their tracks, not even daring to breathe.

He said a few choice words under his breath that would have gotten him smacked by Chatta. The one thing they hadn't been able to predict was what the warlord would do. When Rurick was taken, the man hadn't made a move as far as they could tell. Or if he had, it had taken him several days to put together his army and dispatch it, long enough that they had already re-taken the place and left for dragon territory before he'd moved. They'd assumed that it would take him as long to react this time, so that they had at least three or four more days in Tiergan before they had to do something.

Nolan showed up in that moment, clothes rumpled from sleeping in weird positions, hair standing up a little in the back. His eyes were clear, though. He came to them and asked, "Ehsan said that the warlord is coming."

So he'd overheard that, eh?

"Yes," Danyal said.

"When Trexler comes to re-take one of his cities, how does he attack?" Nolan pressed.

"He attacks front-on."

Trev'nor did not like this answer. "Like it was an enemy city? He doesn't try to…" argh, busted buckets, what was the word for negotiate?

Danyal seemed to understand what he was trying to say and shook his head grimly. "No. He attacks."

He glanced at Nolan and found the same anger and determination in his friend's face that he was feeling. The people here had not welcomed them as openly as the ones in Rurick had, but they were gradually warming up to their conquerors. They were at least not hostile, not after seeing how much work the mages were putting in to improve the place.

Becca half-tripped down the stairs, she was moving so fast, a worried Ehsan hot on her heels with his arms outstretched as if ready to catch her if she did fall. She was fully dressed, although her hair hung in sleep-made tangles around her face. "Ehsan said that Trexler is coming?"

"He's coming," Nolan answered, tone and expression hard. "Apparently he's coming in full force. It's also standard tactics for him to attack any occupied city like it's enemy territory in order to reclaim it."

Her voice climbed several octaves. "WHAT?"

Danyal's eyes darted from one face to another, weighing and measuring. "The warlord believes reclaiming the city from enemies to be worth more than his citizens," he said levelly.

The three mages stood in shocked silence, the other magicians in fearful resignation. Danyal continued to watch them with steadfast intensity.

"No. Absolutely not," Becca announced firmly, her words echoing through the quiet stillness. "We are not about to let him march in here and destroy everything. Really, what kind of warlord is he? Is he an idiot? Is he a child? 'If I can't have it, neither can they' is that what he thinks?"

Without another word, she spun on her heel and started back up the stairs.

Trev'nor knew that look. He quickly sprinted around the table and caught her wrist. "Wait, where are you going?"

"To hurry up my storm system. I'm calling lightning down on that idiot. Maybe a few tornados too. If I blow his army to smithereens, then we don't have anything to worry about." She glanced back and tugged at her wrist. "Let go, Trev."

"She's not kidding," Ehsan breathed, awe in his voice.

To the people who did not understand her, others were quickly translating. Trev'nor tried to cut this idea down before it became permanently lodged in everyone's heads. "Bec, we need a strategy session before we go off and fight this man."

"I just told you my strategy. A little lightning, a few tornados, poof! Army gone."

As tempting as that sounded…. "Bec, where are your tornados coming from? North? South? East? West? Do you remember that we spent a full day going completely around this city creating canals, wells, and planting? Do you want to destroy all of that hard work and start from scratch again?"

She opened her mouth on a hot protest, paused, and growled in aggravation. "No tornados?"

"I'd really rather you didn't," he said frankly, amused at her vexed expression.

"I hate it when you're reasonable, you know that, right?"

"I know, I know. You can use tornados next time,

promise."

She shook a finger at him. "I'm holding you to that."

As they moved to sit back at the table, Trev'nor noticed that Danyal's posture had relaxed, some of the hard edges in his expression softening. He got the sense that they had passed a test somehow, though what test he wasn't sure. The validity of their determination, perhaps?

"Ehsan, get Azin for us," Nolan requested, now that Becca saw sense. "And Commander Danyal, please sit with us. We need information and we need it quickly. I don't want to fight anywhere near Tiergan. We'd planned to bring this battle to Trexler's doorstep, but if the warlord is coming out to meet us, then we'll fight him in the desert."

Trev'nor sat at the table in the inn's taproom and waited as everyone settled into place. Danyal had commandeered a map from someone and spread it out on the table for everyone to see, the ends weighted down with cups and forks and knives to keep them from curling up. Azin sat next to him, looking small and shaken, her hands clenching and unclenching in her lap. Facing the warlord terrified her—it was written all over her face.

Under the cover of the table, Trev'nor put a hand over both of hers and squeezed. She started in her seat, coming half out of it, head snapping around. "Relax," he murmured to her, for her ears only. "There's no need to be nervous."

"Sanjar Trexler is not a good opponent," she whispered back, voice shaking. "He's a petty sort of man with an ugly temper. He's coming with the largest army that you've ever seen, I promise you that. Few can stand in his path."

"You've met this man before?"

She shook her head roughly. "Not face to face. I was working on the defenses for Trexler when he walked by. I saw him from a distance. He's a cruel, spoiled man."

"Good. Spoiled men make stupid mistakes." Trev'nor had to smirk when she gave him that patented 'are you joking' look. "Azin, I'm not worried about defeating his army."

The room was still enough that his words carried past the table and he could hear people creeping in closer. To bolster their morale, he repeated in a louder voice, "I'm not worried about defeating his army. Five Mages alone are an army by themselves. That doesn't even include the dragons. Plus, this idiot was foolish enough to leave his protective walls and come out in the open to lay siege against us. He'd have lasted a little longer behind them."

"The only thing we're worried about is leaving you defenseless while we're gone," Nolan stated, glancing up from his study of the map. He was leaning half over the table, but straightened enough to look around the room in general. "I think the dragons will protect you, in case this march of Trexler's is a diversion to draw us out, but we want to make sure that nothing happens to you while we're fighting."

They'd made that mistake once. No one cared to make it again. "Can we do a ward here?"

"Well, we can," Nolan admitted, although his tone indicated doubt. "But it will interrupt trade if we do that and I'd rather not impact the city's economy that way. I mean, if it's a temporary thing, say a day or two, then I don't think it would do much harm."

"Ward?" Ehsan repeated the foreign word carefully, mouth maneuvering around the syllables.

"A protective shield that will cover the city as a whole," Nolan explained. "It will keep enemies out."

"Only people the ward recognizes can go in and out," Trev'nor sought to further explain. "We left a ward on Rurick to keep it protected."

Danyal made a sound of enlightenment. "Is that what that is?"

Trev'nor cocked a brow at him, still holding onto Azin's hand, although she was losing some of her nervousness under their calm discussion. "You know what we're talking about?"

"Yes, I do. Warlord Trexler was very angry about it. He wanted to retake Rurick but couldn't get any men through."

That was interesting news. They'd assumed, as they hadn't seen any evidence of it, that the warlord was not interested enough in Rurick to come and reclaim it. Apparently he had tried only to be rebuffed so thoroughly by the ward that he was forced into a retreat. At least a temporary one. Still, to not even leave a few scouts? Was the man that arrogant, or what?

"Wards make him mad?" Becca gave a happy sound of evil delight. "Then I vote yes. Wards?" she asked, holding up a hand for agreement.

Nolan lifted a hand immediately. "Wards."

"Wards it is," Trev'nor finished with a lifted hand. "Hey, do either of you know if a witch or wizard needs a focusing wand for the ward spell?"

Becca ventured uncertainly, "I don't think they do…?"

"They don't," Nolan stated with certainty. "The spell itself is their focusing tool. Why? Do you think we should include everyone in this?"

"Wouldn't that make the ward that much stronger?"

"Can't disagree with you there." Nolan thought about it a second before offering, "And actually, that's a really good thing to teach them before we leave."

It really was, now that Trev'nor thought about it. It was the ultimate way to protect themselves even if they didn't have the means to fight. "Then let's do that today. Alright. What do we know about his way here?"

"He will take the trade route," Danyal informed them, tracing a finger along the road. "It's the most direct path."

"How long will it take?"

"Three days."

Nolan asked, "How big of an army? Do we know?"

"It depends on what is happening up north. Also how many he chooses to leave behind to guard Trexler. I would venture a guess of three to four thousand."

"What about this land? Is it flat? Rocky?" Becca asked.

"Yes, both of those," Danyal confirmed.

Azin found her voice enough to speak up. "I've traveled up there a few times. It's mostly flat, with some craggy sections and a few minor hills that are mostly sand dunes. There's no one living in that section. Water is impossible to find."

"Perfect place for a battle, then," Trev'nor observed. Judging that Azin had summoned up her courage, he let go of her to tap the map. "We don't have to worry about hurting people or damaging anything out here. We can cut loose."

Becca eyed the map as if envisioning the landscape. "So if that's the case...still no tornados?"

Nolan glanced up at her from under his eyebrows. "Bec. I'll let you discuss that with your dragon and see what she says."

"Oh," Becca said with dawning realization. "Right. Tornados and flying would not mix well, would it?"

"Understatement, Bec, complete understatement."

"Shrieking hinges," she swore. "I did not think of that. Alright, no tornados. So what do we do?"

"First, we need to divide this up." Nolan tilted his torso to look at the man hovering at his side. "Commander, how much of that army is likely mounted?"

"About half. It is routine for every force to be half-mounted, half on foot. Our tactics work best that way."

Nolan turned to the rest of the table. "I can dismount them and cause some havoc in the ranks first thing. I'll be in charge of an aerial attack. Also, I think I should be point of contact for everyone as I can communicate with all of the dragons."

That made sense to Trev'nor. "Shall I create some fatal funnels, then? Break up the ranks, give us some dividing lines so that we know who should be attacking which part? I'd rather we didn't bumble into each other." Bad things would follow.

"Sounds good," Nolan agreed. "You do that before the army even gets there, I think. Then fight as you see fit. Becca?"

She didn't answer immediately. Instead, her focus was on the other two mages at the table. "I think we need them to get their feet wet with this. Azin, what can you do?"

The Elemental Mage looked jarred to be suddenly called out and was not one bit thankful for it. She stammered, eyes darting anywhere but to the person speaking to her, and paused for several long and awkward seconds. "Um, weapons?"

"Oh? Good thought, that one. Disarming them will help us later."

Azin blushed at this small praise and sat a little straighter. "I will deal with their weapons."

Nolan nodded in approval. "Ehsan, from the description of this place, I'm not sure if you'll have any water to work with. We might need you to go ahead with Trev'nor and create some water traps."

Becca negated this with a shake of the head. "My storm will give him all of the water he needs. He can fight with the rain I call."

Trev'nor was very glad she offered that as he felt like Ehsan would be a formidable fighter, given some more experience and practical application with his magic. "In that case, you two better stick close to each other and coordinate what you're doing."

The man didn't give any overt signs of relief, but the way he relaxed into his chair instead of sitting at the very edge of it gave his emotions away. Ehsan was ready to fight at any time but that didn't mean he had any confidence of how to go about it.

Danyal lifted a questioning finger. "What can we do?"

"Help us after we've defeated them," Becca answered promptly. "Once they're disarmed, round them up, take charge of them. Our magic can't be sustained forever. It's best if we hit them first and you handle cleanup this round." She must have seen the slightly dissatisfied look on his face as she assured him, "We can learn how to fight with each other for the next battle later, after we deal with this situation."

"I understand, Raya. I will explain this to my men and make preparations."

"I think we more or less know what to do, then." Nolan stabbed at the map. "Here. I think we need to meet him about here. It's a day away from Trexler and Tiergan, so the odds of us accidentally damaging anything is very low. That also gives us the rest of the day to prepare before leaving. On dragon-back, we should be able to catch the army about noon tomorrow. Any objections?"

"Wait, you think we can teach magical novices a warding spell in the space of an afternoon?" Trev'nor protested.

"If we can't, we use the people that do know how to do it and move on. We don't have a lot of time here, Trev."

Well, granted, that was true but still....

Nolan was already moving on. "Ehsan, Azin, we need to talk to the dragons and see who is willing to give you a ride there. You'll need to be on dragon-back while you fight so I suggest you learn how to ride one today before we leave."

Trev'nor half-expected an objection from Azin, but instead her lips parted with an expression of wonder.

"I can ride one?" she breathed, hands clasped at her heart.

"If you ask, yes, I'm sure one of them will let you." Nolan gave him a pointed look.

Oh, right, in order for them to ride one Trev'nor would have to create more saddles.

"With them, we need the soldiers who agreed to fight with us to also learn how to ride," Becca added.

"Now wait one minute," Trev'nor objected. "I can't create that many saddles all at once!"

"Do as many as you can," Becca urged. "Those that can't ride this trip can be carried over, but it will be easier on our dragons to fight without shielding a passenger or landing with only three paws."

She really made too much sense for him to argue with her. Trev'nor resigned himself to making saddles. Quickly. If he enlisted some help from Azin and some of the leatherworkers in town, then he should be able to make more in a few hours. "I'll get on that. Ah, I take it you'll explain the battle plan to our winged friends outside?"

"They've been listening in," Nolan assured him off-handedly.

Becca propped her chin in her hand, leaning over the table. "Just how good is their hearing, anyway?"

"Like you would not believe." Nolan gave her an enigmatic smile. "Becca, I think you're the only one free to teach people the warding spell."

"It looks like I am. Alright, I'll do that, then. Ehsan, come with me. I know you can't stay for long, you have riding lessons, but at least help translate so that they understand what it is I'm trying to teach them to do."

"Certainly," Ehsan agreed readily.

Nothing went smoothly, of course. Plans never do. Nolan ended up borrowing his and Trev'nor's saddles and putting the new riders on Llona and Garth for the lessons so that the dragons could half-teach the riders. Trev'nor worked feverishly in gathering all of the supplies and making the saddles while that was going on, cursing whenever he hit a snag and cheating outrageously with magic whenever possible. One would think, after making three of these, he would now more or less have the system down. But nooo, things kept going wrong at every possible turn. Likely because he was rushing. Things always went badly when a craftsman tried to rush.

It was nearly sunset when he finally fitted the last saddle to the last dragon. Tired, grumpy, beyond starving (he'd skipped lunch entirely trying to get the saddles done), he thanked the craftsmen that had helped him and trudged back toward the inn. They had managed to make fifty in all, a number far outside of his expectations, but Trev'nor knew that it wouldn't be quite enough. It just would be mean less for the dragons to carry by claw. Hopefully it was sufficient. He was out of materials and energy, so it had better be.

As he walked, he heard the opening note to the warding spell and looked up and around, trying to pinpoint the source. Spaced around the wall in almost even intervals were all of the magicians. Becca stood a little behind and to the right of Ehsan, standing with what looked like a mirror held up to her mouth. Trying to project strongly enough through the mirror so the other side could hear her? Smart.

In one accord, over a hundred voices opened their

mouths and started to sing one of the oldest songs, one of the most ancient of spells, in a hauntingly minor chorus. With the sunset gilding their silhouettes, it made for a stunning image that seared its way into his eyes and memory. They sang with the purest of intentions, and as the words came out of their mouths, the air shimmered with magic.

Every person in the street stopped dead as they saw the air bend and glow golden in tones different from the setting suns. Even Trev'nor, who had seen more wards than he could possibly remember, felt awed at the sight. It was like the barrier in Q'atal, it shone with so much power. He'd never thought he would see another ward that could rival that one, but this one did. It possibly outshone it.

The spell came to a close, the last word spoken more than sung, and the ward solidified into a firm presence with an almost audible hum of its own.

A woman behind him clutched her toddler to her legs and stared at the ward with trepidation. "Is…that…?"

"A ward," Trev'nor answered her. Seeing that most of the people on the street looked petrified, he sighed and made his voice loud enough to be heard by most of them. "That is a ward! It will protect the city from attack! Do not fear it!"

The toddler was the only one brave enough to ask him, "Won't hurt?"

"Even if you touch it," Trev'nor assured him. "Won't hurt."

They didn't look sold, but he didn't try to add anything more to this. Experience and time would show him right.

Becca caught a quick lift from Cat, cradled against her scaly chest long enough to alight on a nearby rooftop and be lowered to the ground. Fortunately Khobunter liked flat roofs. The dragons had many options for landing pads. "What do you think?" she asked Trev'nor before her feet were even properly under her. "Isn't this amazing? I've never seen a ward this strong."

"It is amazing," he praised, meaning every word. "How did you teach them all that fast?"

"I actually had a few that gave up. They just couldn't pronounce all of the words well enough, so they left it up to the ones that could."

"It is a lot of foreign words to learn in a short amount of time." Trev'nor, in their place, was not sure if he could have managed it. Back when he was still a student, they'd been given a week to memorize this spell.

"Don't I know it," Becca responded, sounding tired. "But it was definitely worth the effort."

He couldn't argue there. "Dinner?"

"Dinner sounds great. I skipped lunch trying to do everything. Did you get the saddles done?"

"By some miracle, yes."

"I'm sensing some frustration there. I take it things did not go well."

"Let's say I've had better days making something and leave it at that, shall we?" Trev'nor grumped. "How do you think Nolan did?"

"I'm perfectly willing to track him down and ask, but only after I get food."

Deserts were very strange, temperature-wise. It could be blazing hot during the day, so much so that it felt like you were baking, and then when the suns set it was cold enough to feel like winter. Becca disliked the extremes, as it played havoc with her system, and she was never sure whether to put on extra layers or doff them. It became even more of a guessing game when riding on dragon-back. Flying like this made it colder but at the same time, the suns were just as strong and heated her up. Especially on her right side.

Azin and Ehsan had been more than a touch nervous mounting on dragons that morning. Not to mention all of their soldiers. A half hour of practice didn't an experienced rider make. What eased everyone's minds was that they could communicate with the dragons vocally if they needed to, and the dragons knew where to go and what the plan was. They didn't really need much in the way of direction. If it had been otherwise, they'd never have gotten Azin on.

Master Sosa and Rikkshana Yasmina had volunteered to go as well. Rikkan Akbar was deathly afraid of heights and absolutely refused to go, which was just as well, as he and his wife were needed in Tiergan more than with them. The city was still in upheaval. But the others would be the judges for Trexler after the battle. They'd also help sort through the soldiers. Becca had no desire to lock up thousands of soldiers at a time. That would drain their resources drastically and be a waste of time and manpower to boot. She would rather send all of them home, if she could.

They flew straight north for nearly four hours. Becca ate and drank sparingly as there wouldn't be any chance for a bathroom break until late this evening. She drank enough to keep from being completely dehydrated, ate enough to keep her stomach from growling, and made do with that.

The day warmed quickly, and by the time it hit noon, she sorely regretted her choice of wearing a light jacket. But shrugging it off would be impossible as she had nowhere to put it later. She wasn't about to try tying the sleeves around her waist, the wind force would whip it off again. Oh well, sweating wouldn't make her melt.

"See them," Cat informed her, loud enough to carry over the wind in her ears.

"How many?" Becca shouted back.

"Lots," the dragon answered truthfully, if unhelpfully.

Garth darted ahead, his speed belying his size. He must have seen them as well.

The first part of their plan depended on Trev'nor raising up walls. He would not only create barriers along the road, breaking up the ranks, but do it in such a way that the army would funnel off in different directions. Each mage (or mage pairing, as the case may be) had their own section they were in charge of. They were depending on Trev'nor's walls to be the dividing lines.

Cat let out a satisfied roar. "Walls up!"

Becca tapped her neck twice in acknowledgement and then concentrated on hanging tight as her dragon tucked in her wings and dropped quickly towards the earth. Her eyes teared up at the pressure, so she closed them in defense, only opening again when Cat's descent slowed.

'Lots' about covered it.

Becca had faced off with soldier-priests, been around guards and sailors, but had never seen an army on the move. Danyal's predicted thousands of men marched along the road. Or they had been, until Trev'nor's walls, thick and tall, cut in between them and forced them to scatter.

She took in a moment to gather her bearings and make sure that things were going according to plan. Becca had to time this correctly, as Azin and Trev'nor both needed to see what they were doing. Even though she glided only a few hundred feet in the air now, the people below still looked like ants to her, making it hard to discern details. It was clear enough when Nolan's persuasion worked, and the enemy dragoos threw off their riders and headed off, running full speed to the west. But she couldn't see more than that.

"Cat, did Azin take away weapons?"

"Some gone," Cat confirmed, sounding quite smug.

Becca twisted in the saddle to take a look as Cat did a lazy circle, coming around again. There had to be at least a dozen walls up now. Trev'nor never had told her how many he was planning to build, but hopefully this was all of them, as Ehsan couldn't do a thing until she called down the rain.

Focusing her attention on the clouds rumbling in from the sea, she urged them to come in a little faster. They pitched and rolled, becoming darker and more saturated as they moved. Little flashes of lightning could be seen arcing in the clouds. It wasn't quite a mother storm, but it was far more serious than a summer shower. Becca had made sure of that.

Ehsan flew around on her right, waving to get her attention. She threw up a hand in acknowledgement, showing him that she saw him and was ready.

And then the storm hit.

The rain pelted down, so fast and furious that it blinded. It soaked her within a minute down to her marrow, and cut visibility down to a foot in any direction. Cat had to be navigating by her other senses as they miraculously avoided clashing with any of the other dragons. Even sound was obscured, although Becca thought she heard at least a few dragons roar out.

She let this go on for several minutes, making sure that they had plenty of water to work with, and then she eased up the storm and sent it on, letting it visit the area south of them. The land needed it, what with all of the planting that Nolan had done. By the time it arrived, it should be reduced to a soft, soaking rain that plants would appreciate.

Wiping water from her face, she slicked back any stray tendrils and looked about her. Between the random walls, the dragoos running off, and the storm, the army below milled in complete disarray. She could hear warhorns going off as commanders tried to regain control of their troops, but of course that wasn't happening. The mages attacking wouldn't let it.

Nolan led the charge, still on Llona's back, which surprised her a little as he typically went dragon about now. The dragons were clear on not hurting the soldiers much. Or at least they were supposed to be. Becca watched them dive toward the scrambling humans and wondered if anyone had explained that seeing a two-ton, fire breathing creature bearing down a person might cause heart failure. Some of the more brave hearted managed to fire off arrows, most missing, some connecting only to bounce harmlessly against hard scales. The occasional arrow did seem to strike as she heard intermittent roars of pain.

Ehsan went to work. The water lifted under his control and whirled into motion, creating liquid barriers that flowed and moved like a river that never touched the ground. It kept men from moving, from rejoining their commanders, and terrified them in turn.

Trev'nor started connecting his walls, making barriers, also blocking people into little groups that ensured they wouldn't be moving. Becca nearly missed it, but from the corner of her eye she saw shields and weapons shift again, flying through the air like an invisible hand had scooped them up. Azin taking away another group of weapons. Good.

Between her lightning bolts, Ehsan's barriers, and Trev'nor's walls, they managed to corral everyone in the better part of an hour. The dragons dropped their soldiers into little regimented ranks on top of the walls, as instructed, and they made sure that no one tried to climb those walls. Never had Becca been so thankful that she had Commander Danyal and his men to take care of the captured enemy. It would have been challenging to try to keep track of this many men on her own.

It looked like everyone had finished their jobs. Time for Becca to do hers.

She urged Cat around, looking for the banners that would signify the warlord. He undoubtedly marched at the front of the line, but with all of the disarray, who knew where he was now. "Cat, do you see banners?"

"Do," Cat assured her.

"Go to banners," Becca directed. "And land there, if possible."

Easier thing to say than do, as there were pockets of people everywhere, and it was hard to find a clear enough space to land. Cat eventually straddled two different walls and perched there, as comfortably balanced as her namesake. Becca looked for the most flashily dressed man in the group and found him standing half-behind two burly looking men that must have been his bodyguards. "Are you Warlord Trexler?"

"I am," he proclaimed. "But you. Who are you! Magicians, I can see, but why are you on these…" his lip curled up in distaste but even from here she could see the whites of his eyes.

"I am Magus Riicbeccaan," she introduced herself. "I am one of the three people that took Rurick and Tiergan from your control."

He turned nearly purple with rage, veins throbbing in his temples. "Y-you! How dare you!"

"How dare you," she retorted. "Your prejudices against magicians have locked up and destroyed thousands of innocent lives. What you teach your people is sickening, but it's so engrained in them that they think they can lock up foreign strangers as well! I spent several days in slavers chains thanks to you and your people."

"THAT IS WHERE YOU BELONG!" he bellowed.

Becca's temper spasmed and as it did, lightning shot from the sky and landed not a foot away from him. The warlord, vaunted for his courage and tenacity, squeaked like a mouse and jumped back. The sight made her smile.

Trev'nor walked casually along the top of the wall, joining her. "Why are you bantering with this idiot?"

"I'm issuing a declaration of war," she responded, making a face at him.

"War's over," he riposted, exasperated. "Or did you miss that?"

"It's not like he can do anything," Nolan agreed.

Becca twitched, wondering how she'd missed his approach, when she saw that part of his back still had a tail. Ah, so he had gone dragon at some point. To her amusement, watching a dragon turn into a man made several people nearby faint dead away.

Wimps.

"Trexler," Nolan stated in a formal, royal fashion, "you and your inner circle have violated the laws of this land. That includes committing atrocities I would rather not repeat. For this, we will hold your judgment and execution tomorrow afternoon."

Trexler regained his dignity and marched forward, shaking a fist. "I am Warlord of this state! You cannot execute me!"

Trev'nor snapped his fingers in sudden inspiration. "In Sagar. We should do it in Sagar. That way we don't have to fight or argue them into submission."

Nolan gave him an approving nod. "You're learning. That's a good idea, let's do that."

"We shouldn't do it in Trexler itself?" Becca asked uncertainly.

"She does have a point," Trev'nor admitted. "It will have more impact in the capital. Maybe, the warlord in Trexler, the rest of his inner circle in Sagar?"

"It's not a bad plan," Nolan agreed.

The warlord threw an apoplectic, screaming fit as they ignored him. Becca got tired of it and threw another lightning bolt at him, which promptly shut him up. Now, what to do with the rest of the army? "Cat, how loud can you be?"

"Not loud," Cat denied. "Garth can."

Garth gave a deep, guttural clearing of the throat before lifting himself up onto his back haunches so that everyone could clearly see him. In his very best Khobuntish, he declared in a thundering voice, "WE HAVE CONQUER THIS PLACE. JOIN US, BE FREE. NOT JOIN US, DRAGONS EAT YOU." With a leer, the giant elder dragon gave a dramatic lick of the lips. "WE NOT MIND. HUMANS

GOOD WITH BARBECUE SAUCE."

It took willpower. It took effort. Somehow, Becca managed not to laugh. Now, when had he come up with this speech? All they had agreed on last night was that they would try to get the army to come over to their side and would use the presence of the dragons to scare them into line. For that matter, when had the dragons been introduced to barbecue?

Not a single enemy soldier had a doubt that they would become lunch if they dared to try and fight. In fact, most meekly went to their knees with their hands high above their heads, signaling their surrender. Becca blew out a secret breath of relief. Hopefully this decision would stick and they wouldn't try to rebel later. They really had no idea what they would do with this many enemy soldiers. And truthfully, most of them were just following orders. It wasn't like they were bad people. Misguided, poorly led, with deep prejudices, but not bad.

Becca hopped down off the wall and into the nearest barrier. She did so under Cat's keen eye, as this was risky, to put herself within arm's reach of the soldiers. Still, trust had to start from somewhere.

She held out her hands to the nearest soldier, taking his own and pulling him to his feet. He did not look comfortable with this, not at all, but rose under her persistence although he couldn't meet her eyes for more than a second at a time.

Trying out her best smile, Becca greeted, "Hello. What's your name?"

"O-omid," he stammered out.

"Where are you from, Omid?"

"R-rurick," he managed, looking more alarmed at this question than the first one.

"Are you?" she asked, genuinely happy to hear this.

"Would you like to go home?"

He looked at her as if she were saying something to him in a foreign language, even though she had deliberately spoken to him in his native tongue. "Home?"

"Yes, home. We left Rurick protected so it could not be reconquered."

"That was your doing?" another, younger soldier blurted out. As soon as he had spoken he clamped his mouth shut, appalled he had said anything.

She turned her smile to him in reassurance. "That was us. We were worried about the city being conquered while we were gone. We've been trying to find where all of the people went. We want them to go home again." Phew, that had been close, but she'd managed to think of all the words she needed to explain.

Omid stared at her hard, face like carved stone, his dark skin making him look like smooth obsidian. "What do you want?"

"Magicians to be free," she answered simply. "Khobunter to be free. Help me."

"What you want," another, older soldier said, "is not possible."

"No," his brother soldier sitting next to him denied slowly, "I think it is. They defeated us in an hour. Less. There's only five of them. Commander Danyal follows them. They have dragons. I think they can do it."

Feeling like she'd connected to at least one person, she held out her right hand to him, grasping it firmly when he took it. "Swear to me loyalty. Do that, and you can go home."

The man looked wistful. "Truly?"

"My word as a Riic."

The suns flirted with the top of the horizon, sinking slowly and heralding the night. Trev'nor was so tired that he was flopped next to Garth's side and tried very hard to not just fall asleep right there. How long had it been now since he'd had a full night's sleep? Three? It was hard to remember. Today alone would've been exhausting in anyone's opinion as he had either flown, fought, or walked around talking to soldiers the whole day. This was the first time he had been able to go horizontal.

Trev'nor hovered in that realm belonging to flying elephants and incredibly punch-drunk sleeplessness, in that dicey area of giggling like a child or crying. The only thing that distracted him from doing so was the mesmerizing feel of stubble scraping along the rocky soil under him. He wanted to sleep. Desperately wanted to sleep. He couldn't, of course, there was too much turmoil for his brain to shut off. While they had divided up the enemy soldiers by hometown, and spoken to them about returning home, there were still people to organize and decisions to be made before they could call it quits.

He nuzzled into the ground a little harder. Nice ground. Undemanding. Smooth and rough in equal measure. Smooth, rough.

Smooth.

"Trev, why are you nuzzling the ground?"

He didn't open his eyes as he responded to Becca. "I like it. It likes me. Mutual kinda thing."

"Uh-huh." The exhaustion was clear in her voice, bleeding into her words, but still she tried to stay light and teasing. "Hey, Nolan, I think Trev's lost it."

"He's done more magical work than the two of us combined for three days straight," Nolan pointed out, the words accompanied by the crunch of gravel as he walked over. "Of course he has. Trev, you do realize that your magical level is getting too low?"

Trev'nor cracked open one eye to stare generally upwards. "Noooo, you don't say."

"Sarcasm, sure sign he's gone over the edge," Becca intoned. "Trev, you're hereby banned from doing anything magical for at least a day."

She had a funny idea of punishments. That sounded like bliss.

Fortunately for everyone involved, Trev'nor had an amazing dragon that knew when to let his mage sleep and take over. "Work done?" Garth asked them.

"Mostly." Nolan dropped like a sack of potatoes and grunted at the impact. The grunt sounded like relief. "We've sorted through the leaders and put the dangerous ones all in a separate holding area. The others are clear that they can go home, they're not part of the military anymore. A lot of men are happy about this, actually. Some of them haven't been able to go home in six years or more."

That didn't sound right to Trev'nor. He prodded his brain back into working order long enough to force out a question. "How many of them?"

"About four thousand."

"Trexler must live in a constant state of war-ready, otherwise why keep all of those troops on hand?"

"It does tell you something about his neighbors, doesn't it?" Nolan agreed. "Either that or he's one of those paranoid people that over-prepare. Commander Danyal reports that the warlord left about two thousand troops back in Trexler that will need to be taken care of as well. He suggests having the commanders and captains that joined us ride in on dragons to be visible for the troops and the citizens, show them that they're on our side. He hopes this will lower the casualties when we take over."

"How many were there this round?" Trev'nor couldn't help but ask.

"Sixty-two accidentals, which, while not great, could have been higher. There are also three-hundred seventy-four soldiers who refuse to surrender," Becca said quietly.

"Ah." The three fell into quiet contemplation as the weight of the lives lost and the lives yet to deal with fell on them. Unable to handle the emotional stress, Trev'nor went back to nuzzling the ground.

At some point, who knows when, he fell asleep. He awoke feeling more than warm—almost hot and sweating—with the smell of dragon strongly in his nose. Blinking, he tried to stretch and failed as his arms were trapped, legs tucked up into each other. He blinked again and found that there was a whooshing noise in his ears that he knew well at this point. Was he flying?

Lifting up his head, he glanced around and saw nothing but blue skies and the occasional cloud drifting by. Garth had him firmly tucked up against his chest, like a sleeping child. "Garth?" he called loudly.

The dragon cocked an ear his direction. "You awake?"

"Just now. Where are we going?"

"Trexler." The dragon had a rumble in his chest of amusement. "You not wake up earlier."

Ah, hence why Garth had just picked him up and flown off like this? Just as well. When Trev'nor got truly exhausted, he became impossible to wake up unless he had at least twelve hours of sleep. "How far away are we?"

"Not far. Look."

He turned his head more and craned upright into a half-crunch and found a city sprawled out below. Trexler easily contained a population of sixty-thousand. It had huge walls all around it, wide enough for at least four carts to ride side by side on top. The city seemed crammed to the gills with houses on the inside but there was not one permanent building outside of the walls. That, too, told Trev'nor something about the neighbors of this province. People didn't feel it was safe enough to live outside of the walls for any length of time.

The architecture didn't seem all that different. It was the same type of stucco he'd seen before, thick mud walls that kept the suns and heat out, tiled roofs. The only variation came from the colors, the city painted like a rainbow of every possible color. It was bright enough from here to seem garish.

There was a lot of activity in the streets below. Trev'nor got a better look as they flew over the city itself. They had ninety dragons with them, each dragon carrying soldiers or prisoners in their claws. The guards below were up in arms about that. The citizens were racing for cover.

Trev'nor understood their nervousness as he rather shared it at the moment, although for an entirely different reason. If he had lots of solid earth under him, or was securely strapped into a saddle, he could handle his phobia of heights. But resting in a dragon's claw while flying hundreds of feet off the ground? Not so much. Panic started to clog his throat and he had to fight the urge to latch onto Garth's nearest claw for dear life.

"Do not worry, fledgling," Garth rumbled at him. "Will not drop you."

That didn't really do anything to reassure his taut nerves.

"If I fall," Garth continued, amused—because of course dragons didn't understand fearing heights— "I will hit ground first."

"Garth, no offense, but that's not reassuring. You're not very squishy. Landing on a bunch of scales will not be softer than bedrock."

The dragon gave a gravelly bark of laughter.

This good-natured bickering stopped as Garth back-flapped hard and brought them into the center of the city. Trev'nor caught a glimpse of banners hanging off the side of the building and didn't think it was any coincidence that Garth chose to land on the warlord's castle.

Trev'nor gratefully dropped out of his dragon's clutches and put his boots back on solid rock. As he did so, he looked around and saw that all of the mages had been dropped off on the balcony, although only some of the dragons chose to linger. While the ledge was thick and wide, it could only support two dragons at a time, and the others chose to branch out and perch on the adjoining walls instead. Other dragons swooped in long enough to deploy troops and prisoners in the middle of the courtyard before taking off again, heading off in all different directions. Trev'nor assumed Nolan was directing who went where. They weren't asking for orders, and there wasn't any sign of confusion, so this must have been worked out beforehand.

A man sure did miss a lot while he sleeping.

The unfortunate guards on the wall or in the courtyard

below scrambled to form up and then stopped dead as they were faced with their own countrymen and how to fight several dragons at the same time. They never had a chance to figure out the answer before Azin stepped forward and collected their weapons and shields with a sweep of her arm, throwing them all into the air. Trev'nor expected her to gather them all into a pile like last time, but instead she let them hover, blades down, directly above the men's heads.

Dragons were bad enough. But to be threatened by your own sword? It was a soldier's worst nightmare.

"Commander Danyal, if you would," Becca requested. Trev'nor couldn't see her, Garth was between them and blocking his view, but she didn't sound at all nervous. Conquering cities was becoming familiar to her. Trev'nor wasn't sure if this was a good thing or not.

Commander Danyal must have been riding with her on Cat, as he stepped immediately forward and cleared his throat. In a booming voice, he announced, "WE ARE THE CONQUERERS OF TREXLER. WE HAVE THE WARLORD IN CUSTODY. IN ONE HOUR, WE WILL SIT IN JUDGMENT FOR HIS CRIMES. ALL WHO WISH TO WITNESS ARE WELCOMED."

That said, he stepped back.

Trev'nor blinked. Was that it? Stepping around Garth's, he asked, "Shouldn't we say something more?"

"Oh, Trev, you're awake." Becca looked more than a little windblown, hair in a messy braid over one shoulder, growing circles under her eyes. Still, she seemed perky. "Have a nice nap?"

"I did, yes." And boy had he needed the sleep. "Is that all we're going to say?"

"What more do you suggest?" the commander asked him. "Announcing your names, that you are conquering

Trexler, what your demands are?"

Trev'nor thought all of that was a given. "Well, yes?"

"But if we do that, we sound like every other conquering warlord," Becca explained. "Which we want to avoid doing. We want to give a different first impression."

"That this is more about the removal of a bad ruler than a conqueror muscling their way in?" Trev'nor stated, feeling his way through the concept aloud. "Smart. Hopefully that works."

"Nothing to lose by trying."

Commander Danyal turned sharply left. "I need to get down to the main level and start organizing things."

"I'll take you down," Trev'nor offered. He swirled some of the rock forming up the wall into motion, building a small platform with it.

Danyal did not appreciate this offer at all and he eyed the rock like it was poisonous and would bite him. If he could have refused, he would have, but doing so would send the wrong signal to everyone watching. Trev'nor recognized the stubbornness for what it was and bit down a smile as he escorted the man onto his moving stones. "I won't let you fall," he assured the man softly. The weirdness of repeating what his dragon had just said was not lost on him, and he smiled at the irony.

As they descended, Trev'nor took advantage of the height to get a bird's eye view of the situation. It got confusing quickly as everyone was in the same uniforms, but what it looked like was their troops were taking advantage of the confusion and general dragon-induced panic to subdue Trexler's troops. Anyone that tried to put up resistance was quickly taken down, and it was so isolated that no opposition could get any momentum.

Surprise attacks, when executed right, were a beautiful

thing to behold.

The commander stood at military parade stance the entire trip down. For his sake, Trev'nor made the landing as smooth as silk and pretended not to notice Danyal sweating. Before he could step away, Danyal caught his arm. "Raja. I had a thought on the flight here."

Trev'nor was all ears. This man understood Trexler far better than he did, after all. "What is it?"

"You said that not all of the magicians in Tiergan were actually magical. What are the odds of it being the same here in Trexler?"

"Very good. The odds don't seem to change much no matter what land you're in."

"Can you take some of my soldiers and go free the slaves here? Then bring me all of the ones that are not magical. I wish to prove this point in the trial and it will be easier if I have living proof in front of me."

The original plan was for the mages to be silently subduing threats so that the trial and execution of the warlord wouldn't be interrupted. But Trev'nor didn't think it would really take all of them to manage this. Azin and Becca alone could keep this castle from being re-taken. That didn't even include the dragons. "I can do that, yes. Who do you suggest I take with me?"

"Captain Hadi and his team."

"I'll do that." Trev'nor silently applauded this conversation. It was the first time that Danyal had taken the initiative with them, which was exactly what needed to happen; otherwise they wouldn't be able to leave Trexler and continue on. "Bring them back here?"

"This is where we will hold the trials, yes. You have two hours."

Trev'nor blinked. "Two hours? You think the trial for the

warlord will take that long?"

A hard expression swept over Danyal's face. "I'm yanking certain officials out of their hidey-holes and prosecuting them before we get to the warlord. I know exactly what to charge them with."

Some house-cleaning first, eh? Trev'nor had no problem with that, especially since it looked like Danyal knew exactly what to do. Having a local on their side was certainly speeding matters along. "You have our full support on that. Do you know where Captain Hadi landed?"

Danyal pointed across the courtyard. "There."

Trev'nor's eyes took a second to pick him out of the crowd, as he was clustered in with several dozen other uniformed men. "Ah, I see him. Then, I'll be back in two hours." Or less. "Tell Nolan and Becca what I'm doing, please."

"I will inform them, Raja."

Giving the man a casual salute, he walked off. He couldn't do that sharp salute like the other army men could, but maybe he should learn it. It had bonded them to Becca because she could return salutes and speak in military terminology. Trev'nor had heard whispers last night before collapsing that the men thought of her as 'their' raya. Growing up as the Super Soldier's sister had its benefits.

"Captain Hadi," he hailed, waving the man over.

"Raja!" Hadi immediately stopped his conversation with one of his subordinates and stood to attention. "What can I do for you, sir?"

"Your commander had a thought, and a good one. I need your help to execute it." There, did that sound military enough? "He wants us to track down the magical slaves here and bring the ones born without magical talents back here."

Hadi was quick on the uptake. "For trial exhibitions?"

"Exactly so, Captain. Can I have your help with this?"

"Certainly, sir, but I only know where one of the holding pens is for slaves here in Trexler."

The way he said that made Trev'nor's blood run cold. "How many are there?"

Hadi exchanged an uncertain glance with the lieutenant standing next to him. "A dozen?"

"Not sure if that's correct, sir," the lieutenant denied. "I think there's a few more than that."

Over a dozen? Trev'nor rubbed a hand over his face and fought down the urge to throw up. Or cry. Or rage. "Change of plans. Captain Hadi, what is Captain Nima doing?"

"Guarding the front gate and helping the commander set up a judicial platform, sir."

That wasn't something he could divert the man from. "Alright, let me rephrase. Do we have a team that we can grab? I want Nolan and another team to go out and find the other slave pens and start freeing magicians."

Hadi stared at him for a moment. "Raja. Permission to speak freely?"

Trev'nor wasn't sure where the man was going with this, but waved him on. "Granted."

"Raja, we're all a little confused on why you and Raya Becca and Raja Nolan react so strongly about the magicians. These are strangers to you, correct?"

Did they not know...? No, come to think of it, only the people of Rurick had known of the connection. Trev'nor took a breath and broke it down to the simplest explanation he could. "All of the magical slaves now? Their ancestors came here from Chahir. We share the same ancestors."

"They're family members?" the lieutenant blurted out incredulously, jaw dropping.

"Cousins, yes." Many, many times removed. But that didn't matter in Khobunter. In this land, family was family and if you shared even just one drop of blood then that's all that mattered.

Complete understanding washed over every person within earshot. Trev'nor didn't have to say a word more. These people, at least, knew how to stick with family no matter what the odds were against them.

"Raja, I can spare two teams," Captain Hadi stated firmly. "And sir, in the future, explain things like this before we go into combat."

"Sorry," Trev'nor apologized with a shrug of the hands. "I thought you knew. But in retrospect, it was the people of Rurick that helped us figure all of this out."

"I'll spread the word," the lieutenant promised and turned about immediately to do just that.

"Get Musa and Seyyed!" Hadi called to his back. "Sir, once I've given them their marching orders, we'll go for the nearest slave pen. I know exactly where it is from here. We should be on high alert going through the streets. We have not secured the area outside of the castle."

"Trust me, Captain, that's not going to be much of a problem."

Actually, walking through the streets wasn't as dangerous as Trev'nor thought it would be. Because everyone wore the same uniform, no one looked at Hadi's team and thought 'enemy soldiers.' Also because he walked with them, even though he was obviously foreign, no one questioned Trev'nor either. Hadi and his men were still on edge, of course, but nothing happened to them and no one questioned their right to be there.

Hadi had been stationed in Trexler during his first years in the military and knew this section of the city like the back of his hand. He went straight for the slave pens that were three streets over. Once they arrived at the main door, they finally met opposition from the guards on duty. Hadi's team worked like a well-oiled machine and the guards were under arrest and subdued before Trev'nor could open his mouth and formulate a full command.

"Masoon, Jamshid, you guard the doors. The rest, with me."

"Sir!" six men barked at once.

Military precision. Trev'nor loved it. Grinning, he stepped through the door, his own weapon at the ready just in case a guard was back in the pen. He stepped from the cool interior of the guardhouse into the stuffy warehouse beyond it. The light was dim at best, the air foul. The slaves inside were still and listless, like the ones he had seen before. But as he came into the room, some took notice and their heads came up. When he kept standing there, with no guards trying to restrain him, others cautiously stood and prodded at their neighbors.

Trev'nor panned his head, getting a rough headcount. Sixty? Or roughly that, anyway. He'd have to get a better count of them before leaving here, and full names, otherwise Llona would have his head. She was their record keeper for the magicians.

Hadi leaned in a little and whispered, "Why are they staring at you like that, sir?"

"Because I'm the most powerful magician they've likely ever seen," Trev'nor responded, not even trying to lower his voice. "And I'm walking around freely." Alright, he had an idea of how many magicians and non-magicians were in this room. Time to move. Stepping forward a little more, he said loudly, "My name is Rhebentrev'noren. I am an Earth Mage. I and three other mages have taken Warlord Trexler into custody. We now rule Trexler. You are free citizens of Khobunter as of now."

"Your Khobuntish is improving, sir."

"Thank you, Captain." Trev'nor was a bit lost on what to do next, so he started with the people directly next to him. "This is Captain Hadi. He will help you out of these chains and take you to a better place until we can get everyone sorted. What are your names?"

The slaves stared back at him as if sure he was some hallucination.

Trev'nor didn't let it faze him. He reached out with his hands and wrenched the bars casually aside, making the metal screech in agony. With the bars out of the way, he stepped through and focused on a little girl huddled in her mother's lap. If she were older than ten, he'd eat his boots. There was an amulet on her, just one, as her magic was still in the process of truly awakening. Trev'nor reached out and carefully brought the amulet over her head before dropping it and crushing it under his boot.

"Hello, sweets." He grinned at her. "What's your name?"

"Dana," she whispered. Her dark eyes were wide in a pale, heart-shaped face. "You glow."

"I sure do," he agreed affably. "Is this pretty lady your mother?"

Dana nodded, eyes still wide.

"Dana's mother, let's get that amulet off of you, too." As he took them off, he noted that both of them were witches. The mother sat perfectly still as it was lifted, her only reaction a single tear streaming down a cheek. Trev'nor wiped that away and winked at her before standing and shuffling to the man in the cell with them. "Captain," he instructed over his shoulder, "you can take these off as well. I wasn't sure until I touched them, but the limits are almost up on them, the magic weak enough that a non-magical person can lift them free."

"Ah, yes, Raja, we'll do that. Once they're off?"

"Destroy them."

The last man in the cell reached out and grabbed Trev'nor's wrist in an ironclad clutch. He was older, old enough to be Trev'nor's grandfather, worn thin by years of hard work and not enough food. "Rheben. Did you say Rheben?"

"I did," he answered steadily. What was the respectful word for an elderly man in this country again? Gan, gan-something… "Ganyesh, you know my family?"

Being addressed respectfully brought tears to the old man's eyes. "I do. I do. A Rheben is here."

Trev'nor's breath halted in his chest. "There is a Rheben here?"

The old man stood, a little shakily, and called out, "Parisa!"

A little girl, no more than eight or nine, stood and tentatively waved. "I'm here," she called back in a tremulous voice.

"Go to her," the old man encouraged, pushing Trev'nor that direction. "She has no other family. Take her from here."

"I'm taking you all from here," Trev'nor stated firmly. He made sure that point got across before he moved. He couldn't contain his excitement as this was the first time he had seen evidence that the Rheben bloodline had survived the fall of the city.

Hadi was hot on his heels, apparently unable to contain his curiosity either.

The little girl had not budged. She stood with her hand holding the chain to her wrist, a move that Trev'nor knew well, because if the chain was left dangling, it would chaff the wrist severely.

Trev'nor knelt slowly in front of her, taking in every detail. She had the dark skin of this people, but the rest of her looked more Chahiran. Her hair was more of a brown than black and her eyes…she had Garth's eyes. Clear green eyes looking straight back at him. To look so much like the Rhebens like this, she must be a direct descendant.

"Rhebentrev'noren," he re-introduced himself, using his best smile to cover up his spinning thoughts. "Trev'nor. What's your name?"

"Parisa Rheben."

So the name had stuck, but not the proper Chahiran methodology? That made things a little confusing.

Her eyes wide, she stood up on tiptoes. "I look like you,"

she breathed.

"Yes," Trev'nor answered, voice shaking. "Yes, you're obviously a Rheben. I can see your magic, too. You'll be a powerful Earth Mage once you grow up." She'd rival Garth, easily, he could see that in a glance.

"Raja?" Captain Hadi interrupted with an uncertain glance between them. "I was instructed by Raya Becca to make a list of everyone, but should I list this girl under her Chahiran name?"

Trev'nor nodded emphatically. "Yes. Do that. Also note that she's in my custody."

"You'll take her, sir?"

"I'm not about to leave a member of my family behind, Captain. I mean, they're all related in one way or another, but—"

Hadi lifted a hand. "I understand, sir."

Trev'nor had no idea what he'd do when it came time to leave Trexler, but for now, he wasn't letting this girl out of his sight. "Find me the keys to these cufflinks," he demanded.

One of Hadi's lieutenants slithered around him long enough to unlock Parisa before going back to the cell he had been working on. Trev'nor gave him a nod of thanks and gave himself a mental shake. He had a job to do before he could focus on Parisa.

Because her magical power was too young, she had no amulets on her, which made it easier on Trev'nor. He picked her up and set her on a hip, and walked around with her that way, pointing out the people that were not magical for Hadi.

Three times, Parisa asked him if they really were related, and he answered her patiently each time that yes they really were. When she finally accepted this as a truth, only then did she really settle against him and put both arms around his neck. It tore at Trev'nor's heart. Bad enough to be born into this abysmal place, but to be an orphan in it? He couldn't imagine it. Didn't want to.

In this dim place, time had no meaning and he had no way of marking it. But Trev'nor felt like roughly an hour had passed. Most of the room was unshackled now, sorted into magicians and non-magicians. Trev'nor could see the sorting had unnerved people and went back to the center of the room to explain, so that everyone could hear him. "We're holding a trial for the warlord now," he said, trying to broadcast his voice. "We need to prove he was holding non-magicians as slaves to the people. That's why we separated you. Don't worry, it's…." Argh, busted buckets, what was the word for temporary?

"Todokii?" Hadi offered. "Short amount of time."

Trev'nor inclined his head. "Yes, todokii. We'll reunite families after the trial is over. There is a white dragon at the castle. If you give her your name, she can tell you if we have already freed your families or friends in Tiergan."

There were happy exclamations over this, although some seemed to still be in shock. Trev'nor let them each take things at their own pace. It would all sink in eventually.

Hadi gathered people up, instructing them to stay together as he and his team would escort them to a safe place.

The mirror broach hanging around Trev'nor's neck came alive. "Trev?"

He picked it up and held it closer to his mouth. "What is it, Becca?"

"Are you ready to head back? Our judges are almost through with the last of the officials and they want to do the warlord next."

"We're heading back now. I'm not far, so if they can give us a few minutes? I'm bringing twenty-three with me for proof."

"That's quite the number. Alright, I'll pass that along. How many people altogether? I have Ehsan preparing rooms here in the castle to put people into."

By which she meant Ehsan was scaring the castle staff into line. The man had no sense of humor where former slaves were concerned. "Hold on. Hadi, what was our exact headcount?"

"Sixty-two, Raja."

"I heard him. Any surprises?"

"One," Trev'nor answered, leading the line of magicians out of the door and into the outside. Parisa's hold on him became almost strangling. Wasn't used to going outside? The thought broke his heart all over again. An Earth Mage, no matter how young, should not be cut off so completely from the world. "Becca. I found a Rheben."

Her breath caught. "REALLY?!"

"Rhebenparisaan," he answered. "She's…Parisa, how old are you?"

"Eight," she said confidently.

"Eight years old? Oh my. Trev."

"I know, I know, too young to take with us but old enough that magical accidents might start happening soon. We'll figure something out. But Bec, I'm told that she's the last member of her family. I took custody of her."

"I wouldn't expect you to do anything different. Alright, I'll pass this along to Nolan. We'll figure something out."

Trev'nor already had a hunch of what would need to happen. It would be similar to what he had gone through, when Garth had taken him from the Tonkowacon. As hard as that had been for him, as much as he hated to do it to someone else, he wasn't seeing any other options. "I'll be there soon."

"Alright." The connection abruptly died.

Knowing what would probably happen next, Trev'nor decided to try and prepare Parisa as much as possible. They walked the street toward the castle, the guards herding the slaves along and keeping them away from what few civilians braved the streets. Trev'nor kept an eye out, too, ready to throw up a wall and sink someone into the ground as necessary. As he kept watch, he talked to the little girl in his arms. "Parisa. You actually have a lot of family."

She sat up straight in his arms, attention riveted. "I do?"

"Yeah. Aunts, uncles, cousins, the works. I'm actually your cousin." This news made her happy, which relieved Trev'nor. Alright, maybe this wouldn't be as bad as when he had been forced to leave the Tonkowacon. "We have a cousin that runs a magical academy in Chahir. Strae Academy. Well, he and his wife both run it. His name is Garth."

"Is he like us?"

"An Earth Mage? He sure is. His wife is a witch, though. Her name is Chatta. You'll like her. You'll like them both, actually, them and their kids."

"They have kids?"

"They sure do. Three of them. One of them is an Earth Mage like you are, but he's a little older." The more information he gave her, the more comfortable and curious she became. "You have aunts and uncles and more cousins than that living in Chahir too, mostly in the northern part of the country. So you see, I'm not your only relative. I'm one of many."

"I don't remember my parents," she told him sadly. "They went away when I was a baby."

"Went away?" Trev'nor wasn't sure if she meant died or was separated from her.

"They were sent north," she explained.

Ah, so not dead. Well, possibly not dead. Trev'nor really

hoped for not dead. "I promise to look for them as I go. But for now, kiddo, I think our best option is to send you to your cousin Garth."

Now she finally looked uncertain, peeking up at him through her lashes. "I can't stay with you?"

"I'm going to have to do a lot of fighting to look for your parents, and free all of the other magicians," he explained. "Besides, don't you want to go learn how your magic works? Meet all of your other family? Play with your cousins?"

Being a child, one limited to understanding how the outside world worked, she could only imagine what he meant by this. "Maybe."

"There's flying cats there, you know," he informed her, trying to connect this idea with a little girl's sense of wonder. "And talking horses. You'll live in a huge castle, bigger than this one is, and be surrounded by magic."

While this intrigued her, she wasn't sold on the idea. "Will you go with me?"

"That's the part we have to figure out." Trev'nor really didn't want to go to Strae just now, partially because he would have to face the music, but also because it would take a lot of time. More time than he really had to spare. What he'd likely have to do was send her via dragon to Q'atal and have them notify Garth. Or drop her off in Q'atal himself and have them notify Garth. Either way, Q'atal seemed the best option for a drop-off point.

Even though the logistics of this whole thing made his head hurt, Trev'nor was still very, very glad to have found her. He sent a prayer up to the heavens that he'd be able to find her parents too. But all of this would have to wait.

They had a warlord to deal with first.

Becca put the mirror broach back in her pocket. While she would dearly love to go meet the people that Trev'nor had found, she couldn't afford to move from this spot. They had divided up tasks before the trials started. Azin and Nolan were in charge of defending the castle, Ehsan preparing to deal with the influx of magicians that would come in, the militia were dragging out officials from their offices and riding herd on the trials. Commander Danyal, the Rikkan and Rikkana, and of course Rikkshana Yasmina conducted the trials.

While they were the ones making the accusations, citing laws, and judging, it didn't mean that they could proceed without any oversight. Nolan had been firm on that when they were planning yesterday. Someone, either Becca or Trev'nor, needed to at least stay and observe. As the future rulers of Khobunter, as the new rulers of Trexler, one of them had to sit in judgment over the last warlord.

Becca had a young sergeant by the name of Amir at her elbow, translating for her, as the Khobuntish flew fast and thick. The citizens of Trexler filled the courtyard, watching as the accused were brought up one by one in front of the judgement table, their names and crimes rattled off, and then they had one chance to defend themselves. Just one. After that, anyone in the courtyard could speak against them, and if there was evidence at hand, that was presented.

One could argue about the fairness of the trials, but usually the evidence was so overwhelming of their guilt that even the men accused had a difficult time coming up with a defense. Becca stood three feet behind the table, lending silent support and power to the proceedings but not interfering. She didn't understand enough about Khobuntian law to intervene, and honestly understood only one word in three anyway. If not for Sergeant Amir, she'd be lost completely.

Tilting her head, she whispered to him, "I count ten officers, three ministers, and four retainers sentenced."

"That's correct, Raya."

"Is that the full inner circle for a warlord?"

"Nearly, Raya. But there's three more to be sentenced."

Commander Danyal was clearing out the entire inner circle, eh? "Sergeant, how does Commander Danyal know exactly who to judge? And what they're guilty of?"

"Commander was stationed here from the beginning of his service, Raya, up until seven years ago. He was here for nearly fifteen years before they transferred him to Tiergan."

Something about the way he said that made a bell go off in her head. "He was transferred to Tiergan as a punishment. Wasn't he."

Amir gave her a confirming look. "Yes, he was. He won't tell anyone what for, but when he came, Captain Hadi came with him, and the captain said the commander authorized a release of prisoners when he wasn't supposed to."

She didn't need to ask any further questions. Becca had an idea of what had happened. Trexler had ordered his army to overtake either a town or watchtower, they had succeeded, the local people taken as prisoners as usual. Only Danyal hadn't turned them into slaves but instead let them go. "I knew I liked the man for a reason."

Warlord Trexler—soon to be known as ex-Warlord Trexler—stood from his chair, wrestling with the guards on either side of him, and bellowed like an enraged bull. What, Becca couldn't decipher, as his voice was too thick with rage and slurred his words enough she couldn't make it out. Didn't care to, either. This was the twelfth time he had done this, and she was getting tired of the repetition.

Amir started forward, ready to lend a hand, but she stayed him with one hand. "Sergeant, step back four feet."

Confused, but too trained to not obey a direct order, Amir promptly moved back four feet. Becca snapped out her weapon's shield to the max, knowing that it was visible to the non-magical eye. Hers was a little different than most mage's, as lightning arced along the edges, sparking and vibrating. It was like a light show at high noon, power pulsating in visible waves.

The courtyard went still, shocked and unnerved by the show of power. Becca ignored them all, her eyes locked on the warlord's who stared at her in muted horror. He looked pale under his tan, body shrinking into the guard's hands. With open menace, she commanded, "Be. Still."

Trexler dropped into his chair, eyes nervously on hers, like a rabbit keeping track of a wolf nearby.

The man couldn't stay cowed for long, but Becca hoped this would hold him at least until his own trial. She let her shield drop and said to her judges, "Apologies. Continue."

It took a few minutes, some nervous clearing of throats, and more than one look in her direction before the trial picked back up. Amir hesitantly came back to stand at her side again and she rewarded him with a quick smile. "My weapons shield can hurt someone if they come into contact with it," she explained calmly. "That's why I had you step back."

"I understand, Raya." The expression on his face said he not only noted that for future reference but would pass the word along to everyone else as soon as he could.

Nothing interrupted the rest of the trial for the Minister of Trade, who was more than guilty of human trafficking, and he was sentenced to execution. Becca had not asked Danyal what execution meant in this country. Part of her didn't want to know. She didn't think it would be something cruel, though, not with Danyal in charge of it. For now, that was enough.

From her pocket, there was a buzz of noise and she lifted it to her mouth to say quietly, "What is it?"

"Becca," Azin said clearly, "a situation has developed out here. Nolan and the dragons are dealing with the guards as carefully as they can, and we've announced to about half the city that we're holding trials against the warlord and his officers, but we're not getting the reaction we expected."

Anger? Fear? Panic? That was what Becca was expecting. "What reaction?"

"Some people are demanding to be let into the trials. They want to add to the charges. They're also wanting to know who exactly is being tried."

Just how badly had Trexler managed his people that they would so readily rise up against him? "I'll have a full list of people and their convicted crimes made up and posted outside the gates. Tell the citizens they can come check for themselves."

Amir acted as if she had just given him an order, as he saluted her and then took off to the far side, where three soldiers were frantically making a transcript of the trials.

"That will help, thanks."

"Are they really that ready to throw their leaders under

the cart?"

"As bad as it was in Rurick and Tiergan, I think it was even worse here. They abused their authority pretty badly. All we had to say was that we were releasing the slaves and the army to go home and we automatically had people swearing allegiance."

Becca rubbed at both eyes and suppressed the urge to find a hard surface and bang her head against it a few times. She might not really know how to govern a land, and it would certainly take her time to get the hang of it, but she could never be as bad as the men she was replacing. It took effort to be that hated. "So, no problems?"

"A few," Azin admitted, "mostly from corrupt officials or men with a strong enough sense of patriotism to think that they have to fight back. But we're subduing them quickly. Most people are so scared of the dragons that they don't even want to move or breathe loudly."

"Trev'nor is almost back. Do I need to send him out again to help you?"

"We have a lot of slave pens to empty. We could use the extra hands."

"Then I'll send him out. Which part of the city are you in now?"

"Ah, almost near East Gate. Nolan is at North Gate."

"I'll send him either west or south." She dropped that connection and called up Ehsan. "Ehsan."

"Here."

"Trev'nor is coming with sixty-two people. Get down here, I need your help with them."

"Coming."

Not a man of many words, their Water Mage. The thought made her smile fleetingly.

So, the people of this city hated their leaders and were

terrified of the dragons. No wonder the city had fallen with such little resistance. It had struck Becca as strange, both Rurick and Tiergan had fought back harder than this, but it now made more sense.

Amir came trotting back and snapped a salute. "Raya. A list of the convicted with their crimes is being made now and will be posted immediately. Updates will be tacked on as the trials continue."

It felt strange to do so while not in uniform, but Becca returned the salute with military precision. "My thanks, Sergeant."

He didn't smile but fell back into place at her side, picking up his whispered translations of the proceedings. Still, Becca felt like he was smiling on some internal level. These men liked having a leader that saluted them, showed them respect, and valued them. They had never in the course of their careers had such a leader. It was probably why they had so quickly latched onto her.

Trev'nor and Ehsan arrived at practically the same time. Ehsan was quick to step in and explain things to the ex-slaves, although because he was on the opposite end of the courtyard, she couldn't hear what he was saying. Trev'nor handed a little girl over to him, who must be Parisa, and then gestured for a second group to follow him toward the tables.

Knowing full well who they must be, Becca caught Amir's eye and gestured for him to take care of things. The sergeant immediately went into motion and to Trev'nor, directing where the ex-slaves should sit.

Becca cocked a finger at Trev'nor, and he obeyed the silent summons to stand at her side. "How are things going?"

"Speedily," Becca decided after a moment. "Our Commander Danyal knows exactly who's guilty of what, and it's not taking him long at all to move the trials along."

"I'm very, truly glad that man is on our side."

"Amen to that. Do you have a triangle, by chance?"

"I do now. When the commander told me his plan, I searched the guardhouse and found a few. I figured you'd need them for demonstration purposes."

"You thought right." Becca was glad he'd had that forethought as she hadn't until just now. It would have been hard to prove to the people observing this trial who was magical and who wasn't without a triangle. She waggled her fingers at him and he promptly fished two out of a pocket. "Thanks. Azin called earlier and said that they need help emptying out slave pens. Go either west or south, they've got east and north covered."

"Roger that." With a slight skip, he commandeered a section of courtyard paving stone to carry him up to the wall, and from there, Garth readily picked him up and carried him off.

Becca smiled at seeing how in-tune the two had become. Her Cat had refused to leave and help the other dragons, instead lingering in a corner nearby. Becca hardly thought it was because she found human trials fascinating. Her dragon's concern was heart-warming and Becca fully appreciated having someone watch her back while her attention was on other things.

The last minister's trial ended with a sentencing of execution. Danyal stood and half-turned to look at her. She could read his expression and body language well enough to know what it meant. It was time to judge a warlord.

Though he had planned this, even Danyal seemed to need a moment to gather his courage. The audience in the courtyard held its collective breath as they waited for the official announcement. After listening to these words dozens of times over, even Becca understood him perfectly as he said, "I call for the trial of Warlord Sanjar Trexler!"

Nervous tension went out like a tidal wave, the words having a visible effect on the watchers. Becca held firm and unmovable, silently lending support. Danyal apparently needed it as he gave her a surreptitious look three different times as the warlord was manhandled to stand in front of the table.

Sanjar Trexler was quite the sight. Dirty from marching in the desert, lines of sweat visible on his dusty skin, clothes rumpled and obviously slept in, the back of his hair mussed. He hardly looked like a man of power. The rage in his face aged him another ten years and he leaned ominously forward as he snarled between clenched teeth, "You do not have the authority to try me!"

Becca held up a hand before Amir could translate anything. "That I got."

It was not Danyal, but instead Rikkshana Yasmina that stood to answer this challenge. "In the history of Khobunter, never has a law said that a man is above it. All are equal before it."

Amir whispered, "That too?"

"That too." Her vocabulary was definite improving.

"I AM THE LAW!" Trexler roared.

"You are not," four voices announced simultaneously.

"The law existed before you," Rikkana Shiva stated with a soft finality. "The law will continue after your death. It is beyond you. The only connection that you have with it is that it was your duty to uphold it."

"It is a duty that you failed," Rikkan Akbar continued, tone hard. His hands fisted on the table's top. "For that reason, you stand before us. Commander, read us the first offense."

Trexler growled and roared some more, but they over-rode him and continued. Becca let out a slow breath and listened intently as the trial continued.

It followed much like their conversation in Tiergan, actually. Someone at the table would read off the exact law that he had broken, list his offenses against it, and then give him a chance to respond. Since Trexler wasn't interested in doing so, they would shrug and continue with the next. Becca felt the strangest sense of déjà vu, as if she were repeating the same conversation in a different setting with only slightly different words.

They came to the last offense, that of slavery, and she finally moved out of her spot from behind the table. After standing in place for nearly three hours, her knees stiffly protested a little. It felt good to finally walk. As she moved, she pulled out the triangles and handed Amir one.

"I don't know how to use this, Raya!" he protested in a low whisper.

"You don't need to do anything," she assured him, pressing it into his hand. "It automatically lights up when placed in front of a magician. Just hold it so the crowd can see it."

Relieved and still nervous, he went to stand on the other side of the bench. Becca stood tall and held the triangle in front of her own chest. Carefully, she phrased the words in her mind before speaking, "As you can see, the triangle glows when near a magician. It will not for a non-magical person."

"These people," Danyal thankfully took over at that point and gestured to the group of ex-slaves patiently waiting on his right, "are former slaves. They were with the other magicians until an hour ago. Sergeant, the triangle?"

The crowd stared intently but as Amir went slowly down the line, the triangle didn't react. People started whispering to each other, the tone confused and escalating with each person.

"Not every person in the slave pens was a magician." Danyal waved the sergeant to cease and Amir did so, standing at semi-attention near the judgment table. "This is against the law."

Trexler flung an outraged finger at Becca. "She is a magician! SHE SHOULD BE IN CHAINS!"

With a flex of power, Becca casually broke the triangle. To the naked eye, it looked as if she broken it by willpower alone. She flung it at Trexler's feet with a negligent toss of the hand. "Trexler, you are confused on a vital point."

"And what is that?" he sneered.

"Human beings shouldn't be slaves to begin with. Ever. Your original lawmakers understood this. The first laws written for Khobunter outlawed slavery. Period." Becca had to switch to Solish to say all of this and was grateful Amir automatically translated for her. She paused to let him catch up before continuing, "The new conquerors of Khobunter are reversing the laws and will return to the original ones. They are more humane and uncorrupted than the laws that supposedly serve the people now."

He stared at her with eyes burning in hatred, jaw working. "You won't last. This reign of yours will not continue forever. I give it a week."

"If I were relying on my strength alone, Trexler, I wouldn't last the day." Becca smiled at him, not in the least insulted. "But unlike you, I don't go out of my way to make people hate me. Perhaps, if you had shown kindness instead of greed, your people wouldn't have been so quick to turn on you."

He spat at her, although he was too far away to actually land anything. "You are too haughty, magician!"

"I am not the one that judged you, Trexler. It was your own people that turned against you. I just gave them the power to stand up to you." Tired of this back and forth, she turned her back to him. "Judges, how do you rule?"

"Immediate execution," they said, more or less in unison.

"See it done, then." Becca turned away, heading for Cat, but she paused next to Danyal and murmured, "If I ever become as bad as that man, strike me down. Do not hesitate."

"Warlord, I would promise to do so, but," he grinned at her, his exhaustion disappearing for a brief moment, "I do not dare cross your dragon."

Cat heard this (of course she did, she heard everything) and gave a rumbling chuckle. "No worry. I make her behave."

"A dragon chaperone." Becca snorted, amused at the idea, but knew good and well that her dragon seriously would keep her in line. Shaking her head, she went and slung herself into Cat's saddle. "I think my work here is done for the time being, Cat. Let's go see if the boys need help."

"What is with this office?" Trev'nor stared around with his face screwed up in distaste. "There's gold everywhere."

"Gaudy doesn't begin to describe it," Becca agreed. She stepped into the room as if afraid that that something would explode. "Are all king's offices like this? Well, not that he was a king, but…."

"No," both Trev'nor and Nolan denied immediately.

"My grandfather's office isn't anything like this," Nolan clarified, unable to take his eyes away from the desk dominating the center of the room. It had enough gold trimming on it to feed a small country for about two months. "And King Guin's office is even plainer than Grandfather's."

"Garth's and Chatta's offices looks a lot like King Guin's," Trev'nor offered by way of explanation. Becca had never been to visit either king herself, but they had all semi-grown up in their mentors' offices.

"I'm relieved to hear it." Becca took another three tentative steps forward, staring around with a horrified look. "Gold curtains, gold furniture, gold statues, even golden armor…the man was obsessed with appearances."

"Let's sell the lot," Trev'nor decided on the spot. "We've been spending money left and right anyway, trying to outfit the magicians and feed them. I think this will more than make up for it."

"Splendid plan. For now, though, let's find a different place to talk. All of this—" she waved a hand around "—is distracting me, I can't hear myself think."

Trev'nor glanced about but the office was a square space that had no dividing walls. At least, none he could readily see. "Outside veranda?"

Becca apparently liked this idea as she immediately bee-lined for the large glass doors.

The outside veranda, fortunately, was not covered in gold. There were several plush chairs, a few small tables, and some dormant flower beds. Sinking into one of the chairs, he asked, "How did the trials go?"

"Smoother than they should have," Becca answered sadly. "The people here really hated their government. No one offered up any real opposition."

"On the contrary, we had people volunteering to go and witness against him," Nolan added, letting out a tired sigh as he sank into a plush armchair. "Ah, that feels good. Llona tells me that we rescued four hundred and twenty-one people today. She's already matching up friends and family."

Yes, that had been a funny sight. Trev'nor had come to drop off the last of the magicians and found people clustered around the white dragon, the younger ones actually sitting on her like she was a giant bench. Llona loved it; that was obvious from her happily twitching tail.

"And resistance?" Becca glanced between the two of them. "Commander Danyal hasn't reported any resistance to me, but you saw some signs of it in the city, yes?"

"Some. The population is too large to be one hundred percent on our side, but—correct me if I'm wrong, Nol, you're better with people than I am—I think they're too used to the idea of being conquered. I don't think this city has been fought over for decades, not like the others, but on some level they're always mentally prepared for it. "

"Unfortunately true." Nolan slumped more into his chair. "They've adopted a 'let's wait and see' attitude. I honestly think that as long as we're good to them, we will never get any large resistance. Between cultural norm and corrupt leaders, they're used to not resisting."

"Well, if we don't have to worry about any uprisings right this minute, let's talk about what to do with all of the magicians," Becca suggested. "We have far too many on hand and it's going to be impossible for the three of us to teach them. Even if we didn't have other things to do, which isn't the case, we still wouldn't be able to teach them."

"There's also the matter of a young Earth Mage to discuss," Nolan agreed. "Alright, let's talk about magicians first."

"Earth Mage first, as she'll be easier to solve. So as I see it," Trev'nor started, "we have one of two options. We send Parisa by dragon to Q'atal or I take her by Earth Path to Q'atal."

"Either way, drop her off in Q'atal?" Becca wasn't really asking a question. She spun sideways in her chair to dangle her legs over the arms. "Probably the best move. You don't have the time to go all of the way to Strae, and even if you did, once the adults lay hands on you...."

"They won't let go," Trev'nor agreed, wincing at the mental picture of what would happen when the adults finally did catch up. "Q'atal is neutral, very close to Strae, and they have a way of contacting Garth directly. I think it's our best option."

"I'm not arguing that." Nolan tilted his head down and gave Trev'nor a look that stated he was being obtuse. "But Trev, you need to start thinking like a politician."

"Meaning…?" Trev'nor trailed off invitingly.

"You are Q'atal's new neighbor. It behooves you to properly introduce yourself and establish relations with them now. Before they get worried and jump to conclusions they shouldn't."

That…was a very good point.

"Might I also point out that instead of just taking Parisa, you should take everyone we've rescued?"

"Not Ehsan and Azin," Becca blurted out, sitting bolt upright.

Nolan waved her down. "No, not them. They're already half-trained, they're fine. I meant everyone else."

Trev'nor was just as relieved to hear this as having the other two mages helped tremendously with the workload. Besides, Trev'nor honestly didn't know what they would do without Ehsan. He was the only one that could find water in the middle of the desert. Becca would have to call storms in to keep them supplied with water, which considering the state of the soil out here, wasn't usually the best option.

He turned over the idea in his head. "Shouldn't some of them stay though? How is the culture going to change if there are no magicians? And not everyone may want to go."

"It'd only be temporary. They'd certainly all be free to return once their training is over, but they have to be trained. Half-trained magicians running around without suppressive amulets are a disaster in the making," Nolan pointed out.

Trev'nor blew out a breath. "You're not wrong. I don't think it's fully right, but you're not wrong. We'll go with it for now, but something else will have to be figured out for later on. There's no way Strae and Hain can take all of the magicians from the other provinces as well."

"Perhaps by that point some of the Trexler magicians will know enough to come back and teach the new ones.

We'll worry about it when it happens. For now, we need to take care of the magicians we do have," Becca said.

"Alright, agreed. Man, an influx of over five hundred students at once. Chatta will kill us."

"The new branch academy is supposed to be up and running by now," Nolan pointed out, all innocence.

"She's still going to kill us," Becca opined. "But if it's too much, Garth can take some of them into Hain."

"My grandfather is not going to stand for that," Nolan denied. "He likes having magicians around."

"Then he better give Garth more funding and teachers; otherwise he's not going to be able to handle it."

A thought struck Trev'nor and he frowned. "I can hardly just drop them off in Q'atal like a litter of kittens and run. I mean, shouldn't we write a letter or something?"

Becca and Nolan exchanged looks and then twin grimaces.

"Yes," Nolan said with vast reluctance.

"But what can we possibly say?" Becca asked uncertainly. "I mean, give them even a hint to go off of, they'll be able to track us down."

"I'm not sure if it will matter what we say," Nolan denied after a moment's thought. "They're going to be asking a lot of questions from their new students. They'll learn everything eventually."

Very true. But that meant they didn't really have any good options. Well, no, Trev'nor could think of one. He could honestly say that this whole thing had been Becca's idea.

"Trev, so help me, if you start off with 'This was all Becca's idea' I will zap you."

He did a double take, flinching back into his chair. "Do you read minds?!"

"That was written all over your face," she growled, frown dark, eye twitching. "Might I remind you that conquering Khobunter was not my idea? I came up here to research weather patterns and get a dragon."

Right. Come to think of it…his eyes gravitated to Nolan.

"You can't use me as a scapegoat either," his friend informed him drolly. "You were the one adamant about conquering the country. Man up, Trev."

"But life is so much easier when I have someone in mind to blame."

"Man up," Becca echoed. "In fact, I think it's time we all man up. At our ages, Garth was doing covert operations in Chahir."

"He had backing from a king," Trev'nor couldn't help but point out.

"Dilly-dally, shilly-shally. Same difference. You think if Shad knew about this situation, or Aletha, or Xiaolang, that they would react any differently? You think if Garth or Chatta knew what was going on, they would have hesitated?"

Well, no, likely not. "I suppose we are old enough to not be worried about the parents."

"You can be." Nolan made a face. "I can't."

True, his father and grandfather would not be pleased to have their heir apparent conquering another country. "I'll help you escape before they can catch and skin you."

"You're a true friend, Trev." Resigned, Nolan heaved himself to his feet and went to a nearby desk, rummaging in the drawers for a few moments before giving a soft, "Ha!" of victory. Coming back, he pulled a small table closer to his chair and laid paper and quill out. "Well, let's write a letter. You can explain the situation as much as you need to when you're in Q'atal, but I wouldn't stay there long."

It wasn't like they could keep things in the dark forever.

"What are we going for? Full confession, half-confession, bare basics?"

Becca twirled a strand of hair in between her fingers, staring absently at the floor. "Full confession."

"Full confession," Nolan agreed. "Because otherwise the facts will get warped by other people and who knows what they'll think? I'd rather not have them come after us in a panic, assuming that something has gone drastically wrong."

Trev'nor imagined Garth in full-panic. Or Shad. Or Xiaolang. Yikes, that wasn't a good picture. "Yup, I vote we avoid that. So, full confession it is. When should we deliver our magicians? Tonight?"

"The sooner the better," Becca confirmed. "We don't have enough room to put them all here and if we get them out of Trexler now, then we avoid complications."

Slapping his hands to the armchair rests, he pushed himself up to his feet. "Then I'll leave you two to write."

Nolan paused mid-word and looked up. "Why? What will you be doing?"

"Testing to see who's going to panic on me underground. I'd rather know now who needs to be unconscious. Also, I need to send word to Tiergan and have them ready to go so I can swing by and pick them up on the way."

Nolan gave an 'ah' of understanding and bent back over the letter. He paused barely a word in. "Wait, Trev, I have an idea. Get Azin up here to melt down some of the gold, or at least take it into market and sell it. We should send at least some money with our magicians so Garth isn't scrambling to financially support all of them."

"Genius, Nolan. I'll send her up to you." Trev'nor was firmly of the mindset that anything they could do to ease the potential wrath of the adults was a good thought.

Becca scooted over to sit next to Nolan, leaning over

his shoulder to read as he wrote. Before Trev'nor had even cleared the door, they were already disagreeing on what was being written. Trev'nor was just as glad to skip that little debate.

Finding an open window in the hallway, he stuck his head through it and called out, "Garth?"

"Hear you fine, fledgling."

Of course he did. "Can you relay the message to the dragons in Tiergan and have people get ready? Tell them I'll come and get them, oh," he did some quick calculations in his head, "about two hours from now."

"Will."

Satisfied, he withdrew and headed down the stairs. He rather hoped that neither Nolan nor Becca would think to tell Garth that he now had an older dragon namesake. That reaction he'd rather see in person.

In the course of Trev'nor's life, he had only been in Q'atal a handful of times. Mostly to visit with Xiaolang, once to help re-do the ward with Garth to make it larger than the original. His last visit had been nearly three years ago and he had grown considerably since then. Having changed the wards with Garth, he knew exactly how they were created and where the sole doorway into the country was.

There were no magicians in Q'atal, of course, so no one had any mirror broaches. Instead, they had a pillar in the middle of town that could communicate with a similar one in Strae. It wasn't capable of passing along much, just an impression of needing Garth and how urgent the need was. Communication magic, over that kind of distance, without a magician on both ends to operate it, had its limitations. But for Trev'nor's purposes, that pillar would do the job adequately enough.

The problem was, he had nearly five hundred people with him. That was a lot to drop on someone unannounced, even if they did know who he was. Worse, the timing had worked out so that he was coming in at nearly six in the evening, which meant imposing on people even further. If the situation hadn't been as chaotic in Trexler, they wouldn't have immediately taken all of the magicians out, but instead waited until morning.

He took everyone to the door and ushered them just inside. Then he hopped up on a short bench so they could all see and hear him. "Everyone, as discussed, just wait here! It might take a good hour for me to return, but you're perfectly safe here!"

"We understand, Warlord," several people assured him.

Hopefully they did. Blowing out a breath, he hopped down again and headed for the country interior. He barely made it to the first row of houses before coming face to face with the Remcar-ol. Trev'nor put on a game smile. "Ah, hello."

"Magus Trev'nor, what are you doing here?" An Meiling demanded. She didn't sound upset, but her eyes were a little wide in her face and there was a flush on her cheeks that made her skin look lavender. "I sense a great many people with you."

"You sense correctly." Even though Trev'nor had spent nearly four hours getting here, he still had no idea where to start explaining. "I promise to tell you the full story, but the short story is that Nolan, Becca, and I have rescued five hundred magicians that were enslaved in Khobunter."

The whole Remcar-ol burst out at once, "WHAT?!"

"There's more, a lot more," oh so much more, "but for now, can you let them in for the night? I don't have a safe place to put everyone."

"Of course we can, child," Li Shen was already moving, faster than his elderly appearance would lead someone to believe he was capable of. "An Quon, inform everyone to prepare beds."

"Everyone ate before I brought them here," Trev'nor assured the man, almost belatedly. "And no one's seriously injured, Nolan healed people before he let me leave."

An Quon waved in acknowledgment over one shoulder but didn't slow down.

Trev'nor was ever so glad that this was a country of empaths. The whole nation would feel exactly the turmoil of the ex-slaves and know how to react to them. It also meant he didn't have to go into a lengthy discourse of what had happened, what was wrong, or anything like that. They could read enough from the people to get the gist themselves.

He didn't think that would excuse him from telling the story, though. Not with An Meiling in charge.

Trev'nor doubled back with the Remcar-ol and explained who they were to the waiting magicians, then helped wherever he could. The whole nation came out to see for themselves what was going on, and it was interesting to see everyone's double-takes. On both sides. The empaths were likely overwhelmed by the strong emotional signatures of that many magicians all at once. The magicians were puzzled by seeing a blue aura—not a typical color—that wasn't really magical. Trev'nor probably should have explained more on the way down here, but his main concern had been getting them all here without losing anyone or tripping over a random ley line.

It took hours to find enough beds, and often the couples or parents were doubling up with family to make more room, but eventually they were all settled into different houses. Trev'nor saw several cases of the Q'atalians being overly kind to their unexpected guests, which in turn made people burst into tears, confused and not sure how to respond. They had never experienced anything like this before. Seeing it brought tears to Trev'nor's eyes, as no one should be confused by kindness.

An Meiling came up and gently touched him on the shoulder. "I think you should come sit down with me,

Trev'nor."

"You're only saying that because I'm swaying on my feet," he half-joked.

"That too," she admitted. The look on her face was very maternal, an expression he had seen on his own foster mother when he was being difficult.

It felt so nice to be in a place where he didn't have to make decisions right, left, and center that he followed her obediently to a shaded area that offered cushioned chairs and a small brazier. It wasn't a particularly cold night, but the brazier gave off more light than heat, and he gravitated toward it. As he sat, he realized that most of the Remcar-ol were already there and obviously waiting on him.

Seeing this, he paused and realized that he couldn't continue as just 'Trev'nor' to them any longer. Nolan had made a good argument that morning. He was now the leader of a neighboring country. He had to establish relations with them now. "An Meiling, have you contacted Garth yet?"

"No, I have not found a moment to do so. And I did not want him coming to fetch them in the dead of night; I thought it best to contact him in the morning."

Perfect. That bought him the time he needed. "Good. Before I give you the story, I should properly introduce myself."

Yu Tung gave him a perplexed smile. "We know who you are."

"Not quite, Yu Tung. Things have changed since I saw you last. I am now the Warlord of Trexler."

The Remcar-ol went very still, so still that they resembled garden gnomes sitting around the base of a tree.

It was An Quon that found his voice first. "You—you conquered Trexler?"

"With Becca and Nolan, yes. We had to. It was the only

way to free everyone." Wiping a hand over his face, he tried to scrub away some of the fatigue so he could focus better. "Let me start at the beginning. It'll make more sense that way."

An Meiling took him by the arm and drew him gently into the chair next to hers. "Sit, Trev'nor. Tell us your story."

He started at the beginning, what seemed a decade ago, about Becca's desire to investigate Khobunter and their selfish wish to have dragons. He left nothing out. There was no point in trying to skirt over events or lie to an empath. They felt his emotions as he relived the events, and often one or another would reach out and touch him, soothe the pain as best they could. It helped tremendously and gave him the strength to tell the story all of the way to the end.

When he finished, An Meiling stood and held his head to her chest. "You poor child. What difficult decisions you've had to make. You should have called for help."

"We couldn't," Trev'nor denied, feeling a little hollow with exhaustion.

"You couldn't," Li Shen agreed sadly. "Politically speaking, no one would have been able to come to your aid without serious consequences. Even your mentors would be hard pressed to help you at this point. Although I have no doubt that some of them will want to despite the consequences."

"They can help me. By taking in five hundred students and whatever other slaves we're able to save. I'm sure Garth is going to hit the roof when he hears the full story, but the one thing I want to make clear is that this was my choice. Mine and Becca's and Nolan's. We knew what the consequences were going to be, what people would think of us, and likely how the Trasdee Evondit Orra would react. We chose to forge ahead anyway. All of the countries and magical organizations of the world have had decades, at least, to do something about the situation in Khobunter. They didn't. They can't complain when we chose to resolve the situation ourselves."

"Oh, they'll complain," Yu Tung denied dryly. "At great volume and length. But it is true they will not have the right to stop you."

Trev'nor half-expected an argument from the people sitting here. Why wasn't he getting one? "No one here is complaining either."

"Politically speaking," An Quon started in a particularly droll manner, "we're very glad to have Trexler removed from power. He was a very difficult neighbor. Having someone we know and trust in that seat of power instead is a great relief to us."

Nolan had been dead on. He really had made a smart move coming and introducing himself as the new warlord here. "Thank you?"

"But," An Quon continued, giving him that Look under a bushy set of eyebrows, "I think you have shouldered on more than a seventeen-year-old should be expected to take on."

He was tired enough that this made him laugh. "We were a bit rash in the beginning."

"A bit, he says," Li Shen despaired.

"We have good help now, though," Trev'nor continued. Uh-oh, this was bad. The chair was gaining a death grip on him. He hadn't thought so before, but it now felt perfectly comfortable to sleep in. "The people of Trexler are supporting us, although it's by degrees in some places, and the dragons have been a tremendous help. I really don't know what we'd do without them."

"And now, you want us to help you as well." An Meiling didn't sound discouraging, more amused. "By acting as a relay point for the rescued magicians."

"If you don't mind? You'd cut my travel time in about half that way and honestly, we can't afford for me to take days at a time to settle the magicians in Strae. Nolan and Becca can barely afford for me to be gone a few hours."

"We prefer to help over having those poor people stuck in Khobunter." An Quon was very firm about this point. "But child, we worry for you. You have taken on too much."

"An Quon, I am not," yet, "in over my head. I probably would be without Becca, Nolan, and the dragons, but like I said the people of Trexler were glad to see the old warlord go. They're quite happy with us so far and are slowly coming around to help establish a new rule. I promise you, the minute we feel like things are out of our control, we'll stop and call for help. But we didn't undertake this lightly and we have no intention of abandoning Khobunter. That country is a serious mess."

"And you are the one that is going to fix it?" Li Shen asked doubtfully.

"Someone has to. I don't see anyone else volunteering." More truthfully, Trev'nor added, "Actually it's not really us doing the work. It's the people who are really changing things. All we're doing is providing guidelines and giving them the power they need."

"Trexler was not a good leader. I can see how the people would readily cast him off." An Quon leaned forward, eyes piercing. "But can you say that your success will be just as high in the rest of the country?"

"This might sound strange, but I hope it isn't. The reason we were so readily successful in Trexler was because the people had been badly abused for years. I hope that the rest of the country isn't the same. I hope that it's been better for the rest of Khobunter. But sadly, I don't think it'll be much different. The land right above us and to the right of us seem to have the same bad habits. Half of this country is going to be the same as Trexler." That thought was extremely depressing. While making it easier to conqueror, it also meant that Trev'nor and Becca had more to fix. Fixing was always harder than breaking.

"When you need our help, you will ask for it." An Meiling was not asking. She was commanding.

Trev'nor forced his mouth up into a tired smile. "I promise, we will. We already are."

"While I do not fully agree with everything you are doing," of course they wouldn't, the Q'atalians abhorred death, "I think you are acting with the best of intentions, and it is true that the situation in Khobunter must change. That land is a stubborn one and they respect only might of arms. You have chosen a hard road, young magus."

She had no idea. Well, no, she probably did. "I know it."

Patting his shoulder, she gripped his upper forearm and dragged him out of his seat. "We will talk again in the morning. For now, we all need sleep."

Trev'nor had no intention of lingering long enough for Garth to get here, which was likely her plan, but was honest enough to admit that in his current state he would probably make a costly mistake in traveling back to Trexler. He was too tired to even stand upright without swaying. That wasn't a good sign. They had about seven hours until dawn, and he'd take the rest of the night to get some good sleep before taking off. "If there's still a spare bed to be had, I'll take it. If not, point me to some soft grass and I'll make do."

"Grass?" An Meiling repeated, sounding scandalized.

"I was raised by the Tonkowacon," he reminded her, starting to feel dry drunk. "A blanket of stars and a bed of grass is all we need."

Li Shen put a hand to the small of his back and steered him out. "I think we can at least find a blanket and pillow, young warlord."

Trev'nor hadn't been joking. In his state, just being horizontal would be enough to get him fast asleep. "Well, if you insist."

"We do," Li Shen chuckled. "Ah, what it must be like to be young enough to not worry about waking up with a crick in your neck."

No, he likely would. Trev'nor was just too tired to care. He followed his host amiably through the dark houses. "Oh, I almost forgot. I have a full letter explaining everything and a pouch of money for Garth. Also, separate letters for Vonlorisen, and Shad and Aletha. Can you make sure those are passed over to Garth when he arrives?"

Li Shen cast him a glance. "You will not stay and meet with him yourself?"

"Naw, I'll skip that lecture, thanks all the same. Besides, if I stay long enough to meet Garth, he'll keep me for hours, and I don't have that kind of time."

"I think you will regret it later if you do not stay and properly talk to him now."

"I end up regretting a lot of things, Li Shen. None of them have killed me yet." Although Garth might, when he eventually did catch up with them. Ah, well.

He'd worry about it tomorrow.

Trev'nor had woken and escaped Q'atal before Garth's arrival, which he felt a fortunate thing. Becca felt like he would regret it later, as avoiding consequences never led to anything good, but it had been his decision to make. They heard nothing from Strae, but they had no way of contacting the three mages directly aside from traveling up to Trexler themselves. With the influx of students, they couldn't afford to send anyone after them, and the three young mages used that to their full advantage.

They spent two weeks in Trexler, and while it was chaotic, it was also strangely peaceful. Becca found that the people of the city didn't know how to respond to magicians at all, and oscillated between being extremely polite and letting old habits surface. Sometimes they would say something rude and cutting to her, then realize what they had done, and apologize profusely. It was hard, but she was patient with them, as she realized that it was cultural prejudice that made them react so. Habits were the hardest thing to break and losing her temper about it would not make anything better.

Trev'nor and Azin spent half their time outside of the city, working with the soil and making it ready to return to the fertile land it was meant to be. Once they were done, they turned it over to Becca and Nolan.

Becca spent a good portion of her day training with the soldiers. She realized in taking Trexler that they were accustomed to fighting with magicians, but the only methods that the soldiers knew were to use the magicians like cannon fodder. She wasn't about to let them go into battle again with that mindset. Trev'nor dropped in upon request, helping her train, and had to bite the inside of his lip often to keep from laughing. Becca knew why without even asking. Her training methods were scarily like Aletha's, with a little Shad mixed in.

In between other duties, Nolan snagged them whenever possible and schooled them on running a country. Fortunately Nolan was a kind teacher. Ruthless about homework, though. Becca learned more about governing a country in two weeks than she ever had reading history books at Strae.

At the end of those two weeks, they realized that the city had settled tentatively into a rhythm with their new leaders. The whole of Trexler was still feeling the aftershocks of being conquered, certainly, but no one seemed to mind it much. Between their dragon watchdogs and the new officials running day-to-day matters, they felt like it was time to move onward.

Which brought about the question of their northern neighbor, Riyu.

Becca called for a strategy session with Danyal, Trev'nor, and Nolan in the newly renovated office. Well, she said renovated, but all they had done was take out the gaudy art and furniture and replace it with more sensible choices. Becca was glad to have an office she could work in without feeling blinded by it. She settled at the head of the table, and waited as the men joined her. "Well. Let's start off with problems. Commander Danyal?"

"We are experiencing problems, mostly from people entrenched in the old ways that don't want to change," Danyal started off neutrally. "However, these are minor complaints and easily dealt with. We have more issues with too many officials learning their jobs all at the same time. It's causing gaps and inter-office conflict."

That didn't sound good. "Anything major?"

"No, it's very minor. Anything major and you would already be feeling the effects of it."

Point taken. "Anything else?"

"Sagar seems to be struggling with the new rule more than Trexler," Trev'nor informed her, "but when I visited there yesterday they were making good strides in the right direction. I mean, people were happily melting down slave chains and selling the ore. I think Sagar was worse off than Tiergan because it's closer to Riyu's borders. It wasn't as protected as Tiergan. If we can prove to them that we'll protect them from Riyu, we'll have their full support."

"That's what we'll do, then. Nolan, I assume our dragon watchers in Sagar are doing fine?"

"They are. In fact, they're quite happy, as they have all of that yummy fish in the sea at their disposal." The way Nolan said this indicated he had heard All About The Fish, in more detail than he probably cared for.

"So, anything major enough to detain us from moving on to Riyu?" she looked around the table expectantly.

"Not that I know of," Trev'nor denied, "But how did you end up running this meeting?"

"You want to take over?" she offered, perfectly willing to let him lead.

"No, no, you're doing splendidly," he assured her in grand, rolling tones. "Carry on, fearless leader."

"Hmmm." She stared at him suspiciously, not sure if he

were up to something or not. "To return to my question, nothing major? No? Then let's talk about Warlord Riyu. Commander Danyal, what do you know about him?"

"Not a great deal," Danyal apologized with a slight shrug. "He's ruthless. Unprincipled. Greedy. Much like our last warlord."

Nolan rolled his eyes. "Lovely."

"Warlord Trexler often complained that he was more clever and stealthy than a snake in the grass. I didn't ever meet the man in the field. Most of my time was spent either defending a city from one of his commanders or training. I will say that fighting against his men never led to a good outcome. Even when we won, we lost."

Trev'nor tapped the table with a finger. "Explain that."

"We might win the battle, but usually the body count was so high it felt more like a loss," Danyal clarified. "It might be different with you mages in the mix. You're powerful enough to hit him head on, which we were never able to do. You might be able to defeat him swiftly enough that he can't employ his usual tactics."

Becca started praying that was the case. "Do you think the same battle tactics that we used to defeat Trexler will work on Riyu?"

"At least with the first battle, yes. It's an overwhelming amount of firepower after all."

"Then let's go with the same tactics." Becca stood so she could lean over the table and get a better look at the map. "The question is, which place first? We have two within reach of our territory."

"Alred Watchtower?" Nolan offered. "I think Jashni is too close to Riyu's capital city."

"I'm inclined to agree." Danyal gestured to Jashni as he continued, "We only attacked Jashni once and it went very badly. If you want to see for yourself how this man fights, how he guards his territories, then Alred is a better place to attack first. It's not as large as the sister-cities and even though it is very well guarded, it will be a better place to try an attack. The con to this decision is that Trexler always attacked Alred. They are always prepared for battle."

"Not as many men deployed there, but also more on guard than the other cities." Trev'nor balanced both on open palms, hands dipping and raising like a balancing scale. "Decisions, decisions."

"I think we should still hit Alred first." Becca's mind spun with logistics, battle strategies, and what little she knew of the lay of the land. "It doesn't really matter if they're more prepared and on guard than the other cities. After we attack one, they're all going to be war-ready, if they weren't already."

"No such thing as an easy target, eh?" Trev'nor said rhetorically.

"I'm afraid not," Commander Danyal agreed with what might have been a sigh. "Warlords, Raja, are we set on this course?"

Becca did a visual check with both of her friends, getting nods of agreement. "It seems we are. Then, let's leave two days from now."

"That soon?" Danyal objected.

"We don't need to take a lot of men with us," Trev'nor explained to him. "The same ones that fought with us before, and the ones that Becca has re-trained will do. We need the rest to stay at their posts here and help maintain the orders we've given."

Danyal looked set to argue this but paused, really studying all three of them for a long moment, then shelved what he was going to say. "Two days, then."

"That means that, Nolan? You and I need to get out there

in the desert and make sure that Trev'nor's hard work doesn't go to waste before we leave."

"You need to do that now," Trev'nor added firmly. "You leave the soil baking under the suns much longer, I'll have to go out and re-do everything. And that will not make me happy."

"Right now," Nolan promised. "Ah, Becca, you have a storm coming in already, I take it?"

"It'll arrive sometime tonight. Unless you want me to hurry it along?"

"Just a tad, if you would. It's best to water seeds as soon as you plant them. Hours of delay doesn't help things grow."

She gave him a casual salute. "On it. Well, sounds like we all have our tasks laid out. Meeting dismissed."

The boys readily stood and left the room, discussing soil and nutrients and planty-things as they went. Commander Danyal stayed her with a hand. "My Warlord. About the uniform you requested made for you."

Becca paused just out of her seat. Actually, what she had asked for this morning was a uniform that would fit. Uniforms fit males and females equally well, with some adjustments. She knew that by watching Aletha steal things from Shad for years. How this had become a custom-ordered item, she didn't know. "Yes?"

"The Rikkan and Rikkana have strong opinions about a woman wearing a male uniform," Danyal informed her blandly.

"They need to get over those opinions," she riposted, fingers drumming unhappily against her thigh. "The rest of the known world has female soldiers. Khobunter is the startling exception, and I refuse to let it continue."

"I had a feeling you'd say that, my Warlord. Your uniform will be done by tomorrow, as long as you can do a fitting for it today."

A slow grin took over her face. "You didn't listen to them at all, did you?"

"Warlord Becca is our military leader," he stated succinctly. "It's only right for you to be in uniform."

"I knew there was a reason why I liked you, Commander. Very well, where do I need to go for the fitting?"

"I'll escort you, my Warlord."

This was not the first time she had asked such a question and gotten that as an answer. "Commander, I have learned the layout of the city, you know?" More or less. "You can tell me where it is. I'll be able to find it."

He gave her that patented 'she's being dense but I'll be patient' look that people wore a lot around her these days. "Raya. You are now warlord."

For a split second that statement didn't make any sense at all. Then it did and she rolled her eyes to the heavens in a silent prayer. "Hence I need a bodyguard or escort wherever I go?"

"It is proper to have one."

She eyed him, evaluating the expression on his face and trying to judge just how far she could push this. "You're not budging on this one, are you?"

He gave her a slight smile but didn't say a word.

So uniforms, yes. Bodyguards, no. Becca decided to pick her battles. "Very well, Commander. Escort me, then."

"Yes, my Warlord." Danyal promptly went to the open door and waited for her to join him.

As she passed by him, she observed, "You are a stubborn, stubborn man, Commander Danyal."

"I have no argument, my Warlord. I will reflect on the shortcoming later."

Uh-huh. Suuure he would.

Two days might not have been enough time. Trev'nor realized this as he rushed about at an ungodly hour of the morning, taking care of last minute details that shouldn't have been pushed off to the last minute. But it was too late now, the main preparations were done, and the army formed up and ready to leave.

Half of the holdup was figuring out how to transport the army itself. On the way to Trexler, they had flown the men via dragons, but they now had too many people to make that feasible. On the other hand, Trev'nor could always take them by Earth Path, but that suggestion had gone over like rotten cheese with the dragons. Garth had been fine with him taking the magicians to Q'atal by Earth Path because that had been the best solution. Also the safest as he was going into very peaceful territory. But going north was a different story. When Trev'nor popped up above ground, Garth wanted to be there to make sure that there was no danger there for him to confront.

Krys was right. Having a dragon was pure trouble sometimes.

To answer the demands of the situations and keep the dragons appeased, Trev'nor came up with a middle ground that made everyone but him happy. Instead of going into the earth, he created a large slab for people to sit on. Because it was earth, he could move it above the ground as he wished, transporting as many people as he wanted to. It was more cumbersome than the Earth Path method (although it worked rather the same in principal) and it did nothing to shield people from the suns, but it kept the dragons happy. It made the men happy too as they weren't really comfortable with magic outside of offensive or defensive spells, and spending hours in the ground had not appealed to them.

"Are we ready?"

Trev'nor started, as he hadn't realized Nolan was behind him. Turning, he found the other mage hiding a yawn behind his hand. "Mostly, yes. If we can get everyone on my slab, then we're ready. What's the holdup, anyway?"

"Commander Danyal."

There were so many possibilities that Trev'nor had to ask, "What now?"

"He can't decide if it's better for him to ride with Becca or to ride on the slab with the men."

"Someone explain to me why the military, Danyal in particular, is so enamored with Becca?"

"She's the first military commander they've had that shows consistent worry for their wellbeing?"

"And she's cute."

"And she's cute," Nolan agreed, chuckling. "Men of all ages are weak to cuteness."

"I think she banks on her cuteness."

"I'm positive she does. As long as she uses her powers for good and not evil, we're fine."

Trev'nor was not as sure about that. "Get the man to make a decision and let's go."

"How about I get Becca to make the decision for him? I think that'll be faster."

"Whatever works." Trev'nor shifted from one foot to another impatiently, waiting for Becca to kick the commander his direction. Danyal did so with much muttering under his breath, none of which Trev'nor could understand, nor want to.

Finally, they were able to leave. Trev'nor sat comfortably at the front of his slab, legs crossed, a wide brimmed hat on his head to shield his eyes from the suns. They were well outside of the city—there was of course no room inside the streets for a slab of this size—so it was a simple matter of moving forward.

Garth had scouted out the tower two days before, giving them a bit better of an idea of the terrain, and he acted as the lead now. All of the dragons and people still traveling on the ground followed his lead. In deference to Trev'nor, he flew slower than usual, which the Earth Mage appreciated. Not that he couldn't go faster, but the men sitting behind him were nervous enough even at this speed. They were going as fast as a trotting horse. Trev'nor didn't think that particularly fast but apparently it was.

Even at this relatively slow speed of travel, it didn't take long to reach Alred Watchtower. Trev'nor had passed this way twice before—the Ruins of Rheben sat just north of the place—but they had been underground at the time so he hadn't seen anything. The watchtower loomed in the distance, like a lighthouse on a desert sea, standing tall against the blue sky. Trev'nor saw it from miles away and he kept his eyes peeled on it, alert for any details as they came in closer.

The watchtower didn't seem to have much around it. Judging from the size, its population was likely half of Rurick's. Trev'nor estimated somewhere around twenty-five hundred people lived there. There was a large base wall, and the watchtower stood in the center of it, going up several stories. Trev'nor counted seven, which was an architectural feat considering they were building out of just stone and the adobe mud that was popular here. There was a flat roof on top, a large balcony that wrapped around near the top of it, and hints of several round mirrors that had to be as tall as a man standing. What were those mirrors for?

Almost as if to answer the question, the mirrors were turned and caught the suns, flashing blinding light out in a system of short bursts.

Danyal, sitting directly behind him, swore. "They've seen us."

"Is that what the mirrors are signaling?"

"Yes. This is the reason why it's so hard to fight the watchtower. They can see our approach from miles away."

Impossible to sneak up or catch them off-guard, eh? Well, it wasn't like they had been really counting on that.

Storm clouds rolled in from the west, becoming darker as they came, and the wind picked up. Trev'nor resigned himself to the fact that he was going to get soaking wet soon. Becca's rainstorms didn't differentiate between friend and foe. Ah well, it would actually feel like a relief after sitting under the suns all morning.

Several dragons dove for the watchtower, starting the attack. Trev'nor couldn't join just yet, he had to get the men closer so that he could break the main gates and get the troops inside. Let's see, the main gate was—

Danyal abruptly stood, almost jarring Trev'nor. "They're veering off."

What? Trev'nor's head snapped up so that he could see for himself what was going on. Every dragon had veered sharply to the right, flying immediately away from the city. What were they doing?

"ABORT, ABORT, ABORT!" Becca's voice frantically commanded.

Trev'nor stopped the slab immediately, making people jerk forward and grumble. He paid them no heed, but snatched the mirror broach from his pocket up to his mouth. "Becca, what is going on?"

"I'll explain—ground," she said, the wind snatching away some of her words. "—NOT engage, I—do NOT—"

"We are on standby," Commander Danyal assured her over Trev'nor's shoulder.

Trev'nor had a sinking feeling that something had gone very, very wrong. Stomach churning, he stayed standing and waited as everyone landed around the slab. Nolan and Becca both threw themselves out of the saddles, dropping to the ground with less finesse than usual.

"What happened?" he demanded of them both.

"That whoreson has taken the magicians and are using them like a living shield around the watchtower!"

Trev'nor's eyes fell closed. "Please, please tell me you're joking."

"I really wish I was. He has them in cages, and they're spaced around the top. I think he has archers lined up to shoot them if we go anywhere close."

"He does," Nolan confirmed in a snarl. "It's not just the watchtower, either, I saw similar cages on the far side of the wall. He's got them set up in two locations."

Trev'nor flopped down onto the ground, frustrated and disgusted all at once. "Well, we have our answer. The reason why Trexler was always war-ready was because his neighbor is a conniving, base-court, ratsbane. I've seen snakes with better morals than him."

Becca stared back at him with hollow eyes. "The cost is too high to just charge in."

"He's far too callous with human life," Nolan agreed. He was just as angry, but his anger simmered instead of burned, and cold calculation creased his face. That expression scared Trev'nor a little. He had seen it before. What followed hadn't been good. "Who knows what he's going to do next? We can't just sit here, though."

"No," Becca growled, "I agree we need to move, and soon, but a frontal assault is clearly out of the question."

"He'll just repeat the same tactic," Trev'nor agreed bitterly, mouth curling up as the words tasted foul. "It's very effective and we have no way around it, so of course he'll use it again. He might even kill a few people to make his point and ensure that we don't try again a third time." How had he figured out so quickly that people were their weak point? Had stories of them freeing the slaves spread that quickly, that he could guess what would slow them down?

"We need to think like Shad or Aletha," Becca stated firmly. "We need to be sneaky."

"One problem with that," Nolan started, only to frown and correct himself, "Actually, two problems with that. One, none of us are very talented at sneaky."

Trev'nor grumbled about that one. True, they weren't good at it. Despite all Shad had done to try and teach them.

"Two, we don't have enough information. We can't make any kind of plan as we have a very limited grasp on the land. Trev'nor, how much can you sense from here?"

"From here? Not a lot. I'd have to get closer. I should be able to come up with a rough outline of the city's layout."

"What about the building itself? The soldiers?"

"The building…will take more time. That place is pretty densely packed. I mean, if I had a week to draw it all out for you—"

"A week of sitting here?" Becca objected.

Trev'nor grimaced agreement and forged on "—then I could do it, sure. But who knows what he'd do in that week's time? And you're the Life Mage, you can sense people a lot better than I can."

Nolan gripped his hair with both hands, head bowing under the stress of the situation. "I don't see any good way around this. We can't just forge ahead again."

"No, that will result in a disaster." Becca put both hands on her knees and pushed herself up. "I'm going to talk to the men, see if they can help us. Surely someone here is familiar with Alred."

Trev'nor felt like she wouldn't learn much, they'd asked for information before leaving and hadn't gotten anything, but let her go without a word. Maybe someone had been shy about coming up and speaking with them. Who knew? Even though this militia of theirs was voluntary, it didn't mean that the men were really comfortable with them. Not yet. They still had some bone-deep prejudices they were wrestling with.

For now, it was getting late, and they needed to feed people. Trev'nor knew the ins and outs of traveling better than anyone here, having lived with a nomadic tribe. He rolled back up to his feet and started prodding people into motion, not so much ordering as reminding them of things that should be done before they lost all sunlight. Most of the men seemed grateful for something to do that didn't let their minds dwell on what happened at Alred. Trev'nor was certainly glad for a diversion.

Tents popped up, cookfires were started, but the tension didn't really go away. Trev'nor went around helping as necessary, creating walled latrines and temporary corrals for the dragoos, but there wasn't much he could do about the tension. That seemed to fall more under Nolan's department.

He saw his friend go about and speak to people. A few times, there was muted laughter from that direction. Nolan had always been good at charming people.

Ehsan waved him over and pointed toward the ground. "There's a steady underground river here. Help me create a well."

That was a good thought. Trev'nor readily went to his side. "Where exactly? Here?"

"There's perfect."

Trev'nor had no sense of water whatsoever, so even as he moved the earth to either side in a circular fashion, he asked, "How deep?"

"Two men standing."

The Khobuntian measurement system was very, very odd to Trev'nor. And inaccurate. It was always 'a man's arm length' or 'two heads worth' or something along those lines. He usually took his best guess and went with the flow, which seemed to be what the locals did, so it worked most of the time.

Ehsan didn't ask him what they were going to do, or speak of that day's events at all. He just worked companionably to create three different wells, then went to spread the word to the rest of the camp that they had water. Trev'nor appreciated that silence. He had no answers to offer, so questions of any sort would have been very difficult to deal with.

With all of the work done, he gravitated back toward the commander's tent. Danyal had been insistent on this point—the commander always slept in a bright red tent. That way there was no confusion for the men on where to report. Trev'nor felt like it was sleeping inside a very large target, but at this distance, it wasn't like any arrow or javelin could reach them. At least, that was the argument he used to console himself.

He entered the tent and found Danyal, Becca, and Nolan sitting on the ground with a very rough map of the watchtower sketched onto a large piece of parchment.

"—the division makes this more challenging," Danyal was saying only to cut himself off at Trev'nor's entrance. "Warlord, please sit with us. I have an idea of how to approach this."

Trev'nor was extremely grateful to hear those words. He immediately sat down between Becca and Nolan. "I am all ears, Commander."

"I think we need to do a night attack." Danyal gestured to the open space between the camp and the watchtower with a grimace of frustration. "There's too much distance to cross with no cover. Our only chance of getting to them without advertising it is in the dead of night."

"Can't argue there," Becca agreed, nibbling on the edge of her thumb. "If we go in at night, they won't see us, we'll have a chance of getting to the hostages before they can be killed."

"I think the attack should be three-fold," Danyal continued respectfully. "Have two mages split up, go for either of the hostages, with the dragons dropping off an elite force to tackle the main gate. We have to time it so the mages get there minutes before the attack on the gate."

He thought he saw where Danyal was going with this. "Get the hostages out of danger fast, then create a diversion at the main gate to keep anyone from going after us while we get them to safety. That's what you're planning."

Danyal gave him a shark-like grin. "Precisely, Warlord."

As plans went, this one wasn't a bad one. Trev'nor had thought of worse ideas. Even followed through on some of them. "One question. Who goes for which group?"

"I leave that to you three to discuss. I am not familiar

enough with your abilities to know which one would be best suited to either target."

Trev'nor looked up to find both Nolan and Becca staring at him with a disconcerting expression on their faces. Well, disconcerting for him. He knew those looks. "Am I going to like this?"

"Probably not." Nolan took in a deep breath before looking him straight in the eyes. "The person that can subdue the most amount of soldiers in the shortest amount of time is you."

"Without structurally damaging everything in the area? Is that what you mean?"

"That's exactly what I mean."

Trev'nor shrugged. "I can't argue with you there. You and Becca can do the same amount I can, but your fighting styles usually topple buildings in the process. What are you thinking, Nol?"

"I'm thinking…that the slaves are only around the tower. I'm thinking that if we can sneak just you in, we have a good chance of stopping the soldiers before they can execute the magicians."

It was not arrogance that made him agree. "Even if I can't get to everyone fast enough, it will still be better than trying any other method of attack. But how are you planning to get me in?"

"This is the part that you're not going to like."

"A night drop?!" he squeaked. Realizing he'd gone into an octave he hadn't visited since puberty, he stopped and cleared his throat. "Nolan. Are you insane?!"

"It's a stone roof top," Becca immediately argued. "You can go right through it."

"You are planning to drop a person that is already nervous with heights several feet onto a small, circular roof."

"Garth won't drop you carelessly."

"Garth isn't going to drop me at all!"

Garth, of course, caught this whole conversation and curled around the tent to stick his head inside. "Sounds fun."

"It does not sound fun, you giant lizard!" Trev'nor jabbed a stern finger in his direction. "We're not doing this. No."

Nolan went back to staring at the watchtower. "Only way we'll get in, Trev."

"It can't be."

"Alright, if you feel that vehemently about it, go think. If you can come up with a better plan, we'll do that instead."

Trev'nor stomped off, cursing them both, and thought long and hard. But no matter how he studied the situation, or thought about the things he had learned from Shad and Aletha, he couldn't think of another option. In fact, he harbored a suspicion that if Shad were here right now, he'd be planning exactly the same thing. Only he'd likely make Garth go in with Trev'nor.

There were many possible pitfalls with this plan, but the one that Trev'nor was most nervous about was how fast he would have to subdue the guards. The moment they realized he was there, they would react, and there would be many lives lost. He would have to be almost superhuman quick to make sure that no one died. Even if he was Shad's student, he didn't have that kind of reflexes.

He made a full circle around the camp before coming back to where they sat. All three looked at him expectantly.

"I'm not Shad," he finally stated.

"We know that, Trev," Nolan assured him.

"At least a few people are going to die, no matter how fast I fight the guards off."

"We know," Becca assured him gently. "But no matter how we look at it, sending you in like this is our best chance to keep the casualties to a minimum. Nolan can handle the cages on the walls, he's best equipped to do that, and he can coordinate with the dragons to help him. I can go in with the main force and blow the main gate apart so they can get in. It's the only way to do it."

"Even if things go really wrong, we have to go in." Nolan spat the words out like they were rotten. "We don't dare let him win this stalemate. Things will be so much worse if we lose this battle."

Trev'nor hated the plan, really and truly hated it, but didn't see a better option. "You'll be ready to move in the moment I have them safe?"

"The second you tell us to move, we'll move," Becca assured him, raising a hand in a silent vow. "I'll light up the sky as soon as you people clear. We'll win, Trev'nor."

"I know we will. And we'll execute that dastard the minute we lay hands on him."

"Only if you beat me to it. Or Ehsan. We're both really mad at him right now. I fully plan to fry him on sight."

"And Ehsan?" Charmed by a particular inner vision, Trev'nor grinned. "You think the warlord will be the first case of a man drowning in a desert?"

"That would be a funny tombstone, wouldn't it?" Nolan grinned back, rocking a little on his haunches. "But really, I think Ehsan will kill him on sight. He told me that he has friends that were sent this direction."

Trev'nor stomach turned over in a hard lurch. "Is that why he reacted that way, earlier?"

"I think he's pretty sure some of his friends were in that lineup."

Trev'nor was wrong, earlier. The situation could apparently get worse. "Are we doing this tonight?"

"I see no reason to wait, do you? They saw us setting up

camp, so they think that we're settling in for the night. It's the perfect time to set up an ambush."

That was the answer he was afraid of. "Let's get dinner. And then I want a nap. We'll wait for midnight before moving."

"Fine by me."

"I hate all of you."

"We know you do, Trev," Nolan soothed, and fortunately for his sake, he didn't sound amused or patronizing. Trev'nor would have strangled him if he had.

"I'm going to have nightmares about this for weeks."

Becca patted him on the leg, subtly making sure that he could pop the straps free in a split second. "You'll be fine. Garth won't miss."

It was not Garth missing that Trev'nor was worried about. Much. It was him having a panic attack mid-air while falling onto a dark rooftop. He couldn't even close his eyes and wait for it to be over as he absolutely had to watch where he was going. "This is insane. I hate all of you."

"You've said that." Becca patted Garth's shoulder and stood back. "He's ready. Take him up."

In the pitch darkness of the desert, he couldn't see anyone except the glowing eyes of the dragons. Garth craned his neck around to look at him, and in those golden depths, there was vast patience and reassurance. "It will be fine, fledgling."

He didn't believe that. Well, maybe ten percent of him was convinced that things would somehow work out fine, but the other ninety was equally convinced that this whole thing was a very bad idea. No one was listening to him, though.

Garth took off before he could either complain or try to talk people out of this plan. The takeoff was abrupt enough to snap his head back, and he realized that ready for this or not, he had to focus.

There were lights on in the watchtower, of course, and large braziers on top of the base wall, but other than that there wasn't another speck of light to be seen. In all likelihood, the moon and stars out here were probably brilliant at this time of night. But Becca's storm system still hovered overhead, ready for her use, and it blocked the heavens completely. This was good for Trev'nor and Garth as it meant they had total darkness to fly in.

Garth started out far away from Alred, gaining height and speed. Then, when he felt he had gained enough of both, he turned and headed for the watchtower. He came in silently, not once flapping his wings, but gliding the whole distance. It made his approach completely soundless but also slowed his descent enough that he had time to drop his rider.

The watchtower was so brightly lit that Trev'nor had no trouble marking distance and angle. He kicked free of his saddle, hovering just on top of it, although he had a death's grip on the pommel. When they got low enough, Garth did a half-twist in air, and Trev'nor leapt free in almost the exact same moment. Using every skill that Shad and Aletha had ever taught him, he rolled into a landing on top of the roof and fetched up a little hard against the side. Bruised, winded, but his adrenaline was pumping so hard that he barely noticed.

How in the world had they pulled that off?!

It took two seconds for the dazed amazement to wear down enough for Trev'nor to realize he had to move. Now. Shaking his head, he eyed the stone under his feet, feeling the contents of the watchtower as only an Earth Mage could. The immediate level below his feet wasn't very large, perhaps eight feet circumference. The level under it was larger, much larger, likely somewhere around thirty feet circumference and it had a wide ledge to it that held the metal cages. All of the levels below it were identical in size and shape.

He couldn't really feel non-magical people well, but in an enclosed area like this made of stone, he could feel their vibrations and weight, and that told him where people were. Four below. Sixteen below that, crowded against each other, although none were readily standing, but sitting, it looked like.

No matter what Nolan said, he couldn't defeat sixteen people at once. Not in a round place like this, where he didn't have line of sight on anyone. Trev'nor's mind coldly analyzed the odds, found the probability of him being able to save everyone very low, and knew that he would have to rely on Garth to make up the difference. His dragon would be attacking from the outside, reaching for anyone near the cages on the ledge. He could only do his best and hope that things really did turn out alright, as Garth had said they would.

Closing his eyes, he dropped through the ceiling.

The first four men didn't know what hit them. He used the bon'a'lon at his side as much as he used earth to fight with, and they were down before they could really give him much opposition. Only one of them managed to cry out, but just that one was enough to doom his element of surprise. Trev'nor swore, dropped through the floor again to the next level, and rolled as he landed. Muscles straining, he put every ounce of speed he could into his attacks, taking four men out at once, then ran around the outside of the building, going around the curve enough to see the next set of archers on standby.

Only they weren't on standby anymore.

Trev'nor's heart sank as he heard the twang of several bows snapping, the sounds of arrows whistling, and the cries of people in pain. Not fast enough, not fast enough, notfastenough. Garth roared out in challenge as he flew, coming in tightly around the tower before latching onto it and using his claws to gain a purchase in the stone. The tower shook under the impact, making people stumble and cry out in alarm. The dragon snapped at opponents, his long neck reaching people that thought they were out of reach.

Trev'nor took advantage of his partner's arrival and spun on his toes, shot out earth in every direction, making people duck and cover, which bought him another few seconds, but even as he fought, he knew it was worlds too late for some.

One soldier took advantage of his preoccupation with two other opponents to get a strike in. Even though Trev'nor knew that the man was coming up on his blindside, he couldn't disengage and turn fast enough. All he could do was turn sideways, mitigating the amount of target he was offering, and grit his teeth for the inevitable. The man took a swing, cutting a long gash along his shoulders and back, leaving him gasping as white hot pain shot down his spine.

Snarling, Garth reached in with a claw and grabbed the man. Trev'nor didn't bother to track what happened to him after that as the man wouldn't survive. Dragons had no mercy when protecting their own.

Clamping his teeth, he fought back the pain even as he battled the last ones standing. It took five precious minutes to take all of the archers in the tower down. Without Garth, it might have taken longer. Trev'nor stood over the last body and breathed shakily, something wet streaming over his cheeks. Had someone gotten a lucky head strike in? Was he bleeding? He lifted his hand to his face to investigate, but his fingers didn't come away with blood. Tears.

"Calling Nolan," Garth informed him in a tone that brooked no disagreement.

His shoulders must look pretty bad to get that reaction from his dragon. "I'm alright for a few minutes, make sure he's not in a serious situation first."

The dragon let out a huff that said the serious situation, if there was one, could wait.

"Tell Becca and Commander Danyal to start the attack at main gate. I'm sorry," Trev'nor whispered to the cages still sitting on the edge of the tower. "I'm so sorry. I fought as fast as I could."

From the cage outside the wall, there was a hiccupping sob.

Trev'nor dove for the open doorway, and he demanded, "Is someone alive down there?" Wait, shrieking hinges, he'd said that in Chahirese. He opened his mouth to repeat it again in Khobuntish.

"Help me!" a thin voice cried out tentatively.

Alright, so, just a voice speaking got a response. Trev'nor switched mental tracks to Khobuntish and assured the child (it had to be with that voice), "I will, hold on." Focusing on several cages at once, he used the stone of the tower to lift them up and bring them gently into the watchtower doorways. As he did this, he snatched the mirror broach up to his mouth. "Nolan. Hurry, I have wounded people."

"How many? Any enemies left?"

"I don't know and no. Get up here NOW."

"I'm already coming."

Garth must have been persuasive. That was good. Trev'nor could slap a field dressing on wounds but his healing ability didn't even compare to Nolan's. The Life Mage was the only chance some of these people had of surviving this. Using the training that had been ground into his head, he jerked open the cage doors and started evaluating people. Anyone dead he left in place, anyone wounded, he brought carefully out and put them in the center of the tower. Miraculously, there were a few that had not a scratch on them. As Trev'nor found them, he realized they were all children, all shielded underneath an adult's bodies.

Parents shielding their children.

That brought new tears to his eyes but he blinked them away and kept going. He had to get the most critically wounded into the same area, that way Nolan could work his magic on multiple people at once. He had seen his friend heal two people at the same time, hopefully he could do so here.

He got five cages open and people sorted before he heard Nolan land on the balcony. "Trev, I'm here, what do we have?"

"Center has the wounded," he responded, his focus not wavering. "The ones on the right side are the most critical."

"Got it." Nolan moved a little too fast for a human being, and Trev'nor suspected he'd borrowed the speed of a predator cat for a moment. He did that sometimes.

Outside the tower, lightning started flashing, and the main gates burst into splinters. Becca and Danyal were leading the attack inside, eh? Trev'nor felt viciously glad of that. Trexler had been bad, but this place nearly reeked of evil.

There were, to his mental anguish, exactly sixteen cages. Each one held anywhere between four to five people, sixty-nine in total. Out of that sixty-nine, twenty-three were children and there wasn't a scratch on any of them, although of course they were all crying and mourning the loss of at least one parent. They huddled inside the tower, watching Nolan work with wide eyes. Having two dragons hovering outside the tower, clinging to it like giant monkeys, might have something to do with their reactions.

Trev'nor thought of trying to comfort them but felt wholly inadequate of the task. Instead, he turned to Nolan. "What can I do to help?"

"That person and that person, put pressure on their wounds, they're bleeding out too fast." Nolan jerked his chin to indicate two people behind him.

He promptly did as instructed.

"And wipe that look of guilt off your face, you did the best anyone could do in this situation. How badly are you hurt?"

He ignored the question. "If Shad had been here, we wouldn't have lost this many people," Trev'nor retorted bitterly.

"Not even Shad can defeat...how many people were up here?"

"Twenty-something."

"You and Garth had to defeat twenty-something people in a minute flat," Nolan chided, exasperated but gentle, "there's no way you can do that with such poor visuals up here."

Trev'nor pressed bloodied hands against the wounds and felt anything but victorious.

That must have been obvious to Nolan as he said softly, "I wish we could have given you more help."

"There were thirty-six cages on the wall, according to Llona." Trev'nor lifted his head enough to glance at Nolan, seeing the confirmation on his friend's face. "I had 16. Of course you needed Ehsan, Azin and the other dragons to help there instead of here. They had more to rescue all at once." Even as he said the words, he couldn't help but wish that he'd had more help anyway. His head understood the logistics. It was his heart that was in denial.

There was no argument from his friend. Perhaps he didn't know what to say. Instead, Nolan bumped into him. "Move. Help the ones I healed up and out of the way so I have more room to work."

For the next several minutes, Trev'nor just did as ordered. It was easier that way, as he didn't have to think, just obey. He didn't want to, but his mind automatically kept a tally as they worked, and even with Nolan's magic they couldn't save everyone fast enough. Out of the sixty-nine, they lost twenty-two. To some, that might seem a good number, as it suggested he had almost beaten some very poor odds. But he didn't feel that way about it at all.

Finally, there was no pressing emergency to demand his attention. No one hardly needed his help outside, as five mages and an army could easily handle this small town. Nolan found a moment to heal his shoulders so that the pain left him, although it left behind a bloody and ruined shirt. Trev'nor flopped down and sat there with bloodied hands in his lap, shoulders hunched in, for the longest time. It took a moment until he realized that a woman was sitting next to him. Eyes drawn up, he took in the gaping hole in her shirt, blood around the edges, and realized that this was one of the mothers shot shielding a child. One of the people that Nolan had been able to save.

Tentatively, she reached out, and with her sleeves wiped at his cheeks. The maternal gesture nearly broke what little hold he had on his sanity. Throat tight, words strangling, he still managed somehow to choke out, "I am so sorry."

She shook her head, a sad smile on her face. "Thank you." Reaching out, she drew her own little boy into her side, and he clung to her with an iron grip. "We survived, thanks to you."

Trev'nor wondered if her opinion would change when she learned that they had known they would lose people by taking this place and chosen to forge ahead regardless.

"Trev."

He looked up and found Nolan with a child on each hip, others clustered around him. The sight wasn't surprising. Nolan drew children to him as well as animals. Young magicians especially liked being around him. Life Mages just had that effect on the world. "Trev, let's get them out of here. I checked with Ehsan, and he said that there isn't any fighting left below the tower. The fight at the main gate has just started. The hard part is over, I think. We've basically won."

Then why did this feel like a loss? Trev'nor forced himself up to his feet, drawing both mother and child up with him. "Let's explain a few things before we go down."

"That's wise." Nolan turned to the magicians and switched to Khobuntish, explaining who they were and what they were doing here. There was a rise in attitude as they realized they had just been freed and by other magicians to boot. Learning they wouldn't be a midnight snack to the hovering dragons probably helped relieve the tension as well.

Most were willing to follow Nolan down, but a few lingered, uncertain about leaving the bodies of their wives or husbands behind. To them, Trev'nor assured, "This place is safe for now. No one will bother it. We will bury tomorrow."

Appeased, although with heavy hearts, they followed the rest down the stairs.

Trev'nor hadn't done much in the way of magic, and all told this dreadful situation had played out with the span of two hours, so he shouldn't be exhausted. But every step felt like a mile, and it was all he could do to keep balanced and upright as he took up the rear.

Becca and Commander Danyal used the dragons for communication purposes. Llona and Garth were to tell Cat when it was time for them to move, and until then, they hovered silently in the skies and waited. Most of the dragons were set up in platoons so that they could ferry soldiers to the gate in waves. It was the only way to get everyone inside Alred without dragons landing on top of each other, or soldiers being accidentally crushed from too many bodies trying to be in the same place at the same time. Becca had gone over the deployment several times with each platoon to make sure that they understood who would go in at what timing.

The good commander did not seem at all comfortable hugging a young, unmarried woman who was also his boss around the waist. Especially for an indefinite amount of time. But it was the only way for him to keep a secure perch on top of Cat, and since no one wanted to fall off a dragon, he kept his arms securely around her. Becca could tell, though, from the way he shifted and fidgeted that he felt extremely awkward.

Trying to help the man, she took advantage of the quiet air to talk to him. "Do you have family, Commander?"

"I do, my Warlord. I have two sisters, nieces and nephews,

and my parents of course. Now that you have put us back on full pay, I hope to save up enough to afford a bride."

She blinked, trying to wrap her head around this, and failed. "I'm sorry? Afford a bride?"

"Is this not your country's custom as well?"

"Ah, no. Do explain." Becca hoped that this wasn't what it sounded like, because if she learned men were buying women and forcing them into marriage, she was going to change her mind and burn the whole country down.

"A man must offer his bride-to-be gifts and an assurance that he can provide for her. Her parents will not let him marry unless he can afford to pay for the wedding and buy a house."

Ohhh. That kind of afford. She let out a subtle breath of relief. "Actually, in Chahir, the bridge and groom share wedding expenses. The parents do prefer the man have a stable income, though, that's not different. If you don't mind my asking, how much would it take?"

"It ranges, depending on the class, but for me I think I need about 80 ghani."

Becca did the conversion in her head and let out a low whistle. "That's a significant amount of money."

"Fortunately a man only needs to marry once," he chuckled. "The men that can afford to marry again after losing a wife, them I do not understand. They are more wealthy than a poor soldier like me."

From what she understood of this culture, Danyal was actually overdue by about five years to find a nice girl and get married. She'd grown rather fond of the man by this point and so wanted to help him reach this personal goal. Perhaps she could find a way to get all of the soldiers' back pay to them? That would help him, surely. She made a mental note to investigate after they got back to Trexler. "Do you have anyone in mind?"

"No, but there is a good matchmaker in—"

Cat let out a roar and abruptly dove for the town below them. Becca didn't try to shout out stupid questions, it was obviously their turn to fight. She hung on and let Cat do the flying as she called on the storm overhead, bringing lightning out and blasting the main gates open. The wooden gates splintered in smoldering pieces and blew apart into every direction. Becca kept the impact low enough that it would do the job without flinging giant splinters at the dragons. No need to risk injury before they had to.

With a harsh backflap of the wings, Cat gave her the roughest landing ever, more intent on speed than technique. Becca did not complain, simply gave Danyal a hand down before leaping off herself. With a pat on Cat's neck, she sent the dragon airborne again. It was the dragons' task to shuttle soldiers in and to find the pockets of resistance or any other potential trouble in the air and relay it to her. Or take care of it themselves. She'd given them the autonomy to do whatever their judgement dictated.

Their soldiers charged through the ruined gate, Danyal in the lead. She kept up with them effortlessly, her eyes peeled for any target that would require a magical attack even as she kept a sword in her hand. She wouldn't use magic before she had to. It was too densely crowded in here, no matter how precise her lightning strikes, she risked hitting friend rather than foe. Besides, they had learned their lesson and tried to keep structural damage to a minimum. Trev'nor could only rebuild so much.

Training kicked in as her adrenaline started pumping. Becca's heartbeat was a wardrum in her ears as she fought her way through, spinning, slashing, using little jolts of lightning like arrows. Under flickering torchlight, in the dead of night, the lighting in the streets was beyond abysmal. She was extremely grateful that the soldiers here wore a dark brown uniform and not a light tan as it would have been very easy to mix up friend and foe in these conditions.

Sweat trickled down her temples and back, and she was breathing hard in the cool air, but fighting in battles now felt almost familiar. It was not as terrifying as it had been the first two times. She fought to protect herself, to protect her men, and to protect the ones that were helpless against these whoresons. It came down to might of arms, her training against theirs, and they were good. Seasoned, experienced, well trained.

But Becca had been trained by the very best.

Blood and sweat was strong in the air, mixed in with the dust they had stirred up, and she almost choked on it. Two men blocked her path, and she went for them with cold calculation, only to stop abruptly when they were taken down by Danyal and another soldier she knew by face, but not by name.

Beyond them, it was clear and she blinked in bemusement. "That was it?"

"For the main gate," Danyal confirmed.

Surely not. "I gathered the impression we fought through roughly a hundred men. Surely that isn't all of them."

"That's the count I got as well, my Warlord." Danyal cast an uncertain glance further down the street. "That's what worries me."

It suddenly worried her, too. "You think the rest of the streets are a trap?"

"We'll either be ambushed, or..." his face fell into grim lines, mouth flattening, "worse, they're doing something we don't want them to do."

An uncertain, yawning pit formed in her stomach. "I

don't like either of those options." Raising a mirror to her face, she called, "Azin, Ehsan, someone respond."

A female voice came through, light and a little breathless. "This is Azin."

"You were with Nolan, right? Is he still there?"

"No, he left to help Trev'nor. There were wounded people at the top of the tower."

Becca took in the news with a pang in her chest. Hopefully Nolan would be able to save them, although she was too practical to think he could save them all. "Is there a dragon near you?"

"Yes, several. Why?"

"Ask them to search for me. We didn't fight as many enemies at the gate as we should have. There must be more soldiers in the town."

"I'll ask. Hold on." There was a muted flurry of questions, a deep voice rumbling out answers, most of it too muddled for Becca to pick out. Then Azin returned. "They said the town has people in the houses, but they're not soldiers. How can they tell, I don't know, but they're very sure of this. They did say there's a building further toward the center that has a lot of people. Also a lot of blood. They're not sure what that's about, though."

Becca's eyes flew to Danyal's. The expression there told her half of what she needed to know. "You know what they did, don't you?"

"Sometimes," he said, quiet strain in his voice, "They will take the strongest magicians and kill them rather than hand them over to an enemy. I'm sorry, my Warlord. I did not think of that possibility before because they had the slaves kept in two other places."

A diversion. The watchtower and the cages on the far side of town were only a diversion. It was to keep them from thinking that there might be a third location with even more magicians at risk. She swore, hard and viciously, which made every soldier around her blink. Either in awe that a woman could swear like that, or in approval for her choice in words, she didn't know. Or care to find out. "Azin, tell the dragons to get there now. Do not let anyone leave that building, and if there're magicians alive, get them out."

Azin didn't do more than a garbled acknowledgement before the connection ended. Becca waved for the men to form up behind her and set off at a ground-eating trot for the center of town.

After turning down two streets, she realized that she should have asked for directions, but as it turned out, they weren't that necessary. Cat flew overhead and guided them in, then landed next to a building that was literally crawling with dragons. It was a miracle that it didn't collapse under the weight.

Lined up next to one of the walls were all of the other soldiers. Some dead and stacked up, others kneeling with their hands behind their heads. The dragons had lost no time in taking them captive.

"Cat," she called, "Status?"

"Magicians dead," her dragon responded, the words accompanied by a long, mournful tone that all of the dragons echoed.

No. Becca's eyes closed under the weight of that announcement. Her earlier feeling of misgiving came up to choke her and she felt like throwing up. She fought down the urge. "These are the men who did it?"

Those golden eyes narrowed as she stared at the prisoners. "Yes. No like."

"We'll deal with them later, promise." Becca felt like hugging her, giving and taking some comfort, but the dragon was still draped on top of the building.

On the faint hope that someone was still alive in there, she felt like she had to check. If nothing else, she needed to verify what had happened. She took three steps toward the door and was abruptly checked by Danyal, who stood half in her path.

"I will go," he volunteered quietly.

She opened her mouth on a denial, only to pause without a sound emerging. The look in his eyes was one of worry for her, but also spoke of hardened determination. She wanted to argue that as the leader of this battle, it was her duty to see this through. In truth, she had no confidence that she could walk in there and not lose the contents of her stomach. The smell alone gave her trouble already.

Whether to help her maintain her dignity, or perhaps to shield her from the horrors of battle, Danyal was volunteering to go in her stead. His stance said he would not budge until she relented.

Rather than fight about something that she wasn't sure she could handle, she gave a slight nod. "Please do, Commander."

Relieved he hadn't gotten an argument, he snapped out a salute, called three other men, and walked in. Becca took in a breath, re-focusing on the immediate situation. "Sergeant Mose, let's secure the prisoners. Find me a place to put them."

The grizzled veteran snapped out a salute before turning sharply on his heel, barking out orders as he moved.

They could settle the living well enough, but what to do with the dead? Becca felt like it was a bad idea to ask Trev'nor to bury any bodies. He was likely at his limits already considering what he'd had to do tonight.

Danyal was back before she could find an answer, and even in this poor lighting, the man looked green around the gills. He stopped before her, swallowed hard several times, as if fighting back bile. "No survivors, my Warlord."

Just how bad was it, when a man who had seen action for nearly fifteen years looked like this? Becca was suddenly grateful that he'd gone inside for her. She would have new fodder for nightmares if she'd bulled ahead and not heeded his warning. "Thank you, Commander. We'll set a detail tomorrow for clearing the building and burying the dead."

"I'll see to it, my Warlord."

Cat leaned her head down and informed her, "Trev'nor and Nolan down."

Relieved that she could put off any decisions for a few minutes, she turned toward the tower. "Let's go see how they fared."

They arrived just as people started emerging from the tower. The slaves took in the soldiers with uniforms on and instantly flinched, backpedaling into the tower, or trying to. Then some noticed that Becca glowed as only a mage could, and stopped, confused.

With a winsome smile on her face, she loudly introduced, "I am Riicbeccaan, Weather Mage and Warlord of Trexler. This is my right hand, Commander Danyal. We are here to escort you to a safe place for tonight." Gesturing to the building right next to her, she introduced, "The dragon is Llona. Please give her your names. She is our record keeper."

Llona extended her head down to street level so she could talk to people more easily and before anyone could stop them, three different kids were trying to climb on her.

Some of the adults were too afraid to go talk to a dragon, choosing instead to speak with Nolan and Becca, as mages were more familiar to them. Trev'nor didn't let them shy away but would drag them directly to the dragon himself and make proper introductions. When Llona greeted them with human words, their fears eased a mite, and then disappeared completely as she talked around one child that seemed determined to climb into her mouth. Trev'nor had to haul her out three times and then finally gave up and just perched her on a hip to make sure she couldn't try it a fourth.

Really, did kids have no survival instincts? Becca hadn't been that bad at that age. Or had she? Some questions were safer to not have answers to.

It took several minutes, and then the ones that had talked to Llona were gathered up by Danyal and led off to some building that had been commandeered.

Trev'nor watched them go for a long moment. "Becca."

"Hmm?"

"You did this on purpose, didn't you? You knew eventually we'd pick up magicians, and they wouldn't want to trust enemy soldiers, so you deliberately put on the same uniform so they would link magicians with this uniform."

She grinned up at him. "Now you're getting it."

"That was brilliant. I should be in uniform too, shouldn't I?"

"It wouldn't hurt," she agreed. "I should probably teach you how to salute, too, and military protocol. You'd get more respect from our soldiers if you did."

"Is that why they call you 'my' Warlord? And I'm only Warlord?"

Now that he mentioned it...they did do that, didn't they? "That might have something to do with it."

He gave a decisive nod. "Let's do that later. What needs to be done tonight?"

"Cleanup." Becca grimaced as she said the word. "Trev..." she fumbled to a stop, not sure how to tell him.

He stared back at her, aging a decade in front of her eyes. "Tell me."

"They had a third location with magicians. We didn't know about it until it was far too late." The words felt lame in her mouth, like a poor excuse. "We lost forty."

Trev'nor covered his face with both hands, a sound like raw pain coming out from between his fingers. He stayed like that for a long second before dropping them again. His eyes were bright but no tears fell. "You got the ones responsible?"

"Our dragons do, yes, and they're not of the mindset that those men should be kept alive. I'm inclined to agree." Trying to get things on a slightly better note, she continued, "So they're part of cleanup. But fortunately, there's not much, as it's not that big of a place and it fell pretty quickly. But the sooner it's done, the sooner we can rest. Cat?"

The blue dragon was not visibly nearby but answered clearly enough, "Yes?"

"Arrange for a few other dragons to take first watch, will you? And have someone tell Azin to fix the gates. I'd sleep better with those back up."

"What do you want me to do?"

"I think the slave pens got smashed as we came in, which isn't a bad thing, but it means we don't have any holding cells to use. Find or make something that will hold a few hundred people. After that, go crash. Danyal has already marked a building for us, he'll tell you where to go."

Trev'nor went off immediately, calling for Commander Danyal as he moved.

Becca turned to watch him go and heard Garth call out to him, "You did fine, fledgling."

"I'm not fighting a battle like this again, Garth. The cost was too high. Even if it means we have to sit around for a week and think of a better plan, we're not doing this again."

Becca silently agreed. They would not fight such a losing battle next time.

Becca watched Trev'nor go off with a worried frown. "Nolan. How is he?"

"Not good," Nolan sighed, looking at least ten years older than he actually was. "He was crying when I landed on the balcony. I don't think he was even aware of it. Tears were streaming down his cheeks the entire time I was up there, but he never stopped moving, and he didn't falter. He blames himself for not being fast enough. But there were over twenty soldiers up there, on two different levels."

"Not even Shad can defeat that many all at once," Becca objected.

"I know. I said so, too. I think eventually, once some of the guilt has worn off, he'll see the truth of the matter for himself. But right now it's hard."

Hard didn't even begin to cover it. "Did anyone say something to him up there?"

"A few thanked him. I heard them do so. Bec, not one person has said a critical word against us. I think they were expecting much worse than this."

Now didn't that send chills up and down her spine. "I don't like that theory, Nolan."

"Did I sound happy and cheerful saying it? I just think that something else is going on, something we don't know about yet, and I'd feel better if we interrogated the commander of Alred and found out what."

Now that he had planted the seed of doubt in her mind, Becca wouldn't be able to sleep until she got some answers. Growling, she did an about face. "Follow me. I know where he is."

Nolan fell into step with her. "How was the fight down here?"

"I know why they used such a cheap tactic. They didn't have the manpower to properly guard this place. Oh, there were a good three hundred soldiers, which would be enough in the normal scheme of things. The gates and walls are nice and thick, it would be easy to defend them."

"Against normal troops."

"Against normal troops," she agreed with a feral smirk. "Not against us. I don't know what information they've gotten up here about us, but it was enough for them to realize they didn't stand much of a fighting chance against us. Hence their sleazy tactics."

"Just so you know," Nolan sounded eerily calm, "I might do something nasty to the commander."

"Feel free. I already did."

Nolan gave her a sideways glance. "Do I want to know?"

"Probably not." Becca took a better look at the city as she had been rushing last time to get the watchtower and wasn't paying attention like she should have been. Structurally speaking, the city hadn't been impacted too much. Some buildings, obviously military, had been crushed by the dragons. The gates too. But otherwise, Alred looked alright.

The people here were another story altogether.

Not one had tried to leave the city, which was very, very strange. Fleeing the vicinity made perfect sense when dragons and mages started dropping out of the sky. Most were holed up in their own homes. They had to be dragged out just to talk to. Becca hoped this meant they were too cowed to offer resistance instead of meaning they were plotting something.

Either way, that would take time to deal with.

For now, she had dragons and soldiers watching the houses to make sure no one tried anything tonight. Her attention went to other things until that could be resolved.

The one place large enough to hold all of the prisoners was in the central marketplace. It made for a short walk, as the watchtower was within spitting distance of it. Every soldier was kneeling, hands laced behind their heads, waiting. The commanders were kept separate from the men, off to the side, and under special guard by Captain Hadi's team. She approached and gave the men a salute. "Captain."

Hadi and his team snapped to attention and returned the salute. "Warlord."

"We need to interrogate the commander. Bring him forward."

"Yes, Warlord." With another salute, he gestured for the man to be brought forward.

The commander of Alred was middle-aged, seasoned, and had a dark countenance to him that Becca did not like at all. Looks-wise, he seemed a normal enough soldier, but there was something about him that made her squirm.

"Commander," she started without any segue, "what was your plan for defending this city?"

"My orders were to use any means necessary to keep you from attacking." His lip curled. "You're more ruthless than we were informed. The plan obviously failed."

He had no idea how effective that plan actually had been. Becca wasn't about to correct him. "I want to know your plan exactly."

"Commander Otsu Hamid, serving under Warlord Riyu, all glory to him," the Commander barked out, staring straight ahead.

Wasn't going to answer that question, eh?

Becca rocked back on her heels. Bluffing seemed to be in order. "Commander, do you know that there are different types of Mages? Earth, Elemental, Air, Water, and so on. The man standing at my right is a Life Mage. Anything living falls under his domain. That means he can do unspeakable things to you and keep you alive."

Nolan glanced at her uncertainly. "You mean I really can switch his arms and legs about? You won't stop me?"

The Commander went white, eyes wide.

"Why should I?" Becca returned, buffing her nails against her uniform. "The man won't answer my questions. He's useless to me."

Captain Hadi took a step forward. "Raya, Raja, it would be my pleasure to chop them off for you."

"Splendid man," Becca praised.

"How sharp is your sword, Captain?" Nolan asked, pondering the possibility. "This has to be done with surgical precision otherwise it won't work very well. Even with my magic, he'll be in danger of losing his limb, and even if he chooses to cooperate later, I won't be able to switch them back."

"You're bluffing," the Commander scoffed, or tried to, his voice was shaking too badly to pull the nuance off. "Magic can't do that."

Nolan dug into a pocket and pulled out a handful of seeds. He tossed them into the ground and watched with a bored expression as stalks grew straight out of the soil, leaves formed, and a few blossoms came out in vibrant colors.

"All life," Becca reiterated quietly. "Plant, human, animal, it makes no difference to a Life Mage. Or did you think all of the blood on him was just for show? What do you think he's been doing ever since we breached the gates?"

Those dark eyes fixated on the blood all over Nolan's tunic and he went a few shades paler. "W-we were ordered to use the slaves as a living barrier around the watchtower," he choked out.

"That much we know. What else?"

"If you tried to advance again, we were to take non-essential civilians and put them around the top of the walls."

"Non-essential civilians," Becca repeated, bile rising in her throat. "What does that mean?"

"In order, sickly and disabled, elderly, children, and any woman past child-rearing age."

Becca felt the ground tilt under her. What had he just said?!

"You were going to sacrifice the people in order to keep this place from being overtaken?" Nolan shook his head a little as if questioning his hearing. "Are you mad? Without the people here, this city isn't a city at all, but ruins."

"You should have refused that order, Commander." Becca was nearly shaking with rage and it took all she had to not kill the man on the spot.

"As a man who served Warlord Riyu—" he retorted heatedly.

"YOU SHOULD HAVE REFUSED THAT ORDER!" Becca bellowed. What little activity in the area ceased immediately. "When a country's soldiers have to sacrifice innocent lives in order to keep territory, then they are a fallen nation, and there is no saving it."

He stared stonily back at her. "I obey my orders."

"Pray that the Guardian of this world has mercy on you

because of that. I certainly won't." Sick to her stomach with this whole conversation, she turned away from him abruptly. "Captain. Execute this man at dawn, along with any officer that knew of these orders."

Hadi looked a little sick to his stomach too and was quick to salute her. "Yes, Warlord."

Turning on her heel, she stalked away, fighting the contents of her stomach. She felt like throwing up after talking to that man. "Nolan. Trev'nor is running around here somewhere building holding pens for our prisoners. Track him down and tell him everything we just learned."

"You think that will help?" Nolan asked quietly.

"If we had delayed, it would have meant losing half of the city. I think he needs to hear that."

"I can't disagree. Alright, I'll tell him. What are you going to do?"

"Clean house. There is evil in this place and I want it all gone by dawn."

They spent the next day burying the dead. Becca ran from pillar to post, re-organizing the town and making sure that she had every corrupt official and officer executed. Trev'nor helped as requested and was glad she had taken over that part of the duties here. He didn't have the stomach for it, not yet.

They gave the fallen magicians proper burials, letting the families left behind grieve, and chose not to take them immediately to Q'atal. They had been through enough in the past few days—taking them to a foreign on country on top of it all seemed cruel. Better to give them some time first and heal.

Becca issued orders to Trev'nor and Azin to "Go play in the dirt." By that she meant prepare the land around the watchtower for planting. Trev'nor harbored a suspicion she partially did this to help him get over the trauma of the battle, give him something soothing to do, but he was not about to call her on it. In truth, he needed time with the earth to find his center again. If she was offering that time, he would take it.

When two mages got it in their head to change something, there wasn't much that could deter them. Before Trev'nor could get breakfast down, Azin had already started by pulling minerals out of the soil and stacking them nearby in an impromptu rubbish heap.

Trev'nor handed her a breakfast roll and a mug of hot tea, which she gratefully took, then switched places with her and changed the soil composition so that it could accept water without pooling. Becca, Nolan, and Ehsan joined him, looking a little the worse for wear. Trev'nor had a feeling that no one had really slept that well since breeching the city walls.

He greeted Nolan with, "This enough?"

"A little more, if you would. And create canals so that Ehsan has a way to direct the water."

"Azin can do that," Trev'nor disagreed. "In fact, she'd be better at it. How much further out?"

"To about—" Nolan stopped dead and peered hard into the distance, eyes narrowing. "We have people coming."

"How far out?"

"I can't judge distance all that well out here. But I can feel them clearly, so less than twenty miles?"

Trev'nor looked around for Garth to verify only to realize that most of the dragons had taken off with the dawn light for hunting. There wasn't enough prey to be had here, so they were likely going toward the sea for fish. For them, it wasn't a very far distance to traverse. "How many?"

"Five," Nolan stated definitively. "Four men and one woman. All mounted on dragoos."

So, all wealthy and with some importance. People couldn't afford dragoos otherwise. "If they're less than twenty miles, then it will take two hours more or less for them to reach us."

"If they're regular travelers, we can just let them pass by. But what if they're coming to meet us?" Becca asked.

"We won't know that until they're here." Trev'nor went back to working on the soil. "I vote we do what we can here until they've arrived. No sense sitting around and waiting."

They must have agreed as everyone went back to the task at hand. Trev'nor did notice that the patrols doubled and there was a suspicious amount of activity going on behind him that had nothing to do with chores. Then again, it made sense to be on the alert when out in the middle of nowhere with no backup readily available. Especially with the dragons gone.

In an hour and half, they received their answer. Standing prominently from a saddle holster stood a banner with a crescent moon over three wavy lines. Trev'nor did not know all of the warlord symbols, but he could recognize their type readily.

The militia did know the insignia off hand and were very quick to react, forming up a guard around the mages, weapons at the ready. Ehsan spoke to the two nearest to him, got an answer that Trev'nor only half-understood, then turned to translate, "Warlord Dunixan."

Dunixan. Wasn't that the very north-left territory?

"According to the banner, it's the man himself," Ehsan added.

Trev'nor's eyebrows shot into his hairline. "You're kidding."

Ehsan gave a slow, emphatic shake of the head. He was not joking. In fact the look in his eyes suggested that he wanted to duck away from this meeting.

With them closing in, no one even pretended to be preoccupied with something else. They spread out, ready to close in an instant if there was trouble, but not offering the enemy a grouped target. Trev'nor, since he had a handy way of blocking weapons, stepped out ahead of the rest and called to the earth to stand by.

Ten feet away, the warlord's party stopped. Only one dismounted, the sole woman of the group, and she very carefully kept her hands away from her weapons as she moved. This had all the earmarks of a diplomatic mission. Trev'nor couldn't imagine why the warlord would approach them, though. They hadn't even crossed paths yet. Just how fast did news travel in this country?

He studied the woman as she approached. Late forties, dark hair a little streaked with silver in her temples, strong bone structure, and a rippling musculature that he only saw on professional soldiers. Trev'nor would bet his eye teeth that she knew exactly what to do with that short sword strapped to her waist.

She stopped two feet away and gave a slight bow. "I am Simin, First Guard of Dunixan. I speak for my warlord."

First Guard…meaning, retainer of the warlord? Very highly positioned, this woman.

Nolan stepped up to his side, taking over as speaker, which Trev'nor was grateful for. His Khobuntish likely wasn't up to this. "I am Vonnolanen. I hear you, Simin."

Trev'nor gave him a slight nod of approval. Good, let her know they were listening, but nothing more than that.

"We have heard reports that magicians have broken free of Trexler's control. We have heard they rebelled and executed their warlord. My warlord wants this confirmed."

He highly doubted Dunixan had ridden all the way down here to find out for himself what was going on. The man likely had spies to do that for him.

Nolan weighed her silently for a moment before stating, "That is mostly correct."

Simin leaned forward onto the balls of her feet. They definitely had her attention now. "What was incorrect?"

"Three foreign magicians came in and broke everyone out of their slave chains. They are responsible for inciting the rebellion and the execution of Trexler." Nolan gave her a wolfish smile. "Everyone else just joined in."

In this land of dark haired people, she had no trouble sorting out who the 'foreign magicians' must be. She pointed a finger at Trev'nor, Nolan, then Becca. "You three?"

"That's right," Becca confirmed, coming up to stand next to Nolan.

Simin turned and bowed to her warlord, then took two steps backwards. A tall man, well-built and dressed in the fine leather armor of the extremely wealthy, abruptly dismounted from his dragoo and came straight for them, lifting off the hooded half-cloak he was wearing as he moved. It revealed a man that some would consider handsome, although others would deem him too square-jawed for that. Trev'nor thought he was staring into the eyes of a panther. The man carried himself like a predator on the move.

"I am Roshan Dunixan, Warlord Dunixan. I am here to speak with you."

Trev'nor was now more confused, not less. "Why?"

Dunixan's mouth stretched into a feral smile. "To speak of an alliance. Why else?"

Absolutely no one trusted Dunixan inside of the still unstable Alred. Instead, Trev'nor created a table and benches where they stood, and they cautiously sat across from each other at the table.

"While I know some of what you have done, and what you are," Dunixan started, "I am afraid I don't know who you are. Might I have your names?"

Becca took in a breath and glanced at the other two. Nolan, as usual, took lead for them. "My name is Vonnolanen, Life Mage from Chahir."

Dunixan's eyebrows shot up. "Von? I believe that family is the ruling family for Chahir."

"That is correct." Nolan stared him down and did not elaborate. "With me are Rhebentrev'noren, an Earth Mage, and Riicbeccaan, a Weather Mage, also from Chahir."

"Magi, it is my honor." Dunixan inclined his head to all of them cordially.

Oh? "This is the first time since entering this country that we have been addressed correctly."

"I imagine so," Dunixan agreed, eyes smiling. "I went to Bromany once, on a business trip with my grandfather, and I met many magicians there. I learned much about them at that time."

In other words, he knew better than to agree with the cultural prejudice of Khobunter against magicians? Becca hoped so, at any rate. "Warlord Dunixan, I'm sure you know as well as we do that rumors bend the truth past recognition. Perhaps it would be best if we first told what we know of the other? To make sure our facts are straight."

"I'm inclined to agree. Perhaps, instead, it would be best if you start by telling me how you came to Khobunter? I am highly curious as to how you started on this path of conquering. The Bromany magicians I met were highly against anything political. I find this choice of yours... somewhat strange."

"You mean highly unusual and somewhat against the rules," Nolan corrected. "Well, let me explain." He started from the very beginning and told the full story, leaving little out, which surprised Becca.

Dunixan didn't seem at all surprised at some parts of the story, but highly surprised at others. When Nolan finished, he gave the three a study from under his eyebrows. "Initially I had wildly varying rumors about you. Rumors had it that demi-gods had descended from the heavens and were punishing anyone that deserved it."

Becca preened, buffing her nails against her shirt. "I am as beautiful as a goddess; it's no wonder they made the mistake."

Both boys snickered. Becca, without looking, lifted her hands and flicked them on the sides of their heads.

"Ow!" they protested in near unison.

"Bec, quit doing that, it hurts," Trev'nor scolded, rubbing at the abused skin.

"If you know that it hurts, stop asking for it," she growled at him.

"When a woman says that she is beautiful," Dunixan

drawled, "a wise man smiles and agrees with her."

Becca beamed at him. "Exactly. Warlord Dunixan, I think I like you."

He gave her a little bow from his seat, his hand flourishing to make the gesture slightly sarcastic. "Charmed, I'm sure. After that initial rumor, I was able to get more solid intelligent reports, and it became obvious to me that you were not gods of any sorts, but mages. I hadn't realized that Weather Mages existed until you introduced yourself as such, however."

"We're extremely rare," Becca responded with a blithe shrug. "The Magic War in Chahir nearly wiped out my family line."

It was past time to turn the tables. "Warlord Dunixan, why have you approached us?"

"For several reasons, actually. First and foremost, I do not want to incur your wrath. We have received numerous reports of your attacks on Trexler. I do not wish the same upon my people."

A very good reason all by itself.

"I'm also glad that someone took Trexler down and is willing to fight against Riyu. Trexler did not cause me as many problems—as Riyu's territory divides us—but he was not a pleasant man or a good ruler. No one will mourn his passing."

Becca believed that, too.

"Aside from self-preservation, I've become increasingly curious about all of you. I did not understand why you came, or what has made you stay, but I do recognize dedication when I see it." There was a confidence, an ease of manner, as he put his forearms against the table and continued, "I have seen for myself what you do to an area after you have conquered it. I saw Trexler with my own eyes. You are builders."

Nolan cocked his head slightly. "You admire this?"

"This country is chock-full of warriors. We are good at destroying, but what this country needs most is builders. It is amazing, the change that Trexler has undergone. I walked into an oasis, a fertile land that is sprouting." With a charming, candid smile, he admitted freely, "The dragons did make me nervous, though. One stopped me and asked many questions."

"Did you walk into Trexler with your banners up?"

"Customs and courtesy require that I do so."

"Then that's why. They've learned all of the different banners and will stop anyone that has a banner they don't recognize." Nolan got that inscrutable look on his face that looked eerily like Chatta's when she was negotiating for something she wanted. "So, Warlord Dunixan, to sum up, the reason why you approach us is because we fight your enemies, you prefer to not have your own territory attacked, and you wish to have your own land become green and fertile as well."

"That is the size of it, yes. We might have much to offer each other as long as our goals align."

That seemed like an opening, and Becca took it. "We started this conquest to free all of the slaves. The magicians in particular. We have no intention of leaving after this is done, however. Khobunter is a mess, one that has been ignored for too long. We will stay and revitalize the country after we have gained control of it."

"Do you intend to take control of every territory, no matter what?"

This question was very, very, important. Becca looked to Trev'nor, her co-ruler, silently asking him how to respond. Trev'nor watched her as he answered, "I do not feel that is necessary as long as certain conditions are met. If the warlord

Honor Raconteur

of an area can agree to abolish slavery completely, change the current rules and customs to a more humane practice, and work in conjunction with us, I don't think it's necessary."

Becca nodded, silently concurring.

"I see." Dunixan made a small, circular gesture with his hand that included the whole city. "I was surprised to learn that you've already taken all of the magicians you've freed to another country. Strae, was it? Why would you do so, when they are a formidable fighting force?"

Trev'nor bobbed his head in confirmation. "Strae Academy, yes. Where we were all trained. Well, first off, we took them there because they're not trained. Most of them know some tricks but they don't really know how their magic works. It's better to have them fully trained."

Dunixan opened a hand, palm up. "It's a valid point. Second off?"

"Second off," Becca started, grinning that he was using their phrasing, "they need to learn what it really means to be a magician. They're so downtrodden, so used to thinking of themselves as 'slaves' that even if we get the culture here to stop treating them as such, that mental stigma will stick with them."

"We have full confidence that our old professors will beat the idea out of them." Trev'nor was absolutely sure that in Shad's and Aletha's case, that wasn't a metaphor or exaggeration. "Which is why we sent them all there. We will send all future magicians we rescue there as well."

"You do realize that by sending them off for this training, most will likely not choose to return," Dunixan observed neutrally.

"It could be worse," Becca observed. "We could have skimped their training and they stayed."

At this, he lost his neutral face and gave her a small,

satisfied smile. "So you do understand good business tactics. Excellent."

Becca pointed a finger at Nolan. "His doing."

"You have to be half-businessman, half-politician in order to really manage a country well," Nolan returned, idly tapping the table. "Or so Grandfather always says."

Dunixan pounced on this. "So you are of the Von's of Chahir?"

"Only grandson," Nolan admitted freely.

Simin gave a soft hiss of triumph.

Dunixan gestured between the two of them. "The two of you are acting as co-rulers, I take it? What about you, Magus Vonnolanen?"

"I'm just helping them," Nolan denied easily. "After they've gained control of Khobunter, then I'll return home. I have my own country to run, after all."

"So I need to negotiate with the two of you?"

"That's correct," Becca confirmed. "But I have questions that I need answered as well, Warlord Dunixan. Aside from non-aggression, what can you offer us?"

He spread his hands outward as if to gesture at everything that he was. "My full knowledge of the terrain and the other warlords, to help prepare for battles. My troops, if you need more manpower. My political power, as needed."

Becca internally let out a whistle. What he offered was nothing to sneeze at. If he really could hold to a bargain, then it would give them support that they desperately needed and another territory automatically that they wouldn't have to fight their way through. It was a considerable and highly tempting offer.

But could they trust the man? Dunixan was incredibly hard to read. He'd also grown up in a world were magicians were not valued except as a tool. That he came to negotiate with three mages felt off to her. Was this a ploy to use them as tools, since he had no way of controlling them other than manipulation? Did he actually think of them as human beings? Becca knew exactly how deep tradition and prejudices could run. Her parents had abandoned her because of it.

"Warlord Dunixan, we would like to take some time and—" Nolan started neutrally, only to cut himself off. He abruptly twisted in his seat, eyes wide, nearly vibrating in place.

"What?" Becca and Trev'nor demanded in stereo, alarmed by his actions.

"G-gardener," he stammered hoarsely.

Gardener?! Granted, as a Life Mage, he could feel one approaching sooner than they could, but… "Are you sure?"

The words barely left her mouth when one appeared, standing several yards away from the table. This one did not resemble the one that Becca had met when she was eight years old. For one thing, this one was female. She was a little taller, pale skin more marbled with blue veins, feather-like hair shorter so that it barely brushed her shoulders. She looked at them and beamed, glowing brightly even under the desert suns.

A chorus of startled curses rang from Dunixan's group, and then the female retainer charged.

Trev'nor threw up a wall of stone instantly, blocking her path, even as Becca and Nolan called out to her frantically, "Wait! This isn't an enemy!"

The female retainer stopped dead, not just because of the wall, and peered suspiciously over it. "Not an enemy?"

"A Gardener," Trev'nor explained steadily, belying the wideness in his eyes. "She's a Gardener."

"A what?" Dunixan queried, head pulling back in

confusion.

How to explain a Gardener in fifty words or less? "They are ancient beings, a race entirely different from man, that are the caretakers of this world. They oversee the land, healing damage done when needed, but also influencing the right people to be in the right place at the right time. They take no one's side, as their ultimate goal is to maintain the balance of this world."

Becca felt like even that explanation was lacking, but she really didn't know what else to say that didn't launch into a volume-length essay. Her mouth was dry, heart hammering like wardrums, mind in such a whirl of confusion that she wasn't able to untangle it. The arrival of a Gardener meant one of two things: either they were in the right place, doing the right thing, or....

Or they weren't.

The Gardener extended a hand, beckoning them to her.

Nervous and shaking, Becca, Trev'nor, and Nolan obeyed that silent summons and walked forward. For all of their sakes, she hoped they would be told they could stay in Khobunter.

If not, she might be the first person in history to ever argue with a Gardener.

"Garth, I'm going."

"Shad, I just got handed five hundred students, you are not abandoning me with them. We're so short staffed I'd borrow a cat's paw if it was offered." Garth had learned over the past ten years of teaching how to give someone a look that said 'sit down, shut up, and do what I tell you to' with impressive impact.

It of course had no effect on Shad whatsoever. "I am her Guardian, she's in one of the most dangerous countries in the known world, and you expect me to calmly sit here now that I know where she is?"

"No, I expect you to run around like a chicken with its head cut off, like I am, trying to handle five hundred new students that don't speak any Chahirese or Solish!"

"Hire help," was Shad's unsympathetic response.

"I've hired help and my help has hired help and they can't get here fast enough to suit me. But Shad, you're one of the few that speak Solish fluently, which is the only language we seem to have semi in common with them. At least some of them speak a little of it. None of the new teachers speak Solish or Khobuntish."

They were all valid points, Shad would be saying the same in Garth's shoes, but Becca's letter to him had scared the light right out of him. If Aletha wasn't six months pregnant, they'd have already taken off after her.

Garth ran a hand roughshod through his hair and glanced back toward the building. Shad had hauled him out of it so they could have this argument, as doing so in front of the students was taboo. Shad knew he wanted to leave the outdoor gardens, this argument, and all potential complications behind so he could deal with the ones that had been handed to him by their three problem children. That didn't mean Shad was going to let go of this until he got his way.

"Listen, I know they conquered Trexler, but—"

"Which is going to get them into serious trouble with the Trasdee Evondit Orra," Garth started righteously only to trail off, "Or not, depending on how things go. Honestly I don't think I'd have reacted much differently in their shoes. Their sense of justice was likely so outraged by what's going on they chose to conquer the country to fix matters." Garth gave him an acerbic smile. "I think you might have taught those three a little too well, Shad."

"Shut up, you. If your children were old enough to get into this sort of trouble, they'd likely do the same things."

"Do not say that in front of them or Chatta, she'll skin you."

Shad cackled. "Not denying it, eh?"

"Any of my students would likely make the same choice," Garth responded with a faint sort of pride. "They're that caliber of people. Either way, we're not in any sort of position to do something about this. Politically speaking, if nothing else, but we don't have the manpower to send an army through the Empire of Sol and into Khobunter either. We can support them, we can advise them, but we don't have the means to interfere or try to stop them."

Shad opened his mouth, all ready to object to this, when he remembered what he had been doing at seventeen. It was not much different than what his little girl was doing now.

"You just remembered what trouble you were getting into at that age, didn't you?" Garth intoned drolly. "I was running around in enemy territory as well at seventeen, so I really have no right to throw stones at those three. We just have to trust that we taught them well enough they can manage. It's not like they're out there alone, anyway, they have a hundred dragons aiding them."

Well, that was true.

Standing, Garth found his balance again, brushing grass off his knees. "I need to report this to everyone else and warn them that we're going to be getting even more magicians. Hopefully Coven Ordan can send us help or will agree to take in some of these students. We're already overrun as it is."

Shad followed him in to Strae but he was not as convinced as Garth that 'support' had to be done from a distance. And the Gardener had not released him from his role of Guardian. A Guardian couldn't exactly do their job from this far away. No, Garth might be content to let them do their task in Khobunter and support from the sidelines, but he certainly wasn't.

Shad split up at the doors and went looking for Aletha. He needed to have a little talk with his wife.

Honor Raconteur grew up all over the United States and to this day is confused about where she's actually from. She wrote her first book at five years old and hasn't looked back since. Her interests vary from rescuing dogs, to studying languages, to arguing with her characters. On good days, she wins the argument.

Since her debut in September 2011, Honor has released almost 30 books, mostly of the fantasy genre. She writes full time from the comfort of her home office, in her pajamas, while munching on chocolate. She has no intention of stopping anytime soon and will probably continue until something comes along to stop her.

Her website can be found here: http://www.honorraconteur.com, or if you wish to speak directly with the author, visit her on Facebook.

Made in United States
Orlando, FL
07 January 2023